Good
Intentions

Good Intentions

A NOVEL

Patricia O'Brien

BEELER LARGE PRINT

Hampton Falls, New Hampshire, 1998

Library of Congress Cataloging-in-Publication Data
O'Brien, Patricia.
    Good intentions : a novel / Patricia O'Brien.
        p.   cm.
    ISBN 1-57490-163-X (alk. paper)
    1. Divorced woman—Illinois—Evanston—Fiction. 2. Stalking—
Illinois—Evanston—Fiction. 3. Intergenerational relations—
Fiction. 4. Family—Illinois—Evanston—Fiction. 5. Evanston
(Ill.)—Fiction. 6. Large type books. I. Title.
[PS3565.B73G66 1998]
813'.54—dc21   98-38048
                                                                          CIP

Published in Large Print by arrangement with
Simon & Schuster

BEELER LARGE PRINT
is published by
Thomas T. Beeler, *Publisher*
Post Office Box 659
Hampton Falls, New Hampshire 03844

Typeset in 16 point Aldus Roman type.
Printed on acid-free paper and bound by
BookCrafters in Chelsea, Michigan

To Burt and Babs Joseph
For allowing me to fill their home
with the people of my imagination.

Good
Intentions

PROLOGUE

RACHEL STEPPED CAREFULLY IN HER HIGH HEELS across a broken porch board, trying to hide her impatience from the stout little man fumbling with the lock box.

"Place is falling apart, Mrs. Snow," he said, glancing at her. "Like I told you, nobody's lived here for a few years. Things like that rotting board are why it's being sold 'as is.' "

"Yes, you told me. Look, maybe that lock's broken." Shivering, she pulled the edges of her coat closer to her body and hoped he would not get too chatty.

"Nope, it's just rusty. I don't know if I mentioned that this used to be the home of a big Chicago doctor who walked in front of a train ten years ago, right up here at Main Street. Dunlop, Dunston, something like that—"

"The name was Duncan," she murmured, turning away, afraid now she might have to race for the curb and throw up in the street. She looked around, pushing back the memories. The paint was peeling from the window frames, and the November grass on the front lawn was as dry and cold as dead wheat. The juniper bushes, untended, were winding over the porch railing. That's what she'd do, concentrate on the juniper bushes.

Too late. She was imagining again what the warning shriek of the old 6:05 Northwestern must have sounded like that night—and saw her father in her mind's eye as he registered what was happening

1

and tried to get off the Main Street station track in time. Rachel raised her hand over her eyes, pretending to brush her hair away. But then she spied on the door a deep, ragged scar she had recklessly gouged out with her tricycle a hundred years ago and suddenly felt a heart-thumping animation. She'd be okay.

The agent thrust the key into the lock and cast her an appraising look. She wondered briefly what he saw. Her face was almost square, with a strong chin and wide black-purple eyes that somebody had once told her could stop a person dead in their tracks with a stare. Not now, she hoped. Right now, she wanted bland anonymity. The moist air caught at her dark hair and curled it around her face. He won't notice me, she told herself. I'm wearing very little makeup; not glamorous, nobody recognizable.

"I've been wondering," he said. "Your voice.

"I host a radio show," she mumbled.

"Oh yeah, now I know who you are, you've got that talk show in the morning. I listen to you a lot in the car." His eyes were bright with interest as he gave the key a final twist and the heavy door swung inward. "Say, why don't you have that guy on who says he can make bombs out of cereal grains? No offense, but you ought to juice things up a little. I heard him on the Jerry Tebbins show the other day, and I was wondering—"

But Rachel wasn't listening. She stepped inside the house. She felt a tingling at the back of her neck as she stood in the gracious old entry hall and stared up past the dingy walls at the eleven-foot ceilings. She smelled the faint odor of burnt wood from the fireplace, but there was also the remembered scent of the flowers her mother used to bring in from the

2

garden and scatter around the house with lavish abandon. Roses, tulips, daffodils . . . lush plants and greenery everywhere. She closed her eyes and inhaled the past as deeply and slowly as she could and waited for the pain, the deep, grinding pain that had hit her the last day she walked through this door on the morning of her father's funeral. It didn't come.

"The floors need refinishing, the skylight over the sunporch leaks, and the kitchen needs sprucing up," the agent said with brisk professionalism. "The fellow selling it got his clock cleaned in a divorce settlement and left for Puerto Rico before his creditors closed in. He left a nice house that needs a little TLC. But South Evanston holds value, I can tell you. You can't beat being two blocks from Lake Michigan." He waved his hand dismissively at the sagging ceiling. "A diamond in the rough."

She walked into the kitchen with its sweep of windows opening to the backyard and ran her hand along the scratched and darkened butcher-block countertop, remembering how thrilled her mother had been the day it was installed. There couldn't be many women anywhere, anymore, who held a party to celebrate new countertops, could there? A flash of Camilla Duncan's pale face and trim figure, neat and muted in black, brought the pain out of its box and hurled it directly into Rachel's stomach. Why hadn't her mother cried at the funeral? Rachel pushed the wearying, familiar question away. She turned and moved back into the hall to more smells; more sounds. The damp, woolly smell of her father's lumpy old Irish sweater when he came in after raking leaves . . .

She made her way slowly through the living room, seeing the dull, scratched floors but remembering

3

herself as an adolescent scrunching her bottom deep into a barrel chair in front of the green tile fireplace and reading until the room turned dark. Then it was up the stairs and through the bedrooms. Dark, peeling wallpaper. She lingered, then came down, fingering the old oak banister, her mind racing, her heart pounding.

"This is a bit shabby, I know." The agent was briskly affable. "I can show you a terrific apartment on Sheridan Road—"

"I'd like to walk down to the lake for a few moments," she said, cutting him off. "Just to get a sense of the neighborhood. Do you mind?"

He was instantly alert, sniffing the air. "I should tell you there's another potential buyer, somebody who's really crazy about the place."

Rachel's pulse quickened.

"Five minutes enough?"

"Five minutes is fine."

Safely out on the sidewalk, she glanced back at the house and drank in its lumpy stucco presence, its peaceful coexistence on this block of soaring Victorians. Be sensible, she told herself, it's too big. Too complicated. She walked briskly east on Hamilton, cutting across the strip of park known as Burnham Shores to reach the wall of boulders that held back Lake Michigan's turbulence. She leaned against one and stared at the profile of downtown Chicago etched sharply against the sky, remembering the fairy tales her father would weave about the "magic city" as they sat on this very rock.

His death changed everything. In the years that followed, trust and hope somehow dribbled away. She had finally admitted to herself that even the miracle of her blooming little girl was not quite enough glue for her marriage to Matt—and when divorce engulfed everything that was true, his nastiness confirmed her need to stay wary. Slowly Rachel stretched, reaching her arms up to the sky, still watching the city. *I became cautious when I should have been bold and too fearful when I should have been brave,* she thought. *And now here I am, with a truly crazy idea of how to get my life moving again.*

She took a deep breath. She shouldn't be impulsive about this. But the place was way below market and now that she had the divorce settlement money, she could afford it. Barely. *Thank you for something, Matt Snow, you prick.* There were worse ways to patch up a life than going back to beginnings, weren't there? She turned that one around in her mind to see how it held up, but who was she trying to convince, anyway? If she did this right, she could make it work. She might even get Edie pried away from that expensive private school in Wisconsin Matt had insisted on and get her interested in moving home, this time into a real home with her—Rachel took another deep, almost gasping breath. She was really getting too agitated; the thing to do was—the thing to do was, just do it.

She retraced her route, walking slowly at first, then faster, growing more sure with every step. She mounted the porch steps in two bounds, tasting flakes of snow on her lips.

The agent was pacing the hall, impatient to move on. "Sorry to keep you waiting," she said. "I'm making an offer."

He stared at her, wary. "Excuse me?"

"An offer on the house. I suspect the owners are

very anxious to sell." A burden was lifting.

"*This* house?"

She felt a sudden fondness for him; he seemed so astonished. "That's okay," she said. "I want it. I grew up here. It's my house and I want it back."

He was recovering rapidly. "I'd advise offering full asking price. The other interested party—"

"Fine.

"Well . . ." He seemed to be trying to think of what to say.

"Well, good luck to you," he finally managed. "I'll draw up a contract."

CHAPTER 1

NOBODY THOUGHT IT MADE ANY SENSE. HER FRIENDS argued you didn't do that kind of thing when you were divorced and moving on with your life, and anyway, Rachel should face the fact that she was the kind of person who was oblivious to year-old cottage cheese in the refrigerator and year-old dust under it, so the very idea of taking on a huge, dilapidated old house when she was supposed to be decomplicating her life seemed ludicrous at best. Larry Kramer, the sound technician at WBBW-FM, said at least she'd be hauling out all the books she kept stacking in the studio's tiny corridors and give them some breathing room for a change, which was good news; the cramped quarters on the fifth floor of the Wrigley Building that they all called home were small enough. Then there was Jim Boles, one of the owners of WBBW; the one who ran the place. Jim was a large, heavy-boned man whose shirts were always wrinkled and pulled a

6

little too tight over the slight swelling of flesh above his belt. Graying hair that fell forward into his eyes, and a deep, comfortable voice. He was a widower with a mild manner who missed little at the station, especially Rachel's comings and goings, something more than one set of sharp eyes had noted. Jim kept quiet for a full week before offering the opinion that she spent most of her time here anyway, so why buy a big old house? Her daughter, Edie, certainly didn't think buying the house made sense, but then Edie was sixteen and thought very little her mother did made sense. Berry Brown, her producer and friend, didn't think it made sense either. She complained that Rachel would get sucked in by things like paint chips and floor varnish just when *Talk Time with Rachel Snow* needed total hands-on attention if they were going to stay on the air.

"I don't believe you really think I'd do any such thing," Rachel protested. "Dithering over paint chips? Me?"

Berry pressed her lips together and said no more, but Rachel caught the worry in her eyes before she turned away. Berry was the daughter of a small-time trumpet player who had hauled his family from gig to gig for most of her childhood, and she had grown up with the loneliness of itinerant living carved deep into her soul. Berry had a wonderful, sardonic way of dealing with everything except major moves; that was the problem. She probably figured the sky was about to fall, and Rachel would just have to convince her she worried too much. It made her feel a bit braver about a lot of things.

But it was her mother's testiness on closing day that rankled most.

"So you're doing it? Good luck," Camilla said when Rachel called her at her condominium in Miami. "It's drafty and old and the plumbing was always backing up, but you're something of a romantic, so maybe it all means something to you." Camilla, of course, was not a romantic; indeed, she prided herself on never looking back—which was not helping her daughter at the moment.

"Excuse me for a second, Mother." Rachel cupped the receiver with her hand and took a deep breath, relieved that Berry was hovering at the edge of her desk. Berry had a kind of flat moon face, with freckles sprinkled liberally across the bridge of her nose and wide brown eyes that registered every setback as a crisis. In her baggy sweat suit she looked a little like a billowing parachute, but Rachel guessed this was no time to start joking about her office attire. "Are you here to save me from this conversation?" she whispered.

"Not my primary motive, sorry. That shrink from Northwestern who opposes genetic testing? He's canceled, says he can't do the show today because his dog is sick and that's it for him; he always sounds like his mouth is stuffed with cotton anyway. Sick dog, my ass. Any ideas?"

Rachel grabbed a fistful of hair and tried to think fast. It scared her when a guest canceled at the last minute, even though it didn't happen now as often as it used to. After a full year they were finally getting a little respect. Maybe she was catching on. Maybe.

"Try Larry Whittle at the Circle campus. He's done good stuff on genetic testing and he can talk on anything."

"With your memory, we don't need a Rolodex.

How do you do it? Stop pulling at your hair like that—you'll go bald. Okay, I'm on it." Berry vanished into the hallway as Rachel turned her attention back to her mother.

"Look, I know you think I'm crazy. I know you think it'll be a money pit. But I assure you, I've got everything under control, honest." Her voice was soothing enough—but her stomach was tensing at the thought of the incredible burden of debt she had just taken on, and she wished her mother would lay off.

"I'll bet I know what you're thinking, I'll bet you're planning to talk Edie into leaving that uppity boarding school Matt has her in and transfer to Evanston High. Am I right?"

"I wish you'd quit seeing through me so easily," Rachel managed.

Camilla sighed, a soft whistling sound. "Good luck."

"Don't forget, I have custody." What an empty declaration of power that was. She stared down at the scratches on her old, battered desk, tracing one of them with a finger until it disappeared under a stack of books she should be reading right now, this minute. She *had* to get off this phone.

"Just don't antagonize him. It'll only make things tougher."

The words were blunt, but Rachel reminded herself that her mother's loyalty had never wavered when Matt pounced with the adultery charge. It was Camilla who had steadied her and said it was a device to scare her into accepting a smaller settlement—but the charge, written into those and legal documents, had buried itself like a sharp nail in her heart. "I'll be totally careful, I promise. I've got a show in less than an hour, Mother, and—"

"Then get to work. We'll talk later."

Rachel found herself listening to a dial tone. Why did she never get used to her mother's habit of banging down the phone without properly ending a conversation? It was with mixed frustration and irritation that she hung up and looked into Berry's sympathetic eyes as she walked back into the room.

"Whittle's on his way," Berry said. "So she hung up on you in mid-sentence again? And she thinks you're crazy, too?"

Rachel smiled. "A little."

"How's she doing?"

"She's happy running the gift shop, and everything else is supposed to be fine—not that she'd ever tell me if it wasn't, of course." There had been a funny note in her mother's voice that made her anxious. It still hurt to remember that night six years ago when Camilla called out of the blue and announced she'd had an operation for breast cancer; but not to worry, she was doing fine. Without telling *me*, Rachel thought. She had chewed over with Berry plenty of times the memory of her mother's resolute voice and her own sense of somehow having been cheated of the chance to be there for her. No use going through that again.

"Well, look at it this way—she doesn't tell you much, but she doesn't burden you, either. Unlike my father, who complains about some pain or other every day."

"You are a saint with him, and I'm not kidding. How's the retired nurse working out?"

"Pretty good." Berry flashed a cheerless grin that was all glistening teeth and gums. "She looks in on

10

him several times a day and fixes him lunch. Truth is, if I had the cash, I'd put him in a nursing home."

Rachel thought fleetingly of the irascible, bitter old man who, weakened by two strokes and confined to a wheelchair, had so taken over the center of her friend's life. He was a man who didn't much like his own daughter, but she had taken him in anyhow and she did her best. "One of these days, you and I are going to be rich and famous, and you'll be traveling to Europe instead of filling out Medicare forms," she promised. "One of these days we'll both be on top of the world."

Berry laughed, that wonderful ebullient laugh that had drawn Rachel from the first time she heard it echoing down the corridor outside her new dorm room at Vassar. It had sent her right out into the hall to meet a jaunty, wisecracking classmate who also loved the Grateful Dead and chocolate bars; someone who could talk herself hoarse late into the night about Vietnam and civil rights—and still study long hours to keep the precious scholarship that allowed her to attend the expensive school for which Rachel's father could so casually write out huge tuition checks. But money never stood between them; nothing stood between them. They started out in radio together after graduation, vowing to be best friends for life. But then came Matt, who didn't like Berry; and then came Edie, whose colic and toilet training were not the kind of bonding topics she and Berry could share. When Berry moved to Indiana, they ended up exchanging Christmas cards—until that day four years ago when Rachel heard a sound as she sat in a Michigan Avenue coffee shop eating lunch and staring at her divorce papers. She was hearing the same fabulous, throaty

11

laugh that had sent her into the corridor almost twenty years before to meet her best friend. It was Berry's laugh. She was back. And that turned out to be the best thing that had happened to Rachel in a very long time.

"I still can't believe we stumbled over each other in that restaurant," Berry said, echoing her thoughts. "It was fate. Karma, whatever. We're gonna make this show work or die trying, right? Positive thinking. I'll even quit complaining about that tyrant in my apartment." Berry began fishing into a box of stale cookies on top of the television set, coming up with nothing but crumbs. Her fingers were short and stubby, her nails cut with a nail clipper straight across. "How's Edie?" she asked.

"I'm not sure," Rachel said slowly. "She keeps pushing me away. She's turned into this chilly little stranger I can't reach. I guess some of it is standard teenage angst." She paused. "Who am I kidding? The divorce blew her away, and it doesn't help that I'm glad to be out of it, absolutely *delirious* to be out of it. It just doesn't. Why should it? Now she won't let me in. She's always angry, just under the surface."

"Yeah, well. . ." Berry sighed. "Don't let it drag you down too much. Maybe she's mad at you, but aren't kids always mad when their parents split? Never having been married and with no children, I, of course, am an expert."

"I don't mind 'mad,' I mind 'chilly.' It's worse." Rachel started to say more, but Marcie, the station receptionist, suddenly swept into the room and tossed a yellow message slip on Rachel's desk. Her lips were some strange brown color today. Marcie kept in her drawer a formidable collection of lipsticks, all shades

12

of red and pink and coral in fat gold cases, and no one knew quite what color would be smeared across her lips next. "This came before you got in," she announced in her broad midwestern accent. "The coffee machine's broken again, like everything else in this place." She was gone.

"Marcie will never forgive us for not being ABC News," Berry said.

Rachel hardly heard; she was staring at the piece of paper in front of her. She began some careful deep breathing.

"What's wrong? Who's it from?"

"Amos Curley." Even saying the name was an effort.

Berry stood totally still, the folds of her sweat suit collapsing limply across plump wrists. "So *he's* back," she said flatly. "How long has it been?"

"Oh, a while." She tried to sound casual as she waved the slip of paper. "This is the *Tribune* number."

"So maybe they've hired back their footloose star, though I can't imagine why. And you're going to see him?"

"I'll return his call, Berry. Aren't you being a little nosy?"

"He hurt you, remember? He hurt you a lot. Maybe I wasn't around for all of it, but I feel like I was."

"Look, we're pals. I love you—don't dictate my life."

"Well, *this* time, see if he's wearing a wedding ring."

* * * *

Rachel stepped out onto Michigan Avenue from the Wrigley Building, savoring the tart bite of early

13

winter in her nostrils. She would stay for one drink, twenty minutes, satisfy her curiosity, and then she would excuse herself. She dug her fingernails into the palms of her hands and jammed them into her coat pockets, wishing she had remembered gloves. You have a way, she told herself, of forgetting basic protections. She walked through the glowing brass doors of the glass-enclosed corridor that connected the two sides of the building and headed down a narrow outside staircase that led to the lower level of Michigan Avenue. Wouldn't you know he would pick Lucciano's, their old meeting place? The restaurant looked seedy, like something from a time warp. She could smell the damp under the old carpets as she pushed through the front door. Looming high in a semicircle above the old wood bar were the vividly painted murals she remembered—each an eccentric shriek of imagination oddly out of step with the general aura of dinginess. Men and women in dark coats sat hunched over their drinks, sending wispy trails of smoke from their cigarettes curling into the light. Several of them seemed vaguely familiar—just older; more faded. Everything here except the murals had faded.

She saw him first. Shaggy hair, brown, peppered with gray, a little thin on top now. His face still lean; features taut. He was standing at the bar, wearing faded jeans and a well-worn leather belt. She recognized the belt's silver buckle. She noted with particular interest that he appeared to be drinking a glass of water. Real water, not vodka?

Amos pivoted slowly and gazed straight at her. "Hello, Rachel," he said simply. He didn't reach out, he just waited.

14

"I never thought I'd see you back in Chicago," she said, taking in as many details as fast as she could.

"Neither did I." He gave her a slow smile that wrapped around her like one more curl of smoke.

I will stay only twenty minutes, Rachel reminded herself. She slipped onto the bar stool next to him, smelling the hint of fresh soap clinging to his skin. Same man, same place; with a thousand years gone by. For this man, she would have divorced Matt sooner. She could admit that now and wonder why she hadn't, but it didn't matter anymore. She remembered Amos's enthusiasm for the zodiac. He would say the stars had remained stubbornly unaligned, which sounded very nice, but she didn't really believe in the stars. That was just one thing among the many that had made them so different.

"Are you back permanently or is Venus fiddling around in the third house of Jupiter?" she said, a false lightness in her voice.

His eyes warmed; maybe he glimpsed what this careful dance around intimacy was costing her. "I haven't checked who's fiddling around with whom," he said with equal lightness. "Yeah, I'm back permanently. California makes you homesick for snow and ice and freezing your rear end off in January—anyway, I lost my sunglasses."

She tried to laugh, aware of his steady appraisal.

"You look wonderful," he said quietly. "I hear you've got a great new show that should make you a star."

"You can hold the praise, Amos. I haven't broken through yet. It's a tough market. But hope never dies, and all that." She flushed at the arch, unnatural tone of her voice.

15

"Still like country music?" He gave her a suddenly twinkly look. It occurred to her that maybe it had taken some guts for him to call at all; maybe she wasn't the only one trying to be brave.

"In the car sometimes."

"Been line-dancing lately?"

She reddened, remembering the night when, loosened with wine, she had hooked her thumbs through the belt loops of a pair of wonderfully tight jeans and danced for Amos at a country bar. Sensing he was already drifting away. Feeling a little like the whore that Matt later tried to make her out to be.

"Not lately. Are you still writing poetry?"

"No, that was another time."

His eyes were swallowing her in a few quick glances, and Rachel felt conscious of the touches of gray in her hair. She saw his mouth twitch in amusement at the sight of her glasses perched on top of her head—as always. Her ivory silk shirt was open at the collar, but not unbuttoned as low as it used to be. She hoped he noticed that.

He moved a fraction of an inch farther away. "How's your little girl?"

"No so little anymore. She's sixteen and coming home for Christmas from a very uptight boarding school."

He whistled softly, staring straight ahead at the murals. At this angle, she could see the patchwork of lines angled out from his eyes; the weathered skin. "Sixteen? Hard to believe."

They sat for a moment in silence, then Amos spoke again. "We should clear a few things up, don't you think? My wife died a year ago. Just thought you'd want to know."

16

"What happened?" Her hand trembled.

"Ovarian cancer."

"I'm sorry."

His face twisted into the self-mocking grimace she remembered so well. "Anyway, here I am, the aging wunderkind, back again—"

"Please, no false modesty. You were the best."

"Maybe. Anyway, I got a monkey off my back. I'm ready."

She blinked in confusion.

"I mean liquor," he said quietly. "You don't have to keep glancing at this glass. I just thought I'd like to see you again. To reconnect in some way. This place just made sense." He took a long, thirsty drink from his glass and she reminded herself it was water, but she still shrank away a little inside. She forced her concentration away from Amos, thinking about the house. Her house. It would insulate her with sturdy wood and weighty plaster and provide a haven that not even Amos would be allowed to penetrate. She let these thoughts run through her mind before she trusted herself to open her mouth and say anything. "Well, here we are, reconnecting," she said, flagging the bartender. She would sip her wine slowly, for old times' sake.

* * * *

How fast time went by, Camilla thought a month later as she sat in a chair, staring into the glittering brightness of the Florida sea. It was already December. Her mind turned to Rachel, her headstrong, impulsive daughter, even now crazily pouring money into a house she was determined to reclaim. Camilla covered her eyes briefly against the light. She could have been

17

more honest; she wasn't as critical of Rachel's decision as she had sounded a month ago. And why hadn't she told Rachel what else was going on? The absentee owners in Toledo who showed up once every year to bask in the Miami sun and check out how business was going in the gift shop had been apologetic, but there was too much competition and too many hurricanes in Florida. That had been early November; why were they worrying about hurricanes in November? It didn't matter. Their smiles were bright but fixed—they were closing the shop. The second blow in a month. No, the third. She rose and drifted out onto the balcony, stumbling over the threshold, almost dropping the coffee cup in her hand.

"Hey, cool it up there, okay?" growled a sleepy male voice from one of the window cubicles below.

Those drunks. She held herself almost unnaturally still, then looked down and checked the terrain; what she was. A proud, wiry body that could have passed for a decade younger. Good, even-toned skin; not too tanned. She was wearing her zip-front bathrobe with the green velveteen palm trees, Rachel's jokey birthday gift from last year. It was the wrong shade. Everything in Florida was the wrong shade.

For a long moment she remained motionless, staring again at the sea, thinking about her last phone conversation with Lindy Colson.

"Okay, I understand; things are tight," Lindy had said in that bright, bouncy voice that had called several legions of suburban neighbors to picnic repasts. "You need money and you have to sell your condo, so now is the time to come home. Camilla, I've got four apartments in this building of mine, and I want you to live in one of them. If it weren't for the property, I would've been wiped out when Bill died, just like you."

"I'm not wiped out—"

"Stop it, Camilla, *please*. It was *my* husband who put all your money in that terrible land deal, and I know it."

"You had nothing to do with it."

"Doesn't matter. I think those scaredy-cats from Toledo have done you a favor. Did you call Field's?"

Camilla hesitated. "Yes," she said finally.

"And?"

"They were very—encouraging."

"Wonderful! You were one of the best buyers that store ever had and they'd be lucky to get you back."

"Lindy, I'm sixty-four." The words caught in her throat.

"Right. You and Gloria Steinem. You'll be sixty-four and looking for work in Miami or sixty-four and looking for work in Chicago, so which do you want? You're better off getting your cash out of the condo and renting my place—I know you don't want to tell Rachel, so we'll just say you're investing as my partner—so, will you come on home, please? Lord, if it weren't for the property and that piddly bit of life insurance, I'd be in trouble too. Now tell me the honest truth, don't you *want* to come home?"

Camilla rolled her eyes, smiling in spite of herself; even Lindy didn't know how much she wanted to go home. "I've been thinking about it for a long time," she said. This tin can of a building with its cheap pool, its incessant pool parties, the sounds of morning urine running through thin walls: it might take a while to sell. But she didn't have to stay until it did. This place. Phillip would have hated it. Funny, ten years and her heart still felt suddenly squeezed by a huge, rough hand at the thought of her husband. She had fled Evanston after standing by Phillip's freshly dug grave, haunted by the question of whether he had deliberately put himself there. With no answer to her question, she could not remain in the town that held all the memories of the years they had shared.

"Fabulous, perfect, I'm so relieved." A trilling laugh. "I can't wait! We'll have fun and I promise I won't breathe a word to Rachel about what happened to that investment, although I don't see why not—"

"Lindy, I don't want Rachel to know anything about my financial situation—I mean it. It would put too much of a burden on her."

"Oh, I understand. As soon as you find a buyer for the condo, you won't have anything to worry about. Then you can buy into my building and we'll be a pair of merry widows on the town every night; how does that sound?"

This time, Camilla laughed. It was decided; she was going to do it. She and Lindy had talked half the night, making their plans, and she had listed her condo with a realtor the next morning. That one act had set her free, and now she was ready to go. *This* time, it was happening.

She slowly poured herself another cup of coffee. Was she afraid? Well, what was wrong with being a little afraid? Anybody with any sense would be a bit afraid, but she wasn't one of those women so frozen in their lives they couldn't move. She was going back to Chicago. It occurred to her that maybe Lindy was right: those timid owners from Toledo had done her a favor. She reached for the phone, feeling a sense of both excitement and fear. How would Rachel respond?

"What? What are you saying, Mother?" Rachel was almost shouting, and Camilla knew that she was an intrusion on the whine of an electric saw and the sharp banging of hammers in the background.

"I'm moving back to Chicago, I've been thinking about it for a long time and I'm really excited—"

"What? Speak up!"

"I want to come home," Camilla shouted back, suddenly desperate to be heard.

"Are you sure?" Rachel said inanely, staring at the carpenter on his high ladder as he finished repairs on the crown moldings. The painters would be out of the house in a couple of days and Edie would be home in a couple of hours and now *this*? What was her mother *doing*?

"Of course I'm sure!"

"You don't have to shout. Why didn't you tell me before?"

"I probably won't have too much trouble selling the condo, but I don't want to wait; these things drag on, you know. So I thought I might as well come back for the holidays," Camilla said, wondering if she was babbling. "Can you spare a room? It'll only be a couple of weeks until my new apartment is ready. I've got wonderful plans—"

Rachel sat numbly as her mother gave her the news that she was throwing her lot in with Lindy Colson, the widowed Lindy, the one who always produced that terrible potato salad at neighborhood barbecues on the Fourth of July. A woman as gregarious and sweet-natured as a puppy. Her mother was buying into an apartment building on the North Side and if she had announced she was going to become a bush pilot in Alaska, Rachel couldn't have been more surprised. She heard herself sounding enthusiastic and saying how great it would be to share the Christmas holiday with her and Edie, wondering all the while if Camilla caught the doubt in her voice. If she did, she was pretending not to.

"Whatever you do, don't decorate the Christmas tree until I come, okay? I'd love to do that with you and Edie. You can't imagine how good it feels to know I'm going back to a climate where it's *cold* at Christmastime, the way it's *supposed* to be!"

"When are you coming?" Rachel asked weakly.

"In a few days." In the ensuing silence, Camilla's voice changed slightly. "I'll stay at Lindy's if putting me up right now is too much of a hassle."

"Oh, for heaven's sake, Mother—who would decorate the tree? You know what a klutz I am."

They laughed their way past the bad patch, and said good-bye. Rachel didn't move from her chair, staring blindly at the phone, unsure which emotion was winning out—her resentment or her sudden sense of defeat. Camilla would bring back to this house something she was trying to erase with all her paint and carpentry work—that was the truth of it. She wiped sweat from her forehead and stretched her aching back, too tired after a day of unpacking boxes and moving furniture to give much more thought to anything. The scarf around her hair slipped forward as she sat down heavily on a sofa still shrouded in plastic and watched the carpenter start packing up his tools. Not defeat, damn it. Definitely not defeat.

"Looks great, Mr. Garcia," she said. "Good job."

"I always do a good job, not like those painters you hired." Mr. Garcia was a scornful, proud craftsman with a slightly crabby disposition, who never lost an

22

opportunity to criticize. "You watch them, Mrs. Snow. They're very sloppy."

"Okay," she said wearily. She jumped up at the piercingly loud sound of the doorbell and ran for the door, tripping over a packing box on the way. It couldn't be Edie, it was too early. But she knew even before opening the door that Edie was, as usual, operating against expectancies.

"Hi, Mom; are you braced? I've got a huge surprise!"

Rachel inhaled Edie's presence, scanning her with the lightning-quick eye of a maternal X-ray machine; instantly caught on the hook of enthusiasm in her daughter's voice. Everything physical about Edie was cut small—her hands, her narrow body, even her nose, now rosy with cold. Her long, pale blond hair was half hidden under a wool cap, the rest of it spilling in helter-skelter fashion down over her collar. Rachel reached for her hungrily, hugging the small defiant body as tightly as she dared.

"You're not *looking*, see?" Edie pulled away and waved a small piece of plastic in her hand. "You will *die*, I did it, aren't you proud?"

"What is it?"

"My driver's license!" Edie's eyes were triumphant. "Surprised? I got it yesterday, so Kurt let me drive partway from Milwaukee—oh!" She turned to the figure standing next to her. "This is Kurt Kiley, my friend from the University of Wisconsin. His folks live in Wilmette. He gave me a ride home from Madison; sorry, forgot to tell you he was coming."

Rachel focused on a tall, stringy-looking boy with old eyes who stood there holding her daughter's hand. His mouth was thin and twitched slightly at the edges,

23

giving him the unsettling appearance of enjoying a private joke. He was tall and wore a leather jacket with sleeves that ended well above angular, bony wrists. He had a wide nose, flat and smooth. His eyes were wide spaced, with long, heavy lashes that gave them a theatrical flash. Rachel smiled and shook hands, disliking him on sight.

"I thought you were driving home with Topper," she said as Edie stomped the snow off her boots and closed the door.

"She takes so long to get ready, I couldn't wait. You know how I *hate* waiting."

"You left without her?" Rachel was genuinely startled. Topper was Edie's roommate and Jim Boles's daughter. When Matt had insisted on sending Edie to Langdon, Rachel was delighted to discover Jim already had his daughter enrolled there. Topper's mother had died in a car accident on the Outer Drive ten years ago, rammed from behind by a pickup driven by a drunken eighteen-year-old off-duty soldier who served a total of two weeks in jail before walking away a free man. That was when Jim Boles changed, people at the station told her, that was when he withdrew and became an observer of the passing scene, still gentle and well liked, but with a reserve at the center that no one after that ever penetrated. Rachel wondered if Topper ever had managed it, and sometimes fancied she could see the loss of more than her mother in the girl's eyes. But she and Edie had gotten along very well last year. Now what?

Edie shot an amused glance at Kurt, who grinned back in a sly way that made Rachel bridle. "We're not such good friends anymore," Edie said in a tone that sounded rehearsed. "She's such a kid—kind of dorky.

Don't worry, some other kids were giving her a ride." Edie turned toward the living room in obvious dismissal of the subject of Topper and looked around curiously. "I vaguely remember this, sort of," she said as she peeled off her sheepskin coat. "I recognized the porch from the outside, anyhow. It looks pretty cool."

"Thanks, I think so," Rachel said, happy at Edie's reaction, although still absorbing the driver's license and Kurt. But when she saw her daughter's delicately boned face in the light, her heart contracted. There were purple hollows under her eyes and she looked much thinner than usual; all angles and bones without her coat. "Honey, you look tired. Have you been studying hard?" she said.

Kurt laughed in a way that stopped her short, but Edie was peppering her with questions about the house and acting bouncy, so she let it go. The three of them made a quick tour while Rachel gleaned as many brief tidbits as possible about Kurt—not that either he or Edie seemed shy about sharing them. He was a junior at the university and the son of a diplomat who usually worked in the Middle East but was now on special assignment for the government. And what assignment was that? Rachel asked.

"Mom, you're interviewing again," Edie protested. "That stuff is confidential." As they came back down the stairs and into the living room, she chattered away, clutching Kurt's hand all the while, telling Rachel about how he had studied for two years at Juilliard and was a wonderful painter and knew quite a bit about literature, which he had studied on a grant at Oxford.

"Edie tells me you've got a radio talk show," Kurt said, interrupting Edie's effusive torrent of words. His

25

voice was slightly nasal, his vowels clipped. He was pacing the room with his hands behind his back, studying the carpentry work with a slight frown. "Just what does that mean? Arguing with Joe from Missoula, Annie from Boulder—things like that?"

Rachel wasn't sure whether she was annoyed or amused at his superior tone. "Hey, don't knock Joe from Missoula—he knows more than I do about cattle ranching," she said lightly.

He shrugged; she sensed his interest already evaporating. "What took you to Wisconsin?" she asked pleasantly enough. "You have a rather wide range of interests, so what's your major?"

"Kurt is SO *smart*," Edie cooed, airily ignoring her mother's question. "He's going to help me choose a computer. Kurt knows everything about computers. Tell her, Kurt."

Rachel's eyes glazed over as Kurt for the next ten minutes talked unintelligibly about computers while Edie listened with rapt attention. When he finally rose to leave, Rachel tried not to show her relief. Mr. Garcia and the painters had left long ago, and she closed the door behind Kurt a little more forcefully than necessary.

"How could you be so rude?" Edie whispered.

"Rude? I wasn't rude, he was."

"Mother, he's a wonderful person. You hardly gave him a *chance*." Edie's eyes looked suspiciously wet as she pushed a long strand of hair away from her face.

"Edie. . ." What could she say? "He does posture a bit."

"Well, you're wrong. I can't believe you'd say that about someone so important to me."

"How important exactly is he?" Kurt had been a

surprise, and she felt herself being defensive.

"He's the *most* important person in my life right now." Edie's chin was up, defiant.

"Okay, maybe he was tired."

"Maybe *you* are, Mother."

"All right, maybe I am. So, I apologize. If he's important to you, then he's important to me. Let's not waste time arguing, honey. I'm just happy you're here. Isn't it great to know we don't have to camp out in a rental apartment anymore?"

"It didn't bother me. I wasn't there much anyway."

"Well, now you're home—and with a driver's license no less," Rachel said as she gently took Edie's arm and guided her toward the kitchen. "That certainly was a surprise." She tried to set aside her image of Edie hurtling through space at the wheel of some strange car just one day after getting a piece of plastic that surely she wasn't ready for. But there was no fooling Edie.

"I know you'd disapprove. I got it because I was ready. Kurt said so."

"I'm sure you are, but we'll drive around a little together, okay?"

"I don't see why. I've got my license."

"Well, you know, so you can get used to those short entry ramps on the Outer Drive, for example." Why, only with Edie, did she always stumble? She felt sometimes like a stand-up comic with bad timing, flailing her arms before a hostile audience of one. "We'll go to some garage sales and get stuff after Christmas," she plowed on. "Did you get that clipping I sent you about the live grenade found at the garage sale in Topeka? Oh, and about the poisoned tomatoes in San Jose? I—"

27

"*Yes*, Mother. Why do you *send* me that stuff ?"

"You eat tomatoes, don't you?" She smiled hopefully. Playacting the Hovering Mom scene used to be one of their favorite games. Was it one more connection Edie was scorning?

"Not from San Jose, I promise."

Ah, a right note struck. Or at least not a wrong one. "Very smart. Now, we've got a lot to catch up on," Rachel said, beaming.

"Sit down, I'll fix you some supper and make some coffee. I bought your favorite, from Starbucks, that blend you like so much."

Edie wrinkled her small, delicate nose. "Starbucks? It's too bitter. Kurt hates it."

"Then I'll pull out the Folgers. I've got some in the freezer."

"Some choice." Edie grimaced again, but comically this time. Her cranky mood appeared to be lifting. Encouraged, Rachel quickly filled her in on Camilla's plans, trying to put an enthusiastically positive spin on the unexpected homecoming.

"Grandma's decided she hates Florida, and you know how she is—she doesn't sit and brood for long. She acts."

"I think it's cool. Why should she just sit down there waiting to die or something?"

"Right. She's doing what she wants to do." Rachel suddenly knew she was about to take a pratfall again, but the words began tumbling out on their own. "There's one important thing I want to do," she blurted.

"What's that?"

"Convince you to ditch Langdon and come home and live with me, that's what. Make you a permanent member of this household, with kitchen privileges and everything."

Edie's long fingers fiddled with a lock of her hair; she looked away from her mother. "You mean live here and go to Evanston High?" She sounded stunned.

"That's it."

"In this big old place, with you?"

"Just you and me."

"Dad would be so furious."

"He doesn't decide everything." Rachel pressed her lips together in an effort to say no more about Matt.

Edie frowned slightly. "I don't know for sure what I want," she said. "I've got friends at Langdon. I'm not exactly prepared to uproot my *life*, Mother."

"Will you think about it?"

"You could *order* me, you know. The judge gave you custody."

"I won't do anything of the sort. I'm too much of a wimp anyhow. I want you here, but unless you want to be here, it doesn't work."

Rachel held her breath as Edie digested that. She had planned so carefully, and now she had blown her own strategy.

"I'll think about it, I guess. But don't count on it."

Rachel exhaled. "Sure."

"How come you don't sound happy about Grandma coming back?"

"But I am, of course I am," Rachel said, taken aback.

"Does it have to do with Grandpa? I mean, neither you nor Grandma talk about him very much," Edie persisted.

"Absolutely not." Rachel bridled. "Your grandfather was a wonderful man and his death was a terrible thing—"

"You don't have to get defensive, Mother, I've heard all this before. You've got a habit of it, actually. Kurt says it's a classic coping mechanism."

Rachel put a plate of take-out chicken salad and bread in front of her daughter, and dipped a spoon into the coffee can, tossing out six spoonsful of coffee into the coffeemaker. She used the time to collect her thoughts. Could she just for once this evening hit the right notes? "Thank you very much, Dr. Snow," she said lightly. "Putting *that* aside, I hate to think you have some wrong idea about your grandfather—"

"Okay, I'll drop it. Kurt said you'd react this way if I mentioned *anything* about it."

Rachel was taken aback again. "You've talked to *him* about your grandparents?"

"We are very close, for your information."

"Edie, who *is* this boy? He must be at least four or five years older than you. How did you meet him? What about the boys at your own school?"

"The boys at my school are dorks. Kurt is smarter than everyone else and I don't *care* about his age." Edie put her coffee mug down with such force that some of the coffee splashed over the lip and onto the counter. "I can't believe this is starting this way! Look, Mother, I'm sixteen, okay? I'm here because it's like, Christmas, and Dad is away anyway, and I'm not your little girl anymore. I can handle my own life. And I'm a *good* driver."

Rachel bit her lip and slowly began mopping the butcher block with a sponge. Parenthood. While you still think you've got all the answers, your kid becomes someone different, someone with incredibly good attack skills. This wasn't what she wanted. What she wanted was a reconnection with the loving

30

daughter she knew was somewhere behind this defiant, pinched little face in front of her. "Okay," she said finally.

Edie seemed suddenly to relent. "He's nineteen, if you really want to know. But Dad was ten years older than you."

"Well," Rachel managed, "look what happened to us."

"Yeah, right." Edie sat there, holding her coffee, a blank look spreading across her face. Rachel noted she had not taken a single bite of the chicken salad.

"How's everything else going?" she asked.

"Fine." Edie sighed, suddenly looking very young.

"Grades okay?"

"Pretty good. Not great, but please, don't have a cow over them when they come. You know me and biology."

Rachel stored that for the time being. "So you like the house?" she asked. "Isn't this a wonderful kitchen? Doesn't it glow? Grandpa and Grandma opened up the back and added the windows when I was fifteen—it was considered so daring back then. I'm going to put plants everywhere, the way it used to be."

Edie glanced around the kitchen, taking in the wood cabinets and the row of copper pots hanging from a bar in the center of the room. "Sure, it's okay. You need new countertops."

"It's on my list." She smiled and pushed for more. "Just okay?"

"I liked our old home. Even if you and Dad did walk around hating each other."

Edie's voice was quite distant now, but it held threads of pain that caught at Rachel's heart. It never

31

ends, she told herself, as the phone suddenly began to ring.

"Rachel?" It was Berry, her voice edged with the frenzied energy she always brought to a deadline. "I've got to go over the schedule for the week with you. Sorry to call so late, but you left early—"

"Let's do it in the morning; we'll have plenty of time."

"But that's how we get into crunches like the one today. Oh, the anthropologist from Pakistan says *fine*, but he wants to know who else will be on the show—"

"Berry, I want to talk tomorrow. Edie's here." Rachel watched Edie slide off the stool, her chicken salad still untouched.

"But—"

"*Tomorrow*, okay? Bye. I'll be in early." She hung up, annoyed. Berry could have held back tonight. She knew Edie was coming home.

Edie cast her a weary, scornful look. "Mom, quit *trying* to pretend you're not thinking about the show all the time, will you? I'm used to your crises."

* * * *

Rachel managed to find a pair of matching sheets in a box on the stairway and together they made up Edie's bed, Edie yanking at the edges of the bottom sheet and ignoring wrinkles. Rachel resisted the impulse to smooth out her daughter's work. Instead she nodded over at a stack of red leather-bound books sitting on a chair. "I haven't had time to shelve all the books yet; there's a bunch of yours in that stack."

Edie glanced over and then gave the top sheet an efficient yank, her face solemn.

"I used to read you a lot of stories, remember?"

"You always remember more of that kind of stuff than I do."

"*Charlotte's Web? Sara Crewe? Frog and Toad?*"

Edie allowed her an inch. "I remember *Frog and Toad.*"

"You do? I'm impressed."

"It was cool the way you did their voices. I used to wish you'd tell stories like that on the radio so I could pretend you were talking to me." Edie's pale face was empty of expression.

"I love you, Edie." Rachel leaned over the bed, pursing her lips in the old way that used to make Edie giggle. But Edie seemed not to notice as she bounced down on the bed, testing its firmness.

"What'd you do with my old bed?" she asked. "This one's too soft."

"I'm glad you're with me," Rachel said. "You're still my baby."

"Mother—please." But Edie allowed herself to be kissed goodnight.

Later, Rachel wandered the house. She would get a tree soon and the two of them would decorate it with Mother, and it would all work fine. I'll pull things together again, she told herself. She sighed, glancing up the darkened stairs at where her well-defended, needful daughter was sleeping. You grab for a child when she toddles toward the street, you buckle her into a life jacket when she swims in the pool and you sit up and fantasize about car wrecks when she is out after midnight. But how do you protect a daughter who is too old to hold your hand crossing the street?

Finally the clock struck midnight and Rachel crawled into her own bed and closed her eyes. She was back home again, damn it. If she had to, she could analyze a political debate or lay out in layman's terms the argument of a plasma physicist, but she couldn't explain satisfactorily to anybody—including herself— why she was back here in this house, nor could she say whether or not it was a good move or one of the dumbest of her life. Eventually she fell asleep, dreaming of Edie and her mother and Amos, and somehow they were all mixed together, limbs and heads and voices. It was not a restful night.

CHAPTER 2

RACHEL AWOKE IN THE COOL, WHISPERING CONFINES of what had been her parents' bedroom, watching the morning sun work its way through the Pottery Barn muslin curtains she had hung only yesterday.

"You're making a big mistake." That's what her father said the day she stood in the doorway of this room and told him she was marrying Matt Snow and would support the two of them while he finished his graduate degree in architecture. It had not, of course, taken Matt very long to figure out he'd never get rich as an architect, building shopping malls would do it much more efficiently.

"Why? Give me one good reason," she had said, trying to keep a certain defiance at bay. After all, she was twenty-two, in lust, if not in love, and much more of an expert on what she should do with her life than her father—at least when he was in his somber moods, which was happening more often lately.

She watched him frowning in front of the closet mirror as he swiftly, expertly, tied one of his much-loved Brooks Brothers silk ties before answering.

34

Phillip Duncan was a lean and handsome man with deeply carved worry lines in his forehead that could vanish in a minute when he was delighted with something, and oh, how she used to rejoice when she saw the light dance in his eyes. But you never knew. Sometimes he would literally tap dance down the sidewalk; sometimes he was so weighted down with gloom he couldn't even treat his patients. Like now; this very minute that meant so much to her.

"Because he won't make you happy. The way I don't make your mother happy," he said, and she still remembered the shiver she had felt at the sadness in his voice.

The phone rang, piercing her thoughts.

"I trust Edie made it to your new pad without incident," a male voice said. "I hate to say this, Rachel, but isn't buying back that white elephant a little childish?" Matt Snow was the flip side of her mother. *He* never bothered with preambles like "Hello" or "How are you?" on the phone, so it shouldn't surprise her that his voice was as brisk and dismissive as ever.

"She's here, and we're fine. The house is great. So how's Hawaii?" She would be just as brisk. She could almost see him sitting by his hotel pool with his latest anorexic MBA from Harvard, wearing the most expensive linen shirt he could find in the hotel gift shop, picking up the phone and calling just to horn in on her time with Edie.

"Is she awake? I've got news for her. By the way, you owe a call to Langdon's headmaster as soon as possible, Rachel. He expects both of us to contribute to the fund-raising drive, which I certainly find reasonable, since I've been carrying the brunt of Edie's tuition for a couple of years now. I trust you won't

35

have any problem with that now that you've got the money from me you wanted."

So that officious little runt of a headmaster was keeping Matt posted on her contributions. Rachel's head throbbed. "I'll handle my obligations in my way, Matt; I certainly am glad you and your lawyers finally honored yours. So what's your news for Edie? Aren't you calling awfully early? She's still asleep."

She heard a murmur in the background, the tinkling laugh of a woman.

"We're not in Hawaii," Matt said in his most self-satisfied tone. "We're at the Four Seasons in New York and about to fly to the Big Island—for our honeymoon."

"Honeymoon?" Rachel said stupidly.

"Greta and I were married last night—a spur-of-the-moment thing." His voice was suddenly muffled and she fancied him turning to the invisible Greta and giving her a quick, posturing nuzzle for her sake. She wondered what old bag-of-bones Greta looked like without her clothes on.

"Well—congratulations. But without telling Edie first? Without telling your daughter?"

"I told you, it was a sudden decision. We are quite happy and I'm sure Edie will be happy for us. If you aren't going to wake her up to hear the good news from me, please tell her later. We'll call tonight from Hawaii."

"Matt, I'll do no such thing. I think you should have prepared her for this. When you call, you tell her yourself."

"You do work at being difficult, don't you?" A deep, noisy, put-upon sigh. "But then, you always did. I suspect that's why you blew that anchor job."

Rachel winced. She had a quick memory of how sometimes she used to see Matt's face across a room at an office cocktail party talking to people he deemed important, or studying a menu in an expensive restaurant with his lips pursed, or giving her his increasingly conservative views on politics, and wondering time and again why he was becoming so smug, so banal and suffused with self-importance, so adept at putting her down—so alien. Not in the early years, not during the delicious times when they laughed and talked and had sex two and three times a day at home or on the floor of his office or on the beach under a full moon. No, it developed slowly— spreading over their lives like a poison as she started in radio, moved on to reporting at the *Tribune*, and finally landed a dream job as a noon anchor for the ABC affiliate in Chicago. Culminating when she told him she wanted a divorce. "You're not good enough for that job," Matt had said scathingly, needing to believe it. Maybe he had been right. She had lasted six months, returning, humbled, to radio. And he would never, ever let her forget it. It vindicated him somehow.

"I'll ignore that, Matt. Look, I think it's a mistake for you not to tell her yourself and you should think about that."

"Good-bye, Rachel."

"Good-bye, Matt. Feed that bride of yours some bacon and eggs for breakfast, will you?" She hung up, guiltily pleased with herself.

* * * *

Edie shifted the gears carefully into reverse and began inching her mother's car slowly out of the garage, her

37

hands tightly gripping the wheel.

"Watch out for the paint cans," Rachel said quietly. Edie had begged passionately at breakfast for the chance to drive them both downtown this morning and Rachel finally had, with some trepidation, given in. Now she kept her fists balled tight in her lap, hidden under her handbag.

"I see them, Mother."

The car moved with minimal jerking into the alley. Edie squinted against the sudden harsh sun as she turned the wheel and headed for the street.

"Pull your visor down," Rachel said.

"I was just about to."

Edie turned onto Sheridan Road and merged carefully into the traffic heading for Rogers Park. She shifted into second, and the gears growled loud enough to make her jump.

"Push the clutch in all the way," Rachel said.

"Mom, I can do this." Edie drove slowly, painstakingly past the cemetery and on through Rogers Park in complete silence. Rachel's eyes automatically looked right, seeking her father's grave; her reference point. She said nothing. By the time Edie reached the left turn that took them out onto the Outer Drive, she wasn't jerking the car as much. She made the turn, accelerated, and then visibly relaxed. She was blending smoothly into traffic.

"Perfecto, sweetie."

"Yeah, not too bad, right?"

Rachel smiled, touched by the relief in Edie's voice. With only a little concentration, she could remember what it was like to be sixteen and yearning for a driver's license and all it entailed. "So where are you going today? Want to sit in on my show?" she asked.

"Oh, I've seen you do it a million times; I mean, I like the show, but I think I'll hit a video store, okay?" Edie brushed back a silky thread of hair from her pale forehead. "Then maybe I'll meet a couple of friends for a movie or something."

It was the vagueness of the "or something" that made Rachel pause. "How about checking in with Topper? Just to make sure she got home last night."

"I'll think about it." Edie's right hand moved restlessly for the radio dial. "Wish you had a tape player; this thing is ancient."

"Sorry, I'll catch up one of these days. I'll be ready to go home around three o'clock, so meet me in the lobby of my building. If you want to come up, Berry is dying to say hi."

Edie's hand dropped from the dial. "Mom, I hope you won't go ballistic, but I think Dad's going to marry Greta. You okay with that? I mean, are you going to throw a fit or something when it happens? She said I could be her bridesmaid. Is it okay if I get a new dress for the wedding?"

Rachel slowly relaxed her hands, smoothing down the folds of her coat, watching the road ahead. They were almost at Michigan Avenue. "Do you like Greta?" she asked.

"Yeah, she's okay, I think. She acts like a girlfriend. We talk about diets; she's so skinny she makes me feel fat."

Rachel suddenly ached for her daughter. But she also had a totally selfish thought: better that Edie have a twenty-five-year-old beanpole as a stepmother than someone real who might usurp her place in Edie's heart.

"So can I get a new dress?"

39

Rachel leaned sideways and kissed Edie lightly on the cheek. "Don't buy it for a wedding," she said. "Just go find the prettiest dress in town."

* * * *

Half an hour later, Rachel sank into the chair in her office and began groping in a bottom drawer for a bottle of Advil she knew was in there somewhere; if she ever cleaned out her drawers, she'd find it in a minute. She had a headache again, the Matt Snow Headache Special; when were they ever going to end? Where was the Advil?

"Got a minute?" She looked up and saw Jim Boles standing in the doorway, one of his large hands ("my bear paws," he called them jokingly) resting against the door frame, fingers drumming slightly. There were the usual nicks on his jaw from what must be hasty shaves, and his smile was genial. But his dark blue eyes behind heavy-rimmed glasses were clouded. She smiled automatically; who wouldn't? Jim was a good guy. He had hired her to host WBBW's morning talk show at a time when she was beginning to wonder if she had the right stuff anymore for broadcasting. Nothing she had done after her humiliating television flop had caught on—and for a while, she had been stuck with doing everything from news at the top of the hour to weather reports. She and Jim had known each other casually during the years when their daughters were growing up—meeting at school events; not much more. Now they went out for lunch on occasion and groused together about the expenses at Langdon, and sometimes, in the afternoons, Jim would saunter in and put his feet up on her desk and regale her with old stories about the wild days of

Chicago journalism that made her laugh. His presence always warmed her; she wasn't sure why. Once after a show he particularly liked, he had brought her a huge box of chocolate-covered cherries. She couldn't tell him how much she hated the oozy, sweet things. So they sat on her desk for about a month until she quietly dumped what was left down the trash chute, feeling obscurely sad.

She closed the drawer with a sense of premonition, wondering what was bothering him, and waved him to a battered, straight-backed chair. "You're always welcome," she said. "What's up?"

"You're doing a terrific job, you know that, don't you?" he began.

"Thank you, boss. But you know I don't do it alone."

"Don't get modest," he said with a slow grin. "You come up with the best damn questions, and you never lose control of the show. You've definitely found your niche."

"Thanks again," she said, feeling warier by the second. "But why do I think you have something else to say?"

"We're changing formats, which probably doesn't come as much of a surprise," he said casually.

She stiffened. It was no secret around WBBW that the station's oldies format was getting stale; in fact, they were pulling declining audience numbers. Everybody was nervous. "So what are we now?" she asked.

"Classic Rock with news still at the top of the hour," Jim said. "We don't need the kids, but we do need baby boomers who buy things. This should turn us around."

"Good, I hope so," she said heartily. "But what if we lose the people who like to listen to me?"

"Obviously we don't want to, but we can't make it any more on denture ads. I wish—" A cloud passed over his face. "You've got potential that goes far beyond what you can do here. For you, this place is just a starting point."

So this was how the ax was going to fall. Velvet-coated with lots of meaningless compliments. Rachel's throat went dry as she thought about her new mortgage, about the painters and the carpenters, and all the bills piling up on her desk at home. She squared her shoulders. If there was one thing she'd learned to do, it was take bad news. "I'd appreciate it if you didn't try to let me down easy," she said.

His astonished expression appeared totally genuine. He leaned forward, the chair creaking under his bulk. "No, no," he said. "We're not killing your show. Is that what you think? You're the best thing we've got. The last thing in the world I want to do is replace you with two hours of rock. We'd *lose* revenue."

"I don't believe it."

"I'm not trying to make you feel good. What you've done is attract upscale advertisers we'd risk losing if we folded your show. Whole Foods, Barnes & Noble—we'll always be a music station, but you add the touch of class we want. It's not you, Rachel, it's us. We're limping along and we're taking another budget hit next month. That's what I'm worried about."

"And the numbers for my show aren't building fast enough?" Her stomach tightened; sweat suddenly moistened the skin beneath her breasts. She gripped the arms of her chair.

"You need more time—plus, it would help to have a gimmick of some sort, something to get you more publicity."

"Wait, let me guess—that means you guys are cutting the publicity budget again, right?" This headache was far beyond a Matt Snow Special now. She thought she had forgotten what it felt like when she lost the anchor job, forgotten the panicky feeling of falling through the floor, but she hadn't. The panic had been just sitting inside her in some hidden corner, licking its chops, waiting for another opportunity to strike and take her back down that hole.

"Yeah." Jim stood up, shifting his heavy body uncertainly. "Rachel, I believe in you and your show and I'll do everything in my power to make it fly. Got that?"

Her eyes stung. "Got it."

"This conversation is just a heads-up for both of us," he said firmly.

"How much time do I have?"

He shrugged, watching her. "I figure about another six months, but that's all you need. You're getting attention and with enough time you'll be the best damn investment we've made, a hell of a lot better than just throwing another deejay on the air."

"Thanks for the vote of confidence." She managed a grin.

"I like you, you know that. I want you to succeed." He looked at her with so steady a gaze that Rachel had to look away. She rose then from her chair and walked over to the window, staring out at the frozen terrain. "Did Topper get home all right last night?" she asked.

"She pulled in a little late, but, yeah, everything was fine."

"Jim, I'm sorry for Edie's rudeness. I hope Topper wasn't too upset—"

Jim turned away slightly, shrugging his shoulders, but she heard the troubled note in his voice. "She gets her feelings hurt pretty easy, I guess. I'm not always too good at knowing how to handle this kind of thing, but I think she feels better this morning."

Rachel felt deeply contrite now. "We're going to trim the tree on Friday night, after Mother gets here. Will you and Topper come have dinner with us?"

He cast her a quizzical grin. "You sure you want one overweight and underbudgeted station owner coming to your Christmas party with your daughter's ex-best friend?"

"I want a particular good friend who's in my corner."

"Then we accept. And don't worry about anything, let me worry." Looking slightly flushed, Jim gave her an awkward squeeze on the shoulder and turned and left, passing Berry in the doorway.

"What bad news is Boles dishing out, other than the fact that we're changing formats? Are we losing our jobs?" Berry asked, glancing after him. Her eyes looked unusually strained.

"No, not that. We still don't have the numbers, that's all."

"Surprise, surprise. How come it's so cold in here?" Berry pulled a thin wool sweater of faded mauve across her breasts and shivered.

"Larry tells me the boiler's acting up again."

"Or maybe WBBW's sterling owners are cutting back on fuel along with the publicity budget." Berry clamped her lips together and stomped across the floor. She knew; she always knew.

"Berry—" Rachel leaned forward, pushing papers aside to find room for her elbows on the desk. "I'm worried. We don't have too long."

"I know."

"We're getting better, and we're getting better known. But we need to figure out a way to juice things up."

"Yeah, and how do you do that? Scream and insult everybody like Tebbins over at WMAAT? That's not you. We've got to have enough time to make an impact and here we sit, trapped by these penny-pinching assholes—" Berry seemed suddenly overcome with frustration. "Jesus, I'm putting my life into this show and they're willing to let the competition walk all over us, just to save a couple of bucks. And now you've done a back flip into the past with that old barn of a house. Don't you understand, Rachel? You've *got* to keep everything focused here!"

Rachel pushed back her chair, muscles tensing. "Whoa," she protested. "My house isn't the issue. We're in this together and we'll make it work. Okay?"

Berry didn't answer right away. Instead she stared down at the week's schedule in her hands. "It isn't 'we,' it's you," she said slowly. "You're going to be the best thing on radio. What you need is something that gets you attention, something that makes you stand out, and I'm damn well going to figure out what it is. I'm going to do it, I promise you. Don't try to mollify me. I mean it."

Her intensity was really over the top; so much so, Rachel wondered if something bad was happening at home. But if she asked right now, Berry in her present mood might get even gloomier and she didn't want that.

45

"You know what we should do? We should get out and split a bottle of wine together over dinner and maybe go to a movie, the way we used to. Or the symphony—how about the symphony? Up for it?" she suggested.

"Right, any day now. I'll chain my father to the TV set so he can't roll off the balcony and just go with you on the town. Sorry, not a good idea."

"We'll figure a way, after Christmas," Rachel said comfortingly, thinking of how long it had been since the two of them had done much of anything together away from the pressure of work. She tried to envision Berry in the shabby old South Side apartment with the high ceilings that she had been to only once since Berry's father moved in with her last year. That visit had agitated him so much, she decided not to go back. She wondered what Berry did anymore beside take care of him and stare at television when she wasn't working at the station. This place was her whole life, which made Rachel feel bad for her friend. She reached for the schedule. Her panic was hunched down again, back in its corner; she had to keep it there for Jim, for Berry, for Edie. She shoved aside a stack of books and cleared a small space in the center of her desk. They'd done this so many times now—scrawling ideas and names and juggling themes and trying to put together shows that people would listen to and praise and talk about. "Come on, let's go through the schedule," she said gently, beckoning to Berry to sit down across from her.

"Here's the publicity packet on the Jeri Bloodstone book, for what it's worth," Berry said, pushing a thick, glossy mailer across the desk. "She's on this morning."

46

"I read her book last night. Interesting; a little slick." Rachel leafed through the promotion packet quickly before impatiently tossing it aside. "I don't know why they make up these elaborate question-and-answer sheets—it's insulting. I'll ask my own questions."

"They do them because not every talk-show host reads the goddamn book first."

"What's the rest of the week look like?"

"Tomorrow, theme day: Are the Comic Pages Getting Too Politically Liberal? We've got Congresswoman Ruby Malek and Seth Dubin lined up—"

"Good, one raging conservative, one foaming liberal—anyone in the middle?"

Berry shook her head. "That's you, dearie. Thursday, General Felkman's new book on the Balkan peace breakdown; Friday, 'Is Big Business Out of Control?' I'm still trying to get through to Warren Buffett at the Drake Hotel. If he'd come on the show it would be fabulous—"

Rachel smiled. Berry actually managed to book some unlikely guests, and she had learned never to squelch her ideas. "Good luck. Tell him we have a potential audience of three million listeners," she teased.

"Unfortunately, he can count. Oh well, here's the latest exposé on Ted Turner's deals, four hundred pages. Can you read it by next week? Of course you can. We've got the author lined up with that slightly fusty economist from Northwestern—"

Rachel frowned, the worry lines between her eyebrows creasing deep. "We can't get boring, Berry. We just can't."

"You won't, you never do." Berry stood with a quick, brisk movement. "Five minutes; I'll go see if we've got Ms. Bloodstone in the waiting room."

"Still 'Guns in the Schools' next week?"

"Yep. *That* story doesn't date. I put a Snickers bar in your desk, by the way. How do you stay thin, eating those things?"

Berry was gone, clearly cheered up. Rachel settled back in her chair, opened her desk, and removed the candy bar from its plastic wrapper and bit into the chocolate. Junk food helped her collect her thoughts. She felt a piercing jolt of warmth, and it wasn't just carbos. Tonight she would close the door to this office and walk out of the station and go home with Edie. They would build a fire and eat supper together and the anticipation of those nice and homely satisfactions was enough to keep her fears at bay. She only wished that Berry could have the same.

* * * *

Rachel adjusted her headset and glanced at the engineer in the control room. The atmosphere in the tiny broadcast booth was as close as her office had been cold, which meant the air-circulating system was out of whack in the whole building. Five seconds. She laced her fingers together and smiled reassuringly at her guest, a blond gamine of uncertain age now flacking a bestseller on raising children. Her guest had the slightly glassy-eyed look of an author on tour who knows all the questions already and has memorized all the answers. Rachel reached for a pen and cupped it in her hand. Her challenge was to poke a hole in the programmed spiel and see what interesting things might come out. But what tack to take here? Her mind raced as the engineer's hand came down.

Rachel leaned into the mike, her voice intimate and husky. "Good morning, I'm Rachel Snow, and this is *Talk Time*—the show where you meet your favorite writers, argue with your least-favorite politicians, and share provocative ideas. Are you ready?" She paused; a swell of music.

The woman seated across from her took a sip of water and glanced at her watch and Rachel flashed her a confident, conspiratorial smile. "With us today, Jeri Bloodstone, author of *Don't Give Up the Ship!*, a primer on how to coexist with teenagers and keep your sanity. Just what many of us parents have been praying for, of course." She looked across the table and turned suddenly serious. "Jeri, you've studied a lot of families. Is it true that no matter how hard parents try, love in a family always flows downward, one generation to the next? Should we grieve about that or celebrate?"

Jeri Bloodstone, surprised, sat up straight and blinked her eyes. "Well, sure it 'flows downward,' " she said slowly. "Maybe that's why we've got so many aging parents rotting in nursing homes." She paused. "Or maybe becoming irrelevant is what we're aiming for. Without knowing it."

The board began to light up nicely. Time sped by so rapidly Rachel was surprised when she checked the clock and saw the show had only five minutes to go. She gazed across at her guest, who was now earnestly comforting a woman crying on the phones about a daughter who hadn't called in five years. One more call, she thought. The phones are hot today.

"Hello, you're on the air," she said, flipping a switch.

A voice oddly high and faintly metallic filled the room. "Hi, Rachel Snow. I have a question. Who are you?"

She paused. "I think I recognize your voice, aren't you Jay from Jersey? Weren't we arguing about nitrogen fertilizer a few days ago? You know who I am."

"No, I'm not Jay from Jersey, I'm a truth seeker. Call me that. Call me the Truthseeker. I like that."

Her finger hovered over the on-off switch. An elusive memory was stirring. "Okay, Truthseeker, what's your question?"

"It's about you, Rachel. It's about what you hide behind that fabulous voice of yours. That haunting voice. I ask for everyone, for all the truth seekers, what do you look like?"

"I look whatever way you want me to look," she said, glancing at Larry Kramer in the control room. He was grinning like a monkey.

"Blond. Right, I see you as a blond. Cool, intellectual, you know? Bet you wear red nail polish."

Rachel glanced down at her bare, well-bitten fingernails and smiled. "Sorry, wish I did. Maybe you're thinking about Diane Sawyer. Any questions for Miss Bloodstone?" For just a second, her attention wandered.

The voice slowed. "I'm not playing anymore, Rachel. You didn't quite catch my name, did you?"

"The Truthseeker," she repeated slowly, stalling for time. She remembered now. Was it ten years ago? Nine? A notorious Chicago killer had called himself that—a killer who stalked his victims and taunted police with signed notes. God, yes; she remembered. Amos had worked on that case. In fact, he had interviewed a convict in prison a few years later who claimed his cellmate committed the murders. But then the cellmate was found hanging from a rope in his cell and nothing was ever proved.

"No, I didn't die in prison, Rachel," the voice said. She shivered; he was reading her thoughts. "Nobody ever caught me. I've been here all along."

"You're the man who murdered two women on the Chicago Circle campus ten years ago?"

"Yes."

Rachel had a sense of time slowing down; even Jeri Bloodstone's shock seemed to be registering in slow motion. What should she say? What should she do? She glanced up and saw Larry Kramer's mouth hanging open. She hoped Jim or Berry or somebody was tracing the call and contacting the police. Keep your voice firm, she told herself. Nobody outside this room sees your face, but they hear you. Keep your voice firm.

"You could be just someone who reads old newspapers," she said. "Maybe you are that killer, and maybe you aren't. Why are you calling me?"

The voice oozed poison. "Because I like you. I like your voice."

She glanced at Kramer again. Should she try to keep him on or cut this off? "I don't believe you're the same person," she said. "You're using my show to get attention. Not a smart idea, fella."

"You don't want to take me seriously. I have ways to change that, and I guarantee you won't forget me the minute you flip that switch your finger is on right now. Nor will your listeners. I am fascinated by you. I picture you with lush, thick hair, strategically placed. I can feel it almost, the moist hotness between your

51

legs. Bikini wax. Do you use bikini wax? I'll bet you do. I'll bet—"

Rachel flipped the switch and swung into her sign-off, talking slightly faster than usual. "Well, folks, we pick up some weird ones every now and then; don't let it bother you," she said. Her neck felt hot and sweaty: he had been toying with her, trying to frighten her. She said good-bye to her guest and thanked her for her insights, but her thoughts were on that strange, unsettling voice. It was brittle with cruelty.

"We notified the police," Jim said, the second she emerged from the studio. "They didn't have enough time to trace the call, but they were very skeptical. They claim the Truthseeker is dead, and has been for years. You handled it perfectly."

"He gave me the creeps," Rachel whispered.

Marcie was at her side, shoving a small clutch of messages into her hand as she started back to her office. "Rachel, did you get these? No? I can't believe it. Who's *running* this place? I swear, I never ignore a single one and if there's a breakdown in communications at this dump, it comes at a higher level than yours truly, *that's* for sure."

Rachel scanned the messages quickly as she walked and felt her pulse quicken. Amos had called at nine. He wanted her to join him for lunch at Lucciano's.

"Oh, there you are." Berry came rushing down the corridor as Jim headed back to his office. "Edie called and said to tell you she hasn't been in a wreck yet and she'll pick you up at four; the painter said he's sorry he couldn't send anybody to the house today, they'll be there tomorrow; we've had some calls already about that jerk who's hot for bikini wax; the police say he's most likely the kind of phony who *loves* calling

52

talk shows and pretending to be some kind of menace; don't worry about it, they say. Warren Buffett is sorry, according to some lower-level minion, but he's much too busy to do the show, and—"

Rachel lifted a hand to stop the flow of words, looking quizzically at her friend. She tried to keep an accusatory note out of her voice. "Why didn't you tell me Amos called?" she asked.

Berry clapped a hand over her forehead, looking stricken. "Oh God, sue me, I forgot!"

Maybe she was just still on edge after the strange caller, but Rachel suddenly couldn't hold back her irritation. "I've already got a mother who is sufficiently on my case, remember? Please, don't go around deciding what's wrong for me. I know you don't approve of my seeing Amos, but I don't want anybody monitoring my life. My feeling is, you didn't tell me he called because you want me to think he's not interested and you're hoping he'll just fade away. Am I right or wrong? Remember, I know you pretty well."

"That was a very long speech. Is it at all possible that I just forgot?" Berry said stiffly.

"Come on, level with me."

"Okay, I don't like him. He's going to do it to you again, that's what I think. He's a drunk who mesmerizes women and he's been going downhill for years and now he's going to hurt you again."

"Give me credit for a *little* sense, Berry," Rachel protested, taken aback by her friend's ferocity.

Berry's eyes were getting suspiciously shiny. "Look, I'm sorry. Can we drop it? I can't help it if I walk around with a crystal ball in my head. When he calls again, I'll do a dance on your desk and put his message on top of the stack, I promise."

"Okay," Rachel said. "But let's understand each other—" She stopped. What more was there to say? What was the use of staying mad at Berry? She pushed up the sleeves of her old black sweater and fumbled for a lipstick in her purse before turning to leave the room.

"Where are you going?"

"To Lucciano's, of course." Rachel felt the silence follow her all the way down the hall and out the door.

She saw him before he saw her. She caught his scent at the very door of the restaurant and wondered how that could be, even as she inhaled deeply and moved to join him, almost sitting down before registering the presence of a young woman with bright eyes and very white teeth sitting at his side.

"Rachel, I want you to meet Jeanie Horton," he said, standing slowly, welcoming her with his eyes. "My new partner on the *Tribune* investigative team. She's a fan of yours who wants to say hello. Now I have a hard time imagining anyone in this town not knowing Rachel Snow, but there had to be someone, I guess." He wore an open-collar denim shirt, his usual jeans, a pair of well-worn cowboy boots; the singularly rakish effect was drawing sideways glances from just about every woman in the restaurant.

Jeanie Horton stood hastily and flashed an ingenue's smile that oddly contradicted her reputation as one of Chicago's toughest reporters. She had a narrow, businesslike mouth that scorned lipstick, and her flaming red hair was caught back in a high, careless ponytail. She looked to Rachel something like a schoolgirl, except for her watching eyes. Her investigations of last year's gambling scandal had

54

toppled two powerful aldermen and nailed the most crooked building contractor in Chicago. The word on the street was, don't mess with Jeanie Horton.

"Love your work, Mrs. Snow. I listen to you every morning when I can," Jeanie said. "You really wrap yourself around some good issues, are you planning anything more on sperm-bank scandals? God, that stuff is *great*." Rachel shook hands and babbled pleasantries, noting Jeanie's perfectly manicured and polished fingernails. She was younger than she had imagined.

"Are you joining us for lunch?" she asked finally with a polite smile.

Jeanie all but lunged for her coat. "Oh my, no, I wouldn't *dream* of horning in on you guys, you two must have plenty to talk about after all this time, being old friends and all," she said. She turned her toothpaste-white smile on Amos. "I'll see you back at the office; let's go through those nursing-home contracts and see what we find. Something will turn up, it always does. Bye, have a good one." She gathered her purse and a stack of papers held by a fraying rubber band and excused herself.

"Does she know about us?" Rachel said uneasily as she watched Jeanie head out the door.

Amos chuckled. "Whether we like it or not, we were once everybody's favorite illicit romance."

Rachel unfolded her napkin with great care and smoothed it over the lap of her skirt, first absently picking off a piece of lint. She checked the cuffs of her blouse, noting the button on her right sleeve was loose, before looking up straight into Amos's amused eyes. She started to tell him about the Truthseeker, but he stopped her with his voice.

55

"Are we still avoiding the past?" he teased gently.

"What do you mean?"

"We were a couple, remember?"

"I paid a big price, Amos."

"You wanted out of that marriage for a long time, if I'm not mistaken." He took a sip of what she noted was iced tea this time, a slightly mulish look passing over his weathered face.

"That's true," Rachel said. "As far as it goes." The room felt warm and murmuring; inviting; enveloping them as it had through those intense, sometimes tortured, stolen lunches and dinners they had shared for a long and painful year. She resented his quick thrust into the membrane of their relationship. It was too quick and too casual.

"So you're into team investigating this time around; what will you and Jeanie be working on? Or is that a secret?" she asked, as the waiter handed them their menus.

"We're looking for the right story now," he said with a frown. "We need a big one—something that warrants headlines and makes people sit up straight. It isn't as easy as it used to be."

"Think the town's more honest?"

He laughed, a low, rich chuckle. "No less or more so than anywhere else. From what I can see, TV is skimming the good stuff and we're not probing deep enough. But nothing beats a good investigative piece. Jeanie and I will blow their socks off with the right story."

The waiter arrived and took their orders and for a few moments Rachel felt herself swept back into the sweet shared routines of the past, that short span of time before their frail equilibrium was destroyed.

56

Berry had declared more than once that she would have warned her if she had been on the scene in time, but Rachel knew in her heart she would not have listened—not to Berry, not to anybody. Not even during the terrible time when Matt was threatening to expose her affair to get custody of Edie. Amos had stood by her then. She was sure they would marry when she was free. That had kept her sane while she fought hard for her daughter, all the while presenting to Amos a facade of self-confidence she desperately wanted to be real.

The morning Matt dropped his lawsuit had started blissfully. She met Amos in a tiny coffee shop with red tablecloths and sun streaming through the windows and triumphantly reported her news. She remembered the warmth of his hands as he softly cupped hers and congratulated her. She remembered him saying the warm, comforting words that she had grown to trust for their ability to envelop and cherish. And then, unbelieving, she heard him saying something different; something cataclysmic. He was marrying another woman.

"Who?" she had managed. "Why?" She had grabbed his hands as if she were drowning and reaching for a lifeline.

Amos's face had looked like a puzzle suddenly broken apart. "I love you, Rachel," he said raggedly. "I'll always love you. But I'm no good for you; you're better off without me. I can't give you an explanation you will understand or accept right now."

And he hadn't. Instead he married the yellow-haired daughter of a *Tribune* vice-president and disappeared onto the sun-drenched cliffs of Monterey Bay in Northern California.

"He never had to do anything, the prick," Berry said later. "He went for fresh meat, that's what he did."

The food arrived. Rachel picked at a pasta salad that looked unappetizing.

"You're not hungry."

"No." She stared at her plate.

Amos put his fork down and leaned close, his hands very near hers on the table. "This isn't where we should be," he said. "Rachel, come with me, I've got the key to the *Tribune* suite at the Hyatt Regency."

"No, I can't do that."

"Please." He was speaking low and urgently. "I can't tell you here what I have to tell you. Don't we owe ourselves something?"

* * * *

They made love with a shared yearning that Rachel had not experienced in a long time. They walked in the hotel room and instantly his hands were all over her body, squeezing, stroking; they could not get close enough. They would devour each other, she was convinced of it; the whole world retreated and there was nothing else that mattered. "I can't believe this is happening, I can't believe I'm here," she sobbed as she clutched his head and brought it to her breasts. He mounted her quickly. She licked a glow of salty sweat from her lip and thrust herself up, wanting nothing more at this moment than to merge with Amos, body and soul.

It was over in five minutes. They lay quietly together, the moist skin of their bodies touching, in what was for Rachel too haunting an echo of past intimacy. Then Amos pushed himself up on one elbow

58

and began slowly stroking her stomach.

"Now I have something to tell you," he said.

She heard the sadness in his voice and her muscles tensed. "You don't have to, Amos; it's history. Please, let's not risk spoiling this."

She heard his voice grow heavier and sadder. "You deserve to know why I left you and married Donna."

"You fell in love with her."

"No."

"Okay, that rules out the obvious. Maybe you were hoping to make the leap into management, and she was your route up in the newspaper world." Rachel stared at a torn piece of flowered wallpaper border directly above the bed.

"I don't blame you for still being furious. You wouldn't be human if you weren't. Maybe what I've got to say won't change that, but at least I'll have told you the truth." Amos sat up, his lean and muscular back bent and somehow vulnerable. "She got pregnant and she wanted that baby. Maybe it's an outdated reason, but I couldn't see walking away from my own kid. I figured she and the baby needed me more than you did."

Rachel reeled inwardly. How easily he said it. How easily he told her that during that time when all her love was wrapped around him, when she was in the fight of her life, he was in the process of committing himself to someone else. That she had never had a chance, because he had decided she was strong—and that made leaving her and hurting her somehow a lesser wound to inflict. "So you did it for the noblest of motives; thank you for clearing *that* little question up," she managed to say. How could he think she had not needed him? How could he say something so disconnected from the truth? How could he cut into her like this?

"She lost the baby at six months," he continued doggedly. "We drifted along for a while. Then she woke up one morning with a lump in her groin and I couldn't leave her then. She needed me, and I stuck with her all the way. I haven't seen many things through in my life but I saw that one through, and I think I made her happy. And I'm glad I did it."

For a long moment, the only sound in the room was their mingled breathing. Rachel wanted to pull herself up tight and crouch into a protective ball, but she forced herself to lie still.

"You know what I want to say? I want to say, well, pin a rose on you," she whispered. "But I don't have that luxury. I have to tell you that you did the right thing because you probably did, but how *could* you conclude that I didn't need you?" Her voice shook with the effort to hold back tears she would never again allow herself to shed.

"You're a strong woman, Rachel. Stronger than you know."

"That's easy for you to say." She took a deep breath and squeezed her eyes tightly shut. "I don't want to talk about it anymore. You did what you had to do, and I muddled through. Maybe you couldn't do anything else, I don't know." She heard her own voice and drew confidence from its coolness. If she couldn't truly mean what she was saying, she could at least protect herself by pretending. But when he answered, the tears almost broke through.

"You see, you're proving it right now," he said. "You are strong. I knew you would be." She felt his body shift its weight and move to the edge of the bed.

When she opened her eyes, he was already reaching slowly for his clothes. "It's almost three o'clock," he said.

"Three o'clock?" Her eyes shot fully open and she jumped from bed on the other side. "Lord, Edie's going to be waiting for me if I don't hurry."

"Will you have dinner with me tomorrow night?"

"I can't, Amos. Not with Edie home."

"I'd like to meet her."

Her heart missed a beat or two, but her voice stayed calm. "I'll think about that and let you know," she said.

"It's okay, Rachel. You can tell me to take a walk anytime you want. You're entitled."

There was something too easy about his tone; anger began lapping at the floodgates. "I might have lost custody of my daughter because of you," she said slowly. "Do you understand that? That's where I was four years ago. Matt found out about you and threatened to fight for custody, remember? I was damn lucky he decided to launch a power struggle instead. I am profoundly glad and deeply grateful, because I wouldn't be able to live with myself if he had taken her from me. You drank too much and you slept with another woman and then you left me and married her, and it was the best thing that ever happened to me. Do you hear?" Her voice ended in a thin treble.

Amos turned and reached for her, trying to pull her back down on the bed. "Remember something else," he said urgently. "That guy is a born manipulator, and *that's* why you stopped loving him in the first place. He wasn't going to take your kid away. He was only playing a money game."

"How could I know for sure? The risk was there." How, she thought despairingly, could he not have *seen* past her bravado and into her heart? Not once tapped into her guilt and pain? Because you tried to hide it all, she answered herself. You are just as responsible as he is, but that doesn't make it better. "He might have been able to do it, and if he had, I would've gone crazy. Don't you understand?"

"I do now. I didn't realize—"

"No, you didn't." She hunched herself forward, hugging her knees.

"Are we saying good-bye?" His voice was harsh with tension. "If we are, tell me now so I don't stick around hoping for something else."

"I don't know. Don't pressure me, I have enough pressures."

He stood slowly and collected her panties and bra and the rumpled remains of her good black suit and handed them to her. "Come on, let's get out of here," he said, his tone softening. "I'm glad you came with me. Can I say that? Wherever we go, we start from right here. The past is the past. Okay?"

She looked into his eyes and nodded, wondering how either of them could pretend it was true.

* * * *

"Rachel, where've you been, for God's sake?" Berry said excitedly as Rachel walked into the office. There were two bright spots of pink on her cheeks. "The calls! Wow, have we been getting calls!"

Rachel was momentarily confused. "About what?"

"About that diddle-head who thinks he's a big-time murderer and likes bikini wax, that's what! They did a piece about him on WBBM's afternoon news show—

can you believe it?" Berry laughed at the expression on Rachel's face. "I'm telling you, that guy did us a *big* favor. He really *could* be that Truthseeker murderer, and if he is, *you* brought him out of hiding. People are screaming about the danger of stalkers and obscene callers and praising you for handling it so well—WBBM even interviewed Jeri Bloodstone and asked her to describe what you looked like when he called and she praised you to the skies! She said you were amazingly cool but your eyes were blazing—that kind of thing. Oh God!" Berry threw her hands up in the air. "Today, I could die happy!"

"But that's ridiculous," Rachel sputtered. "It didn't happen like that at all."

She heard a sound behind her and turned to see a frowning Jim Boles standing in the doorway of his office. He was holding a Diet Coke in his huge hand, which meant he was trying to lose weight again. "Well, I don't like it," he said shortly. "That guy might be a lot more than just some kook with a dirty mouth. He could be dangerous."

"Don't knock success, Jim—just get us some decent publicity," Berry fired back.

"This is no crime show, and I'm not going to try and make it one."

Rachel felt compelled to bridge the gap between the two of them as quickly as possible. "Of course it isn't," she broke in quickly. "But good, bad, whatever, the point is, we did get some attention, so what do we do for an encore?"

Before either could answer, Edie suddenly appeared at the far end of the corridor. She looked a bit self-conscious as she approached them with a large red-and-gold Marshall Field box tucked under her right arm.

"Hey, been shopping?" Jim said in a markedly gentler tone.

"Well, yeah, I guess." Edie cast a side glance at her mother. "Got a new dress, that's all."

Rachel watched Edie's hand rub surreptitiously against the box, fingering the silver string.

"Something really nice?" she asked.

"Oh, it's okay," Edie said, shrugging her shoulders.

"Just okay? Or awesome?" Berry said.

Edie surprised her mother. "Awesome," she said softly, a light dancing in her eye.

Rachel reached for her coat. "Then let's get home fast," she said, "This I've gotta see."

* * * *

Edie was bubbly and animated all the way home and Rachel finally just let herself relax into her daughter's pleasure, trying not to worry. She hoped Matt would call quickly and break his news. Maybe it would be all right; maybe Edie wouldn't care that much. She had a new dress she could certainly wear somewhere—and it wasn't as if she was getting some stranger sprung on her by her father. She thought these things and drove home, part of her brain listening to Edie and part of it thinking of Amos. The trip went unusually fast.

Edie slipped into her dress right there in the living room, twirling in a bias-cut swirl of deep midnight blue silk. The bodice was close to the body, outlining her fresh young breasts without being glued to them. Surprisingly, the neckline would have passed muster at a church service. Rachel had to admit it was a good choice and it made her misty to see how lovely her girl looked in the first major dress she had bought on her own without her mother in the dressing room for final approval.

"Honey, you look beautiful," she said. "You don't need a wedding to enjoy it."

"First things first," Edie said airily, whirling again.

"You need shoes," Rachel said, absorbed in the fashion show. "And a strapless bra, I think. Maybe—"

The phone rang and Edie ran to answer it. Rachel waited in the living room, staring at the puffs of tissue paper spilling out of the open Field's box, her doubts suddenly growing. Should she have told her? She was gone a long time.

Edie appeared in the doorway, looking small and miserable inside her new dress. "Well, my ever-loving father managed to renege on another promise," she said.

"I'm sorry."

"They lied to me. They said they would wait and do it when I was with them. I mean, they didn't have to, but they said they would." An angry stain of tears began rolling down Edie's cheeks.

Rachel silently cursed the happy pair in Hawaii and walked forward, reaching out to put her arms around her daughter. But Edie backed away.

"He told you this morning. All this time, all day, you knew. And you let me go out and make a fool of myself over this dumb dress and you still never told me."

Rachel caught her breath at the hurt in Edie's eyes. "I thought the news should come from your father, not from me," she said weakly.

"You should have told me."

"It would still have surprised you, Edie. I didn't

want to be the one to disappoint you."

Edie rubbed the back of her right hand across her eyes, looking ten instead of sixteen. "You should have told me," she said stubbornly. "If you won't tell me the truth, who will? He sure won't. Neither of you are very good at being straight anyhow."

Rachel winced. "I'd like to believe that's not true."

Edie reached her hands up behind her neck and found the top of the zipper of her dress and pulled it down. The blue silk slithered down her body and landed at her feet. She stared dully down at it, then picked up her jeans and pulled them on. Her face was a mask.

"Don't let this take away your pleasure in your pretty dress," Rachel heard herself begging.

Edie looked at her with a glassy stare, then looked away. "It doesn't matter," she said with a shrug. "Why should I care? He said he'd get me a car for my birthday. You won't screw that one up for me, will you, Mother?"

Then she turned and walked out of the room, leaving the dress where it was on the floor. Rachel felt herself shivering with so many emotions she couldn't sort them out.

CHAPTER 3

"OKAY, I KNOW YOU'RE MAD AT ME, BUT I'D appreciate your acting like a civil human being when Grandma gets off that plane." Rachel squinted at the slightly blurred arrival information on the electronic board by Delta's gate twelve, feeling too drained and tired from that morning's embarrassingly thin show on the comic pages to do any cajoling. It hadn't helped when Amos called after reading about yesterday's show in the *Tribune*'s broadcasting column. "I wish you had told me—that's interesting stuff," he said, sounding slightly surprised. "I started to, but we got diverted slightly, wouldn't you say?" she had replied a little quickly.

Edie grunted something unintelligible. She shifted a grimy canvas tote from one arm to the other and hauled out a bottle of Evian water. She was wearing jeans shredded at the knees and across the backside, a dandy outfit for greeting her grandmother, but Rachel was determined not to say anything that might trigger another blowup just before Camilla stepped off the plane.

"You don't have to worry about me being *civil*, as you put it," Edie said, taking a large, wet gulp before spinning the cap back on the bottle. "I'm not a kid anymore. Which, of course, was my point last night."

"Edie, please, not now."

"I saw you hang that dress in the closet and you might as well forget it, because I'm returning it," Edie said flatly.

There was a sudden flurry of activity at gate twelve; a blue-coated airline employee wearing a ponytail held by a red rubber band pulled open the gate doors and passengers began emerging from the jetway. Rachel spied Camilla working her way toward them lugging a large shopping bag and marveled at how small she looked, how unexpectedly tiny in her long blue cotton skirt and denim blazer. She looked very Florida; very casual, except for her usual high heels. Camilla always had scorned flat shoes, something Rachel never was able to understand.

"Welcome home, Mother," she said warmly, determined that Edie should hear no hint of ambivalence in her voice.

"Thank you, I can't believe I'm back for good, but I am, and this terminal is the most gorgeous place on earth!" Camilla said in a breathless, bubbly voice, hugging them both. She seemed not to notice the pouty cast of Edie's mouth or Rachel's slightly strained smile. "I just brought one suitcase—this funny carry-on thing with the long handle. A very nice man shoved it up into the overhead compartment for me. Why don't they make them lighter? Well, actually I have another suitcase I checked, and I'm shipping the rest. But here's Christmas!" Camilla swung aloft the shopping bag filled with gifts. "I'm afraid I hit a few people in the head with this bag getting off; I thought one poor man was ready to sock me. I could hardly blame him, even though they're not too heavy. Honestly—"

"I'll carry it, Grandma." Edie reached out her hand without being nudged by her mother.

"Dear, are you up on computers, that sort of thing?"

"Well, sure. I mean, mostly."

"Will you give your clumsy grandma a lesson or two? It's good you're up on everything, because I need somebody to tell me who the hell all the people are I'm reading about in *People* magazine these days. Rachel, aren't we lucky to have Edie around?"

"Yes, we are," said Rachel. Her mother was putting on quite a perky show, and she saw with relief that the cloud was lifting from Edie's face as the three of them began working their way down the corridor toward the main terminal. Edie kept shifting Camilla's bag of unwieldy packages from one arm to the other without complaint, looking more cheerful by the moment.

Camilla flashed her daughter a big smile as they hurried through the flowing crowd. "Would you mind if I call Lindy Colson and have her come by for lunch tomorrow?" She glanced at Edie to explain. "You'll love her, dear, she's a real hoot sometimes. She's one of my oldest friends and used to put on the most splendid barbecues and she's a wonderful, warm person."

"That would be terrific. I'm looking forward to seeing her," Rachel said automatically. She wondered what message she had sent that compelled her mother to read off Lindy's credentials. But everything was starting smoothly, so maybe things would work out all right.

* * * *

The ride home to Evanston bubbled with light chatter. Camilla asked Edie about school and teased out of her little tidbits about her "cute new boyfriend," and said she couldn't wait to meet him. Edie, in turn, laughed and joked in an astonishingly relaxed way that lifted Rachel's spirits even more. She turned on the radio to catch a rebroadcast of last week's show, most of it an interview with a Carl Sagan type on celestial black holes, and was delighted when Camilla squealed, actually squealed, at the sound of her daughter's voice. "Honey, you've gotten so good, my God, listen to you, you sound like you know everything about those black holes! Edie, listen to your mother. Isn't this terrific!" For a few moments they listened, actually listened, and Rachel was glad it had been a good interview, and not the one earlier in the show on a new obedience-training book for dog owners.

Only when they passed Calvary Cemetery did they fall silent as Camilla turned to gaze at the array of splendid headstones abutting the curve of Sheridan Road. The stone over Phillip Duncan's grave was briefly visible at precisely the halfway point around the curve; this Rachel knew. She slowed down.

"Shall we stop?" she asked. "I thought we could—"

"Oh, goodness no, not now." Camilla quickly altered the sharpness of her voice. "Maybe later, don't you think? I'm dying to see the house, dear."

"Okay." Rachel sped up, but she couldn't stop the thought that crept quickly into her brain. Does she miss Dad anymore? she wondered. And then felt guilty for even forming the question.

* * * *

Camilla stepped out of the car slowly and stood by the curb, staring at the house. She had thought she was prepared and realized she wasn't; she had to resist the impulse to look away. It was awake, alive, almost preening. She tried to blink away the past, but she could suddenly see faces and fluttering muslin curtains in the upstairs windows and toys strewn on the lawn, and none of it was really there anymore. It was all just in her head. But the house was awake, it was alive. She took a deep breath. This was more than she had bargained for, and she wasn't even inside the door yet.

"Are you all right, Mother?"

"Of course I am. It looks just as clunky as ever, but you'll love the porch come summer, unless the wood's rotted away. Have you checked for termites?" Camilla steadied herself, remembering lazy Sunday mornings on the porch swing, as Rachel unlocked the front door and pushed it open. Slowly, Camilla stepped inside. She touched the banister, stroking it, gazing up the stairs as if she expected to see something.

"I had it brought down to the original wood and refinished," Rachel was saying. "You should have seen it, all slopped with black paint. I can't do everything right away, but that paint was too awful to bear."

"I had a big fight with your father over the bill to repair the old thing," Camilla said lightly. "Phillip thought it was outrageously high. He said old houses weren't really worth it." She moved into the living room, looking around, gazing at the ceiling. Rachel and Edie fell silent as Camilla stood in the middle of the room, breathing in the scent of fresh paint and something else. She sniffed.

"Roses?" she asked tentatively.

"The garden's gone, Mother, but I bought a bunch of them—for old times' sake, you know?" Rachel was looking a little awkward. "When you used to fill the house with them for parties?"

"What a lovely thought." Camilla forced herself back to the present and looked fully at her daughter for the first time since they had driven up to the house. This meant a lot to Rachel and she had to snap out of it. She reached out and hugged her, really hugged her. "It's wonderful. I feel welcomed, dear. Thank you."

Rachel beamed, relieved. She started to answer, but the phone was ringing and she ran into the kitchen to pick it up, only to hear a click and then a dial tone.

"You've made it your own," Camilla said softly as Rachel hurried back into the living room. The words hung oddly in the air and Rachel tried to plump them up, like pillows.

"So I wasn't crazy after all?"

"Well, that depends on the state of the plumbing. And I'm not kidding—have that porch checked for termites."

The phone was ringing again, and this time Edie ran to get it, complaining that there should be more cordless phones in the house and how could anybody be expected to run to the kitchen every time the phone rang?

"If it's Lindy Colson, I'll call her later," Camilla said.

A second later, Edie reappeared. "Nobody was on the line. I hate that," she said, annoyed.

The diversion gave Camilla an extra instant or two to collect herself. "Now I want to see the old kitchen," she said brightly. "Come on, I have a lot to tell you about my plans." She grabbed her daughter with one hand and her granddaughter with the other. "Oh, it is such a treat to be here!"

She paused at the kitchen door and caught her breath. Her favorite room in the house. The wood cabinets looked fresh and the space was warm, the way she remembered it, or wanted to remember it. "Well, isn't this nice? I'm glad to see the stove's in the same place. I'll put some water on for coffee. Where's the teakettle?"

"I haven't found one I like yet."

"An old saucepan will do. Where's the instant?"

"I'll just brew a pot, Mother."

Camilla pulled herself up gingerly on the tall bar stool. She smoothed back straight hair that was a bit too dark and in need of highlighting, and tucked her glasses up on top of her head. "Well, you need to know, I'm going back to work," she announced. "Right away. I might be getting my old job back."

"At Marshall Field's? Cool, Grandma."

So Camilla told them she was applying for the job of buyer of men's furnishings, exactly what she used to do; the job was already all but promised, although it wouldn't open up until after the first of the year. Rachel noticed a deepening line of tension around her mother's mouth and wondered why she was telling all this unnaturally fast.

"Anyway, I start the day after tomorrow," Camilla said. "They need some holiday help, and it'll give me a chance to see everybody at the store again and ease into the old routine."

"Holiday help? What do you mean?"

The phone rang again, Rachel picked it up. "Hello?" she said, but there was only silence on the other end. Annoyed, she slammed the receiver down.

"I told you, the job isn't available yet. That's actually fine with me, because I've got mountains of things to do to get resettled. So I'll just help out over Christmas—"

"Mother, you're going to Field's to work as a salesclerk?"

Camilla stiffened perceptibly, but she waved an impatient hand, "Why not? I began as a clerk in men's furnishings and I certainly know how to do the job. I'm just filling in temporarily. It'll be fun."

"Have they actually offered you the buyer's job?"

"I talked yesterday to the new personnel director. He's little more than a kid, but he was delighted I called. He says they're dying to get me back."

"Is it a firm offer?"

"She already said it was." Edie's voice was sharply, warningly loyal.

"It is not precisely a firm offer yet," Camilla said calmly. "They want to see if I still have the right stuff, I suppose. I'm not worried. It's like ice skating: you never forget how." She sat up straight, crossed her legs, and gazed steadily at her daughter, almost daring disagreement.

Rachel put three mugs on the counter, bothered by the set of her mother's mouth.

"Well, it all sounds good," she said. The words didn't come out sounding the way she wanted.

"All Grandma has to do is get briefed on the computers and she'll be off and running." Edie's eyes widened with a sudden thought. "Do you get a discount?"

"I think so. Always did before."

"That is so great. Can I come buy Kurt's Christmas gift from you?"

"My pleasure, sweetie."

The phone rang sharply for the fourth time. All three of them jumped. "Who *is* this?" Rachel demanded into the receiver.

There was a pause—then a small chuckle at the other end. "Sounds like you've had a bad day, Mrs. Snow. Edie there?"

"Hello, Kurt." She thrust the phone toward Edie who grabbed it, pulled the cord taut and moved into the laundry room around the corner from the refrigerator.

"What do we think of him?" Camilla said casually.

"He's a college kid, kind of arrogant, and he's too old for her. But Edie thinks he knows everything, which means I have to be careful when we talk about him."

"Well—" Camilla was toying thoughtfully with her mug—"you dated a couple of those, too."

"Actually, I married one, didn't I?"

They exchanged bittersweet smiles.

"Do you want to see your room, Mother? It's the one to the left at the top of the stairs on the third floor."

Camilla's smile faltered—or was it Rachel's imagination? "Of course, I can't wait for the full tour." Camilla looked around the kitchen with a strange expression on her face. "It's taken me a few minutes to adjust, but you've done good. And the windows"—she gestured, taking in the wide expanse of glass that opened the house to the garden and filled it with light—"I had forgotten how magnificent they were."

Rachel swallowed a lump in her throat. "I've always thought so."

Together they went up the stairs, with Rachel hauling the carry-on suitcase, bumping up one step at a time. Camilla walked ahead of her with puzzling slowness, her stiletto heels leaving tiny indentations on the worn salt-and-pepper carpet runner that Rachel hoped to be able to replace by spring. Maybe she didn't really want to be here. The thought jolted Rachel and made her feel oddly lonely. Should she have put her mother in the master bedroom? Was she feeling displaced? But Camilla was filled with praise for the newly refurbished room and wry observations about the house's idiosyncrasies as she set about the job of unpacking and settling in. And after a while, Rachel relaxed. She found herself telling Camilla about Matt's marriage and Edie's hurt and the discarded dress now packed away, and maybe it was just the fact of her mother listening to her pour it all out, but by the time the light faded from the windows and night settled in, she was feeling a little better about everything and arguing with Camilla, who thought buying an electric teakettle would be a better idea than getting some clunky designer thing that just sat and collected grease on the stove. By the time they got back downstairs, Edie had ordered two large pizzas with double cheese and sausage for dinner and had even remembered to tell them to hold the anchovies. Rachel was happy.

* * * *

It was past midnight, and the house was quiet, more or less. Still some of the same old creaks, Camilla noted as she stretched her legs under the covers, enjoying the feeling of Rachel's new cotton sheets. Rachel always hated polyester, she thought. It helped to think about the sheets; it kept her mind focused away from everything else. Her fingers wandered to the lump in her right breast she had discovered a week ago. It felt like a tiny marble deep under the skin— just like last time. She should have seen the doctor right away, but that would have meant staying longer in Florida. A stupid call, maybe, but she wasn't going to worry about it this minute. Tomorrow. She would dwell on nothing sad or unpleasant tonight. Her resolve lasted only until the moment before sleep, when she felt her spirit drift, unprotected. She was here, back in this house. She turned on her back and stared into the darkness. There was more than change here, there was challenge. Was she up to it? She yanked at her nightgown, turned back on her side, and pushed her face into her pillow. It did not smell of fresh air; a pity that nobody dried linens on a line anymore. A pity that one's life couldn't be hung out to blow clean in a brisk wind. She was drifting again, sliding toward sleep. She could see Phillip standing at the foot of the stairs, calling up to see if she was ready to go to dinner. . . . In the darkness, Camilla made a tight fist and drew her arm up, shielding her eyes.

There were truths to be faced. She would never find Phillip again, not in this house. This was an alien place now. How did history get erased so fast? Nowhere would there be the scent of him or the feel of him or the sight of him, his head bowed under a reading light in the small study on the second floor. He was gone. All those years wiped out with a little varnish and plaster and paint. Maybe she shouldn't be here. Maybe coming back to this house was a big mistake. Because if he's gone, she thought, maybe I'm gone, too. She turned on her side and buried her head in the pillow. She must never tell Rachel.

* * * *

General Felkman turned out to be a ponderous bore the next morning, and Rachel was praying halfway through the show for the hour to end quickly. Hardly anybody called. She envisioned radios being clicked off in cars and homes and offices all over the city even as she desperately tried to get her stolid guest to open up. She was dying today, but there was nothing she could do about it.

"We bombed, God, we bombed. Our second dud in a row," Berry moaned after the show as Rachel pulled on her coat, preparing to hurry out the door. "I should've known he was too available, I really should've known—"

"It's okay. It doesn't happen too often," Rachel said automatically as she moved to leave. She wanted to avoid Berry's post-mortem. They tended lately to become lamentations, and she had promised to get back to Evanston in time to join Camilla and Lindy for lunch.

"Wait." Berry darted between her and the door, her eyes brightly eager. "Listen, I've got an incredible idea. That guy who called the day before yesterday? Think of the response we got—"

"Mr. Bikini Wax?"

"No, no—let's not call him that. Let's call him what he said he was—the Truthseeker. Sounds more dramatic, even if the police are convinced he can't be that murderer." Berry licked her lips nervously. "Please listen, Rachel, and don't say anything until I'm done. I think we've got a *great* publicity gimmick sitting on our doorstep. We've got something that could get us some real attention in this town. We can make Jerry Tebbins look like the sleaze he is and do it by staying *substantive*. Who knows? It could be our ticket out of this operation and into syndication."

"What have you in mind?"

Berry spoke slowly to give time for each word to sink in. "What if we invite him back?"

"Do *what*? Oh, for heaven's sake, Berry, that's crazy."

"Just listen! People were fascinated. What's wrong with them thinking he *might* be a murderer? Anyhow, an obscene caller is just one step away from being a *stalker*, don't you understand? And we had him on this show! He has *got* to be one sick cookie, but what if you invited him to call again and got him

78

to talk about what makes him do this kind of thing? It would be a public service, for God's sake! People would tune in to get some insight into that kind of brain with *no risk*—"

"No. The answer is no. A flat absolute no."

"So you want to just slog along from one General Felkman to another for the rest of your life?" Berry tried to make it sound like a joke, but her voice was too sharp to carry it off.

"Berry, you're working too hard," Rachel said, putting a hand on her friend's shoulder. "I wouldn't mention this to Jim."

"Jim Boles is a wimp who wouldn't know a news story if it bit him on his fat fanny. He's a station manager, that's all he is. We're the ones who have to figure out a way to get this show some decent publicity."

"Hey, don't attack *him*, he didn't do anything. We want to get better known, sure—but inviting this creep to breathe heavy on the show isn't the way. Now quit barring the door, will you? I'm late for a command-performance lunch with my mother. You know what that means." She smiled placatingly. "We'll talk later, okay?"

"Suit yourself," Berry said with a despairing, theatrical shrug.

But as Rachel left the room she caught just a flicker of wetness in her friend's eyes, although on reflection as she drove home she wasn't sure. Berry wasn't the crying type, not at all, and why would her rejection of such an off-the-wall idea trigger such a reaction? No, she must have been wrong.

She walked into the house still enveloped in her thoughts and was startled by the sound of a familiar trilling voice.

"Rachel, it is so wonderful to see you; am I in a time warp or something?" Lindy Colson's voice filled the hall with comfy laughter; the spicy scent of her perfume made Rachel's eyes water even as she found herself scooped up into an exuberant hug. "Look at you, so pretty in your red suit; I wish I had your lovely dark hair, then maybe I could wear red, too. How do you keep it so curly? Shows your ears nicely; your mother always used to say you had the teeniest, flat little ears, unlike my Millie; hers were always sticking out, poor child; she looked like a car with its doors open. You look exactly the same as ever. What is this? And your mother, my God, it isn't fair! She doesn't age and I do." When Rachel was able to move away, she saw that Lindy Colson had grown quite fat. She still looked out of gorgeous, Delft-blue eyes that Rachel remembered most for their lively kindness. Lindy Colson never trashed the neighbors, which was why Camilla had liked her. But the glowing, tanned skin of her barbecuing days had wandered down from her cheekbones and settled into wrinkled folds of flesh around her brightly lipsticked mouth. She wore a watch that twinkled with diamonds and an obviously expensive suit of Italian crepe. Clearly the late Bill Colson—a man Rachel remembered more for his annoyingly hearty laugh than anything else—had done well enough as a real estate developer to leave his wife comfortably well fixed.

Camilla emerged from the kitchen and gave Rachel a brisk peck on the cheek; it reminded Rachel of her mother's brisk little after-school kisses long ago. She was glad, although guiltily so, to see how much better Camilla was aging than Lindy—but she wished her

80

mother had on something a little nicer. She was wearing the same blue skirt she had worn yesterday on the plane.

"I listened to your show while I was making sandwiches, General what's-his-name was a piece of work, wasn't he?" Camilla said, somewhat breathlessly. "I'm glad you made such good time coming home. Lindy can't stay long. She has an appointment downtown with her stockbroker. Oh, I went out and got you an electric teakettle this morning; you'll love it."

"Thanks, Mother. Actually I'm a bit late—"

"Oh, heavens, not at all." Camilla looked a little tired this afternoon. A network of tiny wrinkles was visible around her eyes. Maybe Lindy was already wearing her out, Rachel thought as she helped her mother carry a platter of sandwiches into the sunroom.

"So how do two old friends decide to become property owners together?" she asked lightly as Lindy laid out some paper napkins. She was glad to see Lindy hadn't adopted the tightly waved, blue-tinged hair that she had seen so much among women of a certain age; that wouldn't be her mother's style at all.

Lindy shot a quick glance at Camilla before answering. "I'm going to tell you up front that I'm nervous," she admitted. "A couple of old broads ready to throw our money in one pot even though we haven't seen much of each other for years—who *wouldn't* be nervous? I only wish Bill and Phillip were still here and everything was exactly the way it used to be. Then we'd be planning some wonderful party instead. Aren't you nervous, Camilla?"

"Oh yes—" Camilla's voice wavered a bit as she

opened a jar of mustard and placed it on the table. Maybe it was the way she fussed over where to place it for a millisecond longer than necessary, but Rachel felt a warning prickle under her skin.

"It's amazing that you two managed to arrange something so complicated over the phone," she said. "Is this a condo apartment building or a co-op?" She realized suddenly that Camilla hadn't said a word yet about where the apartment house was located—except that it was south of Evanston—or what it looked like.

"It's a four-plus-one on Sheridan Road, north of Devon."

"Oh—have you had it inspected? I'm sure you have," she added hastily as she saw Lindy's offended look. In Chicago, four-plus-ones were cheap apartment houses built to evade tough building codes by having the first floor partly below ground level; they were notorious for shoddy construction.

"My husband built it back in the sixties and it's *quite* nice, I assure you. I've been living there for years and adore the location, and the apartments are *huge*. My tenants stay for *years* and—"

Rachel opened her mouth to ask another question, but Camilla broke in, waving her hand to take in the room. "Look around, Lindy, hasn't Rachel fixed up the old place nicely? I think the creamy walls and the natural oak moldings are perfect, don't you?"

Lindy's huge blue eyes blinked rapidly. "Of course, what's the matter with me? I'm so excited about seeing you again, I hardly noticed the old place. Oh, it has good bones, doesn't it? The fun we used to have, Camilla—I remember you dancing in the living room on New Year's Eve in something gorgeous. I could have killed you for it. Green silk, I think it was.

82

Remember when I asked you how much it cost, you wouldn't tell me? What a pair you two made; Phillip was so crazy about you—"

"Yes, yes, lots of old memories," Camilla said quickly.

Rachel knew Camilla hated hauling out old memories, but it would be nice if sometimes she indulged in a *little* reminiscing. "I remember that green dress—it was silk shantung," she said. "I think I was fifteen when Daddy bought it for you. Remember, you let me wear it to a dinner dance and I spilled ketchup on it and it didn't come out and you were really upset and Daddy said not to worry, he'd buy you another one—"

"Oh, that. It came out with a little club soda, as I remember." Camilla gave Lindy a bright smile and patted Rachel indulgently on the shoulder and started firmly, quickly pouring tea. "Lindy, do you still take sugar with your tea? Rachel, would you get the sugar in the kitchen?"

"Never mind, I've stopped using it. Too many calories, thanks," Lindy said as she obeyed Camilla's beckoning finger and took her place at the table on the sunporch. "Did you hear about Bob and Sally Cochran?" The wrought-iron chair—another Pottery Barn special—disappeared under the fleshy folds of Lindy Colson's hips and Rachel feared for a moment that it might not be up to the task of holding one so generously proportioned.

"You mean the Cochrans who live by the lake?" Camilla said.

Lindy rolled her eyes. "The very same. They're divorced—isn't that something? Very unexpected, *great* surprise. I hear she wanted it and he didn't, but who knows? *Such* a handsome man, he *used* to be anyway. Getting *very* paunchy, I'm afraid, but so what? He wears pants and he's available."

"Oh, Lindy. Really." Camilla cast an amused glance at her daughter.

"All right, you and I aren't *looking*," Lindy said with a comfortable chuckle. "No harm in thinking, though." She sighed and stirred in her seat, her mercurial mood shifting once again. "You've only been back twenty-four hours, and here I am, conjuring up Phillip's ghost and starting a dating bureau. This must be hard for you, Camilla. To be here, I mean. With those train tracks so close. . . . you could have stayed with me, I would have been happy—no offense, Rachel, dear, but I—"

"Hi." Edie emerged from the kitchen, trying to hide the fact that she had a mouthful of toast. Rachel caught the relief on her mother's face as Lindy switched focus.

"Oh my, Edie!" she exclaimed. "How you've grown! How are you enjoying Langdon? It's my old school, did you know that? Did I hear you're thinking of becoming a doctor, like your dear grandpa? That's wonderful, it really is—"

Edie swallowed hard and looked just baffled enough to send Lindy down another route.

"—although young people change their minds a lot these days, which is good. Nobody should be forced into anything. They still do that in the English system, you know." She turned her attention to Rachel. "I always knew you'd do well, you were such a *busy* girl, all those speech contests. I remember your father sitting in the kitchen with you, coaching you *for hours* for the state tournament while your mother and I sat out here. You won, didn't you? I remember—"

"An honorable mention," Rachel said, feeling a twinge after all these years.

"Oh dear."

Rachel was feeling a little sorry for Lindy by now. "Mother, why don't you show Lindy the rest of the house before we eat?" she suggested. "I'll put the kettle back on." Camilla hesitated for a second and then agreed, proceeding with brisk efficiency to guide Lindy up the staircase. Rachel started to follow, just to stay hospitable, but Edie was tugging at her sleeve. "Mom, the painter, the one Mr. Garcia doesn't like? He was flirting this morning," she said, a frown creasing her forehead. "The skinny one who looks like he's still in high school. Really gross."

"Really?" Rachel frowned, suddenly aware that Mr. Garcia and the painters were nowhere to be seen. "Why aren't they here?"

"Well, I was kind of upset and so was Mr. Garcia. He said everybody should leave and he'd talk to you later."

"I'm trying to get the place finished by Christmas, Edie; I don't want them taking time off. They'll be done in a couple of days if they stay on the job."

"Is that what you care about, just getting the painting done? Don't you mind that he was *flirting*? I felt like he was leering at me, I really did."

"Oh, Edie, surely—"

"I know you think I overdramatize, but I *don't*. You ask Mr. Garcia."

"Did the painter say anything to you?"

"No."

"Did he touch you?"

85

"No—"

"Well, honey—" She didn't want to overreact; Edie *did* have a dramatic streak. But she made a mental note to have a talk with Mr. Garcia.

The doorbell rang, cutting off their conversation. Edie went to answer it, and Rachel saw as she picked up the teapot a florist delivery man handing her daughter a bouquet of tall, elegant lilies—purple stargazers.

She gave a cry of pleasure. "How nice!" she exclaimed. "Who—?"

Edie stood with the flowers in one hand, staring at a white card. "It isn't signed," she said.

"Well, who are they for?" Rachel walked over to the door and peered over her daughter's shoulder. "I love stargazers. What does the card say?"

"It's just got our address on it." Edie handed her the card. In a wavering script that could have been that of a floral-shop employee was this message: "Great performance." That was all. Nothing else.

Rachel smoothed her finger over the handwritten note as if somehow tracing the letters would give her a clue to who wrote it. "Is this a joke? Could Kurt have sent them?" she asked.

"Kurt? Hardly. It's that painter, I'll bet. I told you, he gave me the shivers." Edie's small mouth pulled tight and the ridges of her nose seemed to sharpen.

"Don't fret, I'll ask the florist," Rachel said. She started to say more, but the sound of voices on the steps signaled the return of Camilla and Lindy. And the tea was cold. "Just stick the flowers into a vase while I put the kettle back on, will you, Edie?" she said quickly.

Edie mumbled something and marched off to the

kitchen with the flowers clutched in her hand.

* * * *

Lunch went pleasantly enough. Edie stayed only for a few minutes and then excused herself. Pleading the need for a new pair of jeans, she asked Rachel if she could take the Honda to the Old Orchard shopping center in Skokie. Rachel swallowed hard before agreeing, but told herself sternly to stop worrying. She lingered at the table, letting herself bob along on the waves of the patter of the two older women: Lindy's voice, so rich and rolling and bubbly; Camilla's voice, so crisp and clear. Soon they were finishing each other's sentences. She wondered what they talked about in private—and whether or not Lindy knew her mother better than she did. Had Lindy seen Camilla cry after her husband died? Or had she also been shut out by the stoicism Camilla presented to the rest of the world, including her own daughter? Maybe instead she was privy to Camilla's real feelings; maybe she knew the truth under it all. . . . Rachel felt herself trying to catch the secret, to snatch it from the air, so she could cup it in her hands and study it. And why did that make her feel shut out again?

Rachel watched the winter afternoon begin to darken through the window. The beveled edges of glass lost their sparkle as the light faded, turning flat and cold-looking. Lindy seemed to have forgotten her stockbroker. The day was almost over; she should head back downtown and do something to bolster Berry's spirits. Instead she continued to sit as Camilla and Lindy negotiated the details of sharing their lives. Watching her animated mother, she wondered if

87

Camilla had been looking for the first excuse she could find to move back. The lunch grew increasingly more relaxed, more elastic. Camilla was soon looking at a large batch of pictures of grandchildren Lindy had stuffed into her oversized purse and Rachel was once again the little girl sitting in on her mother's party. The phone rang as they were eating generous helpings of Sara Lee cheesecake. Rachel sprang guiltily from her chair. It was Berry; she was sure of it.

"I'll get it," Camilla said promptly. She disappeared into the kitchen and reemerged a few moments later. She stood for an instant in the doorway, adjusting her right earring and snapping it back on her earlobe, staring through a breakfast-room window at two holly trees she had planted outside, close together, fifteen years ago. Their leaves were waxy green and their berries were a festive red, but they scratched too close to the glass. Phillip had warned her that would happen but, for some reason, she never had bothered replanting them.

"Who was it?" Rachel asked, cutting into her thoughts.

"Nobody important," Camilla said with a wave of her hand. "Just somebody babbling away who hung up. Don't worry about it, dear."

Rachel felt entitled to a little more information. But Camilla obviously had dismissed the phone call entirely and was now listening raptly to Lindy run on about the pros and cons of collagen injections. Rachel's mellow mood faded a bit. It was her house, and right now she had a child's frustrated sense of having been put absentmindedly on hold.

* * * *

Edie did not go to the shopping center. She drove her car out to Sheridan Road and headed north, praying she was driving competently enough not to get stopped. The lake looked sullen and dark today and the clouds were heavy with snow. She shifted to first, impatient for the light to change at Central Street. Kurt would be annoyed if she showed up late. She wished he had come over last night. Maybe he was right, maybe it was better for him not to be hanging around too much right away. What was it about grown-ups anyway? Kurt said you couldn't trust them, especially parents; they were always trying to lead your life for you. It felt weird not telling her mother where she was *really* going. Would Kurt want her to meet his parents? Not likely, she thought. They sounded strange, so strange she'd better warn him not to talk about them around Mother. Kurt said they were repressed, even bloodless. There were things wrong in *her* family, but nobody was bloodless, except maybe skinny old Greta. The light changed and she hit the accelerator, shoving the car into second gear as she turned west. Ten minutes later, she drew up in front of Kurt's home, staring first at the house and then again at the piece of paper with his address. This couldn't be right. The house was kind of dilapidated— tiny and dreary. Startled, she realized Kurt was standing at the car door.

"Well, hello," he said with that neat kind of sexy drawl of his. The sides of his mouth curled upward in the faintest hint of a smile. "Surprised? Welcome to Kiley Manor."

"You said I didn't have the nerve. But here I am."

"Yes, here you are. So?"

Edie's heart was hammering very hard and she felt

weak at the knees. "You know what."

"Well, finally."

Edie's heart was thumping even harder as Kurt led her into the house and over to an old sofa that groaned when they sat down. She thought they would talk awhile. She had been thinking of what to say; trying to figure out how to act so he wouldn't know it was the first time. But he reached for the zipper on her skirt and yanked it down, almost pulling it off its track.

"Come on, take it off. Hey, I think you're gaining weight again. Don't get fat on me, Edie."

"Here?" She glanced around. "Right here?" She glanced through an open door and saw an unmade bed; the room was illuminated by the pale, flickering light of a computer monitor. Was it Kurt's room? She didn't want to ask, because maybe she would sound nervous and he would laugh at her. Kurt's hands were inside her sweater, pulling it off. Suddenly exposed, she shivered. Lots of girls had sex at her age and it wasn't a big deal. She wished she hadn't run out of her diet pills. Kurt could tell immediately when she got flabby. He pushed her back onto the sofa and she felt the scratchy fabric on the cushion clawing at her back. He was on his knees now, pulling her legs apart.

"Wait—"

He stopped and looked at her, his eyes in shadow; she could see only a glint of light from under his thick lashes. "Wait? What do you mean, wait? You've been freaking over this for weeks. Are you telling me you're still not up to a simple fuck? Edie—"

She twisted her head to the side so he couldn't see her eyes because she knew what he was going to say.

"Are you a virgin? Is that what this is all about?"

90

She heard the barely contained amusement in his voice. "No, I'm not. I just don't want to go so fast, that's all."

He leaned forward, more gently this time, kissing her cheek, her eyes, murmuring in her ear. Edie willed herself to relax. She heard him unzip his pants, felt his body come down on her and shivered again at the feel of his naked flesh. His skin grew sweaty and it hurt when he pushed inside her and then he began pumping so hard, the sofa squeaked. She moaned, hoping she had got the sound right. This should be more fun; it shouldn't hurt this much. . . .

It was over. Kurt rolled over on his side and reached over her for a pack of cigarettes on the coffee table. "Cigarette?"

"I don't smoke, remember?" She curled up tight, wishing she felt a little more as if something special had happened.

"Not even after sex?" He actually looked astonished.

"No, not even then."

That funny smile of his was picking at the corners of his mouth. "Well, there's always a first time."

"No, thank you."

"One 'first time' enough for today?" His eyes were half-closed as his fingers moved down her body to her breast. He squeezed her nipple, hard.

"Ouch!" she exclaimed.

Kurt laughed. "It's okay, I'm delighted to be the first one. Hope you didn't bleed on the sofa, although it's in such crummy shape, I don't think anybody would notice."

Edie jumped up, almost in tears. She hooked on her bra, missing one of the eyes, and then pulled her

91

sweater on over her head, wishing she could just curl up under a blanket somewhere far from here, back at home.

Kurt pulled her back onto the sofa. "If you hadn't so obviously turned up your nose at the sight of my unmade bed, we'd be in there. Look, it doesn't matter." He took a deep drag on his cigarette. "Think your mother suspected anything?"

"No, she thinks I'm perfect." It was a pale attempt at an old joke Kurt usually seemed to enjoy, but today he simply grunted. Edie swallowed fiercely; she would not allow herself to be disappointed. She told Kurt about buying the dress for her father's wedding and then finding out that not only had he forgotten his promise to include her, but her mother had known and hadn't told her. How that completely freaked her out. How—

"Oh, put a sock in it," he said abruptly.

Edie's hands flew to her face.

"Listen, what I mean is, you've got to stop caring about that kind of thing. Chill. Forget it. Don't let them know you feel *anything*. It'll drive them crazy."

"My mother wants me to move back in with her and go to Evanston High." She watched for his reaction.

Kurt's thin lips parted, revealing a row of small white teeth. "Why? She'd want to know everything you're doing. You'd be just another high school kid with a nosy mother wondering what you do after school. You want to leave Langdon? Live in dumpy Evanston?"

"I don't know." She hesitated. It was hard sometimes to be cool and still say what you felt. "But I like the house, and it's not so bad being around my mother, especially now that my grandmother is here,

92

too."

Kurt slumped back into the sofa. His voice was lazily scornful. "I need to get something straight, right now. You *want* to live here with your mother?"

"I don't know—"

"Maybe you're more tied to her apron strings than I thought. Maybe I was wrong, figuring you as a sophisticated type. Maybe you've been fooling me about a lot of things, not just the fact that you were until ten minutes ago indisputably one nervous virgin. Maybe you're as much of a nerd as your pal Topper Boles." The side of his mouth twitched into an indisputable sneer.

Edie's face was burning now, but she forced herself to fold her hands in her lap. "That's not true and you know it! Topper doesn't care about any of the things I care about. All she does with her time is read boring novels and play checkers, and I—" She stopped because she suddenly had no appetite for dumping on Topper. And because she wasn't going to tell anybody, least of all Kurt, how Topper got weepy at night and stayed home alone on weekends in their dorm room and actually still slept with a grungy old teddy bear. It was just too embarrassing.

"Well, you've got me wondering."

"I'm just talking about what my *mother* wants, okay?"

"If you stay at Langdon, we can see more of each other," Kurt said. "It's easier. I've got my apartment; nobody to spy on us."

Edie held her knees together, wishing she didn't feel this dull ache between her legs. It took away the thrill that Kurt's words would have given her just yesterday.

He was jabbing out his cigarette now. "You think you've got disappointing parents; you should meet mine."

"Why? What are they like?" She looked around the room, puzzled about the people who lived here. The carpets were cheap Kmart orientals and she could smell something turning bad in the kitchen, the smell you got when meat and stuff were in the disposal and somebody had forgotten to turn it on. Kurt's parents were supposed to be in England. You at least ground up the garbage before going on a trip. How long had they been in England?

"Do they rent this place?" she asked cautiously.

"Oh dear, you've noticed the housekeeping, right? I see that little nose of yours sniffing delicately. Sorry the place isn't up to your standards, but my mother is the world's lousiest housekeeper."

"I didn't mean—"

"Of course you did. Hey, I don't mind. I just hang out here because it's cheaper than a hotel room, you know?"

He was using his phony gangster tone, but she fancied she heard also a wounded note that made her want to snuggle closer. Kurt understood how it felt to have difficult parents.

"Let's go in the bedroom," he said suddenly.

"Why? It's comfy right here."

"No." He was excited now. "I want to wrap you in the sheets, rub you with them—"

"They're dirty!'"

"That's the point, think of them as heavy with semen, okay? Months and months of it. You could lick them, I could take pictures—"

"Gross." Edie sat up, revolted.

He stared at her, blinked, and then laughed. "You are so literal, do you know that? I'm weaving a nice little fantasy, and you go and ruin it by taking me seriously."

"Well, I'm not licking any filthy old sheet."

"But I could write about you doing it," he said, picking up a lock of her hair with one finger and twirling it slowly.

"You wouldn't do that." She pushed back her hair nervously and peered down at him.

"Of course not." He pulled her closer and kissed her neck affectionately, lazily.

But Edie couldn't relax. She looked around the room, trying not to be appalled at the shoddiness. "Should we, maybe, clean up?" she said. "I mean, your folks are due home today, aren't they?"

"I guess."

"Did they call?"

"No, they never do."

"Why aren't there any pictures around? I mean, you know, pictures of you and them and your brother—"

"He's married, gone for years. Lives in Montana."

"Yeah, but you know, pictures of when you were kids."

Kurt flung one arm over his eyes and didn't answer right away. "They don't believe in pictures," he said.

"Why not?"

"Because when you're with the CIA, you have to erase stupid things like that from your life, you little dope."

God, the CIA. How could she be so stupid? Of course, Kurt's family had to protect themselves. Edie felt overwhelmingly privileged that he had confided the truth to her and ashamed of her insensitivity.

"Wow, it must be awful," she murmured.

He started to say something more and stopped, listening. Edie heard it too—it sounded like the coughing engine of an old truck.

"Well, what do you know, they're home," he said, leaping up from the sofa. "Better get the rest of your clothes on fast if you want to start out on the right foot with the Kileys."

* * * *

Rachel checked her watch when Lindy finally hugged the two of them good-bye and left the house in a haze of perfume. It was four o'clock. She closed the door with some relief. She felt guilty about not going back to the station, but the house was so cozy and pleasant. Edie would be home soon, so she might as well treat herself to a full afternoon off.

"So how do you feel about my old friend Lindy? I saw you watching us during lunch," Camilla asked lightly as they cleared the table together and loaded the dishwasher.

"I like her better than I did as a kid," Rachel said. "The two of you seem to bounce off each other pretty well." Why, she wondered suddenly, listening to her own voice, did her response sound as grudging as some of Edie's?

"Yes, we do." Camilla looked pleased.

Her mother was doing the same thing she did: responding only to the positive. "She does go on, but the two of you obviously like each other. That's all that matters," Rachel continued.

"Well, we've shared a great number of things over the years—especially our worries about, you know, marriage, children, husbands," Camilla said with a light laugh. Rachel watched her mother busy herself scrubbing the counter with a sponge, taking an inordinate amount of time to wring it out before tucking it behind the water faucet.

"Actually, I never much liked her husband," she heard herself saying. "He couldn't talk about anything but the stock market and his precious sailboat. I got a bit tired of those monologues on whether vintage teak was worth the upkeep or—"

"You do know we had problems, don't you, Rachel?" Camilla interrupted, not looking directly at her daughter.

Rachel carefully put away a roll of plastic wrap into a drawer. "I know Dad was a little depressed. But the two of you always . . ." The right words weren't coming.

"Loved each other, yes. But things were rocky."

"You sound so—so matter-of-fact." She wanted to say "cold," but that one important word wouldn't come.

"I'm trying to balance reality for you. I think you're having a hard time letting him go."

"Because I don't believe he killed himself?"

The kitchen was silent for a moment. "I think you've got a lot of things tangled up," Camilla said finally. "Your father was not a happy man. Rachel, I have to say it plain. I don't want you dragging this around all your life—"

"You think I bought the house to be close to him in some sick way?"

"Not 'sick,' for heaven's sake. Just needful."

Rachel tried to quell a stirring anger, but it was difficult. "I think it's you carrying around ghosts, not me. I think you've let him go too easily," she said. She leaned against the counter, her head resting against the cupboard door, before turning to face Camilla.

Her mother's face had become quite still. "You have no idea what I've been through," she said.

"I can say the same thing, Mother. So please don't psychoanalyze me." Rachel fervently wished they hadn't stumbled into this. "I've got to say, I resent hearing the assumption in your voice that he killed himself. I mean, we should be—" She was flailing again for words. "We should be protecting his memory."

"Phillip is dead, and we are alive. That's the focus, Rachel." The color was slowly returning to Camilla's face. For a long moment they stood where they were, safely positioned and buffered by dishes and glasses and pots and pans.

"I want something more from you, Mother."

"I would give it if I could," Camilla said simply.

Rachel carefully folded the dish towel in her hand. She felt like a swimmer struggling to reach shore. Only a week or two, she told herself, that's all. Then her mother would be in her own home, and they would be able to establish neutral ground. She plucked a chocolate from a Godiva box resting on the windowsill. "Who called when we were having lunch?" she asked.

Camilla shrugged. "Some character who couldn't seem to get his words out straight. I figured it was a telemarketer."

"I think you should've called me to the phone—just in case it was somebody I needed to talk to. My listeners, you know." Rachel picked up a dirty teacup sitting next to the stove and shoved it into the dishwasher. "They call from everywhere and they're not always totally articulate."

"Would you rather I didn't answer the phone?"

Rachel was trying to think of what to say to that when the back door flew open.

"Mom? Grandma?" Edie was standing in the doorway. Her eyes were wide and questioning, and Rachel felt a twinge of alarm. She hoped Edie hadn't overheard.

"It's okay, Edie, we were just—"

"Mom?" Edie's voice was a little higher than usual.

"What is it? What happened?"

Edie pulled off her knit cap and threw it onto the kitchen counter, holding aloft in her fist the bouquet of flowers that had come many hours ago. "I found these propped up against the back door—is this somebody's idea of a joke?" she said. She held out the bouquet of stargazers, now bitten by frost and limp from lack of water. She and Rachel exchanged glances as Camilla looked from one to the other, confused.

"Where did those come from?" Camilla asked.

"Somebody sent them earlier today, we don't know who."

"I threw them away," Edie said. "I threw them into the garbage and somebody pulled them out and left them at the back door."

"Why would you throw them away?"

"Because the note freaked me out, that's why. There was no signature."

Camilla looked puzzled.

"Look, I attract strange people in this business," Rachel said with an edge to her voice. "Somebody liked my show, or hated it, or whatever—" She felt irritated that she had forgotten about the flowers.

"Well, yeah, Mom. But you've never had somebody

climbing up the back stairs to leave dead flowers at the door."

"A dog, maybe. Or a practical joker—"

"Oh God, you will deny *anything*." Edie turned huffily and stomped out of the kitchen.

* * * *

Later that night, after Camilla and Edie were in bed, Rachel took a copy of *Vanity Fair* magazine into the living room and tried to focus on a story about some wealthy Italian drug dealer she had never heard of. She wasn't having much luck when the phone rang. It was Amos.

"Hi. I needed to hear your voice," he said simply. "If I'm intruding—"

"No, no." A wave of relief swept over her. Maybe it was just her sense of being under siege on all fronts right now, but his voice exuded the calming strength she needed. He had at this moment the blessed relief of neutrality. And so—on Amos—she unloaded the troubles of the day. She curled up tight in the chair and talked. She told him about Berry's proposal to invite the Truthseeker back on the show and the careful dance with her mother and the equally careful dance with Edie. She talked for a long time.

"It could be true, you know," he interrupted finally.

"What could be?"

"That the guy I interviewed in state prison was lying. Maybe this caller is the original Truthseeker."

Rachel pulled her legs up and curled herself into a ball on the sofa. "The police say it's impossible."

"I don't know; I'm not so sure. Remember the mood in this town? It was like New York when the Zodiac killer was on the loose. People panicked after those two girls were murdered. The mayor was up for reelection on a law-and-order platform, and he was dying to close the books on the Truthseeker. The killings had stopped, remember?"

"I remember."

"I'm not saying it was necessarily deliberate—just that it was mighty convenient to declare a notorious murderer already dead. Saved the city a trial, calmed everybody down."

"This doesn't make me feel very good."

"Let's go back to what Berry proposed. Whether he's the original Truthseeker or not, you're in an interesting position. With a little help, you could catch this guy."

She felt her reporter's instincts stirring. "Explain."

"Well—" He paused, as if to mull it over. "If the *Tribune* was running a series on stalkers at the same time—"

"You mean us, working in tandem?"

He laughed. "It's probably a dumb idea."

Rachel stared at her fingers on the blue-flowered quilt. "Maybe not." They shared a comfortable silence. "By the way, did you send me flowers today?" she asked.

Another pause. "No," he said cautiously. "Was I supposed to?"

"Of course not. I just wondered."

CHAPTER 4

CAMILLA HASTILY SWALLOWED A GULP OF SCALDING coffee, wincing as she put the cup down and shoved her arms into an old raincoat of Rachel's that had been hanging on a hook near the back door.

"That thing's not warm enough," Rachel protested. "I'll find you another one if you can hold off a minute—"

"No, no, it has a wool liner and I never liked heavy coats anyway," Camilla said. She grabbed the Honda keys and opened the door, not looking Rachel directly in the eye. A blast of truly frigid air filled the room. "I can't be late this morning," she said over her shoulder. "I used to be a stickler for employees showing up on time, so how would it look if I were late on my first day back?"

Rachel considered offering Camilla her new shearling coat, but couldn't bridge the awkwardness between them quickly enough. "Hope everything goes well," she called out lamely as Camilla began cautiously picking her way across the patches of dull ice on the path to the garage. She closed the door and turned around to see Edie standing in the doorway of the kitchen in her pajamas, yawning.

"So Grandma's already off to work?" Edie said lazily. "I'll go in later and buy a bunch of stuff for Kurt. It is so wild—buying stuff from, like, my grandmother."

"They'll probably run her off her feet today. She's going to find out working the floor at Field's during Christmas is a lot different from running a gift shop in Miami." Rachel pulled her red wool robe close, remembering flashes of long-ago mornings when she stood here as a child, waving good-bye to her mother from this same kitchen window. The memory made her sad. "I can't believe she went off wearing those ridiculous high heels. Her feet will be killing her by noon." Even to her own ear, her voice sounded fussy.

"She isn't exactly a baby, Mother," Edie said as she

opened the refrigerator and stared warily at its contents. "I wish you'd bought some bagels."

"I've got bread. Second drawer to the right."

"Gross—that bread has so much fat in it. I can't believe you forgot about those flowers. It was totally weird to find them at the back door."

"So did you buy something at the mall?"

Edie looked at her blankly.

"Yesterday afternoon? You were over at Old Orchard, weren't you?" Rachel prompted.

"Oh yeah. I looked at some jeans, you know, at the Gap." Edie pushed a piece of bread into the toaster and took the lid off the butter dish.

"Did you get them?"

"No. They weren't the ones I wanted."

"Too bad. Did you go anywhere else?"

"I'm being interrogated, aren't I? Well, okay— yeah, I met Kurt over there. Is that such a big deal?"

"No," Rachel replied. She took a deep breath and plunged in. "But when you came home, I noticed your blouse wasn't buttoned right. Is that a big deal?"

Edie blushed scarlet.

"Oh, Edie—"

"Mom, leave me alone."

"I can't really do that. I'm a mom, remember? I lose my credentials if I don't try."

"I wish you wouldn't try to be so—so hip."

"I'm not hip; I'm worried." One minute, I'm needy for her; the next, she's needy for me, Rachel thought sadly. Even if she doesn't know it.

Edie stole a quick glance at her mother and tried a diversion. "Kurt and I really like each other. You know something? His dad's with the CIA. Isn't that cool? This is absolutely confidential, Mother."

Her eyes were backlit with sudden excitement, and Rachel felt compelled to look impressed. "That's very interesting—" she began.

"Do you smell something?"

Rachel reached past her daughter and plucked the piece of burning toast from the toaster and handed it to her silently. "I've got margarine, but no butter. Sorry."

"Oh, God, I *hate* margarine." Edie's complaint seemed forced as she rolled a tiny curl of margarine onto a knife and began spreading it over the toast.

"Okay, tell me what 'liking each other' means. Is it something more than just being pals?"

"Well—yeah. But guys are different you know?" Edie began distractedly combing her long hair with her fingers.

"They are, a little, at all ages."

"They'll do anything to get you into bed."

"Not the good guys," Rachel said, keeping it light. "They don't force girls to do anything."

"Sometimes they do; sometimes they talk you into doing stuff."

"Not a guy who respects the woman he's seeing." Rachel felt her jaw clenching and tried not to let the sound of her voice change. Looking directly into the guarded eyes of her sixteen-year-old daughter was hard enough, calling her a "woman" was much tougher.

"Well, sometimes a woman wants sex, too."

Rachel again inhaled deeply. Wasn't it too soon, or was she just kidding herself? "Of course, but sometimes the first experience can be a little disappointing," she ventured.

"Well, sure." Edie was sounding more confident as

she munched her toast, leaving a spot of strawberry jelly on the side of her upper lip. "But *nobody* thinks it's great the first time; I mean, that's what I hear."

"Would any smart sixteen-year-old *you* know be smart enough to insist on a condom?"

A startled Edie stood frozen, jelly dripping. "You mean—every time?"

"Oh, Edie, dear. Yes, every time, always; as in forever." Rachel didn't try to hide the alarm in her voice even as Edie looked away.

"Don't freak, Mom," she said weakly.

"Honey, you know about safe sex; we've talked plenty about this in the past."

"I *know*. So don't lecture me."

"I'm not lecturing you, I'm telling you that having sex is a big step and safety starts with a condom. But I'm also telling you that you don't have to do anything you don't want to do. Kurt probably has a lot more experience than you have, and he's—"

"You're saying I'm too young to have sex?" There was a faint mocking light in Edie's eyes.

"I'm not allowed to say that even if I think it, which I do," Rachel plowed on. "Okay, I sound retro, but the older I get, the more retro I feel."

"You mean, the older *I* get, the more retro *you* feel."

"I've decided I'm a very unhip mother. You don't have to follow the crowd. You're stronger than that."

"I don't see what makes you an expert. Berry told me you've got some old boyfriend who just surfaced. Pre- or postdivorce?" Edie stuck out her chin and arched an eyebrow, looking both vulnerable and defiant at the same time.

Rachel silently swore at Berry. "That's really my

business, Edie."

"Well, Kurt's *mine*."

"Look, I've made my share of mistakes. But I care about your happiness and what happens to you more than anything else in the world. And when I tell you to take it slow, I'm trying to open up your life, not shut it down."

Edie wavered. "Well, I want my privacy, too. That's all I'm saying."

"I ask only that you listen to me and use your common sense."

"I'll think about it," Edie conceded as she slid off the stool.

"You'll be saying these things to your own daughter some day," Rachel said, hoping to stomp out the sparks of this particular eruption.

"No way. I'm having boys only; girls are too much trouble."

They exchanged wan, conciliatory smiles.

"I'm getting the Christmas tree today, want to come?" Rachel asked.

Edie paused. "Yeah, I guess," she said, putting one slender hand at the back of her neck and drawing her hair forward, twisting it slowly. "I kind of like slogging through muddy tree lots."

"I'll meet you at Dempster Street at four."

Edie hesitated. "Can Kurt come?"

"I'd rather have you to myself," Rachel said quickly, and then had an inspiration. "Why don't you invite him over to trim the tree later tonight? We'll pick up take-out and have a good time."

Edie nodded slowly, licking the jelly off the edges of her mouth. Most of her toast sat still uneaten on the plate.

"Can I fix you some eggs?" Rachel asked.

"No, thanks, I'm full," Edie said, sauntering from the room.

Did she have any Advil? Just two pills and she'd be fine, if she could find where she'd left the bottle. But when Rachel glanced at her watch she realized she had no time to hunt for it, which meant she would just have to carry this headache into the office with her—which she'd do anyway, because it would take a lot more than Advil to erase her mounting worries about Edie.

* * * *

"Do you know what your enterprising producer is doing?" Jim Boles asked as Rachel stepped through the door of her office. He stood by her desk, jacket off, shirt bulging past the textured suspenders embossed with tennis rackets his daughter had given him last Christmas. His face was more florid than usual and he was frowning.

"No, I haven't talked to her yet this morning. What's up?"

"She's doing her damnedest to bring that creep out of the woodwork again, *that's* what's she's doing."

Rachel sensed Berry's presence behind her in the doorway and turned.

"Boles, you are definitely overreacting," Berry drawled as she moved past Rachel into the room while munching on a powdered-sugar doughnut. A tiny mustache of sugar coated her upper lip. "I think the fact that the morning news shows saw fit to talk about the kind of guy who would harass someone like Rachel is totally legitimate. Blaming *me*"—she hunched thick, rounded shoulders forward and stared at Jim—"is like blaming the weatherman for a fucking thunderstorm."

"Oh, I see. Then you aren't the one who's whipping up interest in this? You deny that you've got a novel little promo up your sleeve?"

Berry rolled her eyes in elaborate disdain. "I neither deny nor affirm; I know my rights. Now bug off, Jim, we have a show to put on the air."

This was too much for Rachel, and she stepped between the two of them. "What's going on?" she demanded. "I'm not going to stand here listening to the two of you bite away at each other for another minute. What's this all about?"

"The person you want to grill is our Miss Brown here," Jim said, clearly furious now. "Ask her why she told the producers of both morning shows that you sympathized with the 'torment' of 'the Truthseeker,' and hoped he would find a way to get help. Ask her how she coaxed them to hint that he should contact you again. And then you might ask her what she plans to do if this gambit goes sour."

"I did nothing but remind the morning shows that we have a strange guy out there who thinks he's a major criminal and who likes to talk dirty on the air," Berry retorted. "If that's a crime, then arrest me."

Rachel stared at Berry in disbelief. "You did all that?"

"Don't talk to me in that tone of voice," Berry said swiftly. "Not if I'm still working for you."

"You're not working *for* me, we're working together, remember? But I'm the one stuck with talking to him when he calls, and I don't want anybody urging him on. I mean it." Rachel couldn't control the alarm in her voice.

"I simply got this show into one more news cycle,"

Berry said with injured fury. "That's more than you've done, Jim."

"You do your job the way you see fit, and I'll do mine the way I see fit. I've said what I have to say." Jim moved stiffly past Rachel, touching her arm gently. She felt the sweaty dampness of his hand through her silk blouse and realized as he stomped from the room how agitated he must be.

The two women gazed at each other for an instant in total silence. Somewhere on Rachel's desk, covered by a stack of papers, a cheap clock ticked noisily.

"I shouldn't fly off the handle like that, but he drives me nuts," Berry said in a tightly controlled voice. "He's overblowing this, I promise you. I had the most innocent conversation with Sari Carling last night. She's the new morning show producer at Channel Seven; we were hashing over old stories and I simply mentioned—"

"All that matters to me is that you and I work as a team," Rachel cut in. "It's got to be that way. You shouldn't have talked to Carling without clearing it first with me."

"You were out of here like a rocket yesterday, and you never came back. And may I remind you that you almost chopped my head off the other night when I called you at home?"

Rachel pressed her lips tightly together at Berry's injured tone. "Something like this is different. You could've called."

"Coulda, shoulda, woulda," Berry said with a small shrug. But she was trying to smile now. "Okay, I'm sorry, but sometimes I feel like I'm the hired help that has to get the job done while you renovate your house and baby-sit your mother and your kid—"

"Surely you know I care about you and never, absolutely never, think of you as 'hired help.' Berry, how can you say that?" Why was she having to protest like this? Jim had made this a needless confrontation.

Berry sighed, a long, tremulous sound. "Well, okay. We're on in fifteen minutes. I hate to tell you, but 'big business' is going to be a pretty flat show unless you can pull something out of a hat. Fast."

* * * *

The air in the broadcasting booth wasn't as close today. Somebody had finally fixed the venting system, at least temporarily, for which Rachel was fleetingly grateful. She concentrated on taking the measure of this morning's guest as the opening music played, her heart sinking. He was an accountant with squinty eyes who worked for a small chain of department stores forced into bankruptcy by a hostile takeover; a sworn enemy of big business. But he had come armed with a two-inch-thick stack of documents that he clearly intended to refer to as much as he could. She would have to coax him away from his notes as quickly as possible. Why was the prospect of once again turning dross into gold suddenly so tiring?

She flashed her guest a bright smile as the engineer signaled.

"Good morning, I'm Rachel Snow," she purred into the mike. "Here we are again, with *Talk Time*, your favorite morning show. And with us today. . ."

The call she half expected came in the second half hour, and she knew the minute she flipped open the switch who it would be. She felt a shiver of—of what? Of excitement, she realized as she worked to keep her

110

voice steady. "Hello, you're on the air," she said.

"Of course I am, you invited me," the voice said. It wasn't as metallic this time, she thought. It sounded instead like a voice from a 1930s movie soundtrack; hollow, as if it were coming through an ancient gramophone.

"You're calling because you wanted to, not at my invitation," she said. "But I have a question. Why do you call yourself the Truthseeker?"

"Because no one tells the truth. It's up to me to tell the world what it is."

The accountant was sitting pop-eyed, hands splayed protectively across his documents. Rachel took a deep breath, uncertain she was ready for this ride. "That's nicely cryptic, but what prompts you to call my show? What are you trying to prove?"

"I am interested in you, because you are my conduit to the world. Through you I bring the truth to your audience about who I am and what I can do. Got your attention last time, didn't I? All it took was a few dirty words—"

"Any obscenity and I cut you off," Rachel snapped. Her finger hovered over the switch, dancing nervously up and down.

The voice chuckled. "So you're going to set the rules, Rachel? That's not how it works."

"I have the power here, not you. If you want to talk to me and to my audience, you do it on my terms." A quiver of excitement raced down her spine as she watched the board lighting up—in a way it rarely did.

"Okay," he said. "So what do you want to know about me?"

"I want to know who you are. You, the flesh-and-blood person. Why should you hide behind your

111

voice? Don't you have more courage than that?" She was feeling reckless now, like a swimmer confident of one mastered stroke, fueled by the giddy sight of her glittering board. "Maybe you think you are a second Unabomber. Maybe that's why you're calling my show. Or maybe you are just a kid having trouble with his girlfriend. Or—"

"Stop trying to goad me, Rachel. Only a fool does that. My voice is my weapon, and my anonymity will draw from you and your listeners what I want to know. But I warn you—I know evil. I know how to hurt people."

Rachel felt herself teetering on the edge of something unknown. "Maybe you do. But what does that prove? Maybe you are just a lonely person trying to be understood," she coaxed. "Am I right?" She could see a happy Larry Kramer almost turning cartwheels in the control room. She had almost forgotten the pop-eyed accountant. She was breathless now, heady with a strange euphoria. He thought he was playing with her, but she was playing with him. Her finger caressed the switch; the switch was safety.

"Poor baby, you don't understand the Truthseeker, do you? I will breathe close into this phone, I will hold you tight with my voice, I have you, Rachel. You don't know it yet, but I have you *trapped*."

She couldn't tolerate this strange game one second more. "What you have *not* got anymore today is an audience," she said crisply. "Good-bye, Truthseeker." She flicked the switch. Then she began taking calls. One woman insisted she recognized the voice of her ex-husband currently serving a life sentence for murder in the Illinois state prison; another said the Truthseeker was speaking in anagrams and they just

112

had to figure out what he was really saying. The show crackled and spun as it never had before. Even the accountant got into the act and accused one caller of being an anti-Semite when he said the Truthseeker sounded like a Holocaust victim.

Suddenly, the show was over. Rachel leaned back in her chair, sweating, her heart pounding. Berry rushed into the room with a glass of ice water. "Way to go, sport," she said cheerfully. "You really rode that one." People were talking excitedly, laughing. Rachel felt wobbly in her heels as she walked out of the booth after saying good-bye to the accountant. She could hear the phone ringing nonstop at the receptionist's desk.

Only Jim seemed still. He stood planted next to the coffee machine, arms folded, staring slightly downward as she approached.

She felt compelled to explain. "He was daring me to take him on, you know that. I couldn't squeak like a mouse and run and hide," she said.

"I think you were expecting him," he replied, not unkindly. "I think you wanted him to call as much as Berry did."

"I never thought about it until I heard his voice again," she protested. She waited, but he said no more. His face looked heavy and tired.

"Are you coming tonight?" she asked.

"If you still want us, we'll be there. Take care, Rachel."

She walked away then, not liking the way he said it.

* * * *

It was almost ten before Edie caught a train downtown and closer to eleven before she finished peeking in store windows and walked through the doors of Marshall Field's State Street store. The store was jammed with Christmas shoppers. The smell of perspiration and winter wool was mixed everywhere with the scent of holiday potpourri, and the usual canned music of the holiday filled the vast, soaring atrium above the still-grand first floor. Edie took a deep breath, surprised at how much she liked it. There had been all those ritual trips down here every Christmas for lunch around Field's Christmas tree with kids jostling each other and screaming and her parents making strained small talk.

Christmas had always had a pall over it, something mother would deny with her dying breath, probably. Now her memory was sharpening too quickly, and she stopped to stare at a counter display of wool scarves. That awful year when she was ten, dancing between them here in this store, holding their hands, chattering, afraid if she stopped or let go, one of them would slip away forever. She had been a Band-Aid, nothing more, just a Band-Aid holding them together. Holding her head high, the purple circles under her eyes more pronounced under the bright lights, Edie began elbowing her way toward the crowded aisles of the men's furnishings department next to the Randolph Street entrance.

"Excuse *me*. Can *someone* wait on me?" The voice was sharp and exasperated. Edie glanced across the main aisle and saw a well-dressed woman standing next to a display of men's dress shirts, drumming her nails on the glass counter. A slight-bodied woman wearing a navy wool dress pinned with a plastic employee tag was hurrying to the customer's side. Edie hardly recognized her own grandmother.

"I'm sorry, we're short-handed," she heard Camilla say cheerfully. "How can I help you?"

"I want a white dress shirt with a sixteen-and-a-half collar and a thirty-three-inch sleeve, nothing fancy. And I don't have much time." The customer had a heavily rouged face with severely arched eyebrows. Her body was squeezed like toothpaste into a too-tight black coat with heavy brass buttons, one of which drooped from weakening thread.

"Coming right up." Camilla lifted a small stack of crisp white shirts from the under-the-counter display and spread them out. "Button-down?"

The woman frowned. She picked one shirt up, shaking it, scattering pins. "Is this stretch fabric?"

"I beg your pardon?"

"Is the fabric stretchy?"

"I have no idea. Let's check." Camilla quickly scanned the labels, then tugged briskly at the material of each shirt. "It appears—"

"For heaven's sake, don't you know the stock?"

Camilla lifted her chin and gazed levelly at the woman. "I know most of this stock very well, but stretch shirts are a bit new to me."

"Well, I don't have any more time to waste. I'll take this one." The customer extracted an American Express card from her handbag and flipped it across the counter. A very practiced gesture.

Camilla flashed a formula smile and disappeared in the direction of the cash register. After waiting a minute or two, Edie followed. She would make her presence known now; they would laugh about the woman's cranky personality and her stretchy shirt.

But when she saw Camilla standing uncertainly by the computerized register, Edie didn't know what to

115

do. It took her only a second to realize her grandmother was poking ineffectually at the keys, brow furrowed, lips clamped tight. With a sinking feeling, she realized what was happening. Somebody probably had given Camilla about five minutes of instruction and she couldn't work the computer.

"Excuse *me*, how long is this going to *take*?"

Edie felt her muscles stiffen at the sound of the petulant voice arcing over the counter, stabbing at her grandmother.

"Be there in a moment." Camilla's voice was firm, but her eyes were darting around in search of another salesclerk, someone who could tell her what she was doing wrong. There was no one around, and the minutes were ticking away.

"Grandma—" Edie edged closer, keeping her voice down.

"Edie!" Camilla jerked slightly. "What are you doing here?" The veins on her hands hovering over the computer bulged prominently.

"Remember? I said I would come."

"Right, of course. Well, I'm glad to see you—"

Edie glanced at the computer and saw a warning blinking in red. "Grandma, punch in your employee number," she whispered. She pointed quickly at the message, trying not to be too obvious.

"Of course; goodness, I forgot." Camilla quickly punched in several digits, her hand trembling.

"Good, now put in the style and price stuff."

"I know what a universal bar code is now," Camilla said with a quick ghost of a smile. "See? I did that right."

"Now insert the card, no, not there. Yes, there."

"It isn't taking it. What's wrong?"

116

"Push 'enter,' " Edie whispered again. If only she could climb over the counter and do it herself. "The key on the left. That's it, right there."

Camilla ran the card through the machine again, but nothing happened.

"Wait—hit 'enter' again."

"Are you sure?"

"Go ahead, try."

Camilla pushed. A lazy whirr stirred inside the machine. "Got it," she whispered back. She moved quickly now, more confident. A few more hesitations, then the sales slip began chugging slowly out. Camilla ripped it from the computer and turned triumphantly toward the counter. Her customer was standing there, glaring, eyebrows drawn close together.

"I've been waiting for fifteen minutes," the woman said. "Give me my card, please."

"Of course, and here's your receipt, I—"

"Give me my card. You can keep the shirt. As far as I'm concerned, if Field's can't hire Christmas help that know how to do the job, I'll shop elsewhere." The woman grabbed her card and walked away.

Camilla looked to Edie suddenly smaller, even slightly bent inside her navy blue dress.

"Oh, Grandma—" Edie was anguished.

"Well. I wonder who yelled at *her* this morning?"

"There's no excuse, that was rotten behavior, I mean, just *rotten*. Who does she think she is?"

"It happens." Camilla brushed her hair back from her forehead with an only slightly shaky hand.

"I should have helped you faster," Edie said.

"I'm a tougher bird than you think, honey. A customer like that is just one more cranky lady with sore feet, mean kids, or a drifting husband. I've seen

117

hundreds of them."

"I don't care, I haven't, and nobody can treat you like that."

"I'm lucky you were here," Camilla said softly. She straightened her shoulders and patted Edie's hand. "Let's keep this to ourselves, okay? No need to upset your mother."

Edie started to say something, but stopped when she saw another customer looking impatiently in Camilla's direction.

Camilla flashed the woman a bright smile and whispered to Edie, "See you later, don't worry." She hurried off, leaving Edie still shaking with an overwhelming feeling of fierce protectiveness that was new to her.

* * * *

It was four-thirty and already getting dark by the time Edie got off the train at Evanston's Dempster Street station. Rachel had been waiting for over forty-five minutes and she couldn't help protesting. "You're so late," she said as Edie climbed into the car.

"I hung around a while. Sorry."

"Wish you hadn't. We've got to buy the tree and get it decorated before eight o'clock. Shall we swing by Boston Chicken afterward? Jim and Topper and Lindy are coming tonight."

"Oh, Mom, *Topper*? When did this become a party?"

Rachel put the car in gear and backed out of the parking lot, swerving to avoid a patch of ice. "How did Grandma do on her first day?" she asked, avoiding a direct answer. "Was she having fun? I can't imagine standing on my feet all day, waiting on people."

118

"She did *fine*."

"Hey, don't chop my head off."

"You shouldn't have sprung Topper on me like that."

Whatever was eating at Edie began to fade as they trudged through the mud at a huge lot near Old Orchard and found a totally gorgeous, thick spruce that Rachel loved immediately. Falling in love with a Christmas tree was an old habit of hers, one that used to irritate Matt because it was never the same one he chose. A wizened man with tattoos on his hands tied the tree onto the top of the car and Edie and Rachel proceeded slowly down the street in their suddenly festive cocoon to Boston Chicken. The tree branches wobbled and swished against the windows all the way home as they sang to Christmas carols on the radio and argued over who would unpack and test the strings of lights that Rachel had unearthed from her packing boxes. It was like old times. She would worry later about Kurt and about the risky step she had taken into the world of the so-called Truthseeker. Right now, she and Edie were celebrating Christmas in grand style.

* * * *

Two hours later the tree was up—in a rusting red stand missing one bolt—ready for the lights and the resplendent ornaments that would bring it into full glory.

"Looks great," Edie breathed, forgetting to be cool. "White lights, let's put white lights on, all over."

"Remember the beautiful old blue lights we used to use—"

"Oh no, Mother, they're so old-fashioned, we *can't*

119

use those."

"Up to you, honey." Rachel stepped back from where the tree sat in its traditional place by the beveled glass doors leading to the screened-in porch, feeling more like who she wanted to be than she had in a long time. The blue lights would be perfect, but it didn't matter. There was hardly a moment since her father's death that she hadn't yearned for something that had taken wing from her soul, something she could not identify. This was the closest hint of what that could be she had found in a long time, and she would hold on as long as she could.

The back door slammed, which meant Camilla was home. "Wait till you see the tree we got!" Edie caroled.

* * * *

Edie sprawled across the bed in her mother's room, picking at a doughnut from a bag Camilla had brought from Dunkin' Donuts. After dutifully admiring the tree, Camilla had peeled off her shoes and slowly climbed the stairs with Edie and Rachel chattering right behind her. Now she was propped up against the pillows on the far side of the bed, looking more tired than Rachel liked. But Rachel still felt constrained by their argument last night, so she contented herself with bringing her mother an extra pillow and said nothing.

"Edie, watch the sugar on the carpet, will you? Anyway, you shouldn't be eating those things—we've got a ton of roast chicken coming up." Rachel peeled off her jeans and reached into her closet for a pair of black tights and a clean white shirt, all the while trying not to eye Camilla too obviously.

"How'd the afternoon go, Grandma?" Edie asked as she licked her fingers.

"Fine," Camilla said, attempting an exhausted smile. "No clones of our friend showed up, dear. No need to worry."

"What friend?" Rachel buttoned her shirt and moved to the dresser. She yanked at a stuck drawer, wondering if the movers had left a piece of tape still holding it in back.

"Just a cranky woman who thinks a salesclerk should be motorized," Camilla said. She rubbed her feet, wincing slightly.

"Well, it's hard to stand on your feet all day. None of us is getting any younger."

Camilla bridled, almost imperceptibly. "I'm far from being the oldest one there," she said.

"I never think of you as old," Rachel said immediately. She gave the balky drawer one more yank. It suddenly popped free, sending jewelry flying in the air. The three of them went down on their hands and knees to collect the scattered necklaces and earrings.

Edie retrieved a gaudy bracelet with huge pink stones from under the bed. "What's this?" she said.

Camilla answered first. "Your mother won that playing Bingo at a church carnival when she was about nine. Remember, Rachel? You were so cute and excited."

It was a peace offering. But why did her mother always rework family stories to suit herself? "Not exactly," Rachel replied. "I found it in the street outside the church."

"No, that was a different bracelet. I remember very well, your father and I were looking all over for you when you came running out of this tent—"

"No, no, you've got it wrong." She saw with a hollow sense of victory that her mother's eyes had turned uncertain.

"Are you sure?"

"Who cares?" Edie interjected. Suddenly she spied a small piece on the floor that had been half-hidden by the edge of the quilt. It was an oval brooch. She picked it up and turned it around in her hand, staring at a delicately painted cameo of a Victorian woman with two diamond chips sparkling in her dark hair. The gold frame of the brooch was ringed in tiny seed pearls.

"This is beautiful. I never saw it before."

"Oh, for heaven's sake, I'd forgotten about that. Don't you ever wear it, Rachel? It was a gift from an old beau I almost married a thousand years ago." Camilla had a faraway look in her eyes as she reached for it.

"Really, Grandma? What happened?"

"We broke up."

"Oh, come on, there must be a story—"

"We were just babies," Camilla said with a laugh. "Anyhow, I met your grandpa and that was that for me."

"Grandma, do you *have* to give me the sanitized version?" Edie asked with an exasperated expression.

Rachel flashed her mother a knowing look; their eyes locked. Yes, Camilla always hid her stories behind proper little homilies. But Rachel's own memories of this brooch were stirring, memories she had never shared, and for once she understood Camilla's artful dodging. Maybe some things should be like childbirth, where you remember only the

122

highlights.

"How come it's in Mother's jewel box?"

"I gave it to her as her first serious piece of jewelry when she graduated from college."

Rachel gave in to a sudden, overwhelming impulse. "Here, Edie," she said, picking up the brooch and offering it to her daughter. "It's for you now."

"For me? Really?"

"It's about time for *your* first serious piece of jewelry. Don't you think so, Mother?"

Edie turned questioningly to her grandmother, who smiled. "It'll look beautiful on you," she said.

It was beautiful. The nicest piece of jewelry she had ever owned, and Edie figured she'd get the full story out of Grandma sooner or later. "I love it," Edie said shyly. She started to say something more, but the phone rang. She scrambled to the side of the bed and picked up the receiver, thinking of seed pearls and romance. "Hello?"

At first she heard only breathing. Deep inhaling; slow, raspy exhaling. Then a voice that sounded like it was coming out of a fog horn. "You didn't like my flowers, so I sent more."

"Who is this?"

"Open your front door, sweetheart."

Rachel saw Edie's eyes grow round with surprise. With a sick feeling of inevitability in her stomach, she reached for the phone. "Give it to me," she whispered urgently. Edie thrust the receiver at her mother, her surprise turning to fright.

All Rachel heard was a dial tone. Questioning, she looked at Edie.

"He said to open the front door. A really strange voice, Mom."

Rachel pulled herself up and moved with as much matter-of-fact authority as she could muster out of the room and down the stairs, but her knees were wobbling. She opened the front door and looked down at the front mat. She saw a bedraggled cluster of lilies wrapped in newspaper and pushed at them with her foot.

Edie, behind her, spoke quietly. "First we get live ones, now we get dead ones."

Rachel stooped to pick the package up, wondering vaguely if she should do this kind of thing. What if there were a bomb inside? But all she had in her hand were dead stargazers, emitting a slightly rancid smell. Some flowers rotted like animal flesh, but this was different. And then she saw the small, stiff corpse of a dead mouse wrapped inside the newspaper.

CHAPTER 5

"YOU'VE GOT A PRACTICAL JOKER ON YOUR HANDS, I'D guess," Jim said in a voice deliberately loud enough for Camilla and Edie to hear, but his eyes turned flat and hard as coins as Rachel told him what had happened. Topper was taking off her coat in the living room and listening, wide-eyed, as Edie related the story in a rapid tumble of breathless words. Camilla, unusually quiet, was stoking the fire. The police had come and gone, courteous, very professional. They would put a watch on the house tonight and a tap on her phone. Still, they conveyed the impression that a bouquet of dead flowers accompanied by a dead mouse wasn't exactly an earth-shattering event. Anybody mad at you, Mrs. Snow?

"That could be. I sometimes have controversial guests on my show," she had said with as casual a shrug she could muster. She felt stung by the faint suspicion that the police viewed her and her family as a group of slightly hysterical women making a big deal out of nothing much.

Jim's burly presence was both relief and reproof. "Thanks, but I'm not so sure," she said in as low as voice as possible. "Go ahead—tell me you warned me."

"About the character calling your show? There may not be any connection. And if there is, you couldn't have anticipated this."

"I wish I had heard his voice, then I'd know." His lack of censure made her feel worse, not better.

The doorbell rang and Rachel swung the door open, glad for Jim's steadying presence behind her. It was Kurt. She tried to wipe away what must have been a grim look on her face, but Kurt still looked slightly startled as the porch light shone down on his black hair.

"Oh, hi, Kurt. This is Kurt Kiley, a friend of Edie's from Madison," Rachel said hastily to Jim over her shoulder.

"You were expecting Freddy, maybe?" Kurt said as he came in and pulled off his leather jacket. He was wearing a black turtleneck and black jeans in what Rachel decided was an effort to ape the carefully insouciant uniform of Hollywood.

"Who?"

"Freddy Krueger. You know, *Nightmare on Elm Street*."

She laughed a little too heartily and offered him to Jim for perusal. But Edie suddenly appeared and

125

grabbed Kurt with her long fingers, pulling him by the sleeve of his sweater into the living room, away from the others. Rachel could hear her once again telling about the bouquet of flowers, the mouse, and the anonymous phone call—but this time in an amused, laconic way that sounded unnatural. Rachel noted Jim checking Kurt out with keen interest, and wondered if his impressions matched her own.

"Need any help, Mrs. Snow?"

It was Topper, speaking in a strained voice that Rachel didn't recognize. Jim's daughter stood with hands shoved into the pockets of an oversized man's tweed blazer that looked like something picked up out of a rummage shop. It gave her a junior high school look, even though it also hid the chunkiness of her figure. Her hair was burnt orange, the dull color of a fading nectarine. Her thin, pale eyelashes blinked rapidly behind large, steel-rimmed glasses. If she'd just use a little mascara, Rachel thought in sympathy, and then was irritated with her own sexism. "Thank you, I have a plate of pâté and crackers ready in the kitchen you could bring out," she said with a warm smile.

"Oh, good; you do have water crackers, Mrs. Snow?" Kurt turned to her with an eyebrow raised.

"There are no water crackers," Edie said flatly. "You never buy them, Mother, you always forget."

"Some fresh French bread would be fine."

"No French bread, either."

"Oh dear."

Rachel stared at Kurt. Had he really said "Oh dear"?

"We'll go get the water crackers," Edie said quickly. "Come on, Kurt."

126

"Can I come, too?" Topper said with a smile, showing large, glistening teeth.

"Oh, we'll be back soon, don't bother."

"But I want to come, it's no problem."

Edie and Kurt were opening the door as they pulled on their coats and rushed out giggling, pretending not to hear.

"Topper, why don't you help me get the other snacks ready," Camilla said quickly. "Trimming a tree is hard work and we need as much fortification as we can get."

Topper turned with flushing cheeks and followed Camilla into the kitchen like a spanked spaniel. Rachel glanced at Jim and saw a look on his face that made her want to apologize for her daughter's bad manners, but she was afraid she would only make things worse. He began busying himself with the lights, and she convinced herself it was too late anyway.

By the time Edie and Kurt came back, the atmosphere had mellowed. The sound of the Supremes singing "Jingle Bells" was swelling through the living room and Rachel was seated on the floor, carefully peeling off the paper wrapped around each fragile ornament. Camilla was dressed in a black dress with a red enameled Christmas tree pin on her right breast, and setting the table with Rachel's wedding silver. Topper sat on the sofa scanning a book, her red hair now burnished by the light from the floor lamp.

Edie rushed into the kitchen and emerged a moment later with the pâté and crackers on a plate, and Rachel began to relax. She and Jim sat down together on the floor and untangled the strings of electric lights.

"Are you sure you haven't changed your mind?" she asked Edie hopefully. "You want the white ones,

127

not the blue ones?"

"Oh dear, are you still insisting on those old blue lights?" Camilla said with a smile. "Honey, they're *ancient.*"

"All right, never mind." Rachel gave it up and she and Jim began stringing the electric lights around the tree. The homely task resonated with memories, and she found herself humming along with the music as everyone sat eating and chatting away. Everything would have been perfect, except for the fact that Edie and Kurt were huddled together with their backs to Topper, giggling as if they were sharing a secret joke.

Lindy Colson arrived a few minutes later with her arms filled with Christmas presents, causing a flurry of activity as she bubbled and gushed her way through introductions, adding a warmth Rachel gratefully embraced. But even Lindy's sunny presence didn't manage to crack Edie and Kurt apart.

Edie glanced up and saw Rachel looking at her. "Hey, this pâté's awesome," she said promptly with a metallic cheer that irritated her mother. "Give me some more, Topper, will you?" Topper immediately started scooping some pâté onto a cracker and reached with it toward Edie. A glob of it dropped from the cracker and onto Kurt's arm.

"Oh, for Christ's sake," he muttered under his breath, and Rachel wasn't sure if anybody beside herself had heard him.

"I'm really sorry," Topper said quickly. She beseeched Edie with her eyes, attempting clumsily to change the subject. "Remember when we used to make chocolate chip cookies after school and eat all the dough? And got those awful stomachaches?"

"Topper and I went to grammar school together

before we moved to Chicago," Edie said to Kurt with a slightly pained smile. She wished Topper wasn't here. Nobody would ever convince her that Jim's daughter hadn't been haunting her all her life. She knew it was awful of her, but did she have to treat her like a best friend just because their parents worked together?

"Do you remember?"

"Yeah, vaguely."

"What're you getting in biology?"

Edie sighed. "I don't know yet."

"I'm getting an A."

"Wow," said Kurt. "That's really fabulous."

Topper flushed, this time happily.

"I guess that means honor roll, huh?"

"I guess," Topper replied, trying to be modest.

"Wow." Kurt poked Edie with an elaborately clandestine motion. "You know what they do at Langdon when you make honor roll?"

"No, what?" Edie asked, wide-eyed.

"They let you clean *all* the erasers after class, all by yourself."

"Ooooh, cool," Edie said, clasping her hands together.

"Well, I never heard of any such thing," Lindy interrupted, blissfully oblivious. She had wiggled her ample bottom into a chair facing the tree and glared now at Kurt. "I spent four wonderful years in that school and those of us who made good grades did *not* clean erasers."

Topper squirmed. Jim was standing on the ladder, taking great care placing the top ornaments, not looking at any of them.

"And you know what else?" Kurt was ignoring Lindy.

"Wow, there's more?" said Edie.

"If you're *really* good, they let you take a dissected frog home. For *keeps*."

"Edie, hand me those bulbs," Rachel interjected, staring coolly at Kurt. "And get the garlands from the box in the dining room."

Edie couldn't hold back a high-pitched giggle as she rose to comply. Jim and her mother looked so ridiculously glum. "We're just joking, Mother. Topper can take a joke, can't you, Topper?"

"Sure," Topper said quickly.

Jim's face was stitched so tight, it pulled like a puckered seam. Rachel busied herself with the ornaments Edie had made of dough and water in the fifth grade, unwrapping each childish creation with a pang of longing. Suddenly the Supremes gave way to the sweet sounds of Ray Charles, and she realized that Jim had climbed down from the ladder and was now standing next to her.

"Hey," he said quietly. "Can I have a dance with the prettiest girl in the room?" He gripped her hand and moved her slowly around the Christmas tree, his step surprisingly light and sure—and for a few brief moments Rachel was able to close her eyes and imagine the evening she really wanted. The others fell silent. When Rachel opened her eyes, her gaze fell first on Camilla, and she saw that her mother's unguarded face had a haunted quality. Her gaze traveled then to Edie, who was busily untangling knots of silver garlands and didn't seem to be paying any attention. Edie's shoulder blades stood out sharply against her thin cotton shirt.

"I can't believe this. Dad, you're acting like a kid." Topper's embarrassed voice broke the spell first.

Rachel stumbled, losing the beat. "Nothing like a little editorial comment to ruin a good thing," Jim murmured into her ear. She laughed, reluctantly moving away from his encircling arm. They walked self-consciously to the sofa and sat down.

Camilla blinked as if awakened from a reverie. She turned to Topper, who was sitting looking owlish and stuck like a tree stump next to her on the sofa. "Did I hear from somewhere that you want to be a writer?" she asked. "I'm sure I did, didn't I?"

Topper flushed again, but answered readily enough. "Did Dad tell you? I'm writing a novel."

"Autobiographical? The story of your life?" Kurt's eyebrows went up and his expression turned rapt.

Topper was more wary this time. "No, it's a story about two girls in boarding school who are best friends—"

"Oh, definitely *not* autobiographical," Edie said, and then tried a quick laugh to show she was only kidding, but the damage was done.

Over the top edge of her glasses, pale lashes fluttering, Topper stared at her and then directly, balefully, at Kurt. "I write fiction, just like Kurt," she said. "Maybe mine is just ordinary, but has Kurt told you what he writes?"

"Topper—" Edie was warning her.

"No, he hasn't," Rachel said, leaning forward now. "What *do* you write, Kurt?"

Kurt took his time responding, stretching back on the sofa with proprietary languor. "I write short stories, romantic kinds of stories," he said finally.

"I like romantic stories," Camilla said.

"So do I. Tell us about them," Rachel urged.

"Some romance!" snorted Topper.

"Isn't it time for dinner, Mother?" Edie said. She jumped to her feet, looking like a small wraith in her aged blue jeans. "I'll put the chicken out. Where do you keep your hot pads?"

Camilla stood, too. "I'll go open the wine."

Rachel didn't budge. She watched Kurt, tracing with her eyes the shadows of his young-old face as he carefully picked bits of invisible lint off the sleeve of his black sweater. "Give us an example," she urged softly. "I like romantic stories, too."

"You wouldn't like mine."

"Oh, go ahead, try me. Why not?"

Topper giggled semihysterically, refusing to look at Edie. "Because they're really dirty, Mrs. Snow. Kurt writes porn."

"You don't know what you're talking about," Edie snapped.

"Come on, Edie. He writes the filthiest stories anybody's ever seen and he puts them out on the Internet and he's *notorious*, and you just don't like admitting it." Topper's voice bubbled like porridge on a stove, thick with the resentments of the rejected.

"Have you read any of them? If you're going to be a critic, you gotta read the stuff." Kurt's voice was still languorous, but his eyes had narrowed.

"No, but I've heard about what you do. The kids at school talk about it *all the time*," Topper replied primly, taking her glasses off and looking him straight in the eye. "I have to be familiar with all kinds of writing if I'm going to write fiction, so I know *exactly* what you do."

"Pornography? Is that what's going on?" Rachel moved to the edge of her chair.

"Maybe some people think I write dirty stories,

because they have dirty minds," Kurt replied. "They're not 'filthy.' Sure, they have sex in them, but what doesn't? I have different selves. One self writes porn."

"Right," Edie said furiously, reaching for Kurt's hand. "That's what writers do."

"All writers?" asked Rachel.

"I assume you interview writers who write a lot about sex, Mrs. Snow. Does that make them filthy?" Kurt said with a challenge in his eyes.

Rachel wondered fleetingly if he might actually be trying to protect himself from her. What possible power did she have? Certainly not over Edie. "I even *read* books with sex scenes, Kurt," she said. She kept her voice lightly neutral, not directly answering his question, but it was an effort. They shared a glance, a rather long one. He didn't like her and she didn't like him, and they were letting each other know.

"Topper probably thinks The *Velveteen Rabbit* is filthy because the toys don't wear any clothes," Edie lashed out suddenly. "If she's read it, that is."

This was greeted with total silence.

"That's enough. Pornography is too heavy a topic for a tree-trimming party," Lindy said, breaking the silence. Rising quickly from the sofa, she walked over to Topper and tugged gently at her arm, pulling her up. "Come on, enough on this, let's you and me get dinner on the table." Looking totally stunned, Topper followed her into the kitchen.

Jim made a move to follow his daughter and stopped. He glanced at Rachel with regret and turned to face Edie. "Hurting a friend isn't smart and it isn't sophisticated," he said evenly. "Maybe you ought to be thinking about that, Edie. You whomped my

133

daughter right now, and I hope you didn't really mean it, because I don't like it."

Edie winced.

Rachel moved with instinctive speed to Edie's side and protectively encircled her daughter's shoulders. "Hold on, Jim, she didn't mean—" But she didn't finish because the doorbell was ringing again, and she hurried to answer it. She missed the triumphant glance Kurt shot in Edie's direction. But Jim didn't.

"Amos?" Rachel drew in her breath. She couldn't quite believe it: Amos Curley was standing on her front porch. He was wearing an ancient school jacket emblazoned with a basketball letter, giving him the appearance of a slightly faded college athlete. His hair was hidden under a knit cap and his thin, angular nose was bright red. He looked frozen. He must have walked from the El, Rachel thought in surprise.

"Impulse visit," he said affably, making no move to come in. "If my timing is bad, say so. But I had to tell you to your face how gutsy you were this morning. I was in Rogers Park for an interview and thought I'd just hop the El and come up here. I suddenly had the urge to put you in context." He waved his hand to take in the house. He was smiling in his usual, relaxed way, but she saw the sides of his mouth working. His voice had the sound of gravel being ground underfoot; his eyes were questioning.

Rachel was squeezing the doorknob so tightly, her fingers began aching.

"I can hear voices, you've got company." He stepped back. "Hey, I'll call tomorrow—"

"No," she said, making up her mind. "I'm really glad to see you. Won't you come in? And—and meet my family and friends?" She swung the door open wide. Amos had on his cowboy boots and she watched his body as he moved past her into the living room. She flushed, feeling both aroused and endangered. What the hell was she doing?

Camilla's eyes froze when she introduced Amos. She cast a baffled look in Rachel's direction as she went through the motion of shaking hands. Topper and Lindy were still in the kitchen, and they could all hear the muffled sound of sobbing. Edie stared at Amos's cowboy boots with frank curiosity and Jim studied him with such baleful animosity that Rachel was embarrassed. When Camilla started moving toward the kitchen, she walked with her.

"Rachel, it's him, isn't it?"

"Yes, it is; but I can explain."

Camilla stared at her daughter, aghast. "I can't believe it, you're seeing him again? For God's sake, I would've thought you had more sense."

"Thanks for the support," Rachel shot back. A scolding from her mother was not what she needed right now.

She turned back toward the living room, hoping Amos wouldn't notice the coolness of his reception. He didn't seem to.

"Rachel did a great job with that stalker this morning," he said to Jim as he shed his ancient jacket. "The Women's Crisis Hot Line was swamped with calls. Apparently the whole town's buzzing, which makes it a nice story for us. You don't often get a chance to flush that kind of nut out into the open. Was engaging him your idea?"

Edie's eyes flew open. "What stalker?"

"It's not a stalker, just some anonymous caller," Rachel said quickly.

"No, it wasn't my idea," Jim replied shortly.

"Mother?" Edie's voice was rising. "You didn't say anything about some stalker at the office. Is it the same guy who called here?"

"I don't have a clue."

The smile vanished from Amos's face. "He called *here*? What happened?"

Rachel filled him in on the phone call and the dead mouse left at the door and watched his eyes grow thoughtful. "It sounds like your Truthseeker is expanding his territory, which makes things a little dicier for you," he said finally. "But it means you're getting to him, Rachel, and that makes an even better story. It must be—"

"Hey, this isn't about a story," Jim interjected. "It's about Rachel at risk."

"I think you overestimate the danger," Amos said, taken aback. "What Rachel did was provide a public service. The police can take care of—"

"Public service, my foot. You don't play around with a stalker, even to provide the *Trib* with a good story. Why are you pushing Rachel on this?" Jim's face was flushed again, a web of bright spider veins exploding across his cheeks. Rachel looked away, astonished and embarrassed at his tone.

"That's a little insulting to Rachel. I kind of suspect nobody 'pushes' her to do anything on her show that she doesn't want to do," Amos said levelly.

"Dad?"

They all looked up at Topper standing in the doorway. "Can we go home?" she said. The edges of her mouth trembled. "I'm sorry to mess up your dinner, Mrs. Snow, but I just want to go home now." She cast a long look at Edie, who ducked her head and

136

started studying her fingernails.

Jim blinked; his anger suddenly evaporating. He pulled himself up from his chair slowly, looking suddenly very tired. "I think I do, too," he said. "Get our coats from the hall closet, Topper."

"I'm sorry if I embarrassed you," he said quietly to Rachel as he stood in the shadows at the front door. There were scooped hollows of gray under his eyes as he took his coat from Topper and gave her a quick hug, telling her he would join her in the car in a minute. He turned back to Rachel. "I wasn't implying that you were letting yourself be manipulated."

"You skirted the edges," Rachel said, lifting her chin. "I don't need you as my protector, Jim."

"That's not the real issue, is it?"

She hardened her heart in the face of his supplicating glance and told him what truly angered her. "You shouldn't have embarrassed Edie like that."

"Rachel, she deserved it."

"It's Kurt leading her on."

"She's old enough to know what she's doing. She's sixteen, for God's sake. That kind of behavior went out with grammar school."

"You don't know girls, you just think you do. Your own daughter—"

He stiffened. "I do my best, Rachel."

"Edie had a terrible day, don't you see that? She was shocked when she picked up the phone and heard that man's voice. And then to see that dead mouse wrapped in the newspaper—it was too much!"

"That's a separate problem."

"Well, I believe it's all connected and it's a parent's job to look at the whole picture."

"I don't disagree with that. But you'll help Edie

137

more if you don't make excuses for her."

"You don't know my daughter. I'm sorry, Jim, but you don't know Edie. You can't imagine what it's like dealing with a kid by yourself—" She put her hand to her mouth. "What a stupid thing to say. I'm sorry." What flashed through her mind was the unguarded moment last year when Jim had described his awkwardness at buying Topper her first box of tampons. How at sea he had felt in a female world. How much he had missed his wife. Who else was going to do it? How could she be so insensitive, especially when she too was irritated by Edie? But Jim had no right to chastise her daughter in public like that. That was *her* job.

"Oh hell." Jim pushed a long strand of hair back from his ruddy, suddenly bleak face. He yanked at the belt disappearing beneath his bulging waistline. "Let's just call it a night, okay? See you Monday."

Rachel watched his sturdy figure tromping across the porch in black rubber boots until it disappeared. She turned back to the still warm and glowing living room; to the now glittering Christmas tree; to her daughter and mother. She caught in the light the crisp lines of Amos's profile as he talked amiably to Edie and remembered how she used to tease him about his looks. She decided to ask him to stay for dinner.

* * * *

It would have been a total disaster if he hadn't been there. Camilla sat upright in her chair, barely conversing, her eyes flicking back and forth between Amos and her daughter in a way that made Rachel acutely uncomfortable. Lindy Colson took it into her head to wonder if they should have sent plates of food home with Jim and Topper until Camilla silenced her with a raised eyebrow. But the chicken was on the plates, the candles were lit, and the tree was finished. Edie and Kurt began an earnest discussion about cyberspace reporting with Amos, and Rachel felt warmed by occasional glances from Amos's steady, unclouded eyes. She would settle for that, she told herself.

The phone rang sharply and they all paused, a frozen tableau. Edie sprang from her chair to answer before Rachel could head her off. Amos thrust forward a steadying hand as she rose to follow Edie to the kitchen.

"You'll know soon enough," he said.

"Who was it?" she asked a few moments later as Edie returned and slumped deep into her seat.

"Dad." Edie's voice had a muffled quality.

"What did he want?"

"He wants me to fly out to Hawaii for Christmas. To spend it with him and Greta, because they're sorry they got married without telling me."

"Well, he's got his nerve—" Rachel began, nascent fury rising.

"So how come you look so miserable?" Amos interrupted, his eyes narrowing.

"Because he never lets anything be. I mean, he chews everything up." Edie lowered her head, using her fork to pick ineffectually at a drumstick.

"Do you want to go to Hawaii?"

Rachel rested her wrist on the edge of the table to keep her hand steady as she waited for Edie's response. How was Amos able to get this from her daughter with one tug? She felt her own tug, one of jealousy.

"Well—no," Edie said after a split-second hesitation, her eyes darting in Kurt's direction. "I kind of like it here right now."

Amos began stabbing at his own drumstick. "You know, my dad was like that," he said quietly.

"Your parents were divorced? God, and you lived to talk about it?" Edie was trying for her arch tone again, and not quite succeeding.

"Yeah, you know, divorce wasn't invented by your parents. I was sitting in a lunchroom alone with a bag lunch way before you were born."

"Why'd they get divorced?"

"My dad was a drunk who ran a liquor store and my mother was a drunk who hid liquor bottles in my toy box. What else do you want to know?"

Edie flushed and cast a glance at her mother for a clue to what she should say next. But before Rachel could open her mouth, Kurt spoke up.

"It all sounds like so much whining to me. You were lucky they got divorced. Mine just stay married."

"My goodness, can't we talk about something else besides all that terrible stuff?" protested Lindy.

"Sorry, Mrs. Colson," said Amos. "It just seemed like Edie had to get a few things off her chest and I thought I might be able to offer some help. Mind passing the mashed potatoes?" He cast a grin in Edie's direction. "Just remember, divorced parents can drive you crazy, but that's because a lot of times they're afraid of each other—afraid one of them will be a winner and one a loser with their kids, so don't shoot them down too fast. Give them time to get over it."

"I don't want to choose."

Edie's words hung over the dining room table in all

their honest rawness. Rachel glanced at Camilla and saw the lines of her mother's mouth softening as she picked up the old ironstone platter that had belonged to her grandmother—now heaped with potatoes—and passed it to Amos. Lindy was rubbing fussily at a gravy stain on the tablecloth and Kurt had his head bent far forward as he ate, his black hair grazing dangerously close to his potatoes and chicken. Only Edie seemed still. She sat quietly, one finger tracing the curved edge of her glass of Diet Pepsi, looking directly at no one. Then Rachel glanced at Amos and saw him reaching for the bottle of wine on the table. His hand stopped, suspended in air for an instant, and then he pulled it away and embraced his water glass, curving his fingers around it as if it were a life preserver. Had he seen her glance in his direction? She didn't know.

"Of course you don't," Amos said, lifting his water glass. "Well, everybody, here's to Christmas. Edie, you're right. Who wants a dumb luau when they can have Christmas at home?" His eyes sparkled as he looked first at Edie and then directly at Rachel. She raised her glass, filled with gratitude and a sudden clarity of vision. No matter what happened, she had just heard something directly from Edie's heart that eased the fear inside, and it was Amos who had coaxed it out. He had given her a gift of truth from Edie that lit the room with more than the flickering candles now casting their warm glow from the old wrought-iron chandelier above the table. He had done it by paying attention. And if there was any such thing as an ultimate aphrodisiac, attention was what it was.

CHAPTER 6

"WOW. MOM, DID YOU KNOW THE WHOLE STORY about the call and the flowers and the mouse is in the paper?" Edie said the next morning as she stared at the front page of the *Tribune's* Metro section.

"It is?" Rachel was surprised.

"Who's Jeanie Horton? It's her byline."

"She and Amos are doing investigative pieces for the *Tribune,* and I guess he filled her in." Rachel leaned over Edie's shoulder and skimmed the story, hoping she had said this casually enough, but a knot tightened in her stomach. "Anonymous Caller Stalks Radio Show Host," read the headline. That would surely grab attention. Jeanie had done quite a job, lacing her story with details about past notorious stalkers and plenty of speculation as to whether the Truthseeker was the same man who had murdered the Chicago Circle students. There was even a quote from Berry: "We don't know why he chose us—but people like this always make one call too many. He'll be exposed sooner or later. *Talk Time* will not be intimidated."

Feeling queasy, Rachel folded a filter into the coffeemaker. She could hear the branches of the holly trees outside the breakfast-room windows scratching softly against the panes, a sound she usually loved. This morning it sounded vaguely ominous. Why exactly *had* Amos shown up here last night?

"It's gotta be the same guy," Edie said, eyes wide. "Aren't you scared?"

"Not by some coward who breathes heavy on the phone. Don't worry, I think one thing this story will do is get the police to pay a little more attention and not be quite so dismissive."

"I'm not worried, it's sort of cool." Edie gulped at a glass of milk, shoving the paper aside. "Berry called and I told her everything that happened. She got all excited. Oh, she said to remind you about taping the new promos today. Doesn't it suck to work on Saturday?"

"I'm used to it. Did she read the article?"

"She thought it was great. Got any apples?"

"Bottom bin, refrigerator," Rachel said automatically.

"I liked Mr. Curley. I never think of you dating somebody who wears cowboy boots. Grandma didn't like him. How come?" Edie affected an innocent look as she bit deep into a wizened Winesap pulled from the refrigerator bin.

"Grandma can speak for herself on her likes and dislikes. Now what about Topper?"

Edie froze in mid-bite. "So what freaks you out more, Kurt writing porn or me twitting Topper?" Edie's chin was up, a danger signal.

"You weren't twitting her, you were being unkind." It was like driving in the Indy 500, Rachel told herself. One false move and you hit the wall.

Edie's jaws slowly closed over the apple with an audible crunch. "Okay, I was being, like, a juvenile. But don't ask me to apologize, because look what she did to Kurt. Mom, Topper is a dweeb, a crybaby, a—"

"She's a sensitive kid who may be a dweeb, but she deserves better treatment from her friend."

Edie looked miserable. "Kurt hates her."

"Don't blame Kurt." Rachel suddenly heard Jim's stolid, dogged voice in her ear. "You're old enough to know what you're doing. That kind of behavior went out with grammar school. And where did the two of you go after dinner?"

"We just cruised."

Edie tossed the half-eaten apple in the sink and there was a slurping sound as it slid into the disposal. She stood there, her hair falling forward, pale and floaty as chiffon, staring after it.

"Morning," Camilla said chirpily, emerging from the hall, crisp and bandboxy in navy wool again. "Mr. Garcia just showed up. He said he'll finish the job today. I told them we'd be out of their way in an hour." She peered anxiously out the window, checking the sky. "Those clouds look loaded with snow, don't they? The weatherman keeps saying we're going to have this huge storm, but it never happens. I *do* hope we have a white Christmas. Edie, shouldn't you and Topper find a way to make up? She's been your friend forever."

"I guess I ragged her a little too much last night," Edie said. The head was coming up; the hair floating back.

"Yes, you did. But she was a little over the top herself," Camilla replied.

"She's jealous. She has hardly any friends, and she's jealous of me because I have Kurt, do you know that?"

"How do you know?"

"Kurt told me."

Camilla and Rachel greeted that with silence.

"I've outgrown her, that's the problem. You know how it happens? I mean, she's still such a kid and I'm not anymore—"

"Which means it's up to you to be generous," Rachel said quietly.

Camilla was buttoning her coat very slowly. "Edie, why don't you invite Kurt and his folks over one of these evenings? Your mother and I would enjoy meeting them." She cast a quick glance at Rachel, who nodded assent.

"They travel a lot, I don't think they're around much," Edie said, slumping into a chair at the counter. There was no way she could explain what Kurt's parents were like, and she wasn't about to try. Meeting them had been too disappointing.

"Well, sometime maybe. I'm going to drive Grandma to work this morning. Do you want to ride in with me? Hang out at the station?" Rachel asked, walking over to the hooks by the back door for her own coat. "I have to record those promos, but we could have lunch."

Edie pulled at a strand of hair, wrapping it around her right ear, and smiled at her mother with a fragile sunniness. "I don't feel like it today. Maybe next week, okay?"

"Okay. Hope the painters don't crowd you," Rachel said lightly. "The flirty one took another job, and Mr. Garcia swears he hired the others from a monastery."

Edie rolled her eyes and shrugged her shoulders as if to say a flirtatious painter was yesterday's news.

"I'll be home early, probably around six," Camilla said. "You and I can spend a little time together." She leaned over and gave Edie a soft kiss on the cheek. "Thanks for writing out the instructions for that fancy cash register." She patted her pocket. "I'm going to keep them right with me all day."

* * * *

145

"Berry, I don't like this," Rachel said as she walked through the doorway of her office, holding up the morning paper. "I think we're finished with the Truthseeker, okay? Jim's right, this is too risky."

"Hey, you've got it; now just tell *him*." Berry was sitting in Rachel's chair, wearing a long denim skirt. The freckles sprinkled across her broad nose looked today like fiery red pepper. She waved her hand in the air. "You think you've got an argument with *me*? Who needs dead mice at their front door? Edie says you had a great party last night."

"Jim left angry and my mother was freaked out by Amos and I was freaked out by Kurt. Other than that, it was fabulous."

"Yeah, I heard the whole story." She giggled. "I'll tell you the obvious, Rachel. Isn't that my job in life? Jim is jealous of Amos."

"Oh, don't be silly." Rachel smiled as she peeled off her wool cap and tossed it at Berry.

"Anybody can see it, dearie. You should've invited me, I'd have smoothed everything over—you know how well Jim and I get along," Berry said, dodging the cap.

"So now you're Mother Teresa?"

"I would've told Jim to can it, agreed *totally* with your mother, and asked Kurt to send me printouts of his juiciest stories. Did I miss anything?"

"You never miss anything."

"So why wasn't I invited?"

Rachel's grin wavered slightly at the sudden edge to Berry's voice. "I'm sorry, I didn't think of it," she said honestly. But why hadn't she? Just because Berry rarely got out didn't mean she mightn't have found a way to come. Was there anyone else with whom she had quite the same resonating connection to the past?

146

At one point she could have looked in a mirror and seen Berry laughing back at her; they were that much in tune. Maybe it was all the missed years. Wasn't that the perennial problem at college reunions? Bonds were forged; bonds withered. You only faced the truth when you tried to make conversation over a slightly wilted chicken salad in a slightly wilted restaurant and found you no longer caught the same signals or supported the same candidate for president. Maybe it was more the fact that Berry had not married or had a child; her dark moments had been different and produced different rules of survival. Rachel tried to swallow these thoughts behind her apologetic smile, but Berry seemed delighted with her chagrin.

"God, don't look so stricken, I can't stand it," Berry laughed. "I didn't invite you to my fortieth birthday party, so I'd say we're even."

"Your party? What party?"

"Rachel, I'm joking! I didn't have one. You know why I love you? You take everything so damn seriously." Berry took off her glasses and rubbed her eyes. "Now let's stop kidding around and record these promos; then you can go Christmas shopping and I'll go home and oil my dad's wheelchair. The squeaking is driving me crazy."

"Look, I meant what I said about us going out to dinner together—"

"You know what? It gave me a real charge to see you and the show featured in the *Trib* this morning. High time, and don't tell me you didn't secretly enjoy it, too, because we are in this together, pal. Right?"

"Right," Rachel said with a grin, giving up. She reached into her desk, knowing she would find a fresh supply of Snickers bars, compliments of Berry Brown, the world's greatest producer. Stuffed with chocolate, she could tackle anything.

* * * *

The hours were dragging for Edie, although she wouldn't come right out and admit it, even to herself. Kurt hadn't come over, and when she tried to call his house, no one answered. Maybe last night had scared him away. How could Topper smear Kurt like that in front of her family? I'll never forgive her, Edie vowed, angry all over again. She flopped down on a cushion in front of the TV and watched a half-dozen soaps as the day went by. The painters had some loud Latin American music on upstairs. Finally she turned off the TV and thumbed indifferently through some books, then the newspaper, wishing she didn't feel quite so morose. She could study, that's what her mother would say. But she was no grind like Topper. She wandered through the narrow hall to the dining room, looking around on her own terms for the first time. The antique iron chandelier, filled with fat, creamy candles, was huge. Probably a fire hazard. She walked into the living room, fingering the cameo brooch around her neck. It was so beautiful. She reached around and unfastened the clasp, gazing at the delicately painted face of the tiny figure adorned with tiny diamonds now in the cup of her hand. There was a story to it, she knew there was. She propped it up on the mantel, wondering. Suddenly restless again, she started up the stairs, tracing with the tip of her finger the carvings in the massive old oak banister. Mr. Garcia was standing on a high ladder working on the moldings in her mother's room, shouting instructions to a new helper working on the baseboards. He waved, and she waved back. God, Grand Central Station. She started up the second, narrower set of stairs to the third floor and went into Camilla's room and threw herself on the bed. Now she could think about last night. Now she could be relieved that her mother hadn't pressed harder about where she and Kurt had gone after dinner. She hugged a pillow, smelling the faint fragrance of her grandmother's hair. Something like vanilla and roses. It felt good to know she would be home soon.

She rolled onto her stomach, still hugging the pillow, and shivered, remembering Kurt's empty house last night, the dark room, the bed, Kurt's skin, the tight curls of hair on his chest. It wasn't so bad in the dark, when she couldn't see the sheets. . . .

Edie slept.

When she awoke, it was with a start. What had she heard? Her eyes flew to the clock and saw that it was almost five. She listened again, straining. She could hear the painters moving around downstairs. And another sound, what was it? Noiselessly, she moved from the bed to the door and stood uncertainly at the head of the stairs. It sounded like something banging in the basement. The boiler? Washing machine? Edie started down the stairs, a little flustered. She saw the painters on the landing going down ahead of her, and stopped long enough to hear Mr. Garcia's goodbyes. The job was finished, he declared, beaming. Merry Christmas, tell your mama I'll mail her my bill. She walked down with them to the first floor and watched them leave. She went to the top of the basement stairs and hesitated. She hadn't explored down here at all, and she never much liked basements because they always felt spooky. She listened again; it *did* sound like something rattling in the boiler pipes, and it sounded as if it was going to shake itself apart. Damn. She walked down the stairs, ducking her head at the bottom, and gingerly inspected the boiler. She remembered something about air in pipes, but she hadn't the faintest idea of what to do. She turned the thermostat down, and the rattling grew fainter. Mother would have to figure this one out.

She heard a sudden sharp noise, and looked up. It sounded like a chair scraping back. What room was she under? The dining room? She heard the faint tinkle of swaying ornaments on the Christmas tree, and then a soft, tuneless whistling.

"Mr. Garcia, is that you?" she called up the stairs.

The whistling stopped. There was no sound, no footsteps.

"Hey, answer me! Who's there?"

No one answered. There was only a heavy, waiting silence.

Frightened, Edie backed away from the stairs and tried to remember if there was a phone down here. She looked around quickly and saw nothing. What did she do now? Her heart was hammering when she heard footsteps again, but this time they were more measured. Heavy footsteps. Someone was walking out of the dining room and coming toward the side hall off the basement stairs toward her. She moved backward against the windows. Should she scream for help? Would anyone hear her?

And then another sound. The heavy oak front door was opening; she heard it squeak. And now—oh God, her knees were rubbery—she heard footsteps on the front porch. Whoever it was, was going away! For a long moment, she stood rooted to the spot, listening.

150

The whistling began again, and then quickly faded.

Edie ran upstairs and stumbled on the last step, hitting her head on a hook sticking out of the wall. She kept going, reaching the open door and slamming it shut, throwing the bolt. Stumbling again, she started for the back door, trying to decide whether she should run from the house or lock it up. She peered into the living room and froze.

At first everything looked normal. The Christmas tree, fat and fully decorated, exuded a festive holiday serenity. But a chair stood askew in front of the fireplace, and there they were, on the mantel; just what she had half expected. Another bouquet of flowers. Those same things her mother liked; the purple lilies.

And with another part of her brain, she registered something else: her brooch, the lovely cameo with the sad-faced woman set in gold and ringed in seed pearls, was gone.

"Oh, Grandma," Edie heard herself whisper. Blood was trickling from her temple; her head pounded with pain. "Where are you?"

* * * *

Camilla was relieved when a quick glance at the clock confirmed her shift was almost over. It wasn't just her feet aching, it was her teeth, which seemed a bit silly, but there it was, and it hadn't helped when the store manager had so pointedly asked her this morning how she was doing with the computerized cash register. Someone had complained, obviously. She moved from one foot to another, rubbing each ankle, as she helped two seriously inarticulate teenagers through the laborious process of picking a Christmas tie for their father. One of the girls had three earrings in her right ear and the other sported a skull tattooed on her cheek.

Maybe it was a fake; Camilla couldn't tell. They wanted her to disapprove, so she was bending over backward to be nice. It had been a long, hard day, but she wasn't about to admit it. She wasn't sure what it was, maybe pride, but she wasn't going to give anybody the excuse of making her stamina an issue.

She glanced at the clock again. Five o'clock, on the nose. Camilla pulled out one of the last ties in the last stack and held it up for the girls, concealing her own distaste at its swirling stew of reds and lime green and chartreuse. They loved it. Three minutes more, and she had them rung up and on their way to Gift Wrap. "Merry Christmas!" she caroled as she reached under the counter for her handbag and headed for her locker in the employees' lounge. She would be home by six.

The city glittered as Camilla walked out the door of Field's and down the block to Wabash Avenue. A train roared by above her on the El tracks. She closed her eyes briefly, listening to the sounds of Christmas music and the jingling of the Salvation Army bells; then the roar of another train. I love this city, she told herself. I'm back, that was the thing to keep in steady focus; she was back. She turned north, walking slowly up Wabash, thinking vaguely maybe this evening she would walk a bit to clear her head, then take a taxi home instead of the El. Maybe stroll up North Michigan for a few blocks; see if Billy Goat's was still in business. Peek in at Brentano's. Was there still a Brentano's bookstore? She reached the Wabash Avenue Bridge and started over, gazing up the Chicago River to where its black waters met Lake

152

Michigan. She loved the graceful splendor of the Wrigley Building, glowing with lights, and the *Tribune* Tower beyond. Chicago was a city of visual depth and perspective like none other she had ever seen. Nothing could match this view, nothing in the world. Underneath her, the flowing river shimmered with the reflected lights of the city; everything seemed alive and joyous.

Her eyes misted. She would have to see a doctor soon and let him probe the hateful, rolling, marble-hard lump in her breast. It could mean nothing; it could mean everything. Even now, her fingers moved as if to probe it again and force it not to be. And where was Phillip? Why wasn't he with her? Strange, how the realization of his absence still sneaked up and delivered lightning-fast rabbit punches. She could feel herself immune for days at a time until a single memory burst through—like last night, watching Jim and Rachel dancing around the Christmas tree and remembering when she and Phillip had danced there themselves. She pulled off a glove to wipe her eyes and finally felt the deep piercing cold. She shivered, wishing she had taken Rachel up this morning on the offer of her shearling coat. Working clumsily, she tried to shove her hand back into the glove but her fingers were too numb. She hurried on across the bridge, a bit wobbly on her feet. She had lost sensation in her toes—how ridiculous. Why wasn't she wearing boots? What was she thinking of? Why was she so unprepared? Camilla was getting madder at herself every minute as she inched her way across the bridge.

"Mrs. Duncan?"

She turned, pulling the lapels of her trenchcoat together as tightly as possible, and stared at the man illuminated behind her by the flickering lights of the city that bounced back and forth across the river.

It was Jim Boles. His hands were shoved into the pockets of a heavy overcoat. "Sorry, I didn't mean to startle you," he said quickly. "I didn't think it was you at first, but when I moved up closer to be sure, I just—" He took his hands out of his pockets and waved them helplessly, almost comically. "Anyhow, look, this is as good a time as any to apologize for my behavior last night. I shouldn't have stomped out of there the way I did, spoiling Rachel's evening."

"You didn't have much choice," Camilla said politely, trying to turn her back against the wind. "Topper was pretty upset, we certainly could see that. I'm sure Rachel understands. Did you talk with her today?"

"No, not today." He turned and stared out across the water.

"Well, maybe tomorrow." Her teeth were chattering now, and she wondered how much longer she could bear to stand here. She shivered violently and pressed the tips of her fingers against her face. She could actually feel ice fragments under her skin.

"You're freezing," he said with sudden concern. "I'm really sorry, let's get off this bridge. Can I buy you a cup of coffee or something?"

"Thank you, I'm afraid I have to get home." But he looked so forlorn, Camilla changed her mind. "All right, maybe just a quick cup," she said with a smile.

"Forget the coffee—I'm buying you a drink. We'll go to Lucciano's. Do you know the place?"

"Isn't that the bar where newspaper people hang out? Rachel used to go there."

"We all did," Jim said. "It's kind of a dump now—

154

but it's close, and it's better than freezing."

They hurried past the Sun-Times Building and down the narrow staircase that took them to the lower level and into the dilapidated old restaurant tucked beneath Michigan Avenue.

Camilla pushed herself down into the chipped fake leather of one of the booths and blew on her fingers, hard. She was frightfully cold, frightfully exhausted. She thought at first she would simply catch her breath and have Jim call a cab, but the waiter was looking at her questioningly.

"A vodka tonic," she said after a slight hesitation. All right, one drink. She needed it.

"Nobody drinks Scotch anymore," said Boles as he half-apologetically ordered a Johnnie Walker Black. "But I've always kind of liked it on a cold night. How's your job going?"

"It's hard work being out on the floor again," Camilla admitted. She surveyed the rumpled-looking man sitting across from her, and concluded that she liked the openness of his loose, affable manner. She thought of him dancing with Rachel last night, and wished that he were more Rachel's type. "I like dealing with people, I always have, but it's going to take me a while to get used to the pace, I guess. The truth is, I can't afford to be tired, because they'll chalk it up to my age."

"Rachel says if anyone can do it, you can. She says you're incredibly professional."

Camilla flushed with pleasure. "She said that?"

Jim nodded, but his mind seemed to be on something else. "Look, I meant what I said about apologizing," he blurted. "I went home last night and thought about my own kid's problems, and figured,

155

what the hell was I doing, condemning Edie in front of everybody? Rachel was right, I had no business doing that, and it's been driving me nuts all day. What kind of parent am I, for God's sake? I probably get it right maybe half the time. I don't know what got into me. And when Amos Curley showed up, I blew everything."

Camilla leaned back, surprised at the outburst. "You don't like him, I gather."

"I don't trust him, Mrs. Duncan. He used to have a reputation as one of the best reporters in town, but he would do anything for a story. Rachel probably wouldn't agree with me."

"Well, I'm not sure I trust him, either," she said softly. "Not after the way he treated my daughter four years ago."

His eyes flashed. What did she see in them? Did he know? Yes, she was sure he did. Probably most of the people Rachel worked with in this town knew. Normally that would make Camilla uncomfortable, but not tonight. She felt a fleeting moment of shared intimacy with this awkward, bluff man. He seemed kind.

He glanced past her and uttered a sharp exclamation. Camilla turned and saw a young woman with red hair pulled back into a ponytail sitting behind her on a bar stool, deep in conversation with a wiry little man with unfashionably long sideburns.

"Who's that?" she asked.

"Jeanie Horton from the *Tribune*."

"The one who wrote the story with Amos in the paper today?"

"Yes." Jim was staring at the pair, his eyes thoughtful.

156

"Who's she with?"

"Jerry Tebbins. He has a talk show over at WMAT. Do you know about him?"

Camilla sipped her drink slowly. "No," she said, wondering if she should.

"He's not only Rachel's main competitor, he's a guy who would sell his own mother if it upped his ratings." Jim seemed to be speaking now only to himself. "I'd sure like to know what brings that pair together."

* * * *

Rachel kept her arm tightly around Edie's shoulders as she answered the policeman's questions, not sure who was trembling more, herself or Edie. The intruder had simply walked in through the door the painters had left unlocked, as simple and stupid as that. Except for Edie's cameo, and the appearance of the flowers, nothing was touched or stolen. A skinny young cop with ruddy cheeks was now dusting the wrappings around the flowers and the chair for prints. He was mumbling about the unlocked door. Some people didn't have the sense they were born with, Rachel heard him say.

"Tell me again about the whistling," a second cop sitting in front of them said patiently. His jowls hung loosely over a thick neck and they wobbled when he talked, but his eyes were sympathetic.

"It wasn't any particular tune, it was—kind of daydreaming whistling," Edie said. Her forehead throbbed where the emergency room resident had placed five neatly laced stitches. There was still blood in her hair. "Tuneless, like I said."

"A strong whistle? A soft one?"

"Soft. But he wasn't trying to be quiet."

"If it was a man. Why do you think it was?"

Edie swallowed, trying hard to get rid of the dryness in her mouth. She leaned even closer to her mother, resisting the urge to put her head down on her shoulder. "Because the footsteps were so heavy," she said.

"Young man? Old man?"

"How would I know that? Why are you asking such silly questions?"

He patted her hand in a fatherly way and flipped his notebook closed just as Camilla's key turned in the lock. The door swung open, a burst of cold air preceding her into the room. She started to pull off her coat and paused, staring at Edie's frightened face. "What happened?" she said.

"Someone broke into the house," Rachel said, still trembling. "Edie was alone, trapped in the basement."

"Are you all right?" Camilla was at Edie's side in an instant. She touched the caked blood in her granddaughter's hair, stared at the stitches. "Sweetheart, your head—"

"I hit it when I came up the stairs, but I'm fine," Edie said, burrowing her face into Camilla's coat.

The two cops edged toward the door, and the older one tipped his hat. "We'll be in touch, ma'am, after we talk to your painters," he said. "Lock this door after me, okay?" They turned and left.

Rachel got up and slid home the bolt with more force than necessary. Metal to metal. Now what? A kitchen chair wedged under the doorknob? A loaded rifle in the front closet? In a blinding flash of anger, she saw the future. So this was what coming home was going to mean. Bolted doors and new fears. She whirled on her mother, needing someone to blame.

"You were supposed to be here, you said you would be," she accused. "Why weren't you?"

"Why—" Camilla was momentarily speechless.

"You promised this morning you'd be home and I want to know how you could have promised that and then left Edie alone!" Rachel pointed wildly at the clock on the mantel. "It's almost eight o'clock, Mother. Look at Edie, she's still bleeding. A neighbor had to take her to the hospital. When I walked in that door she wasn't here and there was blood on the floor. Can you imagine how I felt? Where *were* you?"

"It isn't Grandma's fault," Edie protested.

"Calm down, Rachel; I've many times rushed you to the hospital, and I know how you feel." Camilla's voice was filled with distress. "I stopped to have a drink with someone—"

"Who?"

"Mom, drop it, okay?" Edie stood, wavering, holding her hand over the bandage on her forehead, which was already slipping over her left eye.

Rachel couldn't drop it now; it was too late. "I asked you, who?" she demanded of Camilla.

"I'm not hiding anything from you, for heaven's sake. I had a drink with Jim Boles. I ran into him on the bridge after work, and we went over to that old place you used to go to, Lucciano's."

Rachel stared at her, now speechless herself. She turned away in frustration and started upstairs, taking the steps two at a time, vowing that—if Camilla made the mistake of trying to stop her—she would scream out with everything she was now lacing in as tightly as she could.

* * * *

159

Late that night, when Edie and Camilla were in bed, Rachel wandered the house. She checked the boiler; she checked the lights; she scrubbed the counters; she stared at the Christmas tree. And then she went to the window and stared at the darkened houses lining her street. The whole world was asleep. She wandered again, checking the packing boxes that still lined the dining-room wall. She wasn't sure what she was looking for until she found it, and then she wasn't sure exactly what she wanted to do until she did it. The old baseball bat in her hands felt smooth and heavy, nothing like the metal substitutes the kids played with now. It was full size, something she had been proud of when her father bought it for her thirty years ago. She climbed the staircase to the first landing and sat down on the top stair, cradling the bat. Someone had come into this house, her sanctuary, while Edie was trapped downstairs. Why? And why did he neither attack her when he heard her voice nor run away? He had *walked* out, as if he owned the place. That was what was eating at her: the strangely proprietary attitude of the intruder. I did this, she told herself, feeling sick. I left us open for this by playing along with him on the air.

Rachel curled tight against a post and tried to make a small pillow out of the thick collar of her down robe. The alarm system would be installed Monday, the doors and windows were bolted tight, and the police had promised twenty-four-hour surveillance. They were safe. She hugged the baseball bat close. She could not leave the landing.

"Rachel, dear."

She sat straight, muddled and frightened; she must have fallen asleep. "Who—"

"It's me, it's all right." Camilla sat down next to her on the step; the faint scent of vanilla from her skin enveloping them both. Her hair was sectioned neatly and rolled tight onto sausagelike foam curlers, giving her a slightly comic fifties look.

"I'm scared," Rachel whispered. She balled her right hand into a fist and rubbed her eyes. "If anything terrible had happened to Edie—"

"Nothing did."

"It would be my fault."

"You had no way of anticipating a break-in; stop torturing yourself."

"Mother—"

"I remember that bat," Camilla said softly, tapping the wood with a fingernail. "I remember the day your dad gave it to you."

"You probably think I'm crazy sitting here with it."

"No, I don't."

"I got pretty good with this; remember my first home run?" Rachel stroked the bat as lovingly as a new bride stroking her wedding silver.

"Down at the sandlot behind the tennis court, I remember. Your dad was really proud."

Rachel's eyes faded slightly. "Yeah, for a while."

Camilla cupped her hand over Rachel's. "You lost him early."

"I wish he had stuck with the lithium."

Camilla let out a deep sigh. "So you knew."

Rachel waited before replying, and then did so with difficulty. "I think the whole time I was growing up I knew. It was easier to say Daddy was too excited or he was feeling blue than to say he was manic-depressive. He tried to fake getting better, to make it okay for me."

"He loved you very much." Camilla hunched her shoulders together and tucked her feet deeper into her fuzzy mules.

Rachel leaned her head against the post, thinking that the curved wood felt almost as comforting as the solid presence of the bat. She formed the words in her brain: manic-depressive. Never said, never hinted at. Not even on the night when she was seventeen and found her father ranting and raving in the kitchen with a knife in his hand and the ambulance came and her mother told the ambulance crew to leave quietly so the neighbors wouldn't be disturbed; please, don't use a siren. And it all still made her sick and, in a funny way, angry. "That night in the kitchen—remember?" she asked.

"There's no way he wasn't going to end up in the hospital sooner or later. You were off to college after that, and never saw the worst of it."

"I used to hear you yelling at him to take his medicine."

"I didn't yell."

"Saying it loudly, then."

"You thought I was too hard on him."

Rachel's silence went a little too long. "Sometimes," she said finally.

"Hey, I have a pair of moccasins for you to walk in. Size seven, double A." Camilla's voice was gentle. "But you're entitled. After the treatment I gave you about Amos last night? Be my guest."

"I know you think he's bad for me and maybe I'm supposed to think so, too. But he isn't. He made his mistakes and I made mine; at least he doesn't drink anymore. What can I tell you? I'm not going to let him mess me up the way he did before."

"What holds you?"

"Oh, Mother—" Rachel felt her cheeks flush. "Look, he was the first man to make me feel sexy and totally special. Can you understand?"

"Just figure out if that's enough to build on; then you'll know whether you can let him safely back in your life."

Rachel studied her fingers, taking time to pick at a chipped nail. She smiled up at Camilla. "I remember you," she said. "You're the one who used to wear white gloves and prissy little hats with veils—have I got the right generation? So how come you're so up on the jargon? This could be very threatening, Mother. You're not *supposed* to understand."

"Oh, right. I forgot." Camilla hugged her knees, staring down at the delicate spidering of blue veins on her feet and ankles. "What happens to Edie is more important than my war stories or yours," she said softly.

"What do you think of Kurt?"

"A vain, posturing, not completely authentic young man, deeply invested in retaining Edie's adoring infatuation."

"Hey, not bad." Rachel glanced swiftly at her mother, a look of respect. "So should I try to break up the two of them?"

"Don't even think about it. If you do, you'll turn them into Romeo and Juliet."

"The police want to talk to everybody who knows Edie or might have been here," Rachel said slowly. "I gave them his name. I'd feel more comfortable knowing more about him, anyway."

Camilla raised an eyebrow. "Did you tell Edie?"

"Not yet. It's touchy; she knows I actively, totally

163

don't like him. This pseudo-intellectual act he puts on? I think he's trying to put a wedge between me and Edie. Now am I acting like a child, or what? It seems ridiculous to feel this way about some strutting, self-important kid, but there it is."

"Because he's writing pornography?"

"That's part of it."

"Kids do that kind of thing, they test. He wants to be outrageous, it could be his way of looking special in Edie's eyes."

"What if you're wrong?"

"I'm not clairvoyant. I'm trying to give him the benefit of the doubt—for a little while, anyhow."

Rachel rubbed her eyes again, smearing the remainder of the day's mascara down onto her cheeks. "Do you think I'm too protective?"

"Sometimes, a little," Camilla admitted.

"Jim thinks I am," Rachel said. "Maybe I am, but I'm trying."

"I love you, Rachel."

"I love you, too, Mother."

Rachel reached for her mother's hand, and they held each other, wordlessly offering support. "Do you feel uncomfortable being here?" she asked suddenly.

"Dear, will you understand if I answer that in a kind of round-about way?"

"Of course." This was new and awkward, asking each other permission to speak their minds.

Camilla's voice turned gentle. "I don't want to make you feel bad, I just want to be honest. This is your home now, and you've made it a wonderful place, and I love visiting. I wish it were still mine, but it isn't, and from the day I moved out, it never could be again. Mine is gone. I sold it to people who let it go to seed after their marriage fell apart, and you bought it back, but it's not for me. Do you understand?"

"I'm trying."

"You can't cling to what's gone, you've got to move on and not look back. Do I sound like a broken record?" Camilla paused, hands laced together. She turned to her daughter. "Can I ask you something? After Edie goes away to college, you'll be rattling around alone in this place. Is that such a good thing?"

"I don't mind being alone. I've always loved this house; that's why I bought it." It sounded a little incomplete, saying it this way. She wished she could say it better.

"Well, I'm glad to hear that," Camilla said. But a note of doubt was in her voice. "Just don't waste time trying to make it into what it never was, or never can be."

"I want this for Edie."

Camilla pushed her legs out and stretched, gritting her teeth at a sudden, sharp cramp in her leg muscle. "You're not the only mother who feels she let her child down, you know," she said. "Maybe you have less to make up for than you think you do."

The words hung for a while in the still, quiet air.

"Let's go to bed," Camilla suggested, reaching over to kiss her daughter on the cheek.

"I can't, Mother. I know it sounds stupid, but tonight I want to stay right here."

"Okay, then I'll stay with you." Camilla reached in back of her. "I brought a couple of pillows down."

"I'm sorry I blamed you for not being here."

"I wish I had been."

They sat in silence for a few minutes, and then Rachel actually giggled. "Are we a couple of dopes, or

165

what?"

"We're a couple of dopes," Camilla said complacently, curling up on the landing, her head on one of the pillows. "But you get to be the dope with the baseball bat. Good night, dear."

* * * *

Edie found them there on Sunday morning: two crumpled figures caught in the rays of the early morning sun as they huddled together on the top step of the second landing, still asleep.

"Mom?" Edie touched Rachel's shoulder and stared wonderingly at the baseball bat. Then she peered into the face of her grandmother. Asleep, she looked kind of faded, sort of like a houseplant that needs water, "Grandma?" she said urgently. "Grandma, you okay?"

Camilla opened her eyes and stared sleepily at Edie. "Morning," she yawned.

"You guys are freaking strange." Edie was wearing a pair of blue plaid pajamas with long, floppy arms that made her look ten years old. Relieved, she settled down on the top step and stared at her mother and grandmother. "Does this mean I'm supposed to make breakfast?"

Rachel stirred, her back aching. She reached up and grabbed a lock of Edie's hair and tugged playfully. "Pancakes," she whispered. "Make 'em with milk."

* * * *

The pancakes turned out pretty well, they all agreed. The police called and told Rachel the painters had been talking with a neighbor down the block interested in hiring them when the intruder came into the house.

They were in the clear, and they had seen nothing. Edie curled up in the sunroom with the *Tribune* Sunday comics while Rachel and Camilla spent an hour trying to figure out how to hook up the stereo, concluding finally that they were both technological idiots and couldn't do it.

"Of course you are," Edie agreed, hitching up her pajama bottoms and digging her bare toes into the sofa. "You're both too old. I'll get Kurt to do it when I see him tomorrow. Grandma, let's go see your apartment. Okay?"

"It's being painted," Camilla said quickly.

Edie shrugged. "Big deal. We've had painters crawling all over this place, too. Come on, Grandma, you haven't shown us where you're going to *live*. What's it look like?"

"Not too big, two bedrooms. The windows look east and south—" Camilla stopped, a look of consternation on her face.

"What's the floor plan?"

"Oh, I'm no good at describing that kind of thing—"

Rachel heaved herself up from the tangle of wires on the floor and stepped deftly over the scattered papers, not looking directly at Camilla. "A great idea, just what we need—a Sunday outing! Edie, go get your clothes on and I'll stick the dishes in the dishwasher. Is this okay, Mother? We'd love to see it."

Camilla nodded as she slowly began stacking the papers. "I'll call Lindy and tell her we're coming," she said in a flat voice.

Rachel hurried to the kitchen, chattering brightly over her shoulder, knowing she had saved her mother from having to admit something that would have baffled Edie and, in fact, baffled her: Camilla didn't *know* the layout of her new apartment because she hadn't even *seen* it. Nor did she seem to be in any hurry to do so.

* * * *

"What a wonderful idea, all three of you at once, this is great! Wonderful timing, they finished painting your living room yesterday and things are moving along, although the tile man told me he can't come till next Thursday; isn't it always the way? Come in, come in, I'll get the keys." Rachel looked at Lindy filling the doorway of her apartment, huge and vital in a green caftan splattered with red felt roses, and saw immediately that she was almost as nervous as Camilla.

They stepped through the doorway and were greeted by a chorus of song from a cluster of blue-and-white parakeets in a brass cage hanging on a hook near the west windows. The apartment was spacious, but so crammed with furniture it looked like an antique shop. Aging sofas with worn tapestry unholstery and at least five Regency tables glittering with gold trim competed with two huge bombé chests and a ceiling-high ficus tree. It was the home of a widow downsizing her life who couldn't relinquish enough possessions, Rachel thought as she looked around. It gave her a wrench.

"Camilla, here's your key." Camilla was wearing her thin raincoat again, over her daughter's objections. She reached out and awkwardly took the key from Lindy, whose huge eyes were riveted imploringly on her friend. "Now you remember,

Camilla, it's the apartment on the second floor on the left, the door next to the elevator—oh dear, I'll go with you."

The four of them trooped toward the elevator. Edie glanced inquiringly at her mother, and Rachel shook her head as imperceptibly as possible. This was Lindy and Camilla's show and they had to play it out, even though they were both so clearly making it up as they went along.

The key turned in the lock and they stepped inside. Rachel's first emotion was relief: it was a good size with good light exposure. Also, the building actually did seem to be reasonably well constructed. If Camilla had indeed taken this leap sight unseen, she hadn't totally messed up.

Edie walked into the living room and turned around, then gazed at her grandmother with a puzzled look on her face. "It's nice," she said tentatively. "But, Grandma"—she waved her hand at the walls—"what gives? You *hate* this shade of green. You used to call it *vomit* green."

"It can be changed," Lindy said, wringing her hands in obvious distress. "Now that you say it, it is a terrible color, I think they didn't understand that Camilla wanted *mint* green, wasn't that it, Camilla? Or was it maybe *avocado*? I'm terrible with colors, really, and I—"

Camilla raised her hand, stopping the torrent of words. "Stop, Lindy, it's okay. Edie dear, I checked out on this part of the redecorating, if you must know. And actually, I like the color."

But Rachel saw her expression as she turned her head and moved further into the apartment. There was no question about it, Camilla seemed detached as

169

she walked through the place she had moved back from Florida to live in—which she was seeing for the first time. There was an oddly casual sense to it all. But did it matter, as long as her mother trusted Lindy?

"You were talking with your real estate agent in Florida this morning, weren't you, Mother? Any buyer yet?"

"One hot prospect, he tells me." Camilla cast her a reasonably jaunty grin. She wore no lipstick this morning, and there were hollows beneath her eyes from their shared night on the stairs with the baseball bat.

"When is your furniture coming?"

"A lot of it I sold to my neighbors," Camilla said, strolling in the direction of the bathroom with her hands clasped behind her back. "I can't be bothered with all that stuff."

Rachel walked after her, obscurely alarmed. "What do you mean? You have nice things. And what about the paintings, you know, the watercolors you and Dad bought in France? And your collection of old photographs?"

"I've got lots of leftover furniture stored in the basement downstairs that Camilla can use. So *much* stuff was in our house when I sold it, it's up on stilts so it won't get any water damage—the furniture, not the house; not that there's been any flooding, mind you—" Lindy babbled.

"I sold the collection, Rachel," Camilla said calmly. "I had a very nice offer that was hard to turn down."

"Why?" Rachel blurted.

"For heaven's sake, because I *wanted* to, that's why." Camilla turned on her heel and walked out of the apartment. Confused, Edie looked at her mother

170

and hurried after her grandmother.

"Oh dear." Lindy swayed in her green caftan; the red roses seemed to dance on their own.

"Lindy, what's going on?"

"You really should ask your mother—"

"Help me out, please. Is Mother in financial trouble?"

Lindy cleared her throat and put one pale hand up to her breast. "She had some investments go bad. It was my husband's fault, but everything will be fine just as soon as she gets the apartment sold in Florida, so don't you worry, dear; she doesn't want you to worry. She'd be coming in as my partner on this place if it weren't for the sale that just fell through—"

"What sale?"

"Camilla thinks you have enough to worry about and I'm not saying anything more." And Lindy shut her mouth with a heaving sigh. Her bulk seemed to collapse as her lungs deflated. The roses fluttered to rest in the folds of the caftan, like flags when the wind dies down.

"Thank you," Rachel said. She started to follow Camilla and Edie out, but was stopped at the door by Lindy's unexpectedly firm voice rising from the collapsed caftan.

"Your mother has to move on in her own way, same as you," Lindy said. "Don't be hard on her."

Rachel turned and stared into Lindy's unblinking eyes. "What in heaven's name makes you think I will be?"

"Intuition."

Rachel walked out with her head high, trying not to look as upset as she felt.

Camilla held herself stiffly on a chair in Rachel's bedroom, staring out the window. Rachel could see webs of bluish veins cording up on her mother's tightly clasped hands and tried to think of what to say first. Was she invading her privacy? How was she *supposed* to respond to a mother who had not even told her when she had cancer surgery? She yearned suddenly for the easy intimacy of last night's vigil on the stairs, but could think of no way to recapture it.

"So you're renting from Lindy until you can sell the condo and make some money?" she began.

"Yes, that's right. I'll be managing Men's Furnishings by mid-January at the latest. It will all work out fine, you'll see."

"I don't like to think of you having to work—" Rachel's voice caught.

"I've worked much of my life, and I don't feel sorry for myself at all. What would I do with myself, for heaven's sake? I intend to work until the day I die, if I can."

"You are welcome to stay here with me. It's your home, after all. And don't tell me it isn't, because I see the way you look around this place when you think I'm not watching you," Rachel said. All her fantasies about hunkering down and creating some kind of perfect retreat from the world seemed ridiculous and selfish now.

"Thank you, dear, I know you mean it. And I'm touched." Camilla's voice trembled a bit. "But you know, it wouldn't be good for either of us. I'm just as independent as you are, and I'd rather start over on my own. Otherwise, I'll just grow old too fast. Do you understand?"

Rachel nodded slowly. "Just as long as you know I'm here."

Camilla fished in her skirt pocket for a tissue and blew her nose loudly. Her eyes were moist as she stood up and walked over to the wall to flick on the lights. "How about if I cook dinner tonight?" she said.

"That depends. What are you fixing?"

Camilla pursed her lips and frowned. "Spaghetti, maybe. Or hamburgers. Or Chinese take-out."

Rachel smiled and slid off the bed herself, stretching and yawning. "Bet I know which one's on the table when I come down."

* * * *

Jim called just as Rachel was dipping a crisp spring roll into the hot mustard sauce. With the phone in one hand and her plate in the other, she moved to the hall stairs. This was a phone call she should have placed first.

"Before you say anything, I want to apologize for Friday night," she said in a rush of words. "You were right about not encouraging the anonymous caller. Something happened here yesterday—"

"I've heard all about it from Jeanie Horton. And so will the rest of Chicago tomorrow morning."

"She's writing a story about my daughter, about her being trapped in the basement?" Rachel pushed her plate to the other side of the step and tried to keep her voice low. "Who told her?"

Even Jim's normally affable tone was strained. "You might ask your friend Amos Curley. I think the break-in at your house was the green light they wanted. They're launching a series on stalking, and they're leading off with you tomorrow. So obviously

173

they've been very busy the last few days. You aren't surprised, are you?"

Rachel swallowed hard, not sure how to answer. Last night she had called Amos and told him about the break-in, anguishing about her fears, before settling on the stairs with Camilla for the night. He had been worried and concerned, and she had felt again the old gravitational pull that nothing seemed to erase. But now she could only think of all the questions he had asked; gentle, probing questions. She felt a chill. Why would he have allowed Jeanie to write this story without telling her?

"Did Jeanie call you? Is that what happened?"

"She wanted to verify a few things, get a few quotes; string the story out. Seems like a perfectly competent, reasonably nice person over the phone. Except for the fact that she and Amos are hanging you out to dry, that is. I just don't get it, Rachel. I may in your eyes be just a station manager with a sagging waistline, but I'd think you'd know a pair of wolves when you see them. I sure do."

"I understand why you're angry, and I'm telling you, I knew nothing about this. I intend to find out what's going on, so please don't harangue me." She slammed down the phone and immediately redialed. No one was at Amos's apartment. She called the office and he picked up on the first ring.

"Working away on deadline, right? On a story about me, I understand. Amos, what is going on?" She was shaking.

"Have you checked your messages?" he demanded. "If you had, you'd know I've called you three times today." His voice was as upset as hers. "You're talking about Jeanie's story tomorrow, right? Damn, Rachel, I would never hit you with that kind of surprise if I could help it. Don't you know that?"

"I've been gone most of the afternoon," she said. "I couldn't believe—"

"I know what happened. Boles got to you, didn't he?" She heard a rustling as Amos cupped his hand over the receiver and lowered his voice. "Rachel, trust me, I am not the guy who would hurt you. Listen, Jeanie picked up the police report; that's how it happened. She checks with the police every day, and she was onto this before I even knew it."

"Couldn't you have stopped her?"

"How? Why?" He was sounding totally baffled and upset now. "You know how it works; you can't put the genie back in the bottle. She's already written about this, and what happened today is a legitimate follow-up. Hey, you've been here, done this—this is not privileged information."

Rachel gnawed at her knuckles. "Then it won't end here," she said. "He'll call again. You're encouraging him."

"Rachel—can I come over? I will not let you be exposed to any danger, that is not going to happen. I promise you that. This is just a follow-up story, nothing more. May I come, please?"

The urgency in his voice picked her up like an insistent tide, pulling gently. She saw him in her mind's eye, his shaggy hair looking even more peppered with gray under the newsroom tube lights; the taut lines of his face, the lean strength of his hands. She wanted him here, next to her. She wanted to be able to see his eyes, hear him argue face-to-face. But something felt wrong. No matter what he said, he must have been planning to use this story when they

175

talked last night. Why had he asked her all those questions? Don't do this, Amos, she prayed. Don't make me wary of you.

"Correct me if I have this wrong," she said. "Are you and Jeanie putting together a big project on stalkers? With ads, media hype, all the rest?"

"Well, sure," he said immediately. "This is a natural for investigative work and, yeah, we're checking it out. We've talked about this, you and I. You've given the issue dramatic focus. People are ready to pay attention, and you should be proud of that. This will do some good, Rachel, I'm convinced of it. Now, can I come?"

She stared at the rapidly cooling orange chicken and spring rolls on her plate. Funny, how unappetizing Chinese food looked when the fat began to harden and yellow. "No, not now," she said finally. "I've got to figure a few things out."

CHAPTER 7

EDIE ANNOUNCED MONDAY MORNING SHE HAD TO work on a term paper, so Rachel dropped her at the Evanston Public Library before heading into town with Camilla. The engine sputtered slightly as she swung left from the narrow canyon of high rises below Loyola University and onto the Outer Drive. Car trouble? She chewed her lip, worrying. There was no replacing this car or the old clunker in the garage for at least another year.

"Am I overreacting?" she asked.

"It's not too bad," Camilla replied. She smoothed out the front section of the Chicago *Tribune* lying in her lap. "Except maybe for leading with the break-in—"

Rachel tapped nervously with her gloved fingers on the steering wheel. "Amos shouldn't have framed the story around us. I keep feeling something is *wrong*. This is escalating too fast. I don't like being described as the object of a 'mysterious stalker's malice'; isn't that the way Jeanie Horton puts it?"

Camilla stared down at the paper again and sighed. "Yes," she said.

Rachel heard something in the sigh that made her steal a quick glance in Camilla's direction. Her mother's face had a slightly overpowdered look this morning and there was more rouge than usual on her cheeks. She looked weary.

"Don't worry, Mother," she said, trying to smooth out the anxiety in her voice. "This guy will be caught. And you'll sell your condo. We'll have a good Christmas—that is, if either of us gets any time for Christmas shopping. So let's both perk up."

"I've *done* my shopping," Camilla said, managing a smile. "Not that I want to rub it in."

"You've always been superefficient; I don't know how you do it." Unfairly, Rachel flashed to the memory of her mother's sturdy gifts of blouses and slips over the years and how disappointing they always were next to the spectacular gifts of huge pandas and elaborate castles from her father. She switched lanes, hurrying through traffic. "I don't like leaving Edie alone in Evanston today, even if the alarm system is being installed and the police are watching the house. But—"

"She'll be fine, dear. The police seemed very competent and they said not to worry. It's you I'm worrying about—you may actually have to talk to this creature again."

"Well, *this* time, I'll have a few choice things to say." Rachel reached out and turned on the radio, switching until she reached an all-news station. She glanced left at Lake Michigan. The waves were high this morning. Once, years ago, after a sudden storm and plummeting temperatures, they had frozen in place all along the Drive—huge waves stopped in mid-curve. She remembered feeling awed as she drove into town with her dad that day: all that water, full of violent, crashing movement—trapped briefly in space.

"Rachel, listen."

She snapped out of her reverie.

". . . what looks like the beginnings of a talk-show food fight," the announcer said. "Popular talk-show host Jerry Tebbins hinted to listeners this morning that rival host Rachel Snow's calls from the mysterious 'Truthseeker' are nothing more than a blatant attempt to beef ratings for WBBW's struggling *Talk Time*—a charge denied by *Talk Time* producer Berry Brown. But Tebbins—who has a lot at stake if *Talk Time*'s ratings go higher than his—points out that *Tribune* reporter Amos Curley is an old pal of Snow's from their early reporting days in Chicago, and happens to be launching a series on stalking at precisely the same time. We—"

"Tebbins?" Camilla said. "I saw him the other night at Lucciano's. He was with Jeanie Horton."

"Oh?" Rachel said, a little surprised. "I wonder what that was about?" She reached over and turned off the radio. "Tebbins must be worried about us," she said half to herself. She pulled the collar of her coat up tighter around her neck, even though the car heater was on high.

* * * *

"We're cleaning Tebbins's clock, that's what's happening, and he's scared shitless," Berry chortled the instant Rachel walked into the office. She sat on the edge of the desk in one of her baggy sweat suits, her dark brown eyes almost backlit; a classic Berry look. She looked happily primed for a fight.

"If we are, it's got to be on the quality of the show and not on hyping the Truthseeker. That's the only way it'll work. We've got his voice on tape. If he calls today, I want the police alerted and I don't want the call to come through on the air. Will you take care of it?"

"I will." It was a man's voice.

She twisted around and saw Jim standing behind her in the doorway. He gave her a sober nod. His eyes narrowed so much as they traveled to Berry that she almost couldn't see them through the steam rising from his coffee.

Berry was unfazed. "Tebbins is a phony who loves taking cheap shots, but this time he's gone too far. He's given us a great opening to take him on—"

"I'm not getting into an on-air fight with Tebbins. Forget it." Rachel hung her coat, keeping her voice calm. "All that'll do is encourage him to spread stories about me and Amos. I don't want any of it."

"Curley could have stopped that. If the 'Master Investigator' had held off, there wouldn't *be* any mud in which to wallow."

Rachel flushed with annoyance; it was as close as Jim had come to saying that he knew about her affair. If he was jealous, that was his problem. She really

179

couldn't help it if he was fixated on Amos; she had more important things on her mind.

Berry had missed nothing, and now she bounced cheerfully off the desk. "We'd better talk fast about this morning's show. We've got that Skokie housewife with the heart transplant who claims she's picking up the personality traits of the biker who donated the heart."

"How does she know?"

"For one thing, she just bought a Harley-Davidson, and she doesn't even drive." Berry's cheery chortle filled the room.

Hearing this, Jim took the last gulp of his coffee in silence and left without a word. Rachel had a pang as his lumbering form disappeared from the doorway, but there was no time to think about Jim. He would have to go off and sulk on his own.

* * * *

"I know it sounds crazy, but who knows just what the heart controls?" the woman from Skokie said. Her thin elbows, bare and angular, rested on the table. She had lacquered gray hair and eyebrows arched in startling upside-down V's with heavily applied brown pencil. She hardly ever broke eye contact with Rachel. "Look at the personality changes people undergo after bypass surgery. Is what happened to me so bizarre?"

The phone line blinked; a cardiologist was calling from Michael Reese Hospital to scoff at this and to point out that depression was the primary personality change in heart patients. Another doctor, a neurosurgeon resident from Northwestern, was on the line next saying he thought the cardiologist was dead wrong; anyhow, cardiologists were too arrogant.

When the call from the Truthseeker finally came, it actually caught her by surprise.

"So much happens in a few days, doesn't it, Rachel?" his voice suddenly purred in her earphones. "Don't cut me off. You have thousands of listeners waiting for me, and they'll be unhappy if you do. You want to know what makes me tick? I'll tell you."

There was an oddly familiar whistling sound in the background that Rachel couldn't place. "How did you get through? Where are you calling from?" she asked.

"From inside your heart, Rachel," the voice crooned. "I'm sorry you didn't like my flowers; it made me angry, I must tell you."

"Did you break into my house?" she blurted.

"I *live* there, Rachel. I live everywhere. Even at the Hyatt Regency. Are you surprised? Ah, I can tell you are surprised; tell us what you were doing there, Rachel."

She began to tremble. She could not have moved her suddenly useless hand to the control switch to cut him off if her life depended on it.

"No," he droned on, "I won't ask you that. We are all entitled to some privacy, and even Truthseekers have compassion. . . ."

"No self-proclaimed murderer has compassion, so please don't insult us by pretending you do," she broke in. She was repulsed by the rapt, loose-jawed expression on the face of the woman with the arched eyebrows staring at her from across the table. Surely the police were getting a chance to trace the call this time; was that enough reason to keep talking?

"Only for you, Rachel. Yes, I can be cruel—but not to you. Is that so terrible?"

He was seducing her, wheedling her, trying to keep

her responding. "You can't choose selectively to be compassionate; if you think you can, you are simply kidding yourself," she said.

He lashed back with swift ferocity. "Fuck that, Rachel, you're not calling the shots here. Your daughter, for example, the lovely, blossoming Edie. She was in the house when I came inside. I knew that. I sensed her fear as I stood at the top of the basement stairs. But I didn't hurt her, did I? Now that boyfriend of hers, maybe he's—"

Something snapped in Rachel's brain. "That's it, no more free airtime," she said furiously. "I know what you're trying to do. You're a twisted human being trying to become famous through me, but it isn't going to work. You're toast, buddy." Her heart was pounding so hard, she imagined the sound of it was going out over the airwaves. She started to rise from her chair, forgetting her earphones. "I have been afraid of you, but I'm not now. You raise one finger against me or anyone else—" she was half-shouting now. "And the police will crawl all over you." The cord tightened and her earphones tumbled to the floor. She hit the switch hard. "That's it for today, folks," she said in a cracking voice. "The show is over." She looked across the table at her gray-haired guest and managed a slightly addled thank-you. Then she marched out of the studio, slamming the door behind her. She stormed down the hallway and turned a corner, walking straight into the arms of Jim.

"Calm down. It's okay," he said, holding her by both shoulders. "You did that just right." She sensed him trembling, too.

"Your partners will want to fire me, you know they will," she gasped. "I've left three or four minutes of

182

dead airtime—"

"What do you think we've got music for? They'll do no such thing. I'll make sure of that." The calm certitude in his voice almost convinced her, but she still wanted to cry.

"How did he get through?"

"That's what's crazy. We screened every call. I don't know how he got through."

She tried to swallow a lump in her throat. "I must check on Edie right away," she said, suddenly panicky. The caller knew everything. He knew that she and Amos had been in that hotel room together. He knew Edie had been cowering in the basement. That cruel, mocking tone in his voice when he mentioned her— was he going to hurt Edie? Who was he? What was he trying to do?

"Go." He released her—but not before bending forward quickly and unexpectedly kissing her on the cheek.

"Rachel, Amos Curley from the *Tribune* is screaming that he really has to talk to you—" A station intern with wide eyes was rushing toward her.

"Tell him I'll call later," she said as she brushed past the intern and hurried to her office. Edie should be home now, she should be there. Let her be there, please let her answer. She punched in the number with sweaty fingers. The phone rang once, twice, three, four times. The answering machine clicked on, and she was listening to her own voice. She imagined the sound echoing through the empty rooms of her fortress, her refuge, the place that was going to make everything in her life whole again. But not without Edie.

She slammed it down and took a deep, calming

breath. She would call the library.

* * * *

Edie tucked her notes for her term paper into a paper binder and hurried down the library stairs. Kurt was waiting, just as he said he would be. She opened the car door and sat down next to him, slightly breathless. "We've got a whole afternoon to ourselves," she said.

He brushed lank black hair out of his eyes and glanced at her with a cross expression. "It could've been a lot more if you'd skipped the library, but, oh no, Mom wanted you to finish your oh-so-important term paper." He parsed the words out in mincing, mocking fashion as he twisted the key in the ignition and backed away from the curb. "This is what you'll be doing if you live with her, don't you see that?"

"I've got dorm curfews at Langdon, too."

Kurt laughed, a not terribly nice sound. "We've done pretty well getting past *them*. Your mother is a different story. My folks are home this afternoon, which is a downer. But they don't get in my way much."

"We could go to a movie," Edie ventured, feeling her sense of excitement dwindling. If she even tried to tell Kurt about how she'd decided to write about the civil rights movement in the sixties and how the librarian had found some cool stuff, he'd laugh.

"I don't feel like sitting in some dumb theater all afternoon." His voice was totally petulant. Edie slumped down into her seat.

Hardly anyone was out on the road; maybe because of the big storm that was supposed to be coming, but it had been predicted for days and nothing had happened. Edie gazed at the homes along Sheridan

184

Road as they drove, wondering how many of the people who lived there were really happy. Half of them were probably fighting over who got custody of the kids. She thought of talking about it, but a quick glance at Kurt convinced her he was in no mood for talk. She could see the flickering light of the television set through the front window as he pulled into the driveway behind his father's battered old pickup truck.

They walked into the house, and Kurt's father glanced up from the Stratolounger where he sat watching the T.V. "Well, well, look who's here, the pretty little gal from Evanston. Come on in, kid. Ever watch *Hard Copy*? Good show."

She wasn't crazy about Kurt's father. He had the same straight black hair and flat nose that Kurt had, but his voice was too loud, and his fingernails were cracked and stained. He was pretending to be an auto mechanic, Kurt said. It was a good cover for a CIA operative.

She saw his mother through the door leading to the kitchen. Mrs. Kiley was wearing some kind of black Spandex jumpsuit and standing by the sink, smoking a cigarette, staring out the window. She never turned around. Edie was glad her mother never hung around the house wearing Spandex jumpsuits.

Kurt grunted something in his mother's direction and led Edie into his bedroom. He sat down heavily on the bed and leaned back, his head propped on the pillows. He looked totally perfect and sexy, Edie told herself. He rolled onto his side and smiled at her. "How did they ever name you Edith, anyway? That's a seriously uncool name for a very cool woman."

Edie flushed, murmured something about how it was her father's sister's name, and sat down on the

185

bed. She started picking nervously at her fingernails, a habit Kurt hated.

"Will you stop that, please?"

"I can't. I feel uncomfortable being in your bedroom with your parents out there."

"Doesn't bother me, doesn't bother them—so why should it bother you?"

"Well, it just does," she said stubbornly.

"Look, I'm not suggesting you pull your panties off, Edie. You don't feel comfortable in here?" He jabbed a finger toward the living room. "I don't feel comfortable out there."

"Why not?"

"Too many secrets. Come here, okay?" He settled back onto the pillows and beckoned her toward him. Edie lay back on the pillow next to him and tried to relax.

Kurt kissed her, then rolled onto his stomach and pulled up his shirt. "Give me a back rub? Nothing more, I promise."

She moved her hands over the muscles of his back, shivering from the feel of his skin.

He groaned. "A little lower."

She kneaded his waist. "Kurt—"

He suddenly pulled himself up on his knees, unzipped his pants and shoved them down. His buttocks gleamed; hard, lean, young. He never wore briefs, she knew that. "Kiss my ass," he demanded.

Edie froze, then jumped off the bed.

He turned and grabbed her hand. "Edie, Edie, I'm just kidding, come here," he wheedled.

She slapped his hand away, tears in her eyes.

"Look, you're overreacting. I know you don't like my folks on the other side of the wall, but it doesn't matter," he said. "Relax, will you? You're a little young for me, Edie. But I think you've got an understanding of things beyond your years."

"Why does it sound kind of dumb when you say it?" she whispered.

Kurt sat up and started to answer when they heard his father yell from the other room.

"Kurt! Get out here!" The bedroom door suddenly opened and Mr. Kiley was glaring at the two of them, either ignoring or not even noticing his son's nakedness. "We've got police here, so you come out and explain why," he said furiously. He glanced down. "And put your goddamn pants on."

Edie glanced past him into the living room and saw to her shock the two cops who had come to the house Saturday after the break-in. One of them saw her, and deliberately looked away. It was the skinny one with red cheeks. Edie thought for one moment she would just fall through the floor and die.

"Who the hell are *they*?" Kurt said, scrambling up. All Edie could think of as he leaned forward and yanked up his jeans was how much his bare bottom looked like a skinned rabbit's.

* * * *

"Mother, how could you?" Edie was standing in the front hall, a forlorn figure, as Rachel opened the door. Her face was streaked with tears.

Rachel slammed the door behind her and leaned against it, weak with relief. Tearing back up the Outer Drive in mid-afternoon—with her foot rammed on the accelerator—was a new experience. "You don't know how glad I am to see you. I guess I panicked, but there was another call—"

187

"Why did you give away his—his secret? Why did you do it?"

"Do what?" Rachel asked. The heat of the house shimmered almost tangibly in front of her face.

"You sent the police to check out Kurt and his parents, that's what. I know you don't like him, but that was way harsh, and—and I'm freaking, that's what."

Rachel moved slowly into the room. She peeled off her gloves and laid them on top of the banister. "They wanted to talk to everybody you knew here, and so I gave them Kurt's name," she said. "They'll probably talk with Jim and Topper—"

"With Topper?" Edie's eyes were wide.

"I don't know for sure. I only know they were interested in talking to everyone who's been here, in the house."

"But Topper—Mom, she's so mad, she'll really trash Kurt." Edie flailed her arms, looking for a moment the way she had in her plaid pajamas. "He's already in so much trouble with his dad—"

A light was dawning. "You were there today when the police came?" Now the windows seemed to be weaving and bobbing in the heat. The security-system installers must have turned up the furnace—

"Yeah, I was. After I left the library." Edie hung her head, hair tumbling forward.

"Why were you there?"

"We were just—just hanging. His parents were there."

Rachel realized this was supposed to reassure her, but it did not. "So, what happened?" she asked.

"The police asked a lot of questions, and then they asked Mr. Kiley if he was with the CIA and he laughed. He said that was ridiculous," Edie said softly. She squinted her eyes, holding back tears. She saw Kurt again, sitting on the couch, his hair in his eyes. Staring at the cops; then, frightened, at his father. "You told the police what Kurt said, that his father was CIA, and Mr. Kiley said he wasn't. He called his son a—a fool. Mom—I told you that in *confidence*."

Rachel stood very still. She had the feeling that if she could see into her daughter's heart, she would discover how deeply she had humiliated her. More than the kids who jeered when Edie couldn't do a back dive at camp, more than the teacher who claimed Edie had cheated on a test when she had not. And there wasn't really anything she could do about it. She had done what she had to do, and her own daughter was a victim. You try, you try to protect, and they end up vulnerable anyway.

"Come here, baby, I'm sorry," she said.

Edie stepped forward and rested her head on Rachel's shoulder. "It's just so positively horrible and humiliating all the way around," she sobbed. "He just looked so—so much like a *kid*, and it's me who's the fool, because I believed his stories. It's *me*."

Rachel folded her in her arms and let her mourn the loss of the glamorous Kurt Kiley who never was. Then somewhere in the distance, vaguely, they both heard the phone ringing.

* * * *

It had been a busy lunch hour with lots of shoppers pouring into the store, and Camilla's feet were tired. So when a slightly tubby mail clerk from the mezzanine-floor offices handed her a message asking her to come up to see Jerry Swardson, she was relieved. The management gears were *finally* moving. She removed a pen tucked behind her ear and dropped it next to the no-longer-intimidating computer register and bent quickly to check her reflection in one of the glowing brass posts by the elevators. Jerry Swardson had been just a kid working in the shoe department ten years ago and now, here he was, the store's personnel manager. It made her feel old, but at least they were on good terms. What a relief it would be to have enough cash coming in finally so she wouldn't have to worry incessantly about selling the condo. She signaled one of the other clerks to take her place in men's furnishings and stepped lightly in her new black low-heeled pumps onto the elevator. She wondered briefly how much money she should ask for.

The offices upstairs, carpeted and with low ceilings, were much quieter than the busy first floor. No stereophonic Christmas music, no buzz from the crowds pressed up against aisle after aisle of glass cases filled with glittering jewelry and handbags. Camilla pushed open the door with the small, tasteful brass plaque that signaled who choreographed the lives of the people working in the store and smiled to herself. He was still such a kid, even though his fingers were manicured and he wore an expensive suit.

"Hi, Jerry," she said.

"Camilla! "Jerry Swardson swiveled in his chair, facing her with a broad grin. "Hey, what a pleasure to have you back with us! Things are getting pretty wild on the floor, right? Jesus, these last few days—" He threw his young, thick arms into the air in a mock gesture of despair and laughed. "Here's the question

190

we in retail ask every year. Why don't people do their Christmas shopping in August?"

"We wouldn't be ready if they did." He was a nice enough guy, but he *was* corny. "How's the family?"

He rolled his eyes. "Jamie wants a computer for Christmas and Kerry wants a trip to Disneyland. How do you deal with kids these days?"

"Jamie's the three-year-old, right? And he wants a computer?"

He hit his forehead with his palm. "Kids these days—go figure."

She chuckled. It was comfortable, sharing his bafflement with new ways, new technology. "So when does my job open up?" she asked, sinking into one of the leather chairs facing Jerry's impossibly wide desk. She remembered the chairs, but the width of this desk made her feel she was alone at the far end of a tennis court. "I'm in no hurry, you know. It'll just help me plan."

Swardson shifted on his haunches and fiddled with a glass paperweight that held pictures of his very blond wife and two very blond children. "Well, it isn't exactly your job," he said, "although it is certainly one for which you are eminently qualified."

The words came so enthusiastically, it took Camilla a second to absorb them. "Really?" she said, just as enthusiastically. "We've certainly been into serious discussions. Has anything changed?"

"Nothing significant," Swardson said. "We're simply keeping our options open, looking, you know, for the best candidate with the most savvy, the most energy—it's a grim world in retailing now, you know that, Camilla. Remember the good old days?" He sighed, inviting her acquiescence. "Life was a helluva lot more civil and we managed to make a little money in the deal."

"That always helped," she agreed with a bounce in her voice, but the sides of her mouth tightened. Why was she here? What did he want?

"You've got a great résumé," Swardson said warmly. He shuffled through the papers on his desk and pulled one out, waving it in the way a patriot would wave a flag on the Fourth of July. "Jesus, we've been lucky you came back. You've only been on the job for a couple of days, but you've made your mark again in men's furnishings."

"Any input from a customer interested in men's shirts?" she asked dryly.

Swardson looked blandly innocent. "None," he said.

"So why am I here, Jerry? I should get back to the floor pretty quick." Her face relaxed into the most cheerful, disarming smile she could muster at the moment.

Swardson leaned forward over the ridiculously wide desk. "We're wondering if this is indeed the right place for you, Camilla," he said carefully. "The retail scene is pretty cutthroat these days, much more than it used to be."

"I'm quite aware of that."

He shifted uncomfortably. "The job means long hours, day and night."

"I've done that plenty of times."

Now he was tapping a pencil on the desk with a certain irritable rhythm. "It takes incredible stamina for this business now," he said. "It takes young people, younger than you and me. Nobody should be in it who can't deliver one thousand percent."

Camilla surveyed his soft, fleshy body with cool

detachment. "That's certainly true, isn't it? Have you joined a health club, Jerry? If not, I can suggest a great one in Rogers Park. The one I used to go to. Ever lifted weights?"

"No." The coolness now went both ways.

"You should." Camilla felt a certain euphoric recklessness taking over, but it had a sweet taste. "Being fat is a problem these days in business. The way things look, you know."

"We've hired someone else, Camilla."

"I know that, Jerry."

* * * *

Camilla marched off the elevator and back behind the counter in men's furnishings, oblivious to the startled glances of her colleagues. She could hardly see. She pulled open a drawer, trying to remember which one held her purse. She would leave so fast; she would be out of here in ten seconds.

"Can you help me, please?"

She glanced up and saw the glazed expression of a middle-aged woman in a tweed coat with a leather collar. "Sorry, I'm busy," she said. The woman looked away, scanning the aisles for another salesclerk. Customers never looked at her directly. They didn't remember if she was black or white or young or old. She was just the salesclerk with the anonymous face who showed them ten pair of men's pajamas before they settled on a pair they saw at Carson's. Camilla kicked a drawer closed; opened the next one; stared inside. A box of tissues, a tube of hand cream; the pair of Rockports she hadn't yet allowed herself to wear. A spare pair of pantyhose in case she developed a run. A copy of *The New Yorker* to read in the lunchroom.

Her purse. This pathetic little drawer was her office, the only office she was ever going to have at Marshall Field's. The week had been a lark—a chance to catch up with all the oldtimers on the floor and feel part of the mainstream again. And all along she had been fooling herself, letting her vanity obscure the truth— she was just a handy hired hand to Swardson. Just an extra body he could plug in for the Christmas season, and she had fallen for it; fallen for his flattery. Her cheeks burned. How could she tell Rachel? What about Edie?

"Camilla? Are you okay?" The floor manager, a dapper little man whose two sons drove delivery trucks for the store, was standing at the counter. "Look, I know you've been on long shifts this week," he said hurriedly before she could answer. "But can you stay until closing on Christmas Eve? We're going to be awfully short-handed, you know what it's like the day before Christmas. We need you desperately."

"I won't be working, Sam," she said evenly.

He blinked, looking a bit chagrined. "I know it's not much money for someone like you, but you've been a great morale booster the last couple of days. Frankly, I don't know what we'd do without you. These young kids come in to work the holidays and they don't give a damn about the customers. You'd get overtime, of course."

How could she tell him? How could she say, I'm not just a salesclerk and this was tolerable only because I knew it was temporary? Joe Reams was standing over in small leather goods; he caught her eye and waved. How could she do that? Wouldn't she be doing it to people like Joe? They were short-handed and everybody was exhausted. I love this store, she

194

thought suddenly. It's old and maybe the people who run it think I am too, but the truth is, I don't believe it, and I'm not going to act like it's true. She could just say good-bye on Christmas Eve and wish everybody a merry Christmas and go home and be out of here. Plus, plus—Camilla felt her body swaying.

"Sam, I've been fired," she said. "Swardson thinks I'm too old."

Sam's face drained of color. "That fucking shithead," he breathed.

And it was precisely with those words echoing in her head that Camilla felt the world swirling around her, too fast. Her legs grew wobbly, then seemed to turn to water; she slipped to the floor and into oblivion.

* * * *

The nurse's aide taking her blood pressure had blond hair and bored eyes and hardly seemed to hear Camilla's argument. "I'm fine. I'm really fine, I just got a little dizzy and I hit my head on an open drawer, and bringing me here to the hospital was absolutely ridiculous—"

"Mrs. Duncan? Camilla Duncan?"

The white curtain swung back and she found herself staring into the astonished face of a former colleague of Phillip's. "Oh, for heaven's sake," she said, pulling herself to a sitting position on the hospital gurney. She clutched the thin sheet thrown over her and balled it in her fists. What other humiliation was in store for her today?

"Don't get upset," the doctor said with a comfortingly professional smile. "You may not remember me; I'm Quinn Rawlins—"

"Of course I remember you." She had sat at banquet tables with Quinn Rawlins and his wife, probably dozens of times over the years. He was one of the many so-called friends who had faded into the background after Phillip's death.

"I'm told you took a pretty good tumble. How are you feeling?"

"Fine, I'm fine." Her face burned at the memory of the scene she'd created. Poor Sam had grabbed her and yelled for help and somebody had called that ninny Swardson down, and the only good thing about the whole episode was the scared look on *his* face. "I was a little upset, and I got dizzy, that's all. I didn't have to be brought to the hospital." She swung her legs over the side of the hospital bed, anxious to get up and get dressed. "Can I go now, please?"

"Apparently you gave everybody quite a fright. The personnel manager insisted we check you out."

"Yes, I'm sure he did," she muttered. "How come you're here?"

"I came in to work and saw your name on the board. I'm head of the emergency room residency program now. It's a small world, Camilla."

"Is there anything wrong with me?"

"Nothing more than exhaustion, they tell me," he said, scanning a chart clipped on the foot of the bed. "May I ask why you're working as a clerk at Marshall Field's?"

She sat up straight and smoothed her hair into place with her right hand. Her lips felt dry and cracked and she wondered where her purse was; she needed lipstick. "I'm there for the fun of it," she said casually. "You know, something to do before the holidays. It's a chance to catch up with a lot of people I worked with over the years."

He gazed at her keenly. "I see you've had breast surgery. What's it been, about five years?"

"Yes," she said.

"Have you had a checkup lately?"

"No, but I will. Soon."

"Lots of women put it off, you aren't the only one," he said gently. "As long as we're here, why don't I take a look?"

Camilla silently and hopelessly leaned back onto the gurney as Rawlins began a brisk, thorough examination of her right breast. He would find the lump any minute now. His hands would stop and hover, just like last time. Then he would probe more, and she would hear him clear his throat and she would know something was definitely wrong. She closed her eyes, waiting for the fear to close in.

"You know about this lump, don't you?"

"Yes."

"Given your history, I think I'll send you upstairs for a needle biopsy."

Her eyes flew open. "Right now? I don't have time. I really can't do it today."

"You'll feel better if we do it right now, no matter what we find. It's the unknown that's most terrifying, Camilla. We can't control everything, but we can arm ourselves with information."

Camilla's head began to spin at his firm, teacherly tone. "All right," she heard herself say.

Surprisingly, it didn't take long. Rawlins came upstairs afterward and told her she would get the results in a couple of days. He advised her to connect with a new primary physician, the basic kind of advice he shouldn't have had to give to a doctor's wife. But he didn't chide her, nor did he try to dredge up past connections, and for those two things she was grateful. He reclipped her chart, tucked his stethoscope inside the front of his white coat, and turned toward the door, glancing at his watch. "If you're ready, I'll have the nurse tell your daughter you're fine and you're able to leave. Take care, Camilla, and don't work so hard."

"She's here? In the hospital?" But he already had disappeared. Camilla slowly slid off the examining table and shoved her feet into her shoes, noticing a large run in her pantyhose. She wasn't ready to tell Rachel or anybody about losing the job. Not yet; maybe in a few days. That meant a better act than she felt prepared at the moment to carry off, so she'd better get to it. She winced. Even now, her feet hurt.

* * * *

Rachel was pacing in back of a cluster of pale green chairs that were mostly filled with men and women slumped down and staring into space or thumbing through old *Field & Stream* and *Redbook* magazines. She stared at her mother walking briskly toward her. Camilla had a big smile on her face, as if they were meeting for lunch or something. She didn't look sick at all. Rachel's heart stopped skittering and she held on tightly for a second to the back of one of the green chairs.

"I've been very worried, Mother. Are you all right?" she managed.

"Absolutely. This is such a waste of time for us both." Camilla checked her watch with a crisp movement of her arm, clucking irritably. "I was dizzy from not eating lunch and I should have sat down, but

198

instead I slipped and hit my head on a drawer, and had to endure the *embarrassment* of being checked out. This is so ridiculous—"

"The hospital called home and said you had an accident and I thought something terrible had happened." Rachel's head was pounding with one more headache; this one compounded by the fact that she had run from the house leaving Edie sobbing on the steps and almost sideswiped a car on the Outer Drive trying to make it to the hospital. She had made the trip Ziplocked inside a bag of fear—haunted by memories of the night she received the other hospital call, the one from a busy Evanston Hospital resident telling her her father had died under the wheels of the 6:05 Northwestern. And now here was her mother acting as if nothing had happened, nothing at all.

"My goodness, you tore down here all the way from Evanston?" Camilla was acting quite nonchalant, abstractly fluffing her hair with her fingers, then rummaging in her purse for a compact. "I'm so sorry they made such a fuss. It was totally unnecessary. Why were you home early?"

And Rachel told her, biting the words out as tightly as possible as she worked to keep herself calm. She reminded herself that it wasn't Camilla's fault that she had raced here on a heart-stopping trip that truly capped a terrible day. But when she was rewarded with the slow fading of light from her mother's eyes, she took a perverse satisfaction at seeing it go. Until she saw the tears that replaced it.

"This person—whoever he is—is eating at us, Rachel," Camilla said shakily. "We can't let him do that."

Rachel pulled the edges of her coat together and

started buttoning up, her cheeks burning. So Camilla knew she had been taking a certain satisfaction in dumping the bad news of the day onto her as some kind of punishment. What had got into her? "Let's go home," she said softly, taking Camilla's arm. "You're right, we can't let that happen. Let's go home and I'll build a fire."

They made their way down the antiseptic, highly polished tile floor of the hospital corridor, walking side by side in silence. And for the first time, it occurred to Rachel that perhaps whatever was going on was an attempt to sabotage her efforts to pull herself and her family together. Suddenly she longed to be back in that sprawling hulk of old stucco by the lake that defined for her all that was good and bad. She would never admit to anyone that she was thinking this way, but it was the only place where she still had a chance of making time stand still.

"Rachel, wait." Rachel turned to see her mother standing at the door of the hospital gift shop staring at a jumble of nightgowns, books, and cheap toys in the front window. "I don't think I've ever seen such a sloppy display," she murmured, half to herself.

"It isn't very inviting," Rachel agreed.

"Lindy volunteers here, did you know that? No, of course you didn't; she says it's very badly run."

"Come on, Mother, let's go home."

"I could fix that display in a minute," Camilla said as she gave the shop one last glance and followed her daughter down the corridor to the parking garage.

* * * *

Rachel fixed pasta with a can of mushroom soup and even Edie loyally told her it tasted pretty good. The two of them hauled in six loads of logs, piling them in front of the fireplace until they began rolling onto the rug, but with the snow coming, who knew how hard it would be later to hack out logs from the woodpile? They ate in the living room, and Rachel took the phone off the hook. She would listen to her messages later; right now she wanted peace. Edie, whose spirits had somewhat revived at the sight of her grandmother walking through the doorway, had no objections. Rachel talked more about what had happened on the show, and Edie told Camilla haltingly about the police talking to Kurt, omitting the fact that she had been there. Camilla picked at her pasta and asked no embarrassing questions, for which Rachel silently thanked her.

Both Camilla and Edie decided, without apology, to go to bed early. The house was quiet by nine o'clock, and Rachel found herself once again restlessly prowling the rooms. She remembered the phone and put the receiver back on the hook. It rang almost instantly.

"I'm really getting annoyed by the environment you're providing back there, Rachel," said a familiar voice. "I also want to protest your allowing Edie to be so rude Friday night. I'm a parent, and I don't have to stand for that kind of treatment."

"Hi there, Matt," she said warmly. "Nice to hear your pleasant voice. How's Hawaii?"

"Greta got a bad sunburn. I told her to send one of the pool boys for more sunblock, but she was too busy reading some Grisham novel."

He sounded fretful. Echoes of the past resonated in her head. "It's your honeymoon, and she's reading

201

novels? Really, Matt."

"Don't 'really' me. As I recall, on our honeymoon you were reading something by Doris Lessing that wasn't particularly appropriate."

"It probably wasn't," Rachel said softly.

"I can sense you raising an eyebrow. Do you still have that old habit of raising an eyebrow when you disagree with something? I saw you do it with me often enough over the years."

"I say what I mean these days. It saves time."

"I've been worried about Edie. Greta heard something on the radio about you encouraging some guy who was calling your show and pretending to be a stalker. That's damn reckless, Rachel."

"You've got it wrong. You know those garbled news briefs," she said. He would know all about it, sooner or later. She had no energy to tell him tonight. "When are you coming back?"

"We're extending our stay a week, because Greta's losing too much sun time. She has to wear a T-shirt out by the pool for the next couple of days. Why won't you let Edie come here for Christmas?"

"I had nothing to do with it. You might've had better luck convincing her to come if the two of you hadn't broken your promise about having her at your wedding. She bought a new dress for it, you should know. It's blue and very pretty."

There was a short silence. "Couldn't be helped," Matt said slowly. "Put her on, please."

"She's asleep."

"Damn it, Rachel—"

"I'm not kidding, Matt. She really is."

She heard his noisy sigh whistle over the wire. "Okay. Listen, tell her I'm sending her macadamia nuts. She's crazy about macadamia nuts. I'm sending a case of the damn things, chocolate-covered. Do you think she'll like that?"

"I think she'd be pleased."

"Blue, huh?"

"She looked very grown-up in it—but still sweet and dreamy. She's on the cusp of many things, Matt, and sometimes I get scared." Rachel swallowed, wishing for the right bridge of words. "It's all moving very fast."

He sighed again, an even longer, raspier noise than before. "Yeah, I know. She's a good kid. I guess we did something right."

"I guess we did." The silence that followed was almost companionable.

"Did you call the headmaster yet?"

"I haven't got around to it. Things have been kind of busy around here."

The fretful tone was back. "Honestly, Rachel, I wish you'd be a little more responsible in your parenting. That donation *must* be made before the new term begins or it looks *terrible*."

"You're having a lousy time out there under the palm trees, aren't you, Matt?" Rachel said sympathetically.

"That's not your concern."

"Maybe you married the wrong anorexic.

The phone slammed down in her ear. And once again she felt guiltily satisfied, but not quite so much as the last time.

She punched in a number slowly, cradling the receiver in the palm of her hand. She leaned back into the sofa cushions and stared at the embers of the still-glowing fire. Outside, the wind was howling. She could see from where she sat the reassuring red light on the wall by the old oak hatstand, indicating the new security system was fully operative.

"Hello?"

"Hello, Jim, I got your messages. Am I calling too late?"

"Nope, I was hoping we'd talk tonight." His voice was husky, sleep-thickened. Was he lying in bed in his pajamas? Had she awakened him? She had no image of the private Jim Boles, which made his voice disconcertingly intimate. Much more so than today's sudden brush of his lips against her cheek.

"I guess I'm calling to find out the obvious. Do I still have a job?"

"You not only have a job, the owners and everybody else in town who's been calling want to pin a medal on you. Nobody could have faked how you responded today. Not even Tebbins can go on insinuating that this is just a publicity ploy. I don't think you'll have any more trouble from him, and if you do, I'll take care of it."

"Thanks, pal." She closed her eyes and let the tears squeeze past her lashes, one by one.

"Look, it's been a bad time at good old WBBW lately and we both need to relax. Think I could talk you into an early dinner tomorrow night? Somewhere in Evanston, if you want."

She gripped the phone, warmed more by his sleepy, comforting voice even than by the still popping, glowing fire. "I know a great little French place on Green Bay Road," she heard herself saying.

CHAPTER 8

"YOUR FATHER CALLED LAST NIGHT AFTER YOU WERE asleep. I think he's lonely." Rachel slid two Eggo waffles onto Edie's breakfast plate and sat down with her own plate in the chair next to her daughter. The morning papers were still stacked on the dining-room table, but she wasn't ready to face them yet.

Edie stared at the waffles. "I couldn't care less, if you want to know the truth. How come you didn't heat the syrup?"

"If you ate anything, I might. But you don't."

Edie's hands hovered uncertainly. "I'm too fat," she mumbled.

"That isn't true, but I'm not going to argue the point. I'm simply going to ask you to think about where that idea is coming from. Remember what happened to that friend of yours in elementary school, what was her name?"

"I don't remember."

"Her name was Chloë, and you were horrified when she was diagnosed as anorexic."

"I am *not* anorexic."

"Fine. But you do not eat enough, and don't think I'm not aware of it. If this keeps up much longer, I'm taking you in for a checkup." Rachel looked directly at Edie and saw her daughter's eyes widen in surprise. Good, she had her attention. She promised herself she would keep it.

"God, Mother, don't go ballistic over cold syrup!"

That she could ignore. "Now, back to your father. I want you to call him because you should. And if you don't, he'll blow up at me, which I can do without. So don't make this simple request so much work, okay?"

Edie glared. "It sounds more like an order than a request. A ploy you *both* use, by the way."

"Quit raising your eyebrow like that, Edie," Rachel said in an even voice. "He loves you, he worries about you. And I wasn't kidding—I think he's lonely."

"With a new *wife*? Jeez, Mom. Are you saying he's blown it again?" Edie put her fork down, making a face.

"I most certainly am not. Now give him a chance, will you?"

"Well, *this* is new, coming from you." Edie's voice rose with righteous indignation. "You guys weren't the most mature parents in the world, you know. Ever think about *that*?"

Rachel propped her elbows on the table and rested her chin in her hands. The books and the divorce therapists didn't prepare you for the time when your child started hurling truths. Crumble? Apologize? Make up for what you did wrong by looking the other way when they walked off with your best silk blouse or stomped sullenly into the house two hours after curfew? "No, we weren't," she said. "And you know what? It wasn't in the job description, so we're still working on it." She studied her daughter. "You're feeling kind of at loose ends today, aren't you?"

Edie rewarded her with a reluctant nod. Her hair was pulled back this morning with a straggly black velvet ribbon that Rachel recognized as coming from one of her old dolls, one now packed away with the rest of Edie's childhood in a closet on the third floor. Rachel had heard her up there this morning rummaging.

"Did you find what you were looking for upstairs?"

She reached over and straightened the ribbon, smoothing Edie's creamy blond hair.

"Yeah, some old pictures and things. My old doll, the rubber one, remember? The one I dragged around for a hundred years?"

"I remember," Rachel said. "You used to tuck it under the covers at night so I wouldn't see you still sleeping with it. I guess you were, hmmm, how old?" Her tone turned gently teasing.

"Probably like twelve." Edie stared at her plate and a trickle of tears began moving down her cheeks like silver inchworms. "I took it back to bed with me this morning. Go ahead—laugh."

Rachel stood and kissed her daughter carefully on the forehead, trying not to convey all the protective, anguished feelings she had tightly stoppered up. "Do you think he'll call?"

"I don't know. Maybe he'll want to explain."

"You don't owe him anything, honey."

"Why did he have to lie? Why was he trying to impress me?"

"Maybe because he's not nearly as grown-up as he would like you to think he is."

"Mother, he's smart, he knows so much more than I do. He's wise and—"

"Oh, Edie, don't give him an identity you've made up for him. It doesn't work."

"Kurt is different."

Rachel held her tongue with an effort and looked into the face of her daughter, a face devoid of the hollows and lines of long experience. She felt like one of those scientists in mask and gloves working a pair of mechanical arms to repair biological damage on human tissue. This would take great care.

"If he's truly different and special, he'll want to win back your trust. And if he doesn't want that, you'll know something pretty significant about his character," she said.

Edie seemed to droop a little more. "I don't know, I don't think I can handle heavy stuff right now," she said.

"You know, Edie—" Rachel picked up her daughter's nearly untouched plate with the other hand as she searched her parental vocabulary for inspiration. "Being mature isn't in your job description, either. You just keep working on it, which is all anybody can do. Now, if you want me to, I'll stick this in the microwave and zap the syrup."

"Then I'll eat, I promise."

Rachel smiled; the sweetness of life's small victories. "I've got an idea—you want something to do? Why don't you finish your Christmas shopping downtown, and surprise Grandma? Maybe the two of you can go to lunch or something."

Edie brightened slightly. "I guess that's better than poking around in the library all day. I won't tell her I'm coming. I'll make it a surprise."

* * * *

There was a buzz in the air, an atmosphere of expectancy, as Rachel walked through the doorway at WBBW The tiny reception area floor had been scrubbed and polished and the magazines were neatly stacked instead of scattered all over the aging sofas. Somebody had even stuck a red poinsettia plant on the battered pressed-wood coffee table. Rachel cast a questioning glance at Marcie, the receptionist, as she pulled off her cap and stuck her leather gloves in the pocket of her coat.

"What's going on?" she asked.

"*You're* what's going on," Marcie said archly, flattening out her vowels even more than usual. She was wearing shocking pink lipstick this morning with matching nail polish and a huge grin on her face. "Can I get your autograph, Miss Snow? You *really* put us on the map yesterday. The *Trib* is sending a photographer over to take some pictures of this charming little dump, so we *had* to clean up."

A few station employees pouring themselves coffee turned and greeted her gaily, raising Styrofoam cups in elaborate homage as she hurried past them, rolling her eyes.

"Well, morale seems to be up around here. Is the secret walking out and leaving dead air? What a screwy world," she said to Berry as she walked in her office and peeled off her coat. She stopped and looked closer at her friend. Berry's flat moon face looked like pastry dough. She sat in a lump in the chair opposite Rachel's desk, her hands thrust deep into the pockets of a pair of old cotton pants frayed at the ankles. It occurred to Rachel that she hadn't seen Berry wearing a dress or even a decent pair of pants in months. It wasn't something you'd notice when she was tearing around with her usual exuberant energy, but it was all too apparent now.

"What's the matter?" she said.

"Boles is bad-mouthing me to the other owners," Berry said. "He wants to get me fired."

"What? Are you kidding?" Rachel sat down on the edge of the desk and peered worriedly at Berry's face.

"No, do I kid with you about serious stuff? Have I ever?" Her freckles were darkened blotches across her

209

pale cheeks. "I heard about him kissing you in the hallway yesterday. You think that was smart?"

"Hey—" Rachel stiffened in surprise.

"Oh hell, I know it wasn't your fault. You were upset and he dove in like the overweight lout he is. Jesus, why is it men always take advantage of women when they're vulnerable?"

Rachel ignored the rhetoric. "What did he say to you?" she asked.

"It isn't what he *said*. It's his all-around *attitude*."

"Nobody fires you; you and I come as a package," Rachel said, relaxing a little. "Got that? So what's going on? The two of you had another spat?"

"Spat? We don't have spats, we have fights. I'll tell you the real problem. Jim is jealous of anyone who gets between him and you, and he's feeling a little encouraged lately, which is *not*, for God's sake, *your fault*." Berry leaned forward, blinking solemnly, clasping her hands together on the desk. She looked suddenly like the fresh-faced girl with big eyes Rachel remembered so well during those late-night dorm discussions at Vassar about the future of the world and what life was all about. Even then, some people had found her abrasive. And now Jim. He didn't appreciate the fact that her manner was central to her fierce honesty. Rachel knew he was jealous of Amos; but Berry? It was too far-fetched.

"I don't believe that, I really don't," she said. "What if you went a little easier on him? He does own the place, after all."

"Okay. Bow and scrape, or just lick his boots?"

Rachel sighed. "I'll talk to him, okay? I promise. Look, I can't make the two of you best friends, but we've all got to work together."

"I know, I know," Berry grumbled.

"Berry, I can tell you one thing I think is happening." Rachel drew a deep breath. "It struck me yesterday. This Truthseeker character is changing all of us. I'm snapping at people more, you are, Jim is—everything's tense. Well, more tense in some cases. I mean, my mother, Edie—we're all affected. Not that it all connects, I don't mean some kind of conspiracy, but—it's like somebody is watching all of us." She looked at Berry helplessly. "Do I sound paranoid?"

Berry stared at her blankly for a moment. Then she smiled, her round brown eyes beginning to tease. "Well, yeah, a little. Are you saying the Truthseeker is somebody you know? Well, who is it? Amos? Jim? Edie's snotty boyfriend, what's his name—Kurt? Your mother, who didn't exactly make things easy by popping back here right now? Marcie, who is agitating this morning for a raise because she's taking so many calls these days? Hey, how about Matt? He's into destabilizing big time."

"All right, maybe I'm dramatizing a bit—"

"Dearie, that *house* of yours could be the culprit."

They were both giggling now.

"You keep me from getting too melodramatic," Rachel said.

"Well, you keep me from going off the deep end with everybody else," Berry said. There was a sudden, sorrowing glint in her eye. "You stand up for me. Like a real friend."

Rachel started to answer, but the door opened. Marcie stood there looking coy, holding a huge bouquet of roses. "For you," she announced grandly, handing them to Rachel. "Hollywood must be getting interested. Oh, and some cop from Evanston is on line two."

Rachel reached quickly for the phone, barely glancing at the flowers. But Berry with two pale pudgy fingers delicately lifted a small card from a plastic prong sticking out of the middle and peered at it curiously. "Amos is on his knees!" she said triumphantly.

"Berry—"

"Okay, I'll be quiet." Frowning in concentration, Berry started flipping through the next week's schedule of shows.

"We thought you'd want a report on our talk with Kurt Kiley, Mrs. Snow." It was the voice of the older cop who had been at the house after the break-in. "Ah—" He cleared his throat. "He's one mixed-up kid, we can tell you that. Ah—"

"Sergeant, it's okay," she said. "My daughter told me she was there when you visited the house."

"Oh well—hey, what do you do with kids these days? I've got a couple of teenagers myself." His voice was kind.

"Thank you." The pause was awkward. "We're working it all out, I think. Is there anything I should know?"

"We haven't found any connection between him and the break-in. He says he was at the dentist at the time, getting a tooth filled. The dentist's office confirms he had an appointment, but the dentist is out of town—we'll get that nailed pretty quick. But there isn't anything linking him to the anonymous phone calls—they weren't coming from his house anyhow." The cop hesitated. "You may want to know, he's no student. The kid never went to college, he never even graduated from high school. He hangs out up in

Madison around the campus and does odd jobs in their computer lab. He's got a reputation for big-man-on-campus stories with girls he meets around town, which probably doesn't surprise you.

Oh, my poor Edie, Rachel thought. "How old is he?" she managed.

"He probably passed himself off to you as older than he is. He's seventeen, Mrs. Snow. As I said, a screwed-up kid with one helluva nasty father, frankly."

"Thank you, Officer," she said. She said good-bye and hung up, then turned and stared out the window.

"What's up?" Berry asked.

Rachel sighed. "Nothing. Other than the fact that now it's up to me to pull what's left of Kurt Kiley from Edie's dreams and boot him out the door. That's all."

"They're all rats," Berry said softly.

* * * *

The show—with the author of a new report on guns in the nation's schools—was filled with statistics guaranteed to scare parents out of their boots. The board, however, lit up only lazily; a ho-hum performance. Rachel wrapped it by apologizing to her listeners for leaving them so abruptly the day before and then signed off before any more calls could come through. It was a relief to be shaking hands with a guest and still talking about the issue at hand, but she could see fleeting disappointment in Marcie's eyes as she said good-bye to the grateful author and headed back to her office. Amos was standing in front of her door with his long, angular arms folded and a determined glint in his eyes.

213

"Okay, here's my plan," he said rapidly as she came to a dead stop. "I go down on my knees in public—maybe in front of the Picasso? Lots of attention there; great photo ops. I make sure I'm miked, so nobody in Chicago misses a word. I invite every TV and radio station in town. I advertise. Then at high noon, I tell the world that I am an insensitive bastard who deserves to be blown away forever by the woman he loves and wants for not protecting her with every ounce of energy he's got. Then I say I am sorry. I say I am so goddamn sorry, and then I just wait and I hope she tunes in and hears—somewhere, sometime, somehow."

They stared at each other.

"Amos, you don't have to do this," she whispered.

The lines around his mouth remained taut. "Oh yes, I do," he said. "I hope you caught the operative word in all of that."

She reached past him and opened her door, wondering why she was turning that word over and over in her mind and heart as if it were some precious and desired jewel she wasn't absolutely sure about. "Come in," she said quietly.

The door closed behind them and he folded her into his arms with the ease of long familiarity. "I love you, Rachel," he whispered into her neck. She felt the faint scratch of his weathered skin against hers and closed her eyes. "That's what I'm saying, that's what I mean. I'm not dodging this anymore. I was a fool ever to let you go in the first place, and if it'll do any good, I will say that to you every day for the rest of our lives."

"Stop, Amos. Not now—" She put her hand up and curled her fingers across her mouth, feeling the warmth of his skin. Could she trust him? Berry's

214

admonitions echoed in her brain. *He'll do it to you, again. You fool, let him in, and he'll do it to you again.*

He kissed her hand and cupped it in his. "All right. I've declared my intentions. And I will do so again, at the first opportunity—"

"I'm overwhelmed right now." It sounded lame, even to her.

Amos gently led her to her chair and then pulled one up next to her. "I heard you on the air yesterday and I thought I would explode with pride," he said. "I was also scared. You know why? We did help unleash that character on you. And I have a plan to propose." His eye caught the bouquet of roses, and he grinned for the first time, nodding briefly in their direction. "You know that's the first time I ever sent anyone roses?" he said.

"I'm honored." She managed a smile.

"Listen, Rachel." His face turned serious again. "I'm convinced this so-called Truthseeker is someone we can nail. A classic stalker keeps tightening the screws on his victims until he makes a mistake and gets caught. That's what we can get him to do. And if he's the *real* Truthseeker, it's even better, because you'll have brought a murderer to justice. Can you imagine a more satisfying outcome?"

"He knew we were together at the hotel," she managed. "Doesn't that frighten you?"

Amos didn't respond immediately. "Let's say I don't like it," he said finally. "It shows that he's very clever. Sure, it could be someone we know—we can't rule that out. But I doubt it." His right hand moved restlessly to his shirt pocket and stopped.

Rachel remembered the gesture well. "Are you

215

smoking again?" she asked.

He smiled shamefacedly. "You know me too well. Yeah, I've started again; the sign of an addictive personality, I guess. Better than liquor."

"Yes, better than liquor," she agreed.

His mind had gone back to her question. "Just for the sake of argument, let's say someone *is* watching us. It could be some guy who lost his job at the station or a listener who's developed an obsession about you or one of my enemies from the old days. Stalkers come in all shapes and sizes. Remember the chief judge of the New York State Court of Appeals? When his girlfriend dumped him, he went off the deep end and even threatened her daughter. And remember the president of American University? He was stalking some woman with obscene phone calls. And just what exactly *is* stalking?" Amos was clearly warming to the topic. "One guy was finally caught who sent letters for years taunting a woman whose daughter had disappeared, telling her he knew what happened—"

Rachel's face went still. "I don't really need to hear this kind of thing," she said.

"I'm sorry." He took a deep breath. "You know I love my work. Sometimes I get carried away."

"I remember the habit."

"It's more likely to be someone you don't know than someone you do—remember, your voice is familiar to a lot of radio listeners. What you should do is follow up on what we were talking about before. Devote an entire show—maybe two shows—to the crime of stalking. The cops have been cooperating with Jeanie and me on this series, and they think it's worth trying. Bring in authors and counselors and victims—you'd have a huge array of possible guests to

216

choose from. Rerun the tapes of his voice. You'll have everybody in town listening. It'll flush him out—wait and see. He'll be dazzled by his own celebrity. The *Trib* will help with the publicity, that I know we can do—"

"I don't want to, Amos."

His eyes widened slightly. "Are you hearing what I'm saying? Because, if you are—"

"Don't you understand why?"

He let the silence stretch out between them for a long moment. A pulse on the side of his neck was visibly throbbing. "I know you're afraid, I'm just trying to tell you that you—of all victims in this position—have a major opportunity. But it means facing down your fears. You know, fighting back with everything you've got."

"It means exposing Edie to danger. And my mother, too. This isn't just about me, it's about my family. He got dangerously personal yesterday, and I take that very seriously. You've met my daughter—you know how important she is to me. She was very drawn to you Friday night, do you know that? She listened to you. You gave her something to hang on to."

"I did? I'm glad." Amos searched her eyes. "I thought she was a great kid. But this is bigger than—"

"Bigger than one sixteen-year-old girl?"

He started to answer and then stopped when he saw her eyes darkening.

"As far as I'm concerned, there's nothing bigger than one particular sixteen-year-old; if that makes me a coward, too bad," she said coldly. "And if you were—"

"If I were a parent, maybe I'd understand your position. Is that it?" He straightened. She noticed the collar of his blue denim shirt was slightly frayed. She concentrated on that longer than necessary, to give herself more time to reply.

"Maybe you would," she said finally. And saw a shadow move across his eye like a cloud across the sun.

"Oh, Rachel." He sighed heavily and pulled himself up from the chair. "You won't save yourself from anything, you know. He'll keep after you. Calling when you least expect it. I wish I could convince you to fight."

"I did. Yesterday. And I did it by cutting him off." The memory of Jim's praise flashed through her mind.

Amos gazed at her with a troubled look as he prepared to leave. "He'll find another way, probably. His kind usually do. Meanwhile—"

"Meanwhile, you'll do great without me," she said more firmly than she felt. "Your series will be first-rate—why wouldn't it be? You're a first-rate reporter. It'll get you plenty of attention. But I can't cooperate without being personally at risk. Please understand." Oh God, Amos, drop it now, please, she thought. Was she wrong? Was she just inviting more trouble? Was she resisting because he seemed too ready to expose her family for the sake of a good story—without thinking about the safety of her child? She fastened her eyes on the spot where his shirt was frayed, and wondered what it would be like to be the one in the morning who noticed it first and pulled a fresh shirt out of his drawer in that normal, everyday way of people who love each other and take care of each other. What had always tinged this relationship with a taste of sadness? The knowledge that this would not be a natural way for Amos to live.

"Okay, I won't badger you, I promise. You've got to do this your own way. But everything I said about us stays true." He started to lean forward to kiss her forehead, and thought better of it. Maybe she was sitting too stiff and tight and fierce. Instead he smiled and nodded again toward the roses. "Keep 'em watered, will you, Rachel? And think of me?"

She nodded and sat staring at the door after he closed it behind him. Berry would probably spot him going out and tear in any minute with some well-chosen scathing words, but right now she was alone with her thoughts. And one of those thoughts, perverse as it was, came totally unexpectedly. He hadn't asked when he could see her again.

* * * *

Edie walked out of the State Street entrance to Marshall Field's and wrapped her wool scarf tight around her face against the biting wind. Now what should she do? Some fry-brain with a crew cut selling jockey shorts said Camilla wasn't working today, but he didn't seem too sure. Why wasn't she? She'd left the house this morning all brisk and businesslike in her navy suit and she'd never said anything about having other plans. Edie frowned, her forehead puckered in thought. Grandma must've carved out some private time for herself, maybe to go see the apartment or something? But why didn't she say anything? Feeling decidedly unsettled, Edie headed north toward the Chicago River. Maybe she'd pass a cool jewelry store where she could find something Grandma would like for Christmas. The stuff she wore was totally boring, just pearls and one plain gold chain. She waited at the corner for the light and crossed in the midst of a jostling crowd of Christmas shoppers and then trudged on for a couple of blocks, feeling more aggrieved than worried. She passed a familiar-looking coffee shop and glanced idly through the glass door, wondering why she recognized it. It was adorned with one of those stained menus that promised twenty-four-hour-a-day breakfasts. Maybe she should get a cup of coffee and warm up. Suddenly she stopped in her tracks, staring through the slightly fogged plate glass. She hardly noticed the people who bumped into her, who mumbled and dodged and went on their way. She saw Camilla sitting in a booth by one of the windows, drinking a cup of coffee. And she had on her face an expression so distant, Edie almost had not recognized her.

"Grandma?" Edie felt timid as she tapped on the window. Intrusive, almost.

Camilla started, looking confused. Pulled out of reverie. She clung a second more with both hands to her coffee mug as if it were some sort of anchor, and then she smiled and beckoned Edie inside.

"What are you doing here, honey?" she asked as Edie slipped into the narrow booth facing her. "I thought you'd be busy on that term paper—"

"I decided to surprise you," Edie said almost shyly. Grandma looked different somehow. Kind of pinched and small. "I went to the store, but some spacy guy said you weren't working today. Are you feeling okay?"

"Oh, I'm fine. I just needed a break, that's all. Thought I'd do a little shopping on my own, that kind of thing." Camilla's smile was very bright. "Now I'm going to insist on buying you some lunch, because if I know you, all you did was pick at those terrible waffles this morning. Am I right?"

"Okay, I'll have a cheeseburger," Edie said, unwilling to argue. She looked around, taking in the long Formica counter lined with hunched-over regulars munching on bagels with little plastic containers of cream cheese tipped at an angle on their plates. Why did this place look familiar?

"So have you heard from Kurt?" Camilla asked as she peeled the top off a blue packet of Equal and dumped it into her coffee. She did not look directly at Edie.

"Well, no. Not yet. Maybe he won't call."

"Why not?"

"Because he was totally embarrassed when the cops showed up yesterday, that's why."

Camilla sipped carefully from her thick-rimmed mug, watching a slight dribble of coffee work its way down the side. "Were you there when they came?"

Edie glanced at her with a sharp, questioning look. "Mom told you?"

Camilla shook her head firmly from side to side. "No, Edie, your mother said nothing to me. I made my own assumptions from what you said last night."

Edie scrunched into her seat and stared out the window, feigning interest in the flow of people hunched deep into their coats outside. "I don't know why I still like him. He told some stupid stories, but he thinks I'm smart for my age and kind of interesting." Her cheeks turned a dull red.

"All of which you are," Camilla said agreeably. "That doesn't excuse his lying, of course."

The waiter, a harried man with a stained white apron and a pencil behind his ear, suddenly thrust

221

himself into their space with such authority that Edie hastily ordered her cheeseburger, medium rare, and asked for French fries with extra ketchup. As the waiter hurried away, she decided suddenly to confide. "He thinks I'm a prude about sex, which I suppose I am, a little," she ventured. "But sometimes he can be pretty gross."

Camilla frowned and sipped her coffee, saying nothing.

Edie cleared her throat. "Sometimes he can be almost insulting."

"Almost or actually?"

Edie hung her head. "Actually."

Camilla studied her granddaughter for a long moment before answering. "You don't have to put up with insults, Edie," she finally said in a voice so low that it wavered slightly. "If that's what you're talking about. You'll be respected more if you don't give an inch on that."

"It's hard sometimes to know what to do, you know?"

Camilla nodded understandingly, her eyes focusing on a time far away. "It's like trying to figure out what to do when the man you're dancing with lets his hands wander," she said. "A woman can't let down her guard."

Edie was trying to decide whether to smile or nod respectfully, but Camilla gave her no clue, so she decided to play it straight. Even though Grandma's advice was beginning to sound like something from another century, Edie didn't want to hurt her feelings. "Men want sex more than women," she said bravely, affecting a jaunty smile.

Camilla's expression didn't change. "Nonsense,

actually. Don't let him get away with insulting you, or you might make a habit of putting up with it."

Edie greeted with relief the arrival of her cheeseburger. She cut the thick bun, which was oozing with ketchup, in half and buried her teeth in its savory contents. The conversation was making her feel like a real adult. God, talking sex with *Grandma*. "Did any guy ever do anything like that to you?" she asked, her mouth half full.

"Well, of course. Didn't you know? It's a rite of passage." Camilla traced the edge of her coffee mug with a finger and stared into its black, sluggish depths.

"A rite of passage to *what*?"

"To being a grown-up with enough maturity to make intelligent choices."

"Grandma, you aren't really old-fashioned," Edie said with sudden earnestness. "But right now, you sound it, just a little. I mean, I know about sex. And I know the code: you're telling me I should stay a virgin and watch out for guys like Kurt until I'm older and wiser. But I don't see many wise grown-ups. Did you see Mom and Dad fighting in those last couple of years? I'll never think of them as grown-up *again*."

"Oh, stuff it, sweetie, of course you will," Camilla said with great crispness.

Edie choked and then cleared her throat. "I beg your pardon—"

"What I'm saying is, you'll find they knew more than you thought they did at the time."

"Grandma—" Edie felt quite reckless now. "How old were you when you first had sex?"

Camilla sighed. "I used to think your mother would ask me that, but she never quite worked up the nerve." Her eyes crinkled in a smile. "Remember, I told you about the man who gave me that beautiful gold-and-pearl cameo brooch?"

"Aha! I knew there was a story."

"Well, he wanted to have sex before we were married. I was seventeen."

Edie looked disappointed. "Is that all?"

"What do you mean, is that all?" Camilla blinked her eyes with indignation. "That was a *very* big thing, and don't tell me it isn't."

"Well, sex is something totally natural and everybody does it—"

"Oh, it never works out that easily." Camilla leaned back, exasperated.

"Well, what happened? Did he force you, or something?"

"No, I was perfectly happy to go along with it." Camilla found an invisible stain on the Formica tabletop and began vigorously rubbing it with her napkin.

"Are you going to tell me you got pregnant?" Edie leaned forward, fascinated by such a confidence. There were things to learn from grown-ups if she could figure out when it was worthwhile to pay attention.

"No." The years in Camilla's face lifted somehow and she looked suddenly very young. The story she told was simple enough: the man she planned to marry—after getting drunk on a few beers—told another man who happened to be the brother of her best friend that Camilla was "great in bed." The brother spread the news among his friends. And before Camilla knew it, she was the laughingstock of the small neighborhood in New Jersey where she grew up, and that was that. She could do only one thing.

"*Marry* the creep?"

"No," Camilla said quietly. "I broke our engagement. He said he was sorry, but I knew I would never feel the same about him again. You see"— Camilla struggled with a way to say it that would be understandable to Edie—"you see, you lost your reputation and that was all you had. I didn't feel good about myself until I broke up with him, even though it hurt terribly. I knew I'd always be pretending to myself that it hadn't happened, but it had. I'm sure this all sounds terribly antiquated to you, dear."

Edie was mesmerized now. "Do you think you did the right thing?"

Camilla nodded firmly. "But that doesn't mean I ever completely forgot him. Who forgets a first love? I went on from him, but I learned about myself, and the brooch reminded me of that. I feel bad that it's gone."

"Me, too." Edie put the final bite of her cheeseburger in her mouth and chewed thoughtfully. The black ribbon in her hair had loosened again, and hung limply to one side, over her shoulder. The crowded coffee shop was cozy and warm. She was beginning to remember what it was that made it so familiar.

"You know something?" Camilla leaned forward and gently picked up the two ends of the ribbon and retied them in Edie's hair. "You've just eaten an entire cheeseburger, more than I've seen you eat at one time since I came home. Why is that?" She settled back into her seat with an inquiring look.

Edie looked down at her plate. "I've been taking diet pills," she said softly.

"Why? You're thin as a rail."

"Kurt says I'm too fat."

"He's wrong, you know."

225

"Yeah. Well, he's wrong about a lot of things, I guess." She paused. "Grandma, I've slept with him. A couple of times. And I feel funny about it. I didn't even enjoy it all that much. If Mother knew, she'd have a cow, she really would."

"Oh, Edie dear." Camilla reached across the table, shoving the empty plate aside, and took both of Edie's hands in her own. The two of them sat for a long moment—wrapped in silence within the cheery, comforting noise of waiters shouting orders and customers laughing and talking at the other booths.

"Are you disappointed in me?"

"I think you're too young, but I'm not disappointed in you. Don't you see what I've been saying? We all make mistakes. It's what you do afterward that counts."

Edie gently pulled one hand away and wiped at her eyes. "You won't tell Mother?"

"Not if you don't want me to."

Edie stared at the small, steel-straight woman sitting across from her. "I've told you my innermost secret and what I'm afraid of"—she mustered her courage—"now, you tell me. Why aren't you working?"

Camilla paled slightly and sat back in her seat. Her eyes became suspiciously bright. "Well, the fact is, they dumped me," she said softly. "I didn't get the job. I didn't get it because they think I'm too old, and I'm scared about what happens next. That's it, Edie. Now you have my innermost secret." Except one, she told herself. Except one.

"Oh, Grandma." Edie's own eyes filled with tears. "Those jerks. I'm so sorry."

"I don't want your mother to know yet. She has too

much to worry about right now."

Edie nodded her complicity. She tried to think of some comforting words to say, but what this meant for her grandmother was frighteningly beyond her. What could she do? How could she help?

"Why do you keep looking around this place like you recognize it?"

Edie gulped so deep her throat visibly bobbled.

"Come on, honey. Tell me."

"Because I was here with Mother and Grandpa when I was six," she said in a rush. "He bought me a balloon on State Street and when we came in here, the manager said we had to leave the balloon outside because it was bouncing around and hitting people in the face. Grandpa started arguing. Mom told the manager we would take it outside and Grandpa said absolutely not and I was crying and then Grandpa untied it from my wrist and it went up and hit the ceiling fan and exploded." Edie looked up at the ancient, whirring fan above their heads. "Grandpa was furious, he said it was the manager's fault. He yelled and yelled. I think it's the same fan."

"I can see why you would remember that."

"I wish Mom had done more. I wish she hadn't tried to smooth it over and pretend to me later that it hadn't happened."

"Your mother is trying to balance the truth with her memories of her father. Do you know that, Edie?"

"But she pretends, that's what I'm saying." Edie fidgeted with her fork, stabbing at tiny shreds of tomato still on her plate.

"You struggle trying to figure out your father, don't you? Well, you're old enough to face the fact that she does, too."

Edie liked the feeling of being treated as an equal. "Was Grandpa crazy?" she asked hesitantly.

"He was manic-depressive, that's the fact of it. And you know what? I used to pretend it wasn't happening myself. In those last few years, the highs and lows became extreme. Your mother didn't want you to suffer from that." Camilla spoke as if she were reading an old laundry list.

"She should've—"

"She should've *what?*"

Edie took a deep breath. "Known more," she said. "Been smarter. I don't know." She started flipping the metal holders that held the names of Golden Oldies on the dented old miniature jukebox in the middle of the table.

"Edie, I've got an idea," Camilla said, breaking into her thoughts. "Let's forget our troubles and go see a good movie. I'm up for anything, except Bruce Willis and Sylvester Stallone."

Edie blinked. "You didn't like *Die Hard?*"

"Loved it, not in the mood. Or maybe we could go ice-skating at that place on State Street."

"Let's do both," Edie suggested with a lightening heart.

* * * *

The 6:05 train roared by over Rachel's head precisely as she drove under the trestle crossing the intersection of Central Street and Green Bay Road; a wretched coincidence of timing that made her wince and clutch the wheel tighter. Oh God, hold on, she warned herself. She braced against the pain; the flashbacks of her father scrambling to save himself. . . . With one sharp swing, she turned right onto Green Bay. She spied Jim's car parked next to the small French bistro. He was standing next to the car, his square, stocky figure wrapped in a dark wool coat with the collar turned up against the wind, stamping his feet to keep warm. He lifted his eyes, saw her, and grinned. Only after she made a U-turn and parked in back of him did she realize: the pain was not spilling out of its box, not engulfing her totally. She waited for her mind and body to double in agony. It wasn't happening. Astonished, she listened to the fading roar of the train as it moved on to Wilmette, disappearing into the night.

"You seem deep in thought," Jim said in an overly hearty voice as she started to open the door.

Rachel felt a bit giddy. "It's nothing," she said. "I mean, I—"

"I'm afraid we're out of luck on your restaurant." He nodded in the direction of the bistro. "They don't take reservations and the place is crammed with people waiting for tables. We can wait—it'll be at least an hour—"

"Oh, that's too long. I don't want to be gone all evening," Rachel said quickly. Camilla and Edie hadn't seemed to mind at all when she called to say she was going out to dinner, but she still felt a little guilty.

"I've got another idea, if you're interested. How about take-out at my place? There's a great rib joint up at the corner on Central Street. Topper is spending the night with a friend in Winnetka, so we've got the house to ourselves. It's only a few blocks away." Jim shivered; his nose was bright red. His eyes were still startlingly blue, even under the street lights. "With champagne," he added shyly. "Do you like champagne?"

Rachel realized she never had been inside Jim's house, although she had dropped Topper off there after swimming lessons and basketball practice a few times over the years. She glanced at the restaurant and saw through the window how crammed with people it was. Well, why not? And if there was a good reason why not, she didn't have time to figure it out, because right now he was looking mortified and embarrassed, probably at having even *suggested* such an alternative. "Okay," she agreed. "Let's pick up some ribs and I'll follow you over there."

Jim lived on Harrison Street in a small, cream-colored English Tudor with dark brown trim and a sloping, curving roof that looked as if it came straight out of a Disney animation shop. It was a Snow White house, slightly off-kilter and charming. A scrawny hedge separated it from the sidewalk. It sat tucked between two much more serious houses that seemed to suffer its whimsical presence with brooding resignation.

"I hope you like dogs," Jim said hastily as they stepped into the narrowest hallway Rachel had ever seen. One step too many and you'd slam your nose against the far wall. Before she could answer, a blur of gold fur came whipping around the corner and straight at Jim. "Hi, fella," Jim muttered as he bent down to scratch the ears of a great shambling mass of golden retriever. "This is Barbie," he said. "He's an old dog, just like me. Named by Topper when she was three years old—Molly and I didn't have the heart to point out he was a boy, so Barbie he was, and Barbie he remains." Jim smiled somewhat abashedly as he rose, took the bag of ribs from Rachel, and nodded toward a short flight of stairs. "Living room's up there," he said. "I'll go fix this stuff on plates. Mind eating there? The dining room's a bit of a mess."

"No, that's fine," Rachel said automatically. She ascended the stairs and found herself in a surprisingly large, soaring space framed by huge ceiling beams. A balcony looking out toward the fireplace hung in graceful suspension over the room, the kind of balcony where a Juliet might have yearned for Romeo; where a child could stand and spin a dream.

Rachel was totally captivated. It was so unlike the house she would have imagined for Jim, but she knew from Topper that this was where he had lived with his family since Topper was a baby. She gazed around the room, noting the slight shabbiness of the furniture. She studied the bookshelves and saw a somewhat eclectic array: a collection of Auden's poems, a battered high school biology textbook that looked very old, a book on child rearing. Several books on architecture. Was Jim interested in architecture?

"Sorry about the dog hairs, I know they're everywhere," Jim said as he came up the stairs, puffing slightly. She turned and smiled, realizing for the first time how nervous he was. His coat was off, and she could see a button had popped open on his shirt. He was holding aloft a magnum of champagne. "I get one of these every year from my sister out in Des Moines—she apparently thinks I lead a more exciting life than I do," he said with a laugh. "A little sip before the ribs?"

"Sure," she said. It occurred to her that she never had been able to hold the stuff very well, so she'd better take it easy tonight.

"I've wanted this very much," he said simply as he popped the cork and carefully poured the frothy liquid into two wineglasses. "Sorry I don't have the right glasses; I guess you can take the boy out of Iowa but not Iowa out of the boy." He made a quick face. "For Christ's sake, that's an idiotic thing to say. Look, I can hardly believe you're here."

"Was the restaurant really full?" she teased.

"Yes," he said, soberly this time. "But if it hadn't been, I would have lied and said it was."

They talked and drank. Rachel slipped off her shoes and put her feet up on the glass coffee table, feeling increasingly comfortable. Jim loosened his tie; every now and then she saw him surreptitiously picking dog hairs off the sofa. They talked about the anonymous caller—Jim resolutely refused to call him the "Truthseeker"—and they talked about Berry.

"I know she can be brash and abrasive, but she is truly my friend and we work well as a team. I need her, and she needs me," Rachel said earnestly. "I want the two of you to get along better, I really do."

Jim rubbed the back of his neck with one huge hand before answering. "I'm not so sure she operates in your best interest," he said finally. "I'm not saying she doesn't *think* she does, but reality—well, it can be different."

"Will you just try to see her from my perspective?"

He grinned. "Rachel, I'll do anything for you. Even that."

They sipped; they talked some more. After a while, nothing seemed off limits in this quirky living room with its Shakespearean balcony. Rachel told Jim about her father and how much she missed him. She told him about her mother losing her money and she told him about the police report on Kurt. They talked about Topper and Edie and how tough it was to do the

232

right thing for your kids when you couldn't always figure out what the right thing was.

"Why do you think Topper is so young for her age?" Jim asked, bending forward to pour more champagne. "I know she is, and I wonder sometimes if I'm either too protective or too distant—or something."

"Kids develop differently," Rachel replied slowly. "Maybe she's just not ready. You worry about Topper being too young. I worry about Edie trying to grow up too fast."

"I don't think I'm doing a good enough job helping Topper stand up for herself," Jim said. He ran his finger absently around the rim of the glass, watching the bubbles rise. "I thought putting her in Langdon would help. But she still ends up being the class 'dork' or 'nerd,' whichever word is current now."

Rachel flushed at the memory of Edie's scorn for Topper. "I'm sorry for Edie's behavior the other night. And my own. You're right. That kind of behavior should go out with grammar school—"

"That's what I said?" He looked slightly abashed.

"Don't apologize or I'll lose respect," she said with a smile.

"Wish I was always right with my own kid."

"Maybe she needs to be back here with you."

"I've thought of that."

They drank more, forgetting the spareribs. The room began to wash back and forth in a pleasant mélange of color and texture, and Rachel lost track of the time. "When did you leave Iowa?" she asked dreamily.

"After college. My father was a farmer with two thousand acres when I was a kid, but after a couple of

233

bad crops, he had to sell off over half of it. As far as I was concerned, that cut kind of deep into his argument that I should take over. So I headed for New York, which effectively killed his dream of passing the farm on. My sister wasn't interested, either. So he sold it at a loss and sat around with my mother in a Des Moines apartment watching television the rest of his life. It's not that unusual a story." Jim slouched deeper into the sofa, staring into space. "Me, I had this crazy idea of being an architect."

"What was so crazy about it?"

He flashed her a slightly weary smile. "I didn't have the talent. Unlike, I understand, your ex-husband."

"I used to think at Vassar that someday I'd be writing novels in a perfectly decorated, tasteful New York loft with four well-mannered children who adored me and always knew to be quiet when I was working. So what's wrong with dreaming?"

He laughed. "Nothing, of course. I only wish I hadn't hurt my father so bad, that's all. Not that I was ever cut out to be a farmer, which I think he grew to understand before he died."

"So you do the best you can and move on," she said softly.

"I'll drink to that." He raised his glass a bit unsteadily in a toast and Rachel suddenly remembered Amos doing the same thing—always unsteadily. But the memory blurred when Jim stood and moved over to her, cupping her face in his hands. When he kissed her, it seemed the most natural thing in the world. And when he took her by the arm and guided her into his bedroom, she could not for the life of her think of a reason to resist.

He was a tender lover. Gentle. He took his time, his

large clumsy hands suddenly the most sensitive of instruments, searching out and stroking every muscle and nerve in her body. She arched her back and flowed into a hazy realm of pleasure totally disconnected from the frenzied longing of her couplings with Amos. It was whole and complete. And when they were finished, they lay back in the sheets and admitted to each other they were now wildly hungry for those spareribs. Jim gave her a robe and the two of them went down the stairs to the kitchen, stumbling over chairs, giggling as they stoked the ribs with sauce and shoved them in the microwave.

Rachel spied a piece of paper held by a magnet on the refrigerator door. She leaned closer to read the buoyant scrawl, noting a little smiley face sketched across the top. "Add green peppers and plum tomatoes to shopping list," the note read. "I'll make lasagna."

"Did you get the green peppers and plum tomatoes?" she teased. "Topper's promising lasagna."

Jim didn't answer right away. When she turned, he was studiously ladling out ribs and succotash onto their plates. "Molly wrote that," he said. "She put it up the morning of the accident."

"And you haven't taken it down?"

"No. And please don't tell me I should, because it's staying there." He pulled the sash of his robe tighter around his bulky middle and retied it with a ferocious yank. A hank of his dark hair fell forward across his right eyebrow, and he brushed it away.

"I wouldn't dream of it," she said, feeling suddenly almost sober. She wondered if other women had questioned the power of that little scrap of paper in the years since Molly's death.

They took the ribs back upstairs along with a roll of

paper towels. "Let's eat them in bed," Jim suggested suddenly. "I like having you in my bed."

So they propped themselves up on pillows and spread the paper towels around them and proceeded to munch their way through what was as deliciously greasy a meal as Rachel could remember. "You have barbecue sauce on your nose," she said at one point as she licked her fingers, one by one.

"You have a glob of succotash on yours," he said agreeably. They both laughed, and then he told her about Molly. "She was a Lit major working as a proofreader at *The New York Times* when I met her," he said. "I was selling advertising for a radio station on Long Island when I got the offer to come here. We bought this house and conceived Topper the night we moved in. So I put on a new roof and set up a croquet game in the backyard and Topper would toddle around batting balls with us on Sundays—" He had stopped eating now. His smile vanished and his eyes were focused on something far outside this room. "Then that idiot kid hit her. We were happy and the world was opening up, and then it was gone. Totally gone."

"Leaving you and Topper to figure out your lives," Rachel said softly.

He took one sticky hand and pushed his hair back with a sharp, almost dismissive gesture, leaving traces of barbecue sauce on his right temple. "She cried when I took down the croquet set," he said. "But I couldn't keep doing the things we all did together."

Rachel put her arm around his thick shoulders and they sat in silence. The room was redolent now of ribs and sauce. "I stopped going to church," he continued. "It was more than I could do to believe in a God who would take away someone as loving and good as

Molly. Jesus, I've never talked like this." He blew his nose loudly on a scrap of paper towel. "Are you religious, Rachel?"

"I believe in God, but I don't trust any church," she said slowly. "I don't like telling anybody that, because either they think I'm intellectually soft or they think I mean the kind of comfy God who watches everything from some far-off kingdom in the sky. I don't believe God is looking out for me. I think I have to look out for myself, but I see myself as part of something much larger, less personal. And it awes me." She hugged her knees together, not looking at him. The champagne-induced giggliness was fading, replaced by a sense of intimacy that made her shiver with longing for more. "Jim, I—"

The phone rang with the piercing forcefulness of a school bell and they both jumped, upsetting their plates of ribs.

"Damn," Jim said irritably as he grabbed the receiver. "Hello?" He listened and suddenly froze. Then he turned to Rachel with a look in his eyes that made her whole body go weak. "It's your mother," he said, handing her the receiver.

"Rachel, we're fine, all right? I'm sorry to bother you, but I wish you would come home." Camilla was half-whispering, her voice trembling with agitation.

"Oh God, Mother, what's happened? Edie—" Rachel shoved everything aside and leaped from the bed, shivering in her nakedness.

"Edie and I are fine. But that man's called three times now, and he says he'll keep calling until you get home. He's very angry. The police are trying to trace the calls, but he's calling from pay phones or something—"

237

"What do you mean he's angry?" She was pulling on her panties, then trying with clumsy haste to snap her bra. Jim, she saw in a blur, already had his pants on and was groping for his car keys. "How did you know where to reach me?"

Camilla moaned in her agitation. "Honey, he said you were at Jim's. He gave me the number. He was furious. He said if you didn't get out of there"— Camilla pulled in a long, constricted breath—"if you didn't get out of there and come home, something might happen to us."

CHAPTER 9

THE HOUSE BLAZED WITH SO MUCH LIGHT IT LOOKED torched from the inside. Jim and Rachel hurried up the porch stairs, their feet clattering hollowly over the wood planking. Rachel shoved the door open and barely heard it hit the wall. She looked up. Edie and Camilla were sitting close together at the top of the stairs, almost fused in place under the full wattage of the hall chandelier.

"I'm afraid you'll have a huge electric bill this month," Camilla said apologetically. "I absolutely overreacted, I'm sure—" She sat with one hand resting on Edie's shoulder. Rachel caught a flash of wood on the stairs. Her old baseball bat had been tucked under a fold of Camilla's robe and now lay exposed.

"You don't have to be brave, Mother," Rachel said through a blur of relieved tears. "Are you all right?" She mounted the stairs and put her arms around them both, feeling Edie's body flutter at her touch. She

238

tightened her hold.

"We're fine and I'm not scared, I'm just cold," Edie said. There was a resoluteness in her voice that was new. She seemed to be hovering protectively close to Camilla and Rachel wondered fleetingly who had been bolstering whom through their nightmarish evening.

"What's going on—the two of you have a *pact* to be brave? That is not required," she said gently.

"I'm glad you're home," Edie said. She glanced past her mother and spied Jim standing at the foot of the stairs. "Hi, Mr. Boles," she said with a wan smile. "I'm sorry about the other night. I was a shit."

Jim cupped both hands over the heavy oak balustrade and gazed up at her in a matter-of-fact way. "It's okay, nobody's perfect."

"You know, you think about those things on a night like tonight," Edie continued. "Your whole life flashes before your eyes when you've got some lunatic screaming in your ear, sort of."

"Well, we're safe now," Camilla announced as she stood and shook out the folds of her robe. "The police will be outside all night and you're home, Rachel. We're all going to be fine. So now I'm going to go into the kitchen and make some tea." But she moved slowly down the stairs.

"We're both spooked in the kitchen," Edie explained. "We thought he might be watching us through the windows."

"Then we'll all go," Jim said promptly.

"He'll call, Mom, you know that," Edie said, taking her mother's hand and squeezing it as if she were the one in charge of comforting tonight. "He knew you were at Mr. Boles's house and he'll know you're home. He's got some way of spying on us, that's the scariest part."

Camilla quickly brewed a pot of tea. Without talking about it, the four of them took their cups into the back alcove of the living room, away from the windows. My beautiful leaded-glass windows, Rachel thought sadly. Tonight I am afraid of them. Edie and Camilla then told them about a bizarre evening of haranguing calls from a man who seemed increasingly out of control. "The police said to keep him talking, and I tried, but it was awful," Camilla said. "He has this funny, cold voice—"

"He called himself the Truthseeker, I suppose," Rachel asked. When Camilla nodded, she felt the blood begin to pound in her temples.

"He said he knew everything." Camilla lifted her cup to her lips, her elbow braced against the arm of the chair.

"Was there anything he said or did that offered any clues?" Jim asked. There was no awkwardness in his manner. Why Rachel had been at his house seemed of no interest to either Edie nor Camilla at the moment.

"The third time he called, I noticed a funny whistling sound in the background," Camilla said hesitantly. "It was distorted somehow."

"I heard the same thing when he called me on the air last time," Rachel said. She started to say more, but the phone rang, and the words died on her lips.

They all stared at each other. Would the simple ring of a phone ever seen totally innocent again? "He'll want to talk to me," Rachel said finally. The very muscles in her hand seemed to resist as she reached for the phone. "Hello," she said, keeping her gaze fixed on Jim. His blue eyes had darkened to inky black.

"Well, there you are, finally." The familiar voice spat out the words like an uncoiling snake. "What made you think you could go to his house without my knowing? What made you think you could get away with deceiving me, Rachel? Don't you take me seriously yet?"

She felt sweat forming on her forehead. "You threatened to hurt my mother and my daughter, and I find that unforgivable," she said. "Don't get too comfortable, because we'll find you. Soon."

The caller chuckled without mirth. "Now you think you can threaten *me*, but you have no power at all," he said. "Oh, I have many surprises up my sleeve. If you cross me—"

Rachel shut her eyes, straining to hear or sense something that would give her a clue as to who this was. She didn't hear the whistling sound this time. There was nothing. Other than the fact that the voice didn't sound completely—what was it? Completely human. She began to shake uncontrollably and felt Jim's hand close over her own.

"Don't anger him more," he whispered.

"I'm hanging up now," she managed. Again, that terrible dry chuckle. Stopped only by the receiver going back into its cradle. She waited: ten seconds, thirty. The phone rang again. "Hello," she said, nausea sweeping over her.

"It's the police, Mrs. Snow," a voice said. "We've made tapes of all these calls. He's moving fast. We've got the numbers of three street phones he used tonight and we've got detectives questioning people in the area. So far, nobody saw anything unusual." He sighed. "I'm sorry, it happens this way a lot of the time. I doubt if he'll bother you anymore tonight, if

241

that's any consolation. Now that he knows you're home."

"I'm trying to recognize the voice—"

"Don't try too hard, ma'am. He's probably disguised it pretty well."

She said something, she couldn't remember what, then said goodnight and hung up. She looked down and realized dully that Jim was still holding her hand. "It's got to be someone I know," she said. "That's the worst thing of all, but I'm positive this time. And that is—" She stopped; tears began streaming down her cheeks. The remains of the champagne pounded relentlessly at the back of her head.

"That is bloody awful," Camilla said, calmly enough. She stood again, looking oddly regal. "I'll fix us some more tea, and I don't want any of you to come into the kitchen with me. I've got my courage back."

* * * *

Much later, Edie and Camilla said goodnight and retreated to bed. Rachel watched with a tremendous rush of gratitude and thankfulness as they climbed the stairs together. So much so that she knew she wanted Jim to leave now. If she did not take charge of herself and her family tonight, she would feel weakened; she would stay afraid. She would be a victim. He was reluctant to go. He held her close, searching boldly for her mouth with his, and she kissed him back. He pulled away finally, studying her face. "Don't answer the phone anymore tonight, please?"

"I won't," she said.

"Will we still respect each other in the morning?" he asked unexpectedly, smoothing a single finger over her left eyebrow.

Rachel laughed, murmuring something, wanting him now to go quickly. Jim kissed her one more time and left, pulling the door firmly shut behind him. Rachel set the alarm. Then she walked boldly over to the sunroom windows, looking blindly into the blackness outside. If he was out there, she needed to show him she wasn't afraid. Slowly, she ascended the stairs and prepared for bed. Lying once again in the bedroom of her parents, Rachel stared at the ceiling for hours. Around dawn, she dozed to the sound of twittering birds. The alarm went off at seven. She sat up and clutched her head, knowing she would be nursing the hangover of her life today.

* * * *

It did not surprise her that Amos was on the phone the minute she stepped inside the doors of WBBW-FM.

"He said he was staying on the line until you walked in the door, no matter what," Marcie said in an admiring tone. "Now is that man *dedicated*? I'd say so. Rachel, you sure are lucky, he's cute."

"Hello, Amos."

"We got the police report this morning," he said in a low voice.

She closed her eyes. "You want the details?"

His voice was calm, neutral. "I've got them. Jeanie does a good job of dragging what she wants out of the cops."

Then he knew where she had been, Rachel realized with almost surreal certainty. And how did she feel about that? She wasn't sure. She felt she was moving through thick Vaseline; she could feel nothing this morning, not even pain or remorse.

243

"Rachel, I need to see you right away."

"Amos, not now, I just can't."

"I'm not talking about what's happening to us. I think you should come over here to the newsroom because there's something I have to show you on the computer." He sighed heavily, wearily. "I hate to do this, but you need to know. It's about Kurt Kiley—and Edie."

* * * *

Rachel walked into the elevator in the fabulously gothic *Tribune* tower in something of a daze. The elevator sliced upward into the shaft with the same faint swishing noise that Amos used to claim sounded too "corporate" for a newspaper. Amos always had a way of looking at things differently, she told herself. She hadn't been here in several years, not since the time when every minute of every hour of her life revolved around him, and memories pricked like tiny bee stings as she got out on the fourth floor and pushed through the smoked-glass doors leading to the newsroom. The glances they would exchange, saying everything, pretending with their voices to be simply friends and not lovers who wanted nothing more than to fall into bed with each other on every possible occasion. . . .

"Rachel?"

She jumped, jolted from her dazed reverie, and found herself at the National desk rim, staring into the inquiring face of Jeanie Horton. She smelled stale Chinese food.

"I'm sorry if I startled you. Come on, Amos is waiting back in his office. Isn't this place a mess? They're renovating soon." Jeanie's voice was as forcefully energetic as Rachel remembered, making her feel even more drained. She followed her to the back of the newsroom, past rows of the dingy cubicles used by reporters, trying not to make eye contact with anyone. Jeanie's bouncing ponytail of red hair—held today by a bright green ribbon—was like a fiery beacon among the pale hues of the newsroom. Rachel figured if she could focus only on that ponytail, she would find her way.

The ponytail stopped. Rachel was forced to shift focus. She saw Amos standing at the door of a glass-enclosed corner office with windows facing the NBC Building. It was far superior to the cubicle he had inhabited in his last incarnation as a reporter. His gaze caught hers and held, and she drew a quick, surprised breath. The lines around his eyes seemed to have deepened into furrows overnight. He was holding a cigarette and a spiral of smoke rose in a lazy curl above his head.

"Hi," he said with a measured tone to his voice she had never heard before. "I'm sorry to drag you over here for this. I truly am."

"Can I get you a cup of coffee?" Jeanie said, now at her elbow. Her voice was soft and solicitous, and she smelled of some kind of lilac cologne. It smelled like the cologne used by the dental hygienist who cleaned Rachel's teeth.

"No, thank you," Rachel said. She switched her focus from the ponytail to Amos. "What is it you want me to see?"

He hesitated. "This isn't going to be easy." He pulled a chair up for her next to a glowing computer screen; she caught his quick nod to Jeanie, who vanished immediately. The thick, gelatinous depth of

245

the Vaseline in which she continued to swim sluggishly was still protecting her.

Amos pulled up a chair close to hers and she inhaled his presence. He ground out his cigarette with a practiced, twisting motion. "Okay," he said with businesslike precision. "Here we go."

* * * *

Her hands folded in her lap, Rachel watched like a schoolchild sitting in some long-ago study hall. Amos punched a few keys, going quickly onto the Internet and into a website that meant nothing to her. Until she saw Kurt Kiley's name.

"I know he writes pornographic stories," she said.

"Yeah, if that were all," he mumbled. "Look, I don't know how to help you brace for this. Maybe it has nothing to do with your daughter, but you have to be the judge of that." He punched a few more keys as Rachel stared at the screen. She began reading a story under Kurt's name, the white electronic letters dancing off the blue field of the computer screen and into her brain. It took several seconds for them to come together and register.

The story was about a sixteen-year-old girl with long, pale gold hair and small breasts, deflowered by a boyfriend who met her at a posh boarding school named Bangdon in Wisconsin. Her name was Ledie and her parents were divorced. She had a mole on the inside of her left thigh, placed so high that it sometimes chafed from rubbing against her panties. She was tiny with a slightly plump belly and her pubic hair was lush and very blond, and she quickly went from being shy to sexually voracious. She had a habit of routinely twisting her blond hair into a braid with

246

her hands before she sucked the cock of her lover in any number of secret trysts. There was something about making love on an old sofa with a broken spring. She liked to make love on dirty, semen-stained sheets, sucking them afterward. She had a nerdy friend who disapproved of her promiscuity. She was adept at all sorts of positions; details were included, but Rachel could no longer see the screen clearly.

"Enough," she whispered. She covered her face with her hands, wanting instead to cover the screen—to protect Edie somehow, even from Amos's eyes.

"He's apparently done stories on almost every girl he's ever met," Amos said quietly. "Keep in mind that writing porn requires a lurid imagination."

"The physical details—"

"You don't have to tell me."

She became acutely aware of Jeanie hovering at her shoulder with a cup of coffee. "Here, Rachel, you'll need this," Jeanie said, blessedly holding back on the bounce. "We've gotta show you the rest of it."

She wanted to say no, but she couldn't. Amos ran through two more stories, each of them featuring a sixteen-year-old girl named Ledie with pale blond hair and a mole on the inside of her left thigh—the same type of mole Rachel as a young mother knew would always identify a particularly happy, loving infant as her own.

"That's it," she said, raising her hand in front of her like a shield against the sun.

Amos immediately reached forward and clicked off the computer. He turned to her and took both of her hands in his. She couldn't look at him.

"I know this is painful," he said. He cupped her lowered chin in his right hand, forcing her to meet his eyes. "But maybe we've found the Truthseeker.

Maybe the cops are right, and the real one is dead. Stop a moment, Rachel, and think. Is there anything that connects this screwed-up kid with all the calls?"

There had to be, she told herself. Had she missed something? "The first calls to the house came a few days after he brought Edie home. That's all," she said.

"Well, it's a long shot. But keep thinking—maybe you'll remember something." Amos pulled another cigarette out of a package of Camels on his desk and lit it.

"It's a classic way that some stalkers begin," Jeanie said.

She was standing in back of Rachel, by the closed door. Rachel heard her inhale and realized she was smoking, too; between the two of them, smoke was rapidly filling the room. She wondered if she would throw up. "What do we do now? Give this stuff to the police?" she said. "They said he couldn't have been the one who broke into the house because he was getting a tooth filled."

"Maybe." Amos didn't seem too impressed. "Cops don't waste much time on minor burglaries when they think a boyfriend's involved. Nothing was stolen except a piece of Edie's jewelry, right? Do they know she's dating Kurt?"

Rachel nodded and looked away. "She was at his house when they showed up to question him."

"Okay."

He tapped an ash into the saucer that served as his ashtray and had the decency to ask nothing more, for which Rachel was grateful. She was still trying to absorb the brutalizing of her daughter's image on that harsh blue screen; struggling to understand how any normal, sane kid who held hands with her daughter and ate dinner at her house could possibly write such disgusting trash. Was some of it true? Was any of it part of a private life Edie had that she knew nothing about? Were her schoolmates reading this and laughing at Edie's expense? Was—

"I can see what you're doing, but it isn't productive," Amos said gently, breaking into her fevered thoughts. "Remember, these are stories. Edie is a decent kid who is going to do fine. Keep your focus on Kurt right now. We'll give the cops these printouts, but they don't connect him to the phone calls or the break-in. *If* he's the one, we need to do something to flush him into the open."

"Invite him to star on my show, right?" She hardly recognized the sound of her own voice.

"I know, I know. You don't like the idea," he said almost impatiently. "But if the police can't find this guy, working together we have a chance to do it for them. Who else might he be stalking? What other damage should he be free to cause? Maybe it won't work, but you won't know unless you try."

"What if it puts Edie in danger?"

"Rachel, excuse me for butting in, but—I think I'd do it because I have a child," Jeanie said quietly.

Rachel turned in her chair and studied Jeanie Horton's solemn face. She wasn't as young as she had looked originally. Under the neon lights, Rachel saw fine lines sprayed out across her skin like delicate cobwebs, and suddenly the ponytail didn't look quite as effortless as it had before. "Why?" she challenged.

"Because I'd be mad enough to make whoever wrote this kind of stuff eat shit."

"Well, I am," Rachel said.

* * * *

249

By the time she got back to the station, Rachel was fueled with fury. She had made up her mind. She would talk to Berry. They would put together a show that would blast the Truthseeker out into the open. The police weren't getting anywhere. She had to do it; Amos and Jeanie knew how to fight back, and so did she. Hadn't she been a journalist long enough to know that she had the power to make things happen? Back in her days as a reporter, she'd been able to get slum landlords to turn on the heat in the projects just by threatening to write about tenants shivering and kids crying in the cold. She had to fight back. Rachel slammed the door behind her and marched, unseeing, past a startled Marcie.

"Jim's looking for you," she managed.

He was in the control room and waved at her as she walked past. She didn't stop until she reached her office door.

"Hey, you look like a lady with a purpose," Jim said, coming up behind her. "What's—"

"Jim, I'm doing that show. I'm doing *six* shows if I have to. I'm going to force this asshole to overplay his hand and—"

"Whoa," he said, searching her eyes. "What's up?"

It was harder to tell him than she had imagined it would be. It was harder to *think* about what she had seen on Amos's screen than she had imagined it would be. But she told him, watching his face turn pale.

"So the kid is a cyberspace nut," he said slowly. "Porn wasn't enough."

"What do you mean?"

"There's a kind of freedom somebody like Kurt gets on the net. Nothing's tangible or written down. They feel freed of the rules, of moral limits. He probably doesn't see it as much different from thinking to himself. It's happening, Rachel."

"Why do you sound so resigned? Somebody who would do this to Edie could easily be making those phone calls. It's the same thing."

"Don't be too sure." Jim's brow furrowed as he glanced quickly around the hallway. She could see tiny half-moons of sweat on his shirt as he pushed open the door and guided her firmly inside.

She shook his hand off her arm, irritated at his attempt to soothe. "Can you stop and think of how you would feel if you had been reading that stuff and it was about Topper?" she said.

"Of course, I can. You think I don't have some idea of how terrible this is for you? But a troubled kid getting off on his own imagination isn't the same as a stalker threatening your safety." He looked at her almost helplessly. "Just don't mix the two things up too fast, that's all I'm saying."

She lifted her chin, thrusting it forward like a weapon. "You don't think he's the Truthseeker."

"I wish you wouldn't grant him the title he wants. That's Berry's doing."

"I'll call him what I want to call him."

Jim hesitated. "I think the guy we're looking for is sicker and craftier. And I still don't think you should mess with him. Do that show and you risk goading him."

"I'm sorry, but I don't buy that anymore. Maybe it isn't Kurt, but I'm going to do the show regardless. I've been too cautious for years and it's cost me a lot, personally and professionally. If I listen to you, I hide under the covers and stay there and let this stuff keep happening. To me, to Edie—"

"This is not a litmus test for courage."

"Oh yes it is."

They glared at each other.

"I can stop you, you know," he said quietly.

"Right, you own the place. Remember the Unabomber, Jim? Would you have argued against printing his Manifesto? If you had, he'd still be out there making bombs and killing people. I'm sorry, I think this *does* require courage."

She had him; she could see she did. The door opened behind them and Berry's shapeless form filled the doorway. Rachel saw her staring at them with frank fascination.

"Thought I heard a little discreet yelling in here. This doesn't look like the best time for an interruption, but you've got five minutes till showtime, Rachel. Women's History Week, a no-brainer," Berry said. Her gaze traveled from Jim to Rachel and back to Jim again, but for once she didn't demand to know everything that was going on.

"I'll be right there," Rachel said. She swept her hair back from her forehead, feeling sick. But she wasn't floating in Vaseline anymore. "We're doing the stalking show," she said to Berry, holding Jim's eyes with her own. "As soon as possible. Shrinks, victims, cops, ex-cons—whatever. I want it all. Will you get on it soonest?"

"You bet," Berry murmured. She cast a triumphant glance in Jim's direction, but he had already turned on his heel and brushed past her as he left the room.

* * * *

The afternoon was waning fast. Rachel sat in her car watching the needle on the gas gauge nudging "empty" and decided she'd better turn off the engine, which meant waiting with no heat. She shivered as she flicked off the ignition and sat back in her seat, wishing she had remembered her heavy mittens. She gazed at the tired-looking Cape Cod across the street. It was a sad little suburban house, the kind that looked as if it had been unloved from the day it was built. There were bright yellow curtains in the living room window but one of them, missing a hook, sagged in the middle.

She took off her leather gloves and blew hard on her hands, then tucked them up under her armpits. She could already see her breath in the air inside the car. Both Amos and Jim would agree on one thing— she was crazy to have charged up here to Wilmette; crazy to be sitting outside Kurt's house, waiting for him to come home. The minute the idea occurred to her during her show, she had felt better. If Kurt was not the Truthseeker, she would find out. But she would have the satisfaction of letting him know face to face that writing those stories about Edie was cruel and destructive trickery and he wasn't getting away with it.

She looked at her watch. What if his parents came home first? Did she confront them or wait for their son?

At that moment she saw his car rounding the corner and watched as he pulled into the driveway. He got out of the car and walked into the house without glancing in her direction.

Rachel hesitated. Then she slipped out of her car, locked it, and crossed the street. The doorbell screeched out one graceless, warning note, putting her teeth on edge.

Kurt opened the door almost immediately. "Well, well, this is a surprise," he said in his best sardonic manner. His upper lip curled in a smile. "Come in, Mrs. Snow."

"This isn't exactly a social call, Kurt."

He grinned. "Oh, I knew that as soon as I saw you sitting in your car across the street. I just wondered if you were planning a stakeout or a confrontation. Now I know."

She walked in the door and looked around, curious. "Where are your parents?"

"Probably off on some secret CIA business."

"Your father isn't in the CIA."

"So Edie gave you a report on the police visit, right? Was that your doing, Mrs. Snow?"

"Yes, it was."

"Want a cup of coffee?"

"No, I want to talk to you."

"About what?"

"About your stories. The ones I've been reading on the Internet." She reached into her purse, pulled out the copies Amos had given her, and tried to keep her voice steady. "These are about my daughter, aren't they?"

He gazed at her solemnly and scratched his head without answering at first. Then he turned and headed for the kitchen. "Take a seat," he said. "*You* may not want any coffee, but I do."

Rachel sat down on the sofa and stared around the room, recognizing the layout from one of Kurt's stories. She pushed down on the sofa cushion, testing for the broken spring. Yes, there it was. She glanced over her left shoulder and saw an open door leading into a bedroom; yes, she knew what was in there, too.

Her nails scratched deep into the sofa.

He came back in with a cup of something sludgy and black and put it on the coffee table before sitting in the chair opposite her. He crossed one leg over the other, a patch of tanned, hairy skin showing between his jeans and sneakers. "So lay it on me," he said.

She tossed the sheaf of papers onto the coffee table. "You've abused her and you've abused me."

"I make up my stories."

"Don't make me laugh too hard."

He shrugged. "What do any of us work with, if it isn't fragments of real life? That's what writers *do*, you know."

"No, Kurt, you've got it wrong." Her voice shook with something more than anger. "Real writers aren't clumsy and crude. They don't have stunted imaginations. They take those fragments and try to transcend reality and pull truth from the imagination. You, I suspect, don't even know what I'm talking about. You sucked my daughter in by convincing her you were some special, gifted genius, and she was enthralled. You set out to ruin with your feeble efforts the reputation of a young girl barely sixteen who trusted you."

He thrust his hands into his jeans and shot her a scornfully defensive look through eyes hooded with heavy, black lashes. "Hold on, Mrs. Snow. You don't have to like me, and you don't have to like what I write. But I've got the First Amendment on my side."

"That's not the issue. Your stories about Edie are acts of violence."

"Edie's no little kid, and I wasn't trying to ruin her. This is about *sex*, that's all. But then, parents are usually the last to know, I guess." He said it with a

255

labored meaningfulness that disgusted her.

"You think I'm here to find out if you had sex with my daughter? How naive of you, Kurt. I'm here because you are a liar and a phony. You've never been officially enrolled at the university in Madison. You hang out around Langdon, pretending you're a real college student, but you aren't; you are just one more high school dropout without a clue."

He winced. "Stop, please."

She stopped. For a few seconds, the room was totally silent. She could hear the drip-drip of a leaky faucet from the kitchen; from somewhere outside, a dog barked.

"It's not what you think. It's different. You want the truth? Okay, you won't believe this, but I'll tell you anyway." He brushed his hair back with sudden alacrity and looked at her, eyes wide. "My dad fingered a Mafia head. You know what that means? It means that when I was twelve the government put him in the federal witness protection program. A little training and, presto! He was an auto mechanic. My whole life is phony. You know what that feels like? Nothing's real, everything's made up. My name is made up. I can't even tell you my real name, it could hurt my father." His eyes were glistening with excitement as he waited for her reaction.

"Kurt, have you ever thought of doing something real—like going back to school and graduating?"

He stared at her. His eyes darted around the room, then fastened again on her. "How can I do that?" he asked. "Then everybody would know. We may be disappearing again."

"Kurt, you're a liar. Do you really expect me to believe you?"

"I'm a liar because I have to be," he said earnestly, speaking more rapidly now. "You know the truth now and you could wreck us. God, I just couldn't stand hearing those things you were saying; I shouldn't have told you—"

"Sorry. Nice try." She said it flatly, but she held her breath.

"You don't buy it?"

"No."

"You're making a terrible mistake. I'm putting my life and the lives of my parents in your hands."

"I'm waiting for you to get desperate enough to tell me the truth."

"That *is* the truth."

"No, it's not."

The silence that followed dragged on for a long moment. Then he shrugged. "Well, give me credit for trying."

A shiver went through her body. "Have you ever seen a psychiatrist, Kurt?"

"I just like making up stories, Mrs. Snow," he said. "You see, out there in cyberspace, I mean something. I'm important, people read what I write. I had a teacher in high school who said I could be a writer if I got through school, but I didn't have to. I can make *myself* famous, I—"

"Are you the Truthseeker?"

"You mean the guy making those phone calls to your show?"

"And my home."

"No, thanks, that's trouble. I don't break laws."

She walked slowly to the window, staring out at the pinched, frozen terrain, and then turned to face him. He didn't frighten her; he was pathetic.

257

"Maybe you're lying again," she asked in a steady voice. "If you are, you'll be arrested and go to prison."

"Me?" He looked up with surprise, and she feared with a sinking heart that it was genuine. "No," he said. "I keep telling you, don't you see? I tell stories. I *create*. I don't threaten."

"Your stories threaten my daughter."

He looked honestly puzzled. "But why? I can think what I want to think, can't I?"

Rachel remembered Jim's description of the mentality that saw cyberspace as simply an extension of private fantasy and suppressed a shudder. "It's kind of ironic, isn't it?" she said finally. "Here you are, a smart young man wasting all you have for the thrill of faking your way through life. And now you say you want to tell the truth. What if I don't believe you? What if the police don't believe you?"

The sides of his mouth were twitching nervously, no longer pulled up in a smile. "When I was twelve years old, I was given a new identity," he said slowly. "I couldn't play soccer anymore, I had to play softball. My name was changed to Kurt Kiley and I had to learn to answer to that. We had a made-up family, and I had to memorize lots of details about them. I came home from school one day and my mother told me I was never going back. I couldn't say good-bye to anybody, because we had to drop out of sight fast. We moved in the middle of the night, and we kept moving every year."

"You just admitted that story is a lie."

"So I'm trying it again," he said blandly.

"What's the matter with you?" she said, troubled.

For just a second, she saw his eyes flicker away; saw uncertainty. "Nothing being born into a different family wouldn't have helped."

"How do you support yourself? Do you work?"

"Odd jobs in Madison and Milwaukee. When I'm out of cash, I come back here." Then, inexplicably, he put his head in his hands.

"How do you get access to the Internet?"

"Through a guy at the university computer lab who lets me log in on his account." He lifted his head and nodded toward the door leading to his bedroom. "Got my computer here hooked up to the net a few days ago. I've got a real identity on the net, you know? It feels good. People are talking about my stories all over the Web."

"Kurt, I'll have to talk to your parents."

"They don't care, Mrs. Snow. Does that mean anything to you? They don't care. They'll care enough to give me hell, but that's just a lot of shouting and hitting. Ask the police. They know what my folks are like."

"I'm sorry, if that's true."

The shadows were lengthening. She wasn't sure what more she could do here; her anger was solidifying into something hard and unmovable, drained of fire. Kurt needed help, but she couldn't give it. Was he the Truthseeker? She felt in her gut that he wasn't, and the disappointment left a sour taste in her mouth.

Rachel slung her bag over her shoulder, picked up the pile of papers from the coffee table, and turned to go. Kurt shoved his hands into the pockets of his jeans and walked with her to the front door, looking right now exactly the age he really was. How had this stringy-looking kid in black jeans ever managed to intimidate her?

259

She opened the door, bracing against the biting cold. Snowflakes were starting to fall and were already leaving a thin pasty cover over the dead grass and bushes.

"Have you told Edie yet?"

She stopped. "No, but I will tonight."

"She'll go ballistic."

"Of course she will. She'll see you as a total user. Not smart, not exciting, not sexy. just a first-class jerk with no moral sense at all."

He kicked at a strip of peeling paint on the door. "Yeah, well. I made up most of the stuff about her, you know. She didn't do those things."

Rachel refused to give an inch. "I almost hate to tell you this," she said as she stepped outside. "But the pity of it is, you aren't even a good pornographer." She glanced back and got her reward. He looked as if someone had just hit him in the face.

* * * *

Rachel had to stop for gas, so she was later getting home than she expected. It was really snowing now. She turned on the wipers, watching the rhythmic sweep of the blades collect the tiny flakes and deposit them as slush in the lower corners of the windshield. She swung around the last curve of Sheridan Road that took her back into Evanston, wishing she could just keep driving, dreamlike, letting the snow cover everything. Letting it smooth the sharp edges of her worries into harmless, flowing drifts . . . She cranked the window down and winced as the wind hit her face. But it did the trick, it woke her up. That would be all she needed, an accident. One accident was enough in this family.

Rachel pulled the garage door shut behind her and started up the walk toward the back door steps. She saw through the windows the kitchen lights suddenly flick on, bringing the wood and the copper pots and her new orchid plants to glowing life. It looked the way she wanted it to look, warm and inviting. She watched as Edie walked into the kitchen wearing the same shredded jeans she had worn to the airport to meet Camilla—how long ago? A week? A lifetime ago. Edie was bending over a book, frowning, chewing on the edge of a pencil. She had a box of pasta next to her and a can of stewed tomatoes. As her mother watched, she turned and pulled one of the big pots from its hook over the central island, settled it gingerly on the stove, and began shaking something into a measuring cup while she studied the book. Rachel smiled to herself. Why, Edie was cooking; she was poring over a recipe. Edie, who thought nuking a potato was too much of a chore? The sight was quite wonderful, and for a moment she forgot the heavy news she was bringing to her daughter. But only for a moment. It occurred to her that anyone standing out here could be watching Edie as she was now. Rachel shivered and hurried toward the steps.

"Mom, you're home early." Edie looked up, startled, her cheeks rosy from the heat of the oven. "I'm making some marinara sauce for dinner. We even went out and got porcini mushrooms to do it right. Where do you keep the flat-leaf parsley?"

"The what?" Rachel said.

"It's *vital* for Italian cooking," Edie sighed. "Oh well, I'll improvise. I was going to make Shrimp Provençal, but Grandma said she wasn't going to stand around all day deveining shrimp for anyone, not

261

even me."

"Isn't she at work?" Rachel asked, puzzled.

Edie seemed to freeze for a moment. "I think maybe they changed her shift," she said. "Are you hungry?"

Rachel nodded and picked up a small knife from the counter and gestured toward two cloves of garlic sitting by the stove. "If you're fixing dinner, the least I can do is chop stuff for you."

Edie wiped her hands on a dish towel with businesslike efficiency. "Be sure to cut them small," she advised. "It's better for the sauce."

"Absolutely," said Rachel, starting to chop away. She would wait. She would not spoil this moment.

* * * *

She told Edie after dinner, up in her room. They sat side by side on the bed. The new mattress was a little too high for Edie's feet to quite reach the ground, giving her the appearance of a small girl on a high perch. Rachel told her the facts as calmly and cleanly as she could.

"He wrote about *me*?" Edie said in a stunned voice.

Rachel nodded, keeping her hands clasped in front of her.

"Show me the stories, Mother."

"Oh, Edie, you don't want to see them—"

Edie slid from the bed and faced her with something unfathomable in her eyes. "I have to read them. I'll take them to my room, please." She reached out her hand.

"I want to help you—"

"I know that, Mother. But I've gotta do this my own way first. I've gotta sit down and read this stuff. By myself."

Rachel handed over the printouts silently. Edie turned and walked from the room, stiff and proud; a flash of pink from her panties showing through the rear of her torn jeans.

For the second time that day, Rachel felt she was about to throw up. She sat very still on the bed and breathed with deep, regular breaths. If she remained extremely still, she told herself, maybe Edie's marinara sauce and pasta would not end up in the toilet.

* * * *

Edie's door stayed closed the rest of the evening. Rachel briefly told Camilla about the stories and about her confrontation with Kurt, but the distress in her mother's face stopped her from pouring out everything. Camilla seemed too fragile tonight. At ten o'clock, Rachel knocked softly on Edie's door.

"I'm fine, just leave me alone," Edie answered in a muffled voice.

It was around midnight, as Rachel lay in bed in her darkened room staring once again at the ceiling, that she heard her door open. Edie glided into the room and crawled into bed next to her mother. She wrapped her arms around Rachel's neck, smelling of soap and tears. "Help me," she said simply.

Rachel cradled her in the crook of her arm. How long since Edie had first rested here, her head still bruised from the effort of being born? How long ago was that? And what Halloween exactly was it when Edie wet her pants trick-or-treating? And when did she give up her T-shirts for training bras? And what now could she say to heal this wound?

"You will survive, I promise you that," she

263

whispered, stroking Edie's head. "No one can knock you down with lies."

"I feel raped."

"You were. In a very real way, you were."

"There's more, I know there is. Please tell me everything."

Rachel told her the drearier truths: Kurt's true age; his pretense of being a college student instead of a part-time maintenance worker; his wheedling of computer access time at the University of Wisconsin computer lab. She told her about his compulsive lying and felt the knot of rage inside her tightening. Why, why had *this* been Edie's first sexual experience?

"I'll have to live with what he wrote for a while," Edie said. "But it isn't me, and I've just got to keep telling myself it isn't me, even though I feel so naked and exposed." She gulped back choking sobs. "I'm trying to hate him, but part of me feels sorry for him."

"Not me, honey. I don't feel one damn bit sorry for him."

"He wanted me to—to do those things, you know. He wanted me to be that girl so much, he could barely change my name. Maybe I was such a blank page he thought he could shape me any way he wanted."

"You can't blame yourself for feeling dazzled. Lots of women are tricked by seductive phonies."

"Has it happened to you?"

Rachel buried her face in her daughter's soft hair. "Sure it has."

"I never thought I'd ask you this, but once when I was a kid and you and Daddy were fighting a lot, I saw some legal papers on the desk in his study. I read them. Was he really going to charge you with

264

adultery?"

"He was very angry."

"Did you?"

"Did I what?"

"You know—commit adultery?"

"Oh, Edie. Don't ask me that."

Edie said nothing, just sighed.

Rachel decided she had no energy to dodge the truth or defend her reasons. "Yes, I did," she said. It took every ounce of self-control she had not to justify herself.

Edie lay very still. "Well, you survived that. I guess I'll survive this," she said finally.

CHAPTER 10

BERRY BURST INTO RACHEL'S OFFICE THE NEXT morning with the flashy exuberance of a circus ringmaster. "*All right*, are you ready?" she asked.

Rachel pushed back from her desk, eager for some good news. "I'm more than ready," she said.

"Here is the lineup of our *lives*," Berry announced triumphantly. "We've got the prosecutor on that New York case, remember, the one where the high school gym teacher made the obscene phone calls to the kid in his class who was going to the Olympics? Turning her into a noncompetitive basket case?"

"That's terrific," Rachel chortled.

"*And*, what about the woman in Michigan whose husband committed *suicide* after a year of nonstop phone calls telling them their missing daughter was working as a whore in Las Vegas?"

"She's willing to be part of the show?"

"She hasn't spoken one goddamn word yet to the media, and she thinks your show is the perfect place to have her say."

"This is sounding really good, Berry—"

"*And*—how about Gina Tolida, the movie actress who had the guy stalking her with a knife?"

Rachel's eyes widened. "She's coming?"

"You bet she is. And Senator Plowfield wants to be on the show to talk about his new bill requiring jail terms for the creeps who breathe hot and heavy on the phone—"

Rachel raised her hand. "Wait a minute, we can't have too many people, we don't have enough time."

"Well, guess what? I've been hustling the owners— who, naturally—want to make as much fucking money as possible, and they are totally impressed with all the people *clamoring* to be on this show. You are going to get extra airtime, but that isn't the best of it—" Berry swept her hand outward in an exuberant gesture that almost knocked one of Rachel's framed citations off the wall. "The best is, National Public Radio thinks we're performing an incredible public service, and they want to carry the show, and they love the fact that it's going to be on Christmas Eve, which is so *symbolic* of family values, and this makes an incredible contrast; oh God, I am so happy I could have an orgasm, standing right here." Berry leaned against the door frame, her cheeks flushed, her eyes glowing. "Rachel, do you know what that means? That means, we have *arrived*. That means, Merry Christmas to *us*."

They stared at each other, not quite believing it.

"Berry, I think you're right," breathed Rachel.

"You *think* I am? Of course, I am! Rachel, old pal,

we have just taken one giant step toward negotiating the deal we need to make it in this damn broadcasting jungle. Don't you see? You don't have to be a jerk like Tebbins to succeed. You can do what you do best and with just *exactly* the right show, you can get that world focused on *you*—" Her eyes were shining.

"Wouldn't that be something?" The back of Rachel's neck began tingling with anticipation. "If it happens, it's because of what *you've* done. How did you get a crew like this lined up so fast?"

"Amos the Shithead has been Mr. Helpful, I gotta say it. He had a lineup of names for me yesterday afternoon—he even called some of them himself, like the actress out in L.A. Look, I'm not saying I've changed my mind about him, but at least he knows how to *deliver* when the going gets tough. Unlike another shithead we know."

"He's been wanting me to do this all along," Rachel said. She began pacing quickly; the adrenaline was flowing. "We need some way to let people know—"

"Amos has that solved. He'll have a story in the *Tribune* tomorrow with the show lineup, and Channel Nine wants an interview with you for tomorrow night's news. We'll have the biggest audience we've ever had for this show. Rachel, think of it!"

Rachel threw her arms in the air and laughed. "I'm thinking, I'm thinking!"

Berry grabbed her hands. "Think *especially* of how many times over the years we've pulled good luck out of bad," she said. Her eyes were glistening. A smear of mascara was dribbling down her right cheek.

"Why, you softie, you're crying. Producers can't cry, you know that." Rachel reached over to a box of tissues on her desk and pulled one out to dab at

Berry's face. How many middle-aged women still had freckles? "Remember, right after college—" she began.

"When we were doing Consumer Alert at that artsy-fartsy university station that had a range of precisely three city blocks—"

"And the home fire extinguisher I was testing misfired and covered the control panel with foam—" Rachel started to laugh.

"And the whole thing short-circuited and we went off the air—" Berry was doubled over now, laughing herself.

"And they *thanked* us, because the station manager thought we'd done it to stop a *fire*?"

Neither of them could stop laughing. Rachel was laughing so hard she collapsed back into her chair. "If we could pull that off, we can damn sure pull this off," she said.

Berry was wiping her eyes with another tissue. "I've got just one question," she said, calming down. "Can Jim stop us?"

"Why would he want to, with that lineup? He's not unreasonable, Berry. He may not like what we're doing, but the last thing he would do is sabotage the show. I'm sure of it." Nor would he sabotage me, Rachel thought. Not Jim.

"I hope you're right," Berry said. "But I don't trust him."

"You don't trust any man."

"This one in particular." Berry said it with a sudden, penetrating gaze.

Rachel shifted position uncomfortably. Where did Berry get this knack of seeming to *know* everything? She half-expected an interrogation any minute now about her night eating spareribs naked in Jim's bed. She felt her face redden and looked down, spotting a book jacketed in glittering gold and black, lying under a scattering of papers. *"Protein Power Versus Carbo Chaos,"* she announced, snatching it up and reading off the title. "Not bad. How about a show on post-Christmas dieting? We'll snag the guilty and the smug at the same time."

"Something's bugging you. What's up?"

Rachel laced her fingers together and leaned back in her chair. She told Berry about Kurt's stories and about her confrontation with him yesterday afternoon. "Don't tell me it was dumb to go up there; I know it was. But I found out what I needed to know. The kid is sick. Now I've got a terribly hurt daughter and I could strangle him for what he's done."

"Probably a bit extreme," Berry murmured.

"Any advice?"

"She's gotta tell herself it happened to somebody else," Berry said.

"How does *that* help?"

Berry frowned and ran the tip of her tongue over her upper lip before answering. "She needs a bit of disconnection. Remember how you used to pretend you could climb out of body and sit on the windowsill and watch when the dentist was filling your teeth? So it wouldn't hurt as much? That's what I mean."

Rachel smiled. "You remember every silly thing I ever tell you."

"Silly? I thought that was brilliant. A kid creates an imaginary playmate; well, you created an imaginary self."

"Good try, but I knew I was playing a game. What Edie is going through is a lot worse than having a

269

dentist drilling my teeth. She needs more connection, not less."

"You don't get what I'm saying," Berry protested with a laugh.

* * * *

"Grandma? You okay?" Edie peered into the sunroom to see Camilla sitting alone with a cup of coffee, staring out the window at the bare-limbed trees. Here it was, already two in the afternoon, and she wasn't dressed yet. That wasn't like Grandma. Edie slowly twisted her hair into a tight braid and pinned it in place with a large tortoiseshell barrette, trying to think of what to say. She had felt bad yesterday when Grandma pretended to head off for work so her mother wouldn't get suspicious—and then only drove around the block a few times and came back. And it made her feel worse to realize she had almost blown Grandma's cover last night when she was making dinner. She sighed. The burden of Grandma's secret was beginning to weigh heavily, along with everything else. She wouldn't break her promise not to say anything, but something had to happen soon.

I'm fine, dear." Camilla managed a small smile. "It's more important how *you* are."

"Mom told you about Kurt, all that stuff." She waved her hand; it was hard to say it directly.

Camilla nodded. Edie looked much calmer this morning than she had expected she would. "I'm glad to see you're feeling better," she said gently.

"I'll survive." Repeating her mother's words made Edie feel stronger. She plucked a green down jacket off the back of a chair and started to put it on. "I just called Topper," she volunteered. "We're gonna meet

270

up at the mall and hang for a while."

"*That's* an interesting development. Good for you, dear."

Edie flushed with pleasure. Calling and apologizing hadn't been as hard as she had feared. Maybe it was because Topper had been pretty decent about it, and hadn't asked any questions. "I thought she'd go ballistic, actually," she said.

"Amazing what an apology can do, isn't it?" Grandma had a funny, far-off look in her eye that Edie couldn't quite fathom, but she was still smiling her approval. Would she start staring in that sad way out the window again as soon as she left?

"When are you going to tell Mother what happened?" she asked tentatively. "Losing a job is awful, but it's not the worst thing in the world."

Maybe not for a sixteen-year-old, Camilla thought. Dear Edie. How could she know how different it was when you were sixty-four? She ran a finger around the edge of her coffee cup, wondering if she had unloaded too much on this child.

"I mean, I know it was terrible, but we love you and you'll be okay. You should tell Mother. Honestly you should." Edie wasn't sure if she was helping, but she couldn't walk out the door without coaxing some reassurance from her grandmother that she was all right.

"I'm going to be *fine*," Camilla said. She stood, realizing that the fact that she was still wearing her nightclothes was worrying Edie. "I'm going upstairs and get dressed as soon as you leave, and then I think I'll start putting a résumé together. Where's the typewriter, do you know?"

Edie looked blank. "The what?"

271

"You know, the typewriter?"

"I've never used one, Grandma. Mother's got a computer upstairs but I don't think it's installed yet."

Camilla sighed inaudibly. When she stood still, the world moved on. "Never mind, I'll probably find Rachel's old portable with the boxes in the basement. You run along, and give Topper my love." She blew Edie a kiss and started busily clearing the dishes. Anything to get Edie unworried.

"Okay—" Edie felt better watching her grandmother moving around. "I'll see you later. I'll pick up a couple of videos for tonight. If the phone rings, don't answer it, okay? Just listen to the messages."

Had she been so visibly unstrung the other night? Camilla smiled and waved Edie off, and felt a little better when the door closed behind her. She kept her word. She showered and dressed, putting on a wool sweater and a pair of cotton pants from Lands' End instead of a dress. It seemed pointless to get dressed up. Then she descended to the basement and spent forty minutes opening boxes and searching for the old typewriter. She was about to give up when she finally found it—in a box marked "Discard." The ribbon looked ragged, but she was by now determined to follow through with her plan. She found a box of computer paper in the room at the top of the stairs where Rachel planned to create an office for herself when she could afford it. Camilla stared at the space, remembering when it had been Rachel's bedroom. Remembering the riotously colored Marimekko comforter on her daughter's bed and the monstrous panda with the lolling felt tongue that Phillip bought Rachel and the sight of the two of them as they read

272

bedtime stories together. Remembering how, when Phillip was the magic parent who could laugh and play and she was the one who cooked and cleaned, she always seemed to be raining on Rachel's parade.

Camilla took the paper downstairs and put the typewriter on the table in the sunroom. She rolled a sheet of paper into the machine and typed her name across the top. She paused. Address? Which address? This one? Lindy's? She hit the carriage return with a little more force than necessary. She was only drafting the damn thing. Work experience: that was easy. Field's, the Miami shop—what else should she put? How far back should she go without making herself look ancient? She stared at the paper and sensed a presence staring over her shoulder: it was Phillip, an invisible Phillip. She imagined him asking her what the hell was she doing—didn't he take good enough care of her? Why was she so insistent on working, for God's sake, when he made more than enough money? Oh, the dances there had been around this issue . . . Because I'm afraid, she whispered now in her soul. You are sick, and sometimes you are somebody I don't know, and someday, something is going to happen to you . . .

She swung the carriage back again, a little too violently. The tiny machine bounced on the table and she typed again: Personal information. Should she put down her age? Did she have to? Wasn't there some law now that said she didn't have to? "Widowed, one daughter, one granddaughter. . ." Should she pretend Edie didn't exist? Next line: references. This time, Camilla felt tears forming. Who, Swardson? *That* would be a good one. Her boss at the store six years ago? Dead of cancer. She started typing out the names

273

of the couple in Toledo, hitting each key as hard as she could. She heard a tiny pop: the ribbon broke.

With a cry, Camilla shoved the typewriter away and held her head in her hands. She couldn't sit here another second. She stood and walked out of the sunroom and into the dining room, remembering suddenly all the happy dinners with the wine flowing and the friends laughing and Phillip's funny jokes . . . and the other dinners, the later ones after Rachel was grown and gone and Phillip sat slumped at the table under the iron chandelier with its glowing votive candles and told her he didn't think he wanted to live anymore. She walked into the living room, watching the winter sun dance across the leaded glass, creating those wonderful sparkling shards of color she and Phillip used to like to sit in here and watch . . . when she told him how precious he was, and how much he meant to her . . . and then the day after his death when she sat in here and learned from some flat-voiced agent that Phillip had let his life insurance lapse . . .

"What am I doing here? Oh God, what's happened to my life?"

Camilla's wail filled the room, bouncing back at her from the walls like breaking glass, and it was an instant before she realized it was her own voice and not some wounded animal's. She picked up a pillow and threw it across the room. She grabbed the morning newspapers and threw them, too, all vestiges of control crumbling. "Phillip, what did you do to me?' she howled. "You left me in the worst way you could! Damn you, damn you!" She paced back and forth between the rooms, hugging her arms tightly across her stomach against the pain. That's what he did, the much lamented Phillip Duncan, the respected doctor, the generous father who bought his little girl the fanciest toys in town, that's what he did! He left her alone, he left her a visitor in her own home, he left her with no money, *He did it all*!

"Does anybody want to know why I can't mourn? Anybody, anybody at all?" she screamed into the still air of the empty house. "This is why!" She stumbled back into the sunroom, ripped the paper out of the typewriter, crumpled it, and threw it into a trash can. "Fuck you, Phillip Duncan!" she screamed finally at the top of her lungs. Then she slumped into the chair and cried, and the house creaked and moaned with her.

A long time later, wrung dry of all passion and pain, she lifted her head. She could barely register a distant, rhythmic sound pulsating through her brain.

The phone was ringing. She looked at the clock and saw it was precisely the time Quinn Rawlins had said he would call with the results of the biopsy. Still in a daze, she struggled to her feet and headed to answer.

* * * *

Rachel pulled a compact of pressed powder out of her purse and applied a few dabs to her nose and under her eyes. She stared at the tiny patch of her face reflected in the compact mirror and was pleased; she didn't feel tired this afternoon, she was euphoric. The show was set. Nobody was vacillating, nobody was canceling; they were on a roll. She'd talk Berry into taking a day off afterward, for however much good it would do. Berry truly never knew when to stop working. She just kept going like that silly pink rabbit in the commercials; she'd always been like that. Amos called just as she snapped the compact closed.

"How's Edie?" he said quietly. "Wiped out by the news?"

"Devastated. I can't imagine how I would have felt at the same age. But she's not falling apart, she's trying to absorb it. I'm proud of her." Rachel groped for the right words to explain. "Kids are usually pretty self-centered, you know? Edie's no exception. But this was different. She was trying to *understand* why he did it. She even felt sorry for him."

She heard Amos snort. "Not too much, I hope. She's not trying to be a saint about this, is she?"

"No, no—not that."

"So are you ready for the big show? It's going to be great. It's going to be terrific." His voice turned ebullient, echoing the Amos of years past.

"You know what's the best of all? I'm engaging him on *my* terms, not his," she said.

"That sounds good, sweetheart. You can explain later what it means." His tone turned teasing. "Meet me at Lucciano's? In an hour?"

The same nonchalant invitation for which she had once put her life on hold still had power. "If I wrap up here soon, I'll stop by, but I won't be able to stay long," she said. The sudden breeziness she heard in her own voice sounded strange.

* * * *

He was already sitting at the bar when she walked into the restaurant, swiveling lazily in his seat, his jeans-clad legs making him look even leaner than he was. Someone shouted hello to her. She watched Amos turn at the sound and saw his eyes appreciatively travel the length of her body. She thought of how she

276

must look: her dark hair bursting out as usual in uncontainable curls, her color high, her skirt short and swingy. Today she had worn the kind of skirt Amos used to tell her she was born to wear. She felt younger, less encumbered.

"Do you ever feel we're reliving the past?" she said lightly as she slid in the seat next to him.

"What do you mean?" he said. "I never live in anything but the present. Here's to you and me." He raised his glass to his lips before leaning forward to kiss her lightly. She smelled the quick, rich scent of Scotch whisky, and did not kiss him back.

Amos studied her for a brief moment. "Why is it that when you stiffen I always know why? Maybe because we know each other too well?" He smiled, the sides of his mouth moving slightly upward. "Bad joke; don't sue."

"I thought you'd stopped drinking."

"This"—he raised his glass with a flourish—"this, is simply a celebratory drink. You're planning an important show and with my trusty computer and the resources of the *Trib*, I'm going to keep Chicago tuned in. How can we not celebrate?" His eyes tossed out a challenge. Vintage Amos. She settled into the bar chair next to his and ordered a glass of white wine.

"You really like that stuff, don't you? I can't understand what anybody sees in white wine; most of it looks and tastes like piss."

"Maybe that's what makes me drink less of it," she said. She printed a moist kiss of lipstick on the rim of her glass and stared at it; it was as good a reference point as any.

He gazed at her with something dark flickering in his eyes. Then he signaled the waiter. "Here, Jose," he

277

said, shoving the drink across the bar. "Toss this, and bring me a Pepsi, okay?"

"Don't do it for me. It's not enough."

"Hey." His finger gently tipped up her chin. "Don't worry. I'm okay."

It would not do to tell him she had heard that before. Rachel felt a strong hand on her shoulder and looked up to see a faintly recognizable man with bleary eyes and a huge wart on his chin. He was one of the grizzled old reporters who worked very little anymore, a lost soul who had become a fixture in the bars of Chicago. "You two back together?" he said. "Hey, it's like the old days again." He wandered off to the end of the bar, slapping a few shoulders companionably on the way and slumped into a seat in the shadows. And that, Rachel thought with a shiver, is what must never happen to Amos.

"It won't be me," he said quietly.

Rachel jumped, shocked out of her thoughts.

"I know you, Rachel. I could see on your face what you were thinking."

"I would hate—"

Amos threw a ten-dollar bill on the counter and slid off his stool. "Come on," he said gently. "I don't think this place is healthy for us anymore. It makes you sad."

"I've outgrown it," she whispered.

"Don't outgrow me."

They stared at each other. Then he took her by the arm and she leaned into the comforting scratchiness of his old tweed jacket. In another life he could have been an academic, forever puffing on a pipe. It used to be one of her longings, that image. Amos as someone safe. His left arm moved easily around her shoulders and they headed for the door, past the booths and tables already beginning to fill with their usual quota of cheery, chattering reporters and photographers newly released for the day from the inky confines of their newspaper world.

Rachel saw Jim coming in the door before he saw her, and held her breath for the instant it took before he edged his way through the crowd and ended up standing directly in front of her. She felt Amos's hand tighten on her shoulder.

"Hello, Jim," she said stiffly.

His eyes widened and he started to say something, but then he spotted Amos. His jaw snapped shut and he looked like someone had hit him. "Hello, Rachel." He nodded a curt greeting in Amos's direction.

They moved on past, the crowd jostling. Rachel felt the softness of Jim's bulk graze her body as Amos guided her firmly through the door. His eyes were on her, she knew it. Outside, the wind blew and Rachel shivered, released and not released from the sorrowful gaze of Jim Boles.

"He's in love with you; you know that, don't you?"

"Yes, I know."

"He's not for you, Rachel. Much too timid a guy."

A tiny flash of resentment crackled in her brain as Amos's hand slipped slightly below her waist, his palm pressing her lower spine.

"I've got a surprise for you," he said.

They climbed the old stone stairs that hugged the edge of the Wrigley Building and turned right onto the pathway that threaded between the river and the Sun-Times, cutting across the IBM Plaza and reaching finally the two circular structures known as the Marina Towers. Amos took them in with a cheery wave of his hand. "I leased an apartment," he announced. "See that balcony above the parking garage? All mine. I'm not an itinerant anymore, Rachel. I'm here to stay." He paused expectantly, but she said nothing. He turned and faced her full, the light from the water playing across his handsome face. "Look, I'd like to pretend I'm inviting you up for consultation on furniture and drapes, but I'm not. I want us to be in a private place together."

"I can't stay. I have to be home soon."

"How soon?"

"For dinner." Rachel's teeth were chattering.

"Half an hour? That's all." His voice was husky and his hands were cupping her chin now, tilting it upward.

Her sigh was lost in the whistling wind. "Okay, half an hour."

The apartment was almost bare of furniture. There were two faded chairs, a scratched coffee table that looked like a sale item from the Bombay Company, and a tired beige carpet that was turning black at the edges.

"I know it's kind of stark, but I don't need much," Amos said with a certain prideful bashfulness.

Then Rachel spotted an antique breakfront so splendid—although it was marred with deeply etched rings—it took her breath away.

Amos followed her eyes, clearing his throat. "Know any easy way to get those rings out? I sold most of the stuff my wife had, but I liked that, except for the fact that I feel responsible for it. Too much upkeep. I'll probably sell it soon."

"Seventeenth century?"

"Yeah, that's what she said. I'll probably get rid of

it pretty soon."

Rachel pivoted slowly. "Maybe you could use a sofa? Some pictures?" What pictures would a man like Amos hang? she wondered.

He collapsed into one of the chairs and swiveled it around to face the curving window. "Forget what it hasn't got, look at the view. Now is this our favorite city, or what? God, it's beautiful. There's more energy in this place than all of California and New York combined, right?" The buoyancy of his voice lifted Rachel from her thoughts and propelled her to his side, where she curled up on the carpet and stared through the window. The city was one of the first thrills they had shared. Amos used to say they were born city dwellers, in love with cars and concrete and lights that formed a blazing carpet of life under their feet every night. She waited for the familiar surge of feeling, but it didn't come. "Right," she agreed.

He pulled her head to his chest and began stroking her hair. "We have only half an hour," he whispered. "I keep my promises."

Why her resistance? Why this sudden heartache? But she was unable to resist, and her hand began to travel. She closed her eyes, thinking of how she loved kissing the hairy softness of his flat belly. Her hand rested on the throbbing warmth between his legs and she licked her lips: marveling, as always.

"Don't let go—" He moaned as he edged out of the chair to the floor, pulling her to the carpet with him. His mouth was all over her face and neck; kissing her eyes, the soft skin behind her ears . . .

"Amos—"

He covered her mouth with his hand. "Honey, it doesn't matter," he said.

"What doesn't?" she managed.

"That you fucked Jim Boles."

Her eyes flew open. "What—" she began.

"Look, it doesn't matter, do you understand? I know why you're holding back tonight." He pulled back and she could see his smile. "You're a very passionate woman, and I love that in you. So you had sex with him, so what? You don't have to worry about how I'd respond. I know you better than he does." He was encircling her again, his fingers traveling lightly, tantalizingly, up the inside of her thighs.

"You found out where I was the other night. From Jeanie, I presume?"

"Yes. But I could smell it when you walked by him. Maybe I've got a better nose for that kind of thing than most."

She pushed his hand away and sat up. "And you don't care?"

"I'm not saying I don't *care*," he said, watching her now. "I'm saying it doesn't *matter*."

Rachel's head began to swim. She bent forward and straightened the right leg of her pantyhose, noting a run in the heel. "I've got to go now," she said. "I promised Camilla and Edie I would be home early. I think something is bothering Mother and I have to get her to talk about it."

"Oh."

She flushed at the dry tone in his voice. "I'm not asking you to worry with me," she said.

"I'm not. I'm surprised because you're leaving so soon."

"Well, at least you're honest."

They smiled at each other. Rachel scrambled to her feet and hunted for her shoes. It was only at the door

282

that he caught her wrist and pulled it to his cheek. "I blew that one, didn't I?" he said softly.

"Yeah, I guess you did."

"Tell me how."

Rachel gazed into his searching eyes and stopped herself from touching his face with her other hand. "I guess I would really want you to feel it matters," she said.

"I don't own you. Much of what I love about you is your independence. Don't you want that?"

"Of course I do."

"Well?"

"I wish you had screamed and yelled and cried."

The hollows under his eyes seemed suddenly to deepen. "Maybe I did, and you just didn't see it," he said.

* * * *

Rachel stopped in bewilderment at the sight that greeted her when she got home. Camilla was sitting cross-legged in the middle of the floor, laughing almost hysterically. Newspapers and pillows and what looked like dozens of sheets of typing paper were strewn around the room as if a fierce wind had blown through the house. The memory of her father's wild mood changes flashed across Rachel's brain. What was this about? And why was Camilla home already? Wasn't she early?

"They sold it," Camilla whispered. Her hair hung around her face, giving her an oddly haggard look that made Rachel uneasy.

"Sold *what*?" She moved closer, barely able to catch her mother's voice.

"The condo. The realtor sold the condo. My condo.

283

Somebody actually came along and bought that cheap, flimsy excuse of a place, and they will pay me money." Tears were pouring down Camilla's cheeks.

Rachel knelt down on the floor and took her mother's hands in hers. "But that's *good* news," she said, still alarmed. "Why are you crying?"

Camilla was sobbing now without restraint. "Because it's over. I don't have to hate the place anymore. I don't have to hate him anymore, I'm free. And there's something else I want to tell—"

Rachel put her arms around Camilla and felt her flutter like a sparrow in the palm of a hand. "Hate who?" she managed. The sparrow suddenly stilled.

"No, no, I didn't mean that—"

"Hate Daddy?" Rachel's voice shook.

Camilla patted her daughter's hand. "No, dear, I'm just babbling, I'm so happy. Listen, I must tell you something. I haven't wanted to say this, to put more on you. My job at Field's?" She paused. The words came out with obvious difficulty. "There *is* no job. They fired me on my third day. They think I'm too old, but it's going to be all right now."

Rachel caught her breath. Somewhere, somehow, she had sensed this, hadn't she? Or had she just anticipated it? "Those bastards," she said feelingly. "Why didn't you tell me sooner?"

"I didn't want you to worry. I'm a big girl, remember? I had to figure out a way to take care of myself."

"You didn't have to go overboard," Rachel gently chided, feeling the old familiar sense of being shut out.

Camilla smiled, a light in her eye. "There's something else. I'm clean. I have a lump in my breast, and I had a biopsy and it's benign." She knew when she saw the shock in Rachel's eyes that she had made a mistake.

"*What* lump? God, Mother, how can you not tell me these things? Do you think so little of me?" It was a cry from the heart.

"Of course not, I'm just—"

"You don't let me in, you try to protect me too much! I'm glad, I'm euphoric about your news, but I should have been able to comfort you. I should have been allowed to!"

Camilla bowed her head. Rachel's words, too long unsaid, were true; she could face that now. She would not argue now about her fear of being a burden; it wasn't the place or time. She would simply tell Rachel every scary, humiliating detail. She would let her in. As matter-of-factly as possible, she told about the lapsed life insurance. The failed investment with Lindy's husband. The slow, systematic selling of her furniture and jewelry; then Lindy's offer, which made it possible to come home after the gift shop closed. The hidden lump buried deep in her breast. And the worst: her sense of having reached the end of the line when the job didn't materialize at Field's. How would she have supported herself if she hadn't sold the condo? What would she have done?

The light outside faded into night, but they continued to sit murmuring together on the floor until they were enveloped finally in darkness. Rachel sat so close to her mother, she could feel the thin bones of her legs through her cotton pants. She watched Camilla's hands and saw the arthritis in her swollen knuckles before they disappeared in the gloom. With the darkness came intimacy; a sharing of secrets she welcomed. But also with the darkness came a realization Rachel absorbed with a heavy heart. She knew now why her mother continued to avoid visiting her husband's grave in the cemetery buttressed by heavy boulders against the pounding waves of Lake Michigan. They each struggled in their memories with a different Phillip Duncan. And that meant they would never mourn for him in the same way.

She was trying to grapple with what this meant when she looked around, suddenly aware of the fact that night had closed in on the two of them and the house was dark and empty. "Mother," she said, her voice edged with concern, "where's Edie?"

* * * *

Edie trudged along the pathways connecting the blocks of stores at Old Orchard, head down against the swirling snow, wishing she were in a closed mall, for God's sake. She glanced at Topper walking next to her, hands shoved into the pockets of her jeans, her nose bright red. We're quite a pair, she thought with some irritation. We shop until we drop. A pair of Reeboks for Topper, a new pair of Gap jeans for herself, and now a frantic search for Christmas gifts before they had to head home for dinner.

"You'd think we would have organized our time better than this," she complained, her voice muffled by the scratchy wool collar of her coat.

"Yeah, well, we were busy. You know, talking."

That was true, and Edie's conscience felt slightly eased. "You're my friend, Topper," she mumbled into the wind. "Remember, you promised never to say a word to anybody."

Topper nodded vigorously. "I'll never say a word,

ever. I'd take a blood oath, honest, I would, if it weren't sort of a dorky thing to do." Ahead of them loomed the bright lights of a computer store, and Topper stopped, considering. "Mind if we go in here?" she asked. "Maybe if I get my dad one of those books that explains computers, he'll have the courage to upgrade. Do you know the PC he uses at home is eight years old? I'm freaking, I can hardly believe it, he is just in another *world*."

They were giggling as they entered the store and started down an aisle packed with manuals and software. When Topper stopped and began thumbing through something called *The Idiot's Computer Handbook*, Edie's attention began to wander. She walked to the end of the aisle, glancing idly around the store. She gasped.

Topper looked up. "What's the matter?"

Edie's finger trembled as she pointed. Kurt Kiley stood not ten feet from them, his black leather jacket hunched up over his shoulders, a scowl on his face. He was staring at a computer monitor, punching instructions onto the keyboard.

"Do you think he knows we're here?" Topper whispered.

Wordlessly, Edie shook her head. She felt the heat building around her neck, spreading upward across her face. She shouldn't feel so flustered: she hadn't done anything. But standing here right now, fully clothed, she decided she was going to wipe the fictional Edie he had created off the screen.

"Come on, let's go." Topper was pulling urgently at Edie's sleeve. Maybe it was in response to Topper's innate caution, but Edie shook her off and stepped forward. She was going to face him with what he did.

287

Otherwise she'd always feel like some kind of whore. Was this what Grandma had felt? she suddenly thought.

"You owe me an apology, Kurt," she said. She folded her arms and planted herself in the aisle with Topper hovering nervously behind her.

He started, then flicked back his black hair and turned to stare at her. The eyes were as bold as ever, but she saw something else, a shadow of uncertainty, and it gave her the courage to stand fast.

"You did a terrible thing to me, and I want an apology," she said.

"I didn't do anything that you didn't agree to," he said flatly. He saw Topper for the first time. "Oh, I get it," he said, his mouth twisting into something like a smile. "We're regressing. Dragged along the dork, did you? I've told you a thousand times she's too young, but I guess you're more of a baby than I thought."

Edie wouldn't have blamed Topper if she'd cried or yelled right then, but she didn't. She stepped closer, standing now silently at Edie's side.

"Okay, you still want to pretend you're superior to everybody else, but I never thought you were capable of doing what you did. I feel sorry for you," Edie said.

"And why is that? Because now you think I'm a glorified janitor? Come on, be honest. You wanted me to be smarter than you are, that's what girls like you always want. I'm not going to apologize for writing stories, you know. You can forget it."

Edie swayed. Why couldn't she open her mouth and tell him he was full of hot air? Why did her tongue feel thick?

"It's got nothing to do with being a janitor and everything to do with being a jerk." Topper's normally high voice was knife-edge sharp. "You don't try to hurt people you care about, that's all there is to it. Even dorks know that."

Edie shot a grateful look in Topper's direction. Now she was released; now she could leave. She took her friend's hand and turned to go when she suddenly saw a man striding up the aisle toward them. She recognized the black hair and red, puffy cheeks immediately and started to speak, but the words died on her lips as Kurt's father grabbed his son by the neck of his collar and pushed him up against a display of computers in their packing boxes. The low growl of his voice shocked her.

"What do you think you're doing, talking to that girl again, getting us into more trouble?" he hissed. "If you think for one minute that I'm going to put up with more fucking around, you've got another think coming, kid. You hear me?" He shoved him a second time, harder.

"Don't do that," Edie whispered, horrified.

Kurt looked over at her, his eyes red and blazing as he dodged his father's thick fingers. "Quit staring," he said hotly. "Just leave us alone, okay?"

Topper tugged at Edie's hand, pulling her away, and they stumbled as they hurried out of the store. Edie hesitated, looking back.

"Come on," Topper whispered. "We can't do anything."

The old Honda in the parking lot was covered with snow and it took them a few minutes to clear the windshield. They worked fast and silently, anxious to be off. Edie slid in behind the wheel and carefully backed the car out of its parking space. The wheels spun slightly; there was more snow on the ground now than an hour ago. She pulled slowly out onto Old Orchard Road, trying to remember if you were supposed to push down on your brakes or just tap them when you skidded. Not that she was planning on doing any skidding, *that* was for sure. The car suddenly fishtailed; she swung the wheel and somehow they straightened out.

"You know, I've got my driver's license, but Dad won't let me drive after dark, isn't that stupid? I can't believe he doesn't trust me. Honestly." Topper was trying to be relaxed about it, but Edie saw her gripping the door handle.

"Well, I'm not supposed to either, but we got kind of held up at that computer store, so don't freak."

"Not me," Topper said. The fingers of her right hand curled tighter around the door handle as Edie turned left onto Grosse Pointe Road and then right onto Central Street, weaving and bobbing until they passed under the Northwestern tracks at Green Bay.

Edie felt the car shiver and arc slowly to the left, directly into oncoming traffic. "Oh shit," she breathed. She yanked again at the steering wheel. They were only about ten or twelve blocks from home, so why wouldn't the car do what it was supposed to do? It wasn't so much the ice on the road but all this blowing snow. "What time is it?" she asked as she wobbled slowly onto a side road off Sheridan. "Is it still okay if your Dad picks you up at my house?"

"Sure. I told you he won't mind."

"I'm not sure my mom and your dad are getting along lately," Edie said, squinting through the snow hitting her windshield.

Topper slumped deeper into her seat. "Yeah, I

figured," she said.

Edie wanted to probe a little and find out if Topper knew anything, but she had to concentrate because she could hardly see. She leaned forward, her nose almost to the glass. The world looked like a screensaver filled with bursts of sparkling light. It was mesmerizing. Suddenly she felt a horrendous jolt. What had she hit? A pothole? The car began spinning lazily in a circle, and Edie clutched the wheel, not sure what to do. Her right foot stiffened and she slammed on the brakes.

"Edie, we're gonna hit the lamppost!" Topper yelled.

The crunch was muffled by the snow, and Edie thought maybe they had just grazed the damn thing until she saw the front fender of the Honda crumpled like tinfoil against the lamppost. "Oh shit," she moaned, "Mom will be so pissed." Then she glanced at Topper and saw a thin spiral of blood trickling from her forehead.

"Are you okay?" she screamed. "Are you okay?"

"I think so. But my head hurts."

"Don't worry," Edie said. "We can walk from here." She opened the driver's side door and stepped into the still, cold world of swirling snow. It wasn't terrible, she told herself. We'll walk home, and everything will be fine.

Topper pulled herself out of the car on her side, clutching the edges of her down jacket with one hand and her head with the other. The two girls began trudging across an empty lot toward Michigan Avenue. The houses around them were dark, which somehow made the night seem colder and more lonely. They were almost past this deserted stretch when Topper suddenly stumbled and fell.

"What's the matter?" Edie was on her knees, trying to pull Topper up.

"My knee hurts, that's all. I think I banged it in the car." Topper scrambled for a foothold in the snow.

"Okay, we're almost home." Edie hoisted her up and glanced past her to see the hazy outline of a person wearing a cap standing in front of them.

"Hey, can you give us a hand?" Edie yelled. The figure made no answer, it just stood there between them and the street.

"It's some guy," Topper whispered hoarsely.

"Hey, excuse me—"

The figure didn't answer, and Edie felt a quiver of fear. "Topper, let's get out of here."

"Maybe he just doesn't hear us?"

Edie felt wobbly in her stomach. "I don't think that's it, come on."

They started running at an angle, floppy silhouettes, snow sucking at their boots with every step. Edie glanced around and this time was truly frightened. The shadowy figure in the cap seemed to be running after them. She ran faster; where were all the neighbors? Why were all these bloody houses so dark? The light was out at her mother's corner, but they were almost there. If they yelled, would anyone hear? The snow was muffling every sound.

"Edie, wait!"

Edie turned around in time to see Topper stumble and fall. The figure in the cap seemed to be standing almost over her. "Leave her alone! Get out of here!" she shrieked. "Help, help!" She heard a door burst open, and then heard her mother's voice.

"Edie? Edie?"

"Over here! Help, Mom, help!" Edie started to cry, knowing that she was losing it. She jumped up and down and flailed her arms.

Her mother burst through the haze of snow, followed closely by her grandmother, holding something long and thick over her shoulder. The baseball bat. "Are you all right? What happened?" her mother yelled. Edie grabbed her arm and pulled her toward Topper. The shadowy figure was gone, and Topper lay groaning in the snow.

"Did someone hurt you?" Rachel knelt in the snow and cradled the girl's head. She peered into the swirling snow. "Who was that person?"

"I'm not hurt. I just couldn't run anymore. Is he gone?" Topper glanced fearfully over her shoulder. "He was right here, he was standing over me."

"I saw him." Edie was trying not to cry. "He ran after us, I'm sure he did. Mom, what is going on?"

They all fell silent, looking around, seeing nothing. The sky was dark; the snow still falling. Rachel gently pulled Topper to her feet and put her arm around Edie, listening as the girls told her about meeting Kurt and the car skidding and their decision to walk home after running into the lamppost. She coaxed them forward, down the sidewalk and toward the open back door. If we can get inside, she thought, we're safe.

Inside, they stopped dead in silence at the sight of wet, muddy footprints trailed across the kitchen floor. It was Camilla who first saw the piece of paper wedged in the handle of the sugar bowl. The scrap torn from a cookbook on the counter was damp and the ink was already running when she smoothed it out. Rachel moved to her side and the two of them read the message, which was printed in large, spidery block letters.

"Don't you know you're supposed to lock your doors when you go out?" the note said. "See you on Christmas Eve."

* * * *

The police stayed about an hour, dusting for fingerprints in the kitchen and asking the same laborious questions they had asked before. Jim arrived and stood stiffly in the living room doorway, arms folded, as Topper and Edie described what happened. The police were particularly interested in their encounter with Kurt and his father at the computer store, to the point where Edie finally protested: "I don't want to describe again what it was like when his father shoved him. I already *told* you, it was *awful*."

Rachel heard Jim make a small strangled noise of impatience as the police plodded on, and was startled at how quickly he bundled Topper back into her coat and headed for the door when they were finally finished.

"Jim—" she said.

He turned and faced her, and she saw the deep lines of worry in his face. "I think you have to take some responsibility for this," he said.

"How can you say that? I can't believe you mean it."

"Look, you gave this maniac a virtual invitation to escalate. Do you see what can happen?"

"I want this to stop as much as you do," she responded angrily. "You think cowering in a corner and doing *nothing* is the way to catch him?"

"If you're trying to imply that I'm some sort of coward, you're entitled to your own opinion. But I don't want my daughter used as bait in Berry and

294

Amos's schemes."

Rachel felt her mouth drop open. "This isn't just about the stalker, is it?" she managed. "It's about us."

He turned. "Let it go, Rachel," he said.

"It's about me being with Amos tonight. That's it, isn't it? Jealousy I can understand. But accusing me of using your daughter—and mine, by the way—as *bait*? That's unforgivable."

He stared at her, his mouth pulled tight into a straight, thin line of misery. "If denouncing each other is the best we can do tonight, I'd better go. Look, I'm tired and I don't like what's going on. Good-bye." He turned on his heel and marched off the porch with Topper into the still-swirling snow.

* * * *

It was three in the morning and Rachel, thrashing in dream-troubled sleep, heard the phone ringing. Befogged, she reached to the side of the bed and picked up the receiver.

"Hello?"

Nothing. No, something worse than nothing. The caller breathed, rhythmically, calmly. She listened and started to speak, but no sound came out. Instead, she pressed the receiver to her ear and sank back into the pillows. She gazed out the window at a changing world. The snow was falling heavily now, and the air and the trees and all the sounds of life outside had gone totally still. Nothing was left except the peaceful, white, unsullied beauty of the landscape . . . and the continued sound of breathing on the phone.

Rachel turned on her side, still holding the receiver. She stared at the ceiling. And with her tormentor still breathing in her ear, she drifted off to sleep.

CHAPTER 11

"JIM'S GONNA DO IT. HE'S GONNA FIND A WAY TO GET rid of me. It's over, Rachel. I'm telling you, it's over. I knew it would happen. I knew—"

"What are you talking about?" Rachel stared at Berry, who sat hunched in a chair under the light of a glittering morning sun, weeping openly.

Berry drew a pudgy hand across her tear-stained face. "He's started a campaign with the other owners to get me fired. He's making calls, writing them letters—"

"What? That can't be true; Berry, I don't believe it." Rachel didn't bother to take off her coat. She simply moved over to where Berry was sitting and knelt in front of her, taking her hand.

"Marcie told me he's been keeping a file on me all along. She saw it on his desk this morning, with a letter to the other owners. I knew he hated me, but I didn't realize how much. This is the real thing, Rachel." Berry had stopped crying and was now speaking with a dull calmness. "I don't have a contract. Remember?"

Rachel's temples throbbed as she stroked Berry's hand once more. "We'll see about this," she said. She stood and strode from the room, slamming the door behind her, and headed directly for Jim's office. He looked up with a startled glance as she threw open his door and walked up to the edge of his desk. Her eyes blazed, red with anger and lack of sleep.

"I can't believe what I'm hearing," she sputtered. "I understand your anger at me, but what are you doing to Berry? You told me she wasn't going to lose her

296

job. That's not true, is it? So you were lying?"

Jim rose to his feet. His face looked haggard and worn, and his eyes were as bloodshot as her own. "She's speaking for you more than you realize, Rachel," he said. "And I'm concerned."

"So you go behind my back to get my friend *fired*? After promising me that would never happen? This is how you get back at me for ignoring your advice?" Now there were tears streaming down her face. She couldn't help it. She was too worn out and too enraged to hold them back.

"I wrote that letter yesterday with no intention of sending it until I talked to you about what's going on. The last thing I would do is break a promise to you, but this Truthseeker bullshit has gone too far. I can't go along with it anymore. Berry thinks she's running a carnival, not a radio show."

"Haven't you've been building a case against her for a long time?" Rachel searched his eyes, looking for some miraculous reassurance that Berry's insecurities were indeed at the heart of this, and not his traitorous behavior.

But he hesitated for a fatal second before answering. "She goes too far. She undermines you, and you don't see it. This show is pure hucksterism—"

Rachel let out her breath in a long sigh, dimly aware that she had held it in until her chest ached. "So that's what this is all about. If you get me to worry about Berry, maybe I'll cancel the show, is that it? You are *way* off base. How can I make this clear? You know what? You fire Berry, you fire me. Think about it."

"Oh, for Christ's sake, why are you so blind? I could stop this cold, but I'm trying to get you to see what's really going on." Jim aimed a swift kick at a trash basket next to his desk, sending its contents tumbling onto the floor.

Rachel turned her back and left, running now on the adrenaline high of self-righteousness.

* * * *

"Okay, Truthseeker," she purred into the mike as she sat hunched in the broadcast booth half an hour later. "We're on for tomorrow. Remember? Christmas Eve is tomorrow. Come on, Truthseeker." It was almost too easy; she could taste her own recklessness. She saw Larry Kramer's doubtful face through the glass and licked her lips. They felt dry and crusted. If she was going over the top on this promo, it was because it was her last chance to goad the stalker out of hiding and she was damn well going to give it everything she had. Her weapon was the power of her voice. "Call me. Call me tomorrow, give me a Christmas present," she wheedled. "We'll have lots of people listening, I guarantee you that." She heard the coaxing, seductive note creep around the edge of her words; what no one else would hear if she could help it was the fury still building inside her. She would prove Jim wrong and root this poisonous presence out of her life, once and for all.

"Jesus, Rachel," Larry said over the intercom after she was finished. She could see him shaking his head in disapproval through the glass. "I dunno. That was gutsy, but—you sure you want to be the Mae West of stalking victims?"

* * * *

She slumped into her seat in her office, exhausted and shaken by her own audacity. It hadn't helped; she still felt sick at heart. And Berry was still so broken up that she couldn't seem to concentrate when Rachel told her about Edie and Topper. The phone rang. She half hoped it would be Jim, even if all he did was protest that every stalker in town would creep out of the woodwork tomorrow after that promo.

"So you told her I was lonely? Thanks for the sympathy, but frankly, I don't appreciate pop psychoanalysis."

"Oh, hi, Matt," she said wearily. "How's Hawaii?"

"I'm flying back to New York tonight. Did the macadamia nuts arrive yet?"

"No, I don't think so."

"What do you mean, you don't *think* so? Don't you check your mail? I thought you'd be a little better at keeping track of fundamentals like the *mail* by now, for God's sake."

"Oh, I shove it in the door once a week or so. I'm glad Edie called you, by the way."

"Well, yes. She was actually civil. Reminded me of my little girl again. Ever miss the kid she used to be?"

"Sure I do." Rachel was surprised at the directness of his question. "Maybe she wouldn't be so hostile sometimes if we hadn't bungled—"

"Oh, don't kid yourself. She's a teenager, remember? Teenagers always hate their parents. I hated mine, you didn't exactly cotton to your mother—"

"We're doing fine," she said quickly.

She sensed him moving impatiently at the other end. Matt rarely liked long conversations; never had.

"By the way, if you're wondering about the donation to the headmaster, I haven't sent it yet. Sorry."

"Of course, you haven't; you're stalling. And I must say Edie is acting *very* headstrong; I told her she was a little too much like you. Staying in Evanston, for God's sake—"

Rachel sat up straighter. "That's what she said?"

"Give me a break, Rachel. She isn't sure she wants to go back to Langdon. You must be conducting quite a public relations campaign back there in the old homestead."

"She said that?"

"Don't act shocked. It's exactly what you want."

Rachel swallowed hard. "Sure it is," she said. "Big surprise, huh?"

"It would save a chunk of money."

She almost choked. Matt, giving up on his precious Langdon that easily? Better not press, she told herself, just wait for Edie to decide. Something he had said earlier suddenly struck her. "You're going back to New York tonight? Aren't you cutting your honeymoon short?"

The silence at the other end was heavy. "Sniffing around for a little news, are you?" he said finally. His voice grew thinner and even more querulous.

"It's not my business, but you haven't sounded like this was a honeymoon made in heaven, that's all."

"Greta is not terribly mature, unfortunately. She seems to think I'm made of money."

"Maybe you should've waited and got to know each other a little better."

"Well, we didn't, so don't gloat." He sighed. "That's why I'm calling you. Greta and I are getting a divorce."

In spite of herself, Rachel was shaken. How long had it been? Ten days? Eleven days? "Oh, Matt, I'm sorry," she found herself saying.

"It's for the best. I hope you'll tell Edie that."

"Wait a minute, you want *me* to tell her?"

"Rachel, I'm heading back to New York to figure out with my lawyers how to get out of this marriage without losing every goddamn cent I've got left to that skinny fortune hunter, so lay off for once, will you?"

Rachel lowered her head into her left hand and closed her eyes. "Ask me how everything's going around here, will you, Matt? Just ask, okay?"

"How's everything going around there?"

"Just fine. Everything's just fine. And I will tell Edie to call you at your office tomorrow, and then you break the news. I am not your messenger."

"I hate breaking bad news to her."

"Hey, maybe you'll be in luck and she won't care that much."

"I'm a coward, that's my problem. When it comes to relationships—"

"Matt, were you really upset when I told Edie you were lonely?"

The silence stretched out, broken only by the faint popping of static on the line. "No," he finally said.

"Good. There's hope for you. Bye."

She gently put the receiver back into its cradle and buried her head in her arms on the desk. And only then did it occur to her that she had no right to deny Matt the news that some anonymous stalker had chased his daughter through the snow last night.

* * * *

The snow stopped by mid-morning, but the weather forecast was for another storm, probably on Christmas

301

Eve. Rachel left the station late, feeling drained of the fury that had kept her going all day. Amos had sent over a second bouquet of roses just before she left and the card was now in the pocket of her coat. "I'll be with you tomorrow, and in your old age," it read. Rachel's fingers curled around the edges of the cardboard, smoothing it down deep into the dark confines of her pocket. She glanced into Jim's office as she walked past his door. He sat hunched in his shirtsleeves under a harsh overhead light, writing something by hand at his desk, and she could see flashes of shiny skin through his thinning hair. She paused, but he did not look up, so she trudged on by. Her steps quickened. She was taking the train tonight, and she'd better hurry.

The El platform was jammed with northbound passengers who had also left their cars home because of the storm. She had to search a moment before she could slide onto one of the old wooden seats, next to a short, heavy man in a sleek cashmere coat with a Persian fur collar. He looked familiar somehow. The train eased around the curves on its ancient steel trestle and headed across the Chicago River. Down below, on the North Side, the snow blew in powdery gusts across the almost deserted sidewalks. The city seemed bowed and hushed.

"Looks like a lot more snow coming," the man next to her said as he too peered out the window. "A monster blizzard, that's what they're predicting."

Rachel glanced quickly at the face above the collar. "You're the man who sold me my house," she said. She searched her brain but could not remember his name.

"Well, well," he said, sitting up straight. "The little

lady who bought that old place in Evanston—how's it going? Still like it?"

"Very much. I told you, I grew up there. Remember?"

"Yeah, I remember. You're the daughter of that Dr. Dunlop—"

"Duncan."

"Sorry, Duncan." He gave her a sheepish, toothy grin. "By the way, I didn't know at the time that your mother had tried to buy it first."

Rachel blinked. "My mother?"

"Yeah. She tried to negotiate a deal about a month before you came along. Thought it was pretty funny that you *both* were interested in going back to that old place, considering. She never told you?"

The train lurched; she grabbed for the back of the seat ahead of her and held on. "No, she never mentioned it."

"Couldn't swing the price, I'm told. Even though the people who trashed it so bad wanted less than she sold it for." He made what was supposed to be a sympathetic clucking sound deep in his throat. "Must be tough on old people to lose—"

"She isn't old."

He cleared his throat with a quick nervous gargle. "No, no, I'm sure. Hey, you're really doing well, aren't you? People are talking about your show a lot lately. You've got this Truthteller coming on tomorrow, right? To give us all a good, shivery scare? I heard you this morning do that great Tokyo Rose imitation, you know the woman who tried to make GIs homesick—"

"Truthseeker," she corrected automatically. "I'm not trying to scare people, I'm trying to pull him out

303

in the open so the police can catch him."

"Yeah, well—even if they don't, you'll make out like a bandit in the ratings, betcha. Whoops, here's my stop." The train was pulling into Rogers Park, the last stop before the Evanston border. The real estate agent heaved himself out of his seat and shot her an almost shy look. "I've always wished I could be a better self-promoter," he said. "You've got what it takes. Nice to see you again." And he was gone, merging into the shuffling crowd exiting onto the windswept platform.

Rachel sat staring out her window, seeing nothing, until the train pulled up to her station. She got off and walked down Hamilton, moving east, slipping slightly on the new snow. Her fingers were freezing by the time she reached the back stairs of her home and fumbled with the code for the safety system. She stood in the kitchen, hearing the sounds of footsteps moving overhead. She walked to the stove and put on the kettle for the tea and waited for her mother.

She didn't have to wait long.

"Well, you were *something* on the air this morning," Camilla said as she walked briskly into the kitchen. "I've never heard you talk like that on the air, what a *performance*. If anyone can pull that character out of the woodwork, you can, but please—be careful tomorrow." The timbre of her voice changed slightly, but she quickly was back on track. "Good, you've put on the kettle. I saved your dinner. It's in the oven. Did I tell you the couple buying my condo is putting up all cash? I'm so excited, I can hardly believe it. Oh, Edie hooked up your computer today and took me into one of those chat rooms—is that what you call them? It's really extraordinary."

Rachel turned and faced Camilla. Her mother's face

had the sheen of a polished apple as she bounced around the kitchen; she looked happy. One of Edie's ribbons was tied around the crown of her head, giving her a slightly Debbie Reynolds look.

"Mother." Rachel knew she was about to drop a rock on that thin, proud back and there was nothing she could do to stop herself. "You tried to buy back this house."

Camilla froze with two saucers suspended, one in each hand. "Who told you that?"

"The realtor who sold me the place. I met him on the train coming home."

"I thought about doing it. I hated to hear from Lindy how rundown it was. I played with the idea—"

"Even before the gift shop closed down?"

Camilla leaned heavily against the sink. "Almost from the moment I left," she said softly.

Rachel waited a second to digest this. "Why didn't you tell me?" she finally asked. "Why did you insist I was making a big mistake when you wanted to do the same thing? Ever since you came back, you've been telling me it's ridiculous to try and recapture the past. You almost convinced me I was doing something backward and Freudian. Why?"

"Well, I was wrong."

Rachel felt her eyes brim with tears. "That's all I get? 'I was wrong'? Maybe this time you could give me a little more?"

Camilla covered her face with her hands.

"Don't you see? How can I trust what you tell me when everything changes all the time?"

Camilla lifted her face at this. "Don't things change with Edie?" she shot back. "Can you tell *me* that everything you've tried to explain to her about your

305

life with Matt is totally consistent?"

"I can tell you I don't live my life the way you live yours." Rachel's voice was trembling. "I don't keep dark secrets for years and years and—"

"Your father's illness was no dark secret. You didn't *want* to see all that was going on between us, that was what happened. And I do not understand how my passing fancy to come back to this house is some kind of betrayal of you! I didn't owe you that information any more than I owed you a strict accounting of my financial situation when—"

"Maybe you didn't owe me the information that you hated my father either. But it makes a difference that you did."

"I knew we'd get back to that." Camilla was holding her stomach as if it hurt.

"You've been pushing it in my face since you came home, that's all. How do you think that feels? The big question isn't whether he killed himself, Mother. It's whether you *hated* him so much that he wanted to!" Rachel instantly wished she could grab the words and shove them back inside her throat. "That's not what I mean. What I mean is, I—"

"No. No." Camilla shook her head, covering her eyes with one hand. She groped her way to the other side of the counter and sank into a chair.

"I didn't mean that, I truly didn't mean that."

"Don't you understand?" Camilla said finally in a barely audible voice. "I didn't hate him, not the way you're painting it. I loved him. We had good times and bad times, and we knew how to comfort each other and we knew how to hurt each other—isn't that like any marriage? Then he got sick. It got worse and worse. He would do crazy things and drink too much

306

and make scenes in restaurants and we lost friends, but the worst was I knew how much you adored him, how you loved the euphoric, soaring side of him, and I resented him because I had to hide the truth from you when he crashed—" She stopped and drew in a ragged, dry-sounding breath. "I had this knot of anger inside of me that never seemed to go away. Can you honestly say you don't understand how you can love someone and be angry at the same time? Don't you see what's happening? It's not that I hated *him*. That's not the question, Rachel. It's the fear that he hated *me*. Because that would explain why he killed himself." She put her head into her hands and began to weep, a dry, painful sound that cut into her daughter's heart.

"He didn't hate you," Rachel insisted. "He loved you. He *had* to love you. He couldn't have deliberately left you!" Or me, she agonized silently.

"Yes, he could have. He was capable of that."

Rachel stumbled around the counter and put her arms around Camilla, resting her face on her mother's hair. It felt wiry and coarse. She wanted to bury herself in it and cry for comfort and forgiveness, but she couldn't. "Maybe it wasn't an accident," she whispered into the small cap of wiry hair. "Maybe it wasn't. I still don't believe it, but it doesn't matter anymore." She thought she had said it softly enough not to be heard, but Camilla's body suddenly trembled and she wasn't sure.

* * * *

It was late, close to midnight, and Edie pulled the covers over her head as Rachel walked into her room.

"What's the matter?" Rachel whispered.

"You're coming in to tell me something awful again, I know it."

"Oh, Edie, what makes you think—" Rachel stopped, irritated at her own placating tone.

Edie's eyes peeked out from above the sheet. "I heard Grandma crying. You guys are good at pretending nothing's wrong, but you must've had some big fight, and I don't know how you can do that; she is so *great*, and I'm *glad* she's here—"

"So am I. We're fine—it just took me a while to figure it out." Rachel sank heavily onto the side of the bed. "I need to tell you something. It's about your father. He's going to call you tomorrow morning—"

"And ask about the macadamia nuts? Honestly, he is so anal. They came today, everything is cool. *What* is his problem?"

"He and Greta are getting a divorce." She hadn't expected to blurt it out and heard her own words with a certain mild surprise. It all sifted through a deep tiredness, which she didn't want Edie to see. It would require the kind of explanations she wasn't capable of giving right now.

Edie sat straight up, her eyes suddenly dark and round. "Just like that? That's how it happens?"

"I don't know the details. Your father is—still searching for himself."

" 'Searching for himself'? Oh, give me a fucking break, that's a lot of bull. Who does he think he is? He's no little kid!" Edie threw her pillow with vicious aim against the far wall, jolting Rachel from her torpor.

"Neither are you, and have you got everything figured out? Okay, your father made a mistake. Give him a little love and support, for God's sake. You

308

don't think he feels like a jerk? Of course he does." Rachel stood and walked to the window, staring outside, a little amazed at her own visceral defense of Matt Snow.

"You can't stand him, why are you defending him?"

"Because he's blundering along like the rest of us, doing the best he can. And he loves you."

"Well, I deserve more from—"

"You are sixteen years old, Edie. You've got two parents who love you and would do anything for you, so grow up."

The silence grew behind her. Then, finally, Edie's astonished voice: "You've never talked to me like this before."

"No, I guess I haven't. But I guess if I have to grow up, you do, too." Was she really saying these things? She turned slowly and walked back to Edie's bed and sat down again.

Edie was sitting bolt upright now. "What happened between you and Grandma?" she asked.

Rachel waited a long moment before answering. "I guess I've been thinking about myself more than her. Sort of consistently, like all of my life."

"Grandma told me that when Grandpa was sick, she didn't tell you enough how much she loved you. You know, to balance things out."

"She told you that?"

Edie nodded slowly.

"Okay. Maybe I've been paying her back."

"She loves you a lot." Edie felt a bit dazzled by her sudden role as a bridge between her mother and grandmother.

"Here's another lesson, Edie." Rachel drew a shaky

hand across her eyes. "Don't figure you know it all, ever. It screws everything up."

"Okay. Is this what they calling learning on the job?"

Rachel smiled into the shadows flickering across the walls of the room. "You could put it that way, I guess."

"Growing up isn't much fun. That's what I'm learning."

"Honey, I wish I could bundle you up and protect you from all the bad stuff, but I can't."

Edie digested that, then leaned over and flicked off the light by her bed. "Mom, are you worried about the Truthseeker calling the show tomorrow?" she asked softly in the dark.

Rachel felt the air leave her lungs in an audible sigh. "I'm worried about all the hype," she said.

"But that's what's supposed to be so good about this. That's what Berry and Mr. Curley have been saying."

It was easier in the dark to express what was bothering her most. "Unless we're just playing into his hands," she said. She heard Edie scrunch back down under the covers, the way she used to when a bedtime story got scary.

"Do you think Kurt is the stalker?" Edie asked in a wavery voice.

Rachel gently traced the outlines of Edie's fingers with her hand. "I don't know," she said. "My gut tells me he's what we know him to be and nothing more."

"I've never seen a parent treat his kid like Mr. Kiley did."

"I hope you never do again. Kurt's probably trying to escape, in his own way." They sat for a long

310

moment in companionable silence, each with her own thoughts. "I'm trying to decide where I want you to be tomorrow," Rachel said, breaking the silence.

"Oh, I want to come," Edie said immediately. "I'm sure Grandma does, too. You can't leave us here. I mean, why should you be there all alone? You know, this guy—"

"I'll be perfectly fine," Rachel said. She was touched by the alarm in her daughter's voice and decided not to share her fears. "It's a long day, Edie; the show might get exciting, but after that you'll be bored out of your skull."

"Maybe if you let me drive the Honda?"

"Forget it, Toots. We got it back in the garage, but the fender is about to fall off."

Edie sighed. "I'll argue with you in the morning."

"Maybe Grandma—"

"Mom, look." Through the dark, she saw Edie pointing out the window.

It was snowing again. Thick, heavy flakes were already building up against the windowpane as the clock downstairs on the mantel chimed the hour: twelve o'clock.

"It's the day of Christmas Eve," Edie said dreamily. "We should be celebrating. You want some macadamia nuts? Dad sent chocolate-covered ones. He remembered they were my favorite kind, which is pretty surprising for the kind of space cadet *he* is."

* * * *

Rachel's stomach was comfortably stuffed with macadamia nuts when she crawled into her own bed an hour later and reached to flick off the light. She saw a note folded on her pillow. "Waffles for breakfast," it read. "Your mother is cooking." Rachel smiled and crumpled the note in her hand as she let her head fall back on the pillow. She might actually get the deep and peaceful sleep she needed so desperately tonight—if she could strip from her memory the sight of Jim's face when he kicked the wastebasket. If she could.

* * * *

They awoke the next morning to a foot of new snow, with more still falling in heavy, wet clumps. Camilla was already in the kitchen making waffles and wearing the robe with the palm trees. Rachel winced when she saw it, remembering how hastily she had scooped it off a clothing rack—not thinking much about the gift or who it was for. Camilla forgot to heat the syrup and Edie broke a plate, but when the three of them gathered around the table on the sunporch for breakfast, it was with a fierce and shared unity.

"I'm glad you don't have a TV talk show, Mother," Edie said, glancing at Rachel with a worried frown. "You look so wiped. At least nobody will see you." She speared a second helping off the stacked plate Camilla had deposited in the middle of the table.

"I should wear a bag over my head, maybe?" Rachel suggested with a small smile.

"You look lovely," Camilla said automatically as she poured the orange juice. "Maybe add a touch of lipstick, that's all." In truth, her heart ached at the tautly drawn lines around her daughter's mouth and the faded light in those marvelous purple eyes that people were already exclaiming over when she was still a baby. She couldn't stop worrying about the pressure Rachel was under.

312

"Mom, that dirndl skirt is kind of awful," Edie said, her eye now traveling over her mother's clothes. "I think—"

"Your mother looks fine," Camilla interrupted sharply. "Today is not a fashion show."

Rachel hardly registered their exchange. "Mom, Edie—I want you both to stay in the house today and not go out at all," she said. "It's important."

"You mean I'm stuck in here all day? That's not fair. Why?" Edie sputtered, licking congealed syrup off the tines of her fork.

"I thought about having the two of you with me downtown—"

"We'd be good moral support," Camilla said quickly.

Rachel smiled, her eyes lighting slightly. "I just feel twitchy, I guess. If you stay here in the house with the alarm system on and the police outside, I will feel"—she took a deep breath—"safer."

The three of them fell silent.

"Don't worry," Camilla said finally, casting Edie a firm look. "If you want us to stay here, we will. We won't budge."

"Maybe Topper can come over later," Edie said. She stared out the window at the snow, thinking of how boring it would be to be cooped up here all day. But that wasn't the main thing. The main thing was, she was going to be listening to her mother's voice on the radio and for the first time, she was going to feel too far away.

"Maybe he won't call," Rachel said slowly. "Then what? Does it look like a party where the guest of honor never showed up?"

"Oh, he'll call," Camilla said. "He's promised us

that already."

"Got a question." Edie's mouth was full of waffle.

"Shoot," Rachel said, arching an eyebrow at Edie's table manners. It was such a relief to see her eating again.

"You know what you said last night? I kind of wondered if maybe in a certain way you were *afraid* this will work. Is that crazy?"

Rachel swallowed a large gulp of orange juice before answering. "No," she managed. But then the front-door bell rang and interrupted their conversation. They all jumped. Camilla hurried to the door and reappeared a moment later with Lindy by her side. Lindy beamed at them. She wore a huge sheepskin coat and a tiny cap with earflaps. Her nose was bright red and tiny spidery veins of purple burst like tiny flowers across her cheeks.

"I thought you all might need a little moral support today," she said brightly. "So I thought I'd just come right up here and maybe share a cup of coffee; my goodness, waffles? I can't touch them—my diet, you know—but they do look good. I'll just stay a few minutes. I've got lots of shopping today. Do you know there are two police cars in front of the house? Rachel, are you going to be all right?"

Rachel smiled as reassuringly as possible. "Of course I will be. We were just talking about how nothing may happen at all."

Lindy's brow furrowed. "Oh, that would be too bad. Everybody is expecting you to bring this Truthseeker person out of hiding and we'll all be so *disappointed* if he doesn't call."

"Rachel isn't responsible for *his* performance, only her own," Camilla said quickly. She was pouring a cup

314

of coffee for Lindy when she said it. Half of it slopped into the saucer.

"Absolutely," Lindy said, gingerly lifting the saucer and pouring the coffee back into her cup. She looked up at Camilla, her eyes brightening. "How about some good news? The Hospital Guild absolutely wants to interview you for that job, Camilla. They're *thrilled* that you're interested."

"Really? Oh, I'm delighted—"

"What job?" Rachel looked from one woman to the other.

"Manager of the hospital gift shop," Camilla said excitedly. "Remember how messy the place looked the other day? It's *just* the kind of place I want to get my hands on and fix up and—"

"And it's the only paid position," Lindy broke in. "Isn't it wonderful? If Camilla takes that job, I'll be working for *her*. Oh, fate."

Something caught in Rachel's throat as she watched Lindy and Camilla beam at each other across the table. For once, she didn't feel excluded from her mother's life. Indeed, she felt warmed.

* * * *

Rachel felt the car fishtailing in the snow almost as soon as she cleared the alley and made it out onto the street. She waved in the direction of the patrol cars parked in front of the house and saw one of the cops wave back. Then she concentrated on the road ahead, squinting into the snow. She maneuvered slowly down Sheridan Road, allowing herself only one glance in the direction of her father's grave as she drove around the curve into the neighborhood of Rogers Park, wondering fleetingly what he would think about today's agenda. Why wasn't he here? He should be here. She was astonished at her own momentary flash of anger, but it evaporated as fast as it came.

There were only a few people at the station when she arrived, all complaining about how hard it had been to shovel themselves out of their driveways. Even Berry hadn't arrived yet. Rachel was still unloading her briefcase when she heard a brisk knock and looked up to see Jeanie Horton smiling at her from the doorway.

"Hi," Jeanie said. Her thick red hair was loose about her face today and she wore tight black jeans and a black wool turtleneck sweater. Her manner was, even for Jeanie, slightly over the top in brightness. "Big day today, I'd say. See our story this morning? I'm kind of pleased I forced Senator Plowfield to promise a hearing on stalkers. He may not be the brightest guy in Washington, but he knows how to ride a good issue, right?"

"I read it, yes, you did a great job; thanks," Rachel said. She decided she didn't much like the lilac cologne Jeanie favored, maybe because it was too pungent for so early in the morning.

"Get him to repeat his promise on the show today, you never know with these pols—"Jeanie's eyes were darting around the room and it took Rachel a few seconds to realize she was looking for an ashtray.

Self-mockingly, she clutched her throat. "My larynx and smoke don't mix. Sorry, hope you don't mind."

"No, of course not, nobody likes it anymore. Amos and I are the only ones at the *Tribune* who still smoke, can you believe it? We'll probably both die of lung cancer, but at least we'll keep each other company."

She laughed and shrugged and plopped into a chair with disarming naturalness. "Can't wait to hear you make these guys dance to your tune. You've got the issue beautifully framed with this gorgeous, juicy mystery. Think your stalker could be that serial killer they're looking for over in Wheaton?"

"Oh, what a silly rumor," Rachel said dismissively. "Different profiles entirely, as you know."

"You never can tell." Jeanie looked a little put out. "Here's something better—a couple of cops are telling me they're suspicious again of Kurt Kiley. That incident with your daughter in the computer store—"

"Who told you about that?"

Jeanie stared at her, a little surprised. "I check police reports every day, and I've got friends on the force who make sure I don't miss anything important. Your daughter was chased the other night and someone broke into your house. I'd be a pretty lousy reporter if I didn't know."

"What makes them think it could be Kurt?" Rachel felt sweat on her palms, remembering Edie's question.

"Ah, that's what's interesting. Have you met his father? The guy has a criminal record. The whole thing is a terrific story, no matter which way it goes. You know, con artist-turned-computer-nerd-with-criminal-father loses his moral compass out in cyberspace. I've interviewed some people at the university who know Kurt and I think I've even got—"

"Are you doing a profile? On Kurt?"

"Sure. Wouldn't you?"

"What if he's nothing more than a mixed-up kid with an abusive father? What about the damage you could do?" She was beginning to feel flattened by

Jeanie's energy; it felt like a freight train roaring over her.

"I'm surprised you say that after what he did to your daughter. Facts are facts, Rachel. And this kid doesn't deserve special treatment, that's for sure." Jeanie's cheery face was looking a touch fretful. "Amos agrees with me, by the way."

Rachel touched Amos's note in the pocket of her suit jacket, tracing the sturdy fold of the cardboard lightly with her fingers. "When is he coming over?" she asked as casually as possible.

"Didn't he call you?" Jeanie's eyes widened just a little too much. "Damn, he'd forget his own head some days if it weren't screwed on. He said he was sorry, but he's checking out a tip on union fraud in Gary. He was really upset about having to go, which is why he sent me over."

Rachel smiled pleasantly. "To give me moral support?"

"That's right, to give you moral support." Jeanie's smile was bright again.

Rachel had the sudden fantasy of pulling the note from her pocket and handing it to Jeanie to see what would happen to her face when she read it. She played with the thought for an instant as she fingered the cardboard.

"That's kind of you," she heard herself saying. "But I'm fine."

"I knew you would be," Jeanie said, standing quickly.

There was an awkward moment as they stared at each other. Rachel wondered what Jeanie saw. Did she see only a middle-aged woman with circles under her eyes and tangled hair that badly needed brushing? I know what I'm looking at, she thought, I'm looking at a woman in love who is trying not to show it.

"Take care," she said impulsively.

Jeanie raised an eyebrow. "With my story on Kiley? Sure, if you say so." A tiny, polite smile flickered at the corners of her mouth as she turned to go. "Good luck with the show. You'll be great."

"Is he worth it to you, Jeanie?"

She saw the younger woman's back stiffen. "What are you talking about? Kiley?"

"I think you know."

Jeanie turned slowly and looked at Rachel, her face guarded and tight. "I don't, really."

"That's because he hasn't told you he loves you yet, but you're expecting him to any minute. You're waiting in this wonderful kind of giddy enthrallment and shivering every time he lights your cigarette—if he does that kind of thing anymore—or touches your hand or says you're terrific. You're waiting."

Jeanie's face drained slowly of color. "Don't make fun of me."

"I'm not," Rachel said. "I'm just saying, be careful."

Jeanie hesitated for a brief second, "I think you should know something. Amos isn't down in Gary, he's at my apartment, drying out."

"What are you telling me?" Jeanie's words swirled around her, leaving her light-headed.

"I'm telling you that he was destroyed when you walked out on him the other night. He told me what happened after he brought you to his place. He couldn't handle it. So he went out and got himself a bottle of vodka and drank the whole damn thing. Around two in the morning, he was knocking at my door with another bottle in his hand. Is that the way you treat a guy who loves you as desperately as he does?"

"It wasn't quite like that."

"I don't mean to be harsh, but you sound a little like a woman who wants to have it both ways. Am I right?"

"Amos told you about Jim, I suppose."

"Yes."

"And he cried on your shoulder and you took him into your bed."

"I told you not to make fun of me." Jeanie's eyes glittered almost dangerously.

"Jeanie, you were at Lucciano's with Jerry Tebbins the other night, weren't you?"

The younger woman's eyes flickered. "I meet a lot of sources over there."

"And I suppose you were the one to tell him about my relationship with Amos five years ago—figuring he'd use it on his show, which, of course, he did."

"Everybody knows about you two back then. I didn't tell him anything new."

"Does Amos know you—shall we say—reminded him?"

"That's none of your business, Rachel."

"You have an interesting way of handling competition." She felt very calm as she said it.

Jeanie's eyes flickered again, this time without fire. "I'm not out to hurt you, if that's what you mean."

What was there to do? Nothing much. "Time moves on," Rachel said, shrugging. "Look, I'm not your enemy, either."

"If I do my job right, everybody's my enemy." With that, Jeanie turned and left. But Rachel had heard the catch in her voice.

Rachel moved out into the corridor after she was gone and walked slowly toward the reception area. More people had arrived—Sam, one of the deejays, was pulling off his coat and talking with Joe Betto, the new guy who read Associated Press news briefs on the air at the top of the hour. Larry Kramer was in the back hall stomping snow off his boots.

"Hey, what a day!"

It was Berry, just coming in the door, looking plump and rosy. A second later she burst into a surprisingly melodious version of "Rudolph, the Red-Nosed Reindeer," singing at the top of her lungs, and everyone within earshot started laughing. Rachel squared her shoulders, still thinking about Amos. There was a little pain, nothing engulfing—nothing more than a mild toothache all through her body. That was all, she told herself. She had a show to do today and it was going to be the best she and Berry had ever done. In another hour, they'd be on the air.

She threw an arm around Berry as the two of them walked back down the corridor. Someone had plopped a Santa Claus cap on Berry's head that bobbed up and down as she talked, and Rachel was filled with sudden, effusive well-being.

"This will be fabulous today, absolutely fabulous," Berry said. "You've got all the background stuff on your guests, right?"

"Righto," Rachel replied. "I've got them memorized up one side and down the other."

"Be sure to get the prosecutor, what's his name?"

"Harold Stichen."

"Be sure to get him to talk about the status of the gym teacher's appeal. Did you know the guy is claiming he was an abused spouse and *that's* why he made those phone calls to the kid?" Berry chortled. "You can have fun with that. And don't forget to ask Gina Tolida about her new movie—she plays Joan of Arc or somebody—"

"Oh, give me a break," Rachel said, laughing.

"No, it's *important*, these people have such teensy-weensy self-esteem, you know, they need a lot of puffing up—"

"Teensy-weensy egos?"

"I wouldn't go *that* far." Berry's eyes flicked left as they walked by Jim's office. It was empty.

"He's not in yet," Rachel said, "You can breathe freely."

Berry skipped a step or two and laughed, two bright spots burning on her cheeks. She looked nothing like the dejected Berry of yesterday. "What, me worry? I'm invulnerable—we're invulnerable. Want to know why?" She opened the door to Rachel's office with a huge grin on her face, pulling it quickly closed behind the two of them. "Guess what?" she stage-whispered. "We're got a syndication nibble. More than a nibble, actually, I think they're really interested."

"Oh, my God." Rachel felt her heart jump. "When? Who?"

"This is top, top secret; it's Kendall Productions— they called me at home this morning. They've been monitoring your show and they're *very* interested in what you're doing today. Can you *believe* all this? Finally, we get our break. I told you all along, we needed one big chance and once we found it we'd run with it and that's how you make it in this business." The fuzzy white ball at the tip of the Santa Claus cap was drooping over one eye, but Berry hardly seemed

322

to notice.

"What if the show doesn't work?"

Berry gave her a puzzled look. "What do you mean?"

"What if the Truthseeker doesn't materialize? What if we don't catch him?"

"Oh, he'll materialize. But don't you see? It doesn't matter if he's caught. Oh, they'll probably catch him eventually, or somebody like him, it's what we *build* off this—"

Rachel curled the fingers of her right hand, digging with her nails into the flesh of her palm. "It *does* matter if he's caught. He isn't just calling this show, remember? He's stalking me and my family. He followed Edie home and got into the house—you think that's not important? Nothing matters to me more than catching him."

"Hey, pal, calm down." Berry reached out and touched Rachel's shoulder, her eyes dark with concern. "I know it was terrible. I'm with you, okay?"

Rachel took a very deep breath. "Okay," she said.

"Of course, we have to catch him. I never meant to imply anything else." Berry lowered herself into a chair and hoisted her feet to the edge of Rachel's desk.

"I'm sorry I snapped at you."

"No problem."

"Maybe we should both take vacations when things calm down. What do you think? We've been under a lot of strain lately."

Berry's eyes began to dance around the room, lighting on nothing. "A vacation?"

Rachel smiled, shaking her head. "I mention 'vacation,' and you think 'end of the world' or something. Do you realize you've *never* taken a day off from this show?"

"Why would I? What else would I do?"

She said it so simply that Rachel was nonplussed. She recovered enough to turn her suggestion into something of a joke. "Oh, maybe go soak up sun on a beach somewhere and pick up a beach boy or two—or go on a shopping spree on Madison Avenue or something."

Berry looked dreamy all of a sudden. "I never had nice things," she said. "That nomadic life we lived ruled *that* out. Anyway, Dad didn't believe we should be carting much stuff around, you know? I had nothing pretty, nothing fancy. It was kind of wrong to want any of it. Remember graduation? Remember what he did?"

Yes. Oh, yes. If Rachel shut her eyes, she could quickly conjure up her long-ago image of the tall, ramrod-straight man with the stiff smile who had so effectively marred his daughter's happiness the day she graduated second in her Vassar class. In truth, she preferred the image of the helpless stroke victim in the wheelchair.

"The brooch," she said.

"Yes, the brooch. That beautiful face, surrounded by those beautiful pearls—"

"It was pretty," Rachel agreed wistfully. "I wish it wasn't gone."

Berry blinked, as if pulled back from a long distance. "I know," she said softly. "But I remember her perfectly—she was an elegant lady encased in glass. And you were letting me wear her for graduation."

"She looked perfect on you," Rachel said, her heart sinking as she saw Berry's pain opening up again.

324

There were very few moments of cruelty she ever had witnessed that she knew she would remember forever. And one was the afternoon Barry's father strode up and ripped the brooch from his daughter's dress—announcing she took no handouts, thank you very much. In front of her friend, no less.

"I was a good daughter, wasn't I?" Berry said. "I didn't cry or yell or anything. He didn't want me to wear something I couldn't afford in case it might damage my character. You never can tell—it probably did anyhow." She smiled widely. "Shall we run through the details about everybody one more time? They should be coming in here in about half an hour if they don't get bogged down in a snowdrift somewhere." She raised her hands to her face in mock horror. "Oh my God, what if *that* happens?"

"It won't," Rachel automatically reassured her. "So when do I meet with the people from Kendall Productions?"

Berry's eyes were happy again. "Later this week. They want to wine and dine you at some fancy restaurant, location to be determined later. They're gonna *court* you, Rachel, how does that feel? God, I wish Jim were here so I could throw this in his face; discreetly, of course."

* * * *

Senator Plowfield—who arrived first—was a slightly built man with pale yellow eyebrows. His staff had done such good advance work that he showed up with precisely enough time to shake hands with everyone at the station before the other guests arrived. Harold Stichen arrived next. He had the frazzled look and winter pallor of a constant traveler and Rachel noted that his bow tie was shredding slightly at the edges—probably from rubbing against the faint stubble on his neck. He had a terse speaking style, which she knew could make coaxing him to talk more difficult. But she also saw the way he eyed Plowfield, and she decided he was ready and able to hold his own with the more voluble senator.

"Hello, Mrs. Snow? I'm Angie Moran. From Michigan?" A tiny steel trap of a woman wearing a flowered dress and heavy blue eyeshadow stood at the door of her office, cold eyes sweeping Rachel and the two men sitting there. Her disappointments all but bristled. "I want to tell you right up front, I'm here only because. I hope your show helps me catch the bastard who forced my husband to suicide. Nothing more, nothing less." She let her gaze rest on Plowfield. "You're a senator, aren't you? You look like one in that expensive suit. I truly hope you're the kind who has enough in his head to do something for us."

"I'm trying," Plowfield said promptly with an easy smile.

Rachel heard Berry give a gurgling sigh in back of her as she reached out to squeeze Angie Moran's hand. She knew what Berry was thinking: so far, no duds. At that moment, the door opened and a woman with wild hair and skinny legs encased in black tights swept into the room.

Rachel stood. "Miss Tolida?"

"No one knows I'm here except my agent," Gina Tolida announced without preamble. "Otherwise this creep stalking me would track me down, I know he would. This is no publicity stunt, do you understand? Is this show serious? That's all I want to know."

Rachel gazed directly into the actress's almost startlingly probing eyes. "It's serious," she said. "It's the most serious show I've done in my life because I have a personal stake in the outcome."

"Good." Gina Tolida slapped a thick stack of papers down on her desk. "Read these before we start."

* * * *

The broadcast booth felt short of oxygen as Rachel and her four guests crowded around the circular table. Rachel glanced into the control room, wondering why Jim hadn't appeared yet. Was he so disgusted he was staying away? Marcie was filling their water glasses with such nervous haste that water slopped over the tops and began soaking into the green felt table covering. She cast a stricken look at Rachel, who waved her away with a reassuring smile. Nothing must interfere with her focus now. She glanced at the clock; fifteen seconds to airtime. Angie Moran was still fiddling with her earphones, and Rachel signaled Marcie to help her get them adjusted. Ten seconds. Plowfield was regaling Stichen with a joke about on-air gaffes that he finished just as Larry Kramer raised his hand and pointed at Rachel. The light above the window separating them from the control room glowed red. They were on the air.

"I wish you all a good morning on this snowy Christmas Eve, my friends," Rachel said. "I am Rachel Snow and this is *Talk Time*, a very special *Talk Time*. Today we'll be talking about a particular kind of crime and a particular kind of criminal—the stalker." She lowered her voice, moving slightly closer to the mike. "It begins innocently, often with a phone call. The stalker, mind you, is a coward at heart. But as many of

327

you know who are listening, the stalker escalates. There is someone out there now trying to make himself part of this show: a twisted person who calls himself the Truthseeker. He boasts of murdering two young girls, but the police call him a liar. He thinks he is stalking me and my family. But he is doing more than that—he is stalking all of us." She took a deep breath and smiled at each of her guests in turn, riveting them with her eyes. Don't get carried away, she told herself.

"And now I want you to meet my guests today, all of whom have experienced this crime in one way or another. We'll hear first from the actress Gina Tolida—"

The show flowed smoothly for an hour. At one point Rachel caught sight of Berry's grinning face in the control room, blissfully signaling a hit. Gina Tolida's throaty voice held them in thrall as she related her story of the stalker with the knife, and Stichen was articulate and compelling as he described how one convicted stalker might yet wriggle free. Plowfield promised hearings and talked about his bill. But it was Angie Moran who had people all over town turning up the volume on their radios. She told of her dual loss: the daughter, still missing, maligned as a whore by a stalker who turned the family's lives into such a nightmare that her husband finally killed himself. She spoke with a level of controlled rage that took Rachel's breath away.

It was time for the phones. Rachel flipped the switch for the first call, feeling a tightening in her chest. "Good morning, you are on the air," she said, bracing herself.

It wasn't the Truthseeker. Nor was he the second or

the third caller; in fact, when Rachel glanced up at the clock and realized she was into the final half hour of the show, she began to worry. Suddenly she saw Larry Kramer raise his hand, holding a piece of paper on which he had hastily scrawled the number five.

She flipped open the line.

"Good morning, you—"

"You've outdone yourself, Rachel. Nice show. So here I am, your Christmas present, just the one you wanted."

She hoped her guests didn't notice her involuntary shiver at the sound of the familiar monotone voice. She heard the same whistling sound in the background again, and searched her memory. What was that sound?

"The police are tracking you as we speak," she said pleasantly. "Have you listened to the stories today? Do you have any inkling of the damage you and your type do, or have you passed the point of caring?"

"I'm not doing damage, I'm making good things happen, that's what a Truthseeker does."

"What good things are you accomplishing?"

The chuckle on the line was startlingly low, without its usual metallic edge. "I'm making you famous, Rachel. We're both becoming famous. How does it feel, partner? Look at your guests today. Could you have gotten that same crew together six months ago?"

"We are not partners," she said steadily. She felt Angie Moran's round black eyes boring into her. "You are what I said you were when this show began: a coward, a sneaking, bullying coward who stalks children and toys with other people's lives. You are—"

"I am what you want me to be," the voice

329

interrupted. There was a thin vein of anger laced through the words that made Rachel pause. She looked up at the glass control booth and saw Jim standing there with his arms folded, staring at her. The sight of him sent a shiver, almost a spasm, of relief through her body. He was finally here, and that was what mattered. What was she seeing in his eyes? And then she knew: a wariness, a fear. Why? A realization nibbling at her soul began to grow and spread through her body, and she felt a sudden, almost overwhelming dizziness.

"Rachel, are you listening?" The voice was still angry. "We're doing beautifully, aren't we? Did you know *People* magazine is interested in doing a piece about us? Everybody wants the Truthseeker. They want you. Don't fight it, Rachel. We will talk again, maybe tomorrow—"

She closed her eyes, listening for the rhythms of speech, straining to hear what she dreaded to hear. "No," she said, "I'm sorry, this is your last public forum."

"You'll change your mind. I can make you change your mind; I know how to do that."

Words hovered dangerously on her lips and she had to restrain herself from leaning out of her chair. "You don't understand what I'm saying, do you? You don't hear my real meaning. I'm cutting you off, for the last time. That means your fame ceases to exist."

"No! I don't deserve that! I've worked to be who I am, I've worked and slaved to be who I am—"

Rachel felt the tears begin to inch down her cheeks and saw the shocked expressions on the faces of her four guests.

"I am the Truthseeker, Rachel, not you, and I will

decide what comes next," the voice snapped, back in control. "I know where to go and I know what to do. You can't make me go away because I am part of you."

Rachel saw from the corner of her eye Jim's bulk moving from the control room. She glanced at the clock, sweat breaking out on her forehead. One minute of airtime left. "That's it for you," she said, and closed the switch with a flick of her finger. She thanked her guests for their contributions with all the calmness she could muster, and coaxed a summarizing thought from each of them. Larry's hand was raised. It came down; the red light went off. Rachel tore the earphones from her head and ran from the broadcasting studio directly to Berry's office at the end of the corridor. The door was closed. Without hesitation she pushed it open and faced an empty room. She glanced wildly around, as if somehow Berry might materialize from the walls. Where was she? What was that familiar whistling sound?

Rachel approached Berry's desk, trying to register everything at once. The Santa Claus cap was sitting on top of a pile of papers. An open drawer. She moved closer and stared at its contents.

She couldn't remember afterward which realization came first: the fact that the whistling sound she had come to associate with the Truthseeker's calls came from Berry's radiator, or the fact that her mother's pearl-rimmed brooch lay partly wrapped in a scrap of Kleenex on top of a box of Snickers bars in the center of the drawer.

She turned slowly at the sound of a cough and focused on Jim standing in the doorway.

"She's been doing it from here," he said. "All the

time, she's been tapping into the telephone lines from here."

"Where is she?"

"Gone. Her car's still in the parking lot, but she's disappeared."

Rachel's body felt like stone. "Jim, I think I know where she's going," she whispered.

CHAPTER 12

THE WINDSHIELD WIPERS, BURDENED WITH SNOW, moved sluggishly across the glass as Rachel pulled her car onto the almost deserted Outer Drive. All power and phone lines were out along the lakefront because of the storm, but the police guarding the house had been alerted. Rachel tightened her grasp on the wheel. Why hadn't she remembered to leave the cellular phone at home? She had no reason not to believe that Camilla and Edie were perfectly safe, but remembering Berry's last words on the air left her neck clammy and her mouth so dry she had to swallow repeatedly.

"When did you guess?" Jim asked quietly from the seat next to her.

She jumped, so deep in thought she had almost forgotten he was in the car. "When she said we were partners. I suddenly had a sense that I knew the person behind that odd voice, and then—I don't know—I heard *Berry* speaking to me. Then I looked up and saw the expression on your face. It told me everything." Including the fact that Jim had stood in the control room hoping she wasn't part of the hoax, but Rachel didn't say that out loud.

"She was using a sound mixer to alter her voice. Worked pretty well." Jim sighed and turned to stare out the window at the sullen, roiling waters of Lake Michigan. "I got the facts this morning," he went on. "That's why I was late. I was doing the kind of background check I should've done a week ago. Years ago she made a series of anonymous threatening calls to some guy in Atlanta who jilted her; after that she spent a brief time in a psychiatric hospital. Don't let that panic you—remember, she's never hurt anyone physically. Nobody described her as dangerous."

"What's wrong with her?"

"The hospital wouldn't tell me."

"That makes two sick people I managed to deny," Rachel said. She took a long, strangled breath. "I still can't believe the things she did. Breaking into my house, chasing Edie and Topper—"

"That wasn't her. The police said this morning that the guy stumbling after the girls in the snow was some harmless old drunk. They picked him up last night. But Berry was hanging around the house, and the commotion gave her the chance to get inside again."

She felt no anger, just a light-headedness in the face of what was coming in the days ahead. Jeanie Horton wouldn't take long to find out what was going on; all she had to do was check in with Marcie at the front desk. There was no way this wasn't going to change everything. How could she have been so blind?

Jim seemed to be reading her thoughts. "Don't be too hard on yourself," he said.

"After all your warnings? Thanks, but I *should* be hard on myself. I've worked with her and I should have seen something. Her mood swings, her angers, her way of making herself my alter ego—instead I just drank it in and let her make me feel I was the best thing ever to hit broadcasting. I was a fool, plain and simple."

"You were loyal—plain and simple. She was your friend from years back, and you stood by her. You can't fault yourself on something you didn't know."

"Don't, Jim. Don't try to make me feel better about this. I seem to be a pretty poor judge of people. I was wrong about my father, too."

They had left the station in such a hurry, Jim hadn't even put on his coat. His shirtsleeves were rolled up, and she could see goose bumps on his arms.

"Maybe you were, and maybe you weren't," he said slowly as he reached to turn up the heat. "Just because you and your mother remember him differently doesn't mean he wasn't the loving father you grieve for. What's truth, Rachel? The night Molly was killed? We had a terrible fight that afternoon. I was angry because she had been flirting the night before with some dashing Type A hotshot at a party. A little thing, maybe. Maybe not. So why did I give her such a bad time? Because I was jealous, that's why. We loved each other but we fought a lot over what seem now to be little things. Would we have made it if she lived? How the hell do I know? Everything wasn't perfect. Is it ever? I choose to remember that it was, most of the time. I don't have to destroy what I remember and neither do you." His voice was breaking.

Rachel was astonished by his outburst. She tapped the brakes lightly as the car slid at an angle over a patch of slick snow. "Molly would have been crazy not to love you," she ventured.

He hardly seemed to hear her, continuing now in a gruffer voice. "As far as Berry is concerned, what makes you think you can be right about everything? You think you're the only person who's been blinded by what you want to believe rather than what you see in front of your eyes? That's arrogance. And if what I've just said sounds contradictory, hell, that's life." He slumped deep into his seat and left her staring at the road ahead with no words left to tell him he was being too kind, for she had been wrong about Amos, too.

* * * *

"What happened? That was his voice—why is the radio dead?" Edie leaped up to fiddle with the volume control of the boom box she and Camilla had placed on the coffee table in the living room. Her eyes darted to the plug. That wasn't the problem. She flicked on the overhead light and nothing happened. "I think the power's out," she wailed, running into the kitchen to check the circuit breakers. "Oh, damn, Grandma, just when the Truthseeker called!"

"Do we have any batteries?" Camilla pulled herself up from the sofa, trying to hide a sudden panicky feeling. She had just lost a critical link to her daughter. The two of them hurried into the kitchen and began rummaging frantically in several drawers, coming up with nothing. They stared at each other.

"We're going to miss the rest of the show," Edie burst out. "I can't *believe* it. I know, I'll call Mother and ask her to bring home a tape." She picked up the phone. "The line's dead," she said uncertainly. They both jumped at the sound of a heavy knock on the front door.

Camilla moved briskly to answer it with a slight

wobble of uncertainty in her step, but found only the cop stationed out front telling them the heavy wet snow had mucked everything up and not to worry. He was certain the electricity and the phones would be working again very soon. "Didn't want you ladies to get upset," he said with a big grin.

Camilla invited him in but he declined, glancing at his watch, telling her they were about to change shifts anyway. "I've gotta hit the stores and buy something for my wife pretty quick," he said, slightly abashed. "They're closing early today because of the storm and I don't want to prove her right again. She always says I wait until the last minute. Which I do. Merry Christmas, ma'am."

He clumped back across the wooden porch in his heavy boots toward his patrol car, and Camilla closed the door after him, the tension in her head only slightly eased.

"This is so disappointing!" Edie complained, throwing up her arms and stomping back into the living room. "We can't even turn on the Christmas tree!"

"I'll stoke the fire and we'll be just fine and perfectly cozy," Camilla said, picking up the poker and jabbing at the fire with a little more force than necessary.

"Yeah, but we should be listening, we should be knowing what's happening." Edie was pacing now, a fretful look on her pale face. "We should've gone with her. We can't even listen in the Honda, because the radio's broken. Grandma, we'll be the last people in town to know if they catch the Truthseeker! This *sucks*!"

"Enough of that language, Edie, we'll find out soon enough." Camilla tamped down her irritation,

336

reminding herself that Edie's anxieties were not that far removed from her own.

"I know what I've gotta do, I've gotta go get some batteries," Edie said suddenly.

"You'll do no such thing."

"Grandma, the power may be out for hours and we don't even have batteries for the flashlight, you know? It would be just too creepy to sit here in the dark! I can walk up to the drugstore at the corner and be back in ten minutes, I promise. If we wait until Mother gets home, the stores will be cleaned out of them or closed—like the cop said."

Camilla hesitated. "Well, you're not going alone," she said finally. "You go tell the policeman outside what we're doing and I'll get some boots on."

"Meet you at the back door," Edie agreed as Camilla hurried upstairs.

Finding the boots took time. It was half an hour before they were inching their way down the back steps, which were slick with packed snow. "You okay?" Edie said, glancing back at Camilla. Her voice was slightly muffled as she stomped a path through the snow out toward the back alley.

"Fine, fine," Camilla replied through chattering teeth. She was bundled up in an old parka of Edie's and some rubber wading boots over heavy socks, and she was already freezing. But there was no way she would let Edie head off alone for the store. What was happening with the Truthseeker? She shivered, not wholly from the cold, at the memory of the last words she and Edie had heard before the electricity went out: "So here I am, your Christmas present, just the one you wanted." That strange, high-pitched monotone voice had done a masterful job of cutting through their lives, leaving all of them edgy and uncertain. She stopped for a second and looked down the length of the alley toward the street and shivered again. The trees lining the alley looked like scrawny, snow-bleached skeletons against a bleak, gray sky. She loved a raw winter day, but she didn't like being out here right now. When they got back, she would bring some wine up from the cellar. They would have a Christmas celebration tonight, the three of them, when Rachel was safely home. She would make sure to keep stoking the fire.

"Grandma, look." Edie had stopped and was staring into the garage at the Honda, which was only half visible under a mound of drifting snow. "Oh God, Mother will be furious. She told me to close the garage door when she left, and I forgot. I'd better shovel it out right now so she can get her car back inside. Are you really cold? Do you want to wait in the house?" Edie cast Camilla a worried look as she dragged out a snow shovel from behind an array of damp leftover packing boxes.

Camilla briefly considered it. "No, I'll help," she said with a sigh. "I'll use the plastic shovel."

They started working as fast they could, but it was slow going. Camilla felt better for the effort, and soon found it necessary to unzip her parka part way. "I'll be sore tomorrow, but this feels good," she said, glancing at Edie's industrious figure. "Not that I can keep up with you, of course."

"There's nothing old about you, Grandma. Now Mrs. Colson, she's different. She looks ancient because she's kind of fat."

"I don't even notice anymore," Camilla said in some surprise.

"Why go to live with her? You should stay here and live with us, that's what I think."

Camilla smiled as she bent her back to the job. "So you are going to stay, Edie?"

"Yes, I am."

"Your mother will be very happy."

Edie pushed her shovel deep into the heavy snow and they heard the faint scrape of metal against the cement garage floor. "She's been telling me things she's never talked about before. I kind of like it. She's just different, somehow."

"Even parents learn."

"Yeah, she's learned a lot."

This time Camilla had to duck her head to hide her smile.

"You and Mom seem to be doing better," Edie ventured in her most grown-up voice.

"Well, yes, I think we are—we're actually doing a little cheek to cheek. Finally."

" 'Cheek to cheek'? Oh, Grandma, how retro."

Camilla pulled a fistful of snow from her shovel, crunched it into a ball and tossed it at Edie, who dodged and laughed. They were both too absorbed to notice a chunky figure appear at the corner and slowly begin walking toward them from the other end of the alley.

"Hi, you two," Berry called gaily. "What are you doing out here shoveling snow while it's still coming down? Mrs. Duncan, is that the way they do it in Florida?" She laughed happily. "Isn't the snow *great*?"

"Berry!" Edie's eyes widened in astonishment. "What are you doing here? Where's Mom?"

"Your mom invited me up for a Christmas Eve

celebration. You know, because I couldn't make it to the tree-trimming party, that's why. She's on her way. Here, let me help." She put down a brown paper bag she was carrying, took the shovel from Edie and began vigorously clearing snow. "I can't believe Rachel sometimes. Leaving the garage door open on a day like this? Honestly."

"The automatic control in the car is broken, that's the reason, and I was supposed to close the door when she left and I forgot," Edie said in a rush. She somehow felt a need to defend her mother. "We missed the last part of the show because the power went out. We're *dying* to hear what happened."

"The whole show was fabulous. Did you hear that prosecutor talking about the gym teacher blaming what he did on an abusive father? Can you think of a more ridiculous explanation—" Berry was puffing now, but still shoveling hard.

"I thought it was an abusive spouse," Camilla said.

"Oh, yeah. An abusive spouse. Wait until you hear the really fabulous news. Rachel is going into syndication. Can you believe it? It's going to happen, nothing can screw it up. Kendall Productions. It's going to happen soon, maybe this week. I'm telling you, nothing can screw it up." Her face was turning red and Camilla exchanged glances with Edie.

"I think we've almost got the job done," Edie said. "You're working too hard, Berry. See? I can pull the door closed now. We need to go buy some batteries at the store, if you want to go inside while—"

"Oh, don't do that, let's all go in and warm up. I'll run out for them later." Berry straightened her back, wincing, and picked up the paper sack. "By the way, I got a couple of bottles of wine at a little place on

Dempster Street, so we can celebrate. You know I caught the last train up here? Too much blowing snow on the tracks. Pretty big stuff for Chicago. I mean, this town can handle anything, but today is different. Today we're going into syndication, that's what's happening. Today—"

"Hey, come on," Edie urged, a little puzzled. She guided Berry back to the house, missing the suddenly wary look in her grandmother's eyes. Camilla unlocked the door and they stepped inside the warm kitchen and pulled off their boots and coats. Camilla took a paper towel and mopped up the puddle of water by the door, listening as Berry chattered on.

"The house looks great," Berry said as she started to wander through the rooms. "I remember being here back when Rachel and I were in college, remember, Mrs. Duncan? I thought it was such a grand place, not at all like the dumps I grew up in. You used to put big bunches of flowers in the hall, I remember. You had nice things, but that's all gone, isn't it? Everything goes, finally. I don't think Rachel understands that, do you?" She disappeared into the hall and Camilla hurried after her, not exactly sure why.

"Are you feeling all right?" she asked softly.

Berry turned, her eyes lit with a particular fire that Camilla thought for a brief moment she recognized— but then it was gone. She stepped back, steadying herself against the wall.

"Of course I am," Berry said. Her lips parted into a wide, fixed smile. "Why would you ask? This is a wonderful day, Mrs. Duncan. Everything worked. People took us seriously and they're never going to take us for granted again, I've made sure of that. I'm wound up too tight, that's all. I haven't slept much lately, and I'll bet Rachel hasn't either." She stared up the staircase with the smile fixed on her face. "Mind if I take a quick peek at the redecorating upstairs? Rachel kept saying I should come over to see the place, and I feel like a bad friend because it took me so long to get around to it. Okay?"

Camilla hesitated for the fraction of a second, but she could come up with no reason to refuse. "Of course, go right ahead," she said. "Shall I fix some hot tea? Cookies? You must be tired after all that walking and shoveling."

"That would be nice," Berry said as she started ascending the stairs. "I'll just take a quick peek and be right down and then we'll all have cookies and tea."

Camilla stared after Berry's pudgy retreating figure with a puzzled frown. She glanced through the long leaded-glass window that opened up onto the screened porch and saw the patrol car parked in front. Maybe she would take some hot tea out to the policeman sitting behind the wheel and ask him if he could get through on his car radio to Rachel. Why had Berry come before Rachel? For that matter, why hadn't they driven together? Was Rachel stuck somewhere in the snow? She walked quickly back to the kitchen, put the kettle on the stove, and stared out the window. The snow had stopped falling. The pristine beauty of untouched snow at the end of a storm had always been a favorite sight from this window, but now a sense of unease was gnawing at her.

"I'm glad Berry came along, she was a big help," Edie said as she pulled cups and saucers from the cupboard. "She sure is strong. I didn't know Mother invited her for the tree-trimming. She never mentioned it. That's pretty awesome news about syndication, isn't it? I can't wait to tell Topper. If only they'd fix the phones! How come it's taking so long, I wonder?"

"What did the cop say when you told him we were going to the store?" Camilla had a sudden vague idea that maybe he would be stomping over the porch any minute to check on them once more.

Edie looked embarrassed. "He was pulling away from the curb and yelled out the window that the cop on the next shift was coming around the block. I waved and came back in so I wouldn't have to waste any time chatting up the new guy."

"Oh. Well, that's fine."

Edie was still chattering as the two of them walked back through the hall toward the living room, Camilla holding a steaming teapot and three cups and saucers on a tray and Edie walking ahead of her, carrying a plate of cookies.

Edie came to a sudden halt. Camilla saw her turn and face the stairs, her mouth dropping in surprise.

"What is it—" Camilla felt her heart beating faster as she hurried forward and looked in the direction Edie was staring.

Berry was descending the stairs, her moon-shaped face painted with heavy makeup and her hair, glistening with gel, standing out from her head. She was wearing Rachel's red wool robe, clutching it together with one hand, the flesh of her heavy body straining against the fabric. In her ears glittered a pair of Rachel's gold earrings. She clutched the banister with her other hand, teetering slightly as she held out one foot.

"The shoes don't quite fit, but it doesn't matter,

343

because I have a pair just like them at home. Rachel never noticed I bought a pair just like hers. Why do you look surprised? I just thought I'd get comfortable, that's all. Rachel won't care." There was sweat on her upper lip, which was covered with a thick smear of awkwardly applied coral lipstick. She continued down the stairs, talking in a high, falsetto voice interspersed with girlish giggles. "I like the earrings, don't you? I always thought Rachel might get the hint when I admired them and give them to me, but she can be insensitive. You know that, don't you, Mrs. Duncan? You know a lot of things."

"I think you should sit down, Berry," Camilla heard herself saying. "Right there, on the stairs. Just sit down and relax for a minute." She stood totally still, unwilling even to bend to the floor to put down the tray of hot tea and cups. She did not want to take her eyes off Berry Brown. No matter how shocked she was, she must stay calm.

Berry frowned, a petulant look crossing her freckled face. Her brown eyes were the color of coffee sludge. "Please don't patronize me, Mrs. Duncan. I really, really hate that."

"I'm not patronizing you. I certainly wouldn't dream of doing that," Camilla said agreeably. She edged forward, acutely aware that an astonished Edie was still standing between her and Berry. "Edie, stick those cookies on the coffee table, will you, dear?" she said in the same relaxed tone. She had to get Edie out of the hall, away from this woman, so she could figure out what to do next.

Edie shot her a sudden knowing glance and hesitantly stepped back. She was moving too slowly and Camilla realized Edie was reluctant to leave her

344

alone.

"Go," she commanded.

But Berry heard the fear in her voice. "Stay where you are, Edie," she said. "I want to talk to both of you. I'm sorry about this, Mrs. Duncan, but your daughter's sense of superiority has gotten too much for me. Do you know, I don't think she's grateful for what the Truthseeker has done for us? I could hardly believe it today. She didn't care. She wanted him gone. Did you realize that, listening? She wanted him not to exist."

"Where is Rachel?" Camilla demanded now, her voice trembling.

"She'll be here soon. You haven't asked the big question, Mrs. Duncan. I expected it sooner. You haven't asked me if we found out who the Truthseeker is."

"Grandma—" Edie whispered.

Camilla took another step forward. "Did you?" she asked, her voice steadier.

Berry sank onto a step and hugged her knees with two chubby hands. "We did," she said dreamily. "We found him. Did you know that, Mrs. Duncan? We found him. Actually, Rachel did, because I've known all along. And now she's going to ruin everything."

"Not at all," Camilla said. She was standing shoulder to shoulder with Edie now. She would shove her out of the way if she had to; it was the only plan she could think of. "Rachel is your friend, Berry. Edie and I are your friends. And friends don't hurt, they help. We can help you. Why don't you go back upstairs and put your clothes on and we'll fix you some tea? Why—"

Suddenly they heard footsteps running on the

345

porch and a key turning in the lock. Rachel burst through the door, her eyes wide and her hair disheveled, with Jim right behind her. "You're all right," she said with relief as she stepped into the hall and reached out her arms to Edie. "The cop outside said everything was quiet, but I have to tell you—"

"You don't have to tell them anything, Rachel, they already *know*." Berry was standing again. She let out another highpitched giggle.

Rachel whirled and stared at the figure on the stairs. Jim started forward.

"Don't come near me!" Berry shrieked.

They froze.

"Oh, *why* did you bring that prick with you, Rachel?" Berry moaned. "It was going to be all right. We could've talked this out, I could've made everything work. You can't handle anything without me, don't you understand?"

"Oh, Berry, you're not well," Rachel whispered. "Why did you do it?"

"Did you tell anybody?"

"The police know."

"Then we're finished. Everything." Berry's eyes widened in horror. "Rachel, you've killed us. You've killed the deal with Kendall."

"We would've made it without you creating the Truthseeker. Don't you understand that? You've been the energy and heart of our partnership. We had it all. This didn't have to happen."

Berry shot her a contemptuous look. "*You* had it all—I never did. You were so magnanimous, offering me the brooch to wear when you knew my father would throw a fit, letting me pin it on and then taking it back—" She had a glazed, faraway look in her eyes.

346

"When I saw it on the mantel, I was thrilled. It was my reward for making your career. It was mine. For once, it wasn't you getting so much all the time. You always did. Except when your father died, but you know what? I still envied you. Why did it have to be your father who died and not mine?"

"It's not your friend talking," Jim warned in a low voice as he reached out with a hand to steady Rachel. But tears had begun trickling down her cheeks and she started blindly up the stairs.

"Wait—" Jim said sharply.

Berry let go of the edges of the robe and thrust her hand into the right pocket. The robe fell open and revealed a pale pink body with loose flesh hanging in symmetrical folds from above the navel down to a small patch of dark pubic hair. One large, pendulous, dark-nippled breast stood revealed on one side of her chest. On the other was nothing but a wrinkled map of pink scar tissue.

Berry spoke politely, almost primly. "Me too, Camilla. I had my operation back when you had yours, but nobody much cared. You never knew, did you? Everybody thought I was deformed enough, being fat."

"I'm not impressed," Camilla blurted.

Berry stared at Camilla without comprehension. She lifted her hand, holding what looked to Rachel like a black flashlight and pointed it at Jim. She heard a sharp crack. Jim fell to his knees. She looked up and saw Berry raise the gun again and point it directly at her.

"No!" screamed Edie. She dropped the tray and threw herself in front of her mother, blond hair flying, thin arms spread wide.

The second report was muffled by Berry's screams as Camilla heaved the tray with its pot of scalding tea in her face.

* * * *

Rachel sat in the surgical waiting room at Evanston Hospital staring at a calming swirl of abstract color framed in white enamel on the opposite wall. She registered its presence without seeing it. All she could see was the shape of Edie's body flying at her through the air; all she could feel was the impact of her daughter's flesh knocking her to the ground; all she could hear was her child's scream. There was nothing else. She laced her fingers together and stared into the swirling pinks and greens and grays and let herself be sucked into their vortex, her brain and will left somewhere behind.

"Breathe," commanded her mother's voice. "Look at me." Camilla's fingers were pulling at her hands, unlacing them. Rachel tore her gaze away from the wall and tried to refocus. Her mother's face was drained and immobile and she looked like a stranger, but there was coming from her a pulsating strength that Rachel needed. She tentatively rested her head on Camilla's shoulder.

"Hang on," Camilla whispered.

A door swung open and Rachel saw a man's figure walking toward them from the direction of the emergency room. She realized with a shock that it was Jim. She flashed back to the sight of him on his knees in the hall but could remember nothing after that, not after she found herself lying on the floor under the suddenly limp weight of Edie's body and realized her daughter wasn't moving or screaming or crying. She saw now his right arm was bandaged and in a sling.

He bent down and kissed Rachel gently on the forehead. "What does the doctor say?" he asked, directing the question to Camilla.

"They think she'll be out of surgery in about an hour. The bullet missed her spine and her heart, that's the good news. That's all we've heard so far." Camilla's voice caught on the last words.

"Berry?"

"In the burn unit, under police guard." Camilla turned her face away.

Jim settled heavily into the chair on the other side of Rachel, wincing as he adjusted his arm.

Rachel straightened and put her hand to his face, touching him, staring into his eyes. "You're all right?" she said. It suddenly mattered desperately that she hadn't focused on Jim at all. How could she have not thought about him?

"The bullet went right through my arm and rests now in your floor, I guess." He gave her a rumpled grin and she saw a crack in his lip. "It's one of those Hollywood injuries; you know, mortal peril one minute and walking into the sunset with your arm in a sling the next. Don't waste any energy worrying about me. You need it all for Edie."

"I can't remember what happened after she was shot," Rachel said in a tremulous whisper.

"Your mother took over. She got the cops and kept pressure on Edie's wound to stanch the blood until the ambulance came." He glanced over at Camilla. "And thanks for calling Topper."

"I didn't tell her everything—"

"I did. I called her a few minutes ago. She's crying about Edie; my poor kid, all alone—"

"Go home to her, Jim," Rachel said urgently. "She

shouldn't be alone and frightened."

"It's okay." He smiled tensely at her. "Right now, you come first. I'm staying until we know Edie is all right, and then I'm going home. Topper understands."

Rachel shot bolt upright, her hands to her face. "Oh, my God, Matt! I haven't told Matt!"

"I did, and he's on his way," Camilla said in a steady voice. Making the call had been hard. Matt Snow, the resident family prick, the man who had wanted to destroy her daughter, had broken down and cried for his own. No recriminations, no petulant complaints. She resisted the impulse to pull Rachel into her arms and simply hold her like a child again. She resisted because she saw the naked yearning on Jim's face to do the same thing. But then she saw his yearning look turn cautious and she looked over her shoulder. Amos Curley and that youngish woman with the red hair from Lucciano's were hurrying toward them down the corridor, their faces tense.

"God, Rachel, finally. You've had a hellish day and I could kick myself for not being with you." Amos strode directly to Rachel and pulled her to her feet, enveloping her in a fiercely proprietary bear hug. Rachel closed her eyes and opened them to see Jeanie staring at her.

"You know what happened?" she said, disengaging herself from his arms.

"Everything," he said soberly. He searched her eyes, oblivious to everyone else's presence. "I meant what I said in my note. I meant every word of it."

Rachel wasn't sure for an instant what he was talking about. Then she thrust her hand into the pocket of her jacket and felt the piece of folded cardboard and remembered its promises.

"Do you hear me, Rachel? Are you okay?"

She was suddenly acutely conscious of Jim behind her. She knew if she turned around she would see him hunched down, stomach swelling over his belt, graying hair in need of a haircut. He was the man you took for granted, the one who got the job done. He was an older version of the boys she had avoided in high school, the ones who not only never played on the basketball team but rarely had enough interest to attend a game. He was the classic second choice: the embarrassing date whose glasses were too thick and whose jeans were too wide. He was not Amos Curley, and he never would be.

"Rachel?"

"I'm all right," she said to Amos, through a lifting fog. "I'm waiting to find out about Edie. I can't think about anything else—"

"Nor can I, absolutely." But his thin face with its angular jaw had stiffened and he seemed to see Jim and Camilla for the first time. He started to say something when a door opened and a surgeon, peeling off a blue surgical cap and mask, walked slowly toward them.

Rachel straightened her shoulders and waited. She reached blindly for her mother's hand.

"Edie is a very lucky girl," the surgeon began. "The bullet broke a couple of ribs and punctured her lung, but remember, it just missed her spine. It was a very close call. She will live and she will not be paralyzed, Mrs. Snow. She'll probably be out of school for a while, but she's young and healthy and she should be fine."

Rachel began to cry. She sensed Jim standing in back of her. and felt his thick, generous arms encircling her. She could let go now, she could feel again. She turned and leaned her head against his

351

shoulder and let the tears come, purging herself of more pain and fear than she had dreamed could possibly flow out of her at one time.

When she turned to Amos she saw only a handsome face pinched tight; she couldn't register anything beyond that. "She's all right, she's going to be all right," she announced tearily.

"That's wonderful," Amos said. His hands hung at his side. His jaw seemed to be working on marionette strings.

"I'm glad, Rachel, it would've been terrible if—" Jeanie cleared her throat. Even in her hazy, euphoric state, Rachel noticed Jeanie glancing surreptitiously at her watch.

"Are you ready to give a statement about what happened today? I don't want to put words in your mouth, but you need to dissociate yourself from Berry Brown as quickly as possible, preferably for tonight's news. We're ready and willing to make an exception on keeping any quotes to ourselves for the *Tribune*—unless, of course, you want to save some details for us—" Jeanie paused expectantly.

"Save details?" Rachel echoed. She realized vaguely she was expected to do something. She straightened herself.

"There aren't any to save," Jim interjected. "The story's pretty obvious. Berry is a sick woman who was living through Rachel and lost it. What else do you say?"

Amos stood to the side, his face carved and still. "I want to hear from Rachel, not you," he said. It was the first intimation of the animosity pulsating from him.

"Let's not do the dueling-banjos bit," Jeanie said with a brisk edge to her voice. She stared full at

Rachel. "I want to hear from you, too. What happened with Berry is sad and tragic, but there must've been signs. What's this about her taking care of a doddering old father who ruled her life? Can you give me some guidance on that?"

"Is anybody with him? Has anybody told him?"

"Some woman who says she's a nurse answered their phone and said the police had been already there. She wouldn't open up on a damn thing."

"I don't want to talk about it right now," Rachel said. "Later. Not now."

"If you don't put out a strong condemnation of Berry tonight you're going to get smeared with the charge that the two of you were hyping ratings and this was a scheme that went awry because she flipped out." All the energy in the room, all the certitude, centered on Jeanie, who stood now with arms folded and lips pulled thin as rubber bands.

Rachel faced her with feet planted. "Is that your take on the story?" she asked.

"I'm not going to smear you, if that's what you're asking. I'm telling you to peel Berry off, and peel her fast."

"She was my friend for many years, and what has happened to her is tragic. I hope she can somehow be helped," Rachel began. Her voice faltered. "But it was a stranger who shot my daughter and Jim. She could have killed both of them. Only a desperately sick person able to hide an acute illness could have done what she did. I was in no way involved in any scheme to promote the Truthseeker as a way of hyping ratings for my show—and I'll quit tomorrow if people don't believe me."

Jeanie was already scribbling in a notebook.

"Good," she said. She looked up with a sunny expression. "My best to you and your daughter. Lots of people are expressing support. I'll tell the TV animals waiting outside the hospital that this is your official statement, but you won't be doing an on-camera interview tonight. Okay?"

"Okay."

"I'm going to hold on to your last statement for an exclusive in the *Tribune* tomorrow. Agreed?"

"Agreed."

"Thanks for being a professional, Rachel." Jeanie flipped her notebook shut and hesitated. "By the way, Jerry Tebbins won't ride this on his show. He has kids, too. 'Bye now."

Rachel nodded and laced her fingers through Jim's. It felt like the most natural thing in the world. It was only with a certain haziness that she saw Amos hesitate and then turn and follow Jeanie back down the corridor. His cowboy boots made hollow clicking noises on the tile as he strode away.

* * * *

Much later that night, Rachel and Matt stood alone in the intensive care unit, one on each side of the bed, staring at the sleeping body of their daughter. The rhythmic wheeze of the ventilator echoed off the bare white walls. Matt's already burly figure had thickened over the past year, but the hands grasping the metal rail of the bed were as powerful as ever. His thick hair, which had once been the color of sherry, had faded somewhat, and his heavily tanned face looked strangely bizarre in the bleached and muted hospital environment. But he mostly rippled with the aura of the successful developer in his expensive Italian suit, and the intensive care nurses darted quick glances at him as they hurried in and out of the room.

He glanced up, catching Rachel staring at him, and their eyes held. She pushed the hair back from her eyes, almost knocking off the glasses on top of her head. She shivered. She had left her coat somewhere in the ambulance or the waiting room and wore now only her thin black cardigan, which was missing half of its buttons.

"That sweater must be a million years old," Matt said.

"Probably. I keep it at the office."

"I gave it to you, didn't I?"

"For my birthday, when Edie was four."

"I guess it doesn't matter what you look like when you're doing radio."

"I'm free to be frumpy, on occasion."

They both fell silent, staring again at Edie.

"She threw herself in front of you," Matt finally said. "That's what we always figured we'd do for her."

Rachel nodded, unable to speak.

"You know what I'm wondering? I'm wondering if she would've done that for me."

Rachel looked over at him and felt all the memories, good and bad, merging into something new. "She would have," she said simply.

"Maybe."

"Matt, I used to be afraid that love only flowed downward. I'm not anymore. She loves you."

For a long moment, the only sound in the room was the rhythmic wheeze of the respirator. Matt cleared his throat. "Nice of you to say so," he said.

She saw the sagging lines of his mouth and marveled fleetingly at how shriveled he looked, even

355

clothed in fine Italian wool. A knot loosened inside her. "Matt, I'm sorry for the haste and the unkindness and the pain. And you don't have to say the same thing, I just wanted to say it for myself."

"Thank you," he answered in a barely audible whisper.

* * * *

The house was dark when Rachel stepped out of the cab and paid a very sleepy driver. Somewhere she heard a single bird; it was almost dawn. She walked up the stairs in snow above her bare ankles and across the porch, brushing back a drooping juniper bush. She had to get somebody here to shovel tomorrow. Maybe next month she and Edie could trim the bushes back, after the snow was gone. She walked with automatic care over the spot where the porch board had been repaired. It still squeaked a little, and she didn't want to wake Camilla. Jim had brought her home hours ago, so she must be asleep.

She stopped and listened to the house, hearing its whispering and its tears, but also hearing it tell her something new: remembering and revisiting the past was one thing; living there was another. She could freeze an image and etch it into her heart, but she couldn't keep it alive, she could only commit it to memory, to the repository for life already lived. Old loves, old hates, triumphs and disappointments all becoming equally hazy. Everything fades, she told herself as she stood listening. History isn't changed, mistakes aren't erased. Wounds resolve and judgments soften and blend, that's what happens. I have held an image of my father that is drifting away, and it is all right to let it go. This house; her house. It was ready for new memories. Maybe they would be hers for a while, but then they would belong to strangers yet to walk across this porch who would hear their own whisperings and be deaf to hers. It could be no other way: if her memories were the only ones to prevail and define, they would sink of their weight into oblivion.

By the door she saw the morning newspaper, bundled in plastic. She picked it out of the snow, pulled it from its protective wrapping, and held it up, squinting to read the headline in the first faint glow of light. A joint byline; Jeanie's above that of Amos Curley's. "Show Producer Shoots Radio Host's Daughter," it read. And underneath, "College Pal Unmasked as Anonymous Truthseeker in Ratings Stunt." There was much more, but she couldn't see it well enough yet. It didn't matter. Rachel unlocked the door and stepped inside. She blinked at the sight of a sheet covering the hall carpet, but understanding only dawned when she saw a bucket and scrubbing brush at the foot of the stairs. Camilla had been cleaning up the terrible sight of Edie's blood, something she could not have faced; not tonight, not ever. She heard a small noise and looked up.

The living room was suddenly glowing with soft blue light. The Christmas tree stood resplendently lit with ornaments shimmering, and Camilla stood next to it.

"Merry Christmas, my Rachel," she said quietly. "I found all the old blue lights and put them on for you."

Rachel walked across the room and put her arms around her mother, not caring at the moment what came next. All of what she had been seeking was here.

Dear Reader:

I hope you enjoyed reading this Large Print book. If you are interested in reading other Beeler Large Print titles, ask your librarian or write to me at

Thomas T. Beeler, *Publisher*
Post Office Box 659
Hampton Falls, New Hampshire 03844

You can also call me at 1-800-251-8726 and I will send you my latest catalogue.

Audrey Lesko and I choose the titles I publish in Large Print. Our aim is to provide good books by outstanding authors—books we both enjoyed reading and liked well enough to want to share. We warmly welcome any suggestions for new titles and authors.

Sincerely,